# MORE THAN JUST US

### A NOVEL

Allie Otoski

ISBN: 979-8-9898376-0-1


Editor: Britt Howard, at Pro Book Edits

Cover Designer: Mary Scarlett, at @mscarlettcreative

Formatting: Kristen Hamilton, at Kristen's Red Pen

# Content Warning

This book includes mature themes and pertains to serious mental health topics, including discussions of anxiety, panic attacks, depression, and suicide. Please keep this in mind while reading.

# Playlist

The Night We Met by Lord Huron
Matilda by Harry Styles
Little Do You Know by Alex and Sierra
Head Over Heels by Rachel Gonzalez
The Moment I Knew (Taylor's Version) by Taylor Swift
Like Everybody Else by Lennon Stella
TALK ME DOWN by Troye Sivan
The Bottom by Gracie Abrams
Something in the Orange by Zach Bryan
you were good to me by Jeremy Zucker, Chelsea Cutler
Locksmith by Sadie Jean
Already Gone by Sleeping At Last
Forever Winter (Taylor's Version) (From the Vault) by Taylor
Swift
Don't Give Up On Me by Andy Grammar
Midnight by Ed Sheeran
Learning How to Love by Colony House
Older by 5 Seconds of Summer (ft. Sierra Deaton)
Daylight by Taylor Swift
Girl by SYML

# 1

## NOW

I always wonder if he knew.

When I dream of that night, floating around that hazy, in-between state of consciousness, when my mind attempts to make its way around the blurred edges of my memory, and my eyes trace the cracks in the ceiling in the early morning hours . . . I can't help but wonder.

Did it mean something, the way those deep brown eyes never left mine? Did he squeeze my hand a little tighter, hold on a little longer? Did he linger in the driveway before he drove off? Or am I imagining it, unknowingly changing subtle details over the course of time to lessen the hurt?

I know how the story ends, yet it's the same question I come back to every time.

Did he know?

I tell myself the answer doesn't matter. Because it can't, not really. I won't let it. Because the second I do, the second I begin to believe that things could have ended any other way, I'm right back where he left me.

And yet, on nights like this—when I can almost feel the evening summer breeze and see the warm, dying light of the early June sunset, when I remember the subtle glow of the city and swear I can hear him laughing next to me—I find myself wondering if he knew. If he saw it coming.

But the answer every time is no. Of course not. He couldn't have, or he would never have let me leave that night.

Which was exactly why I couldn't stay.

I held onto his hand, and he held onto my heart, and we almost made it to the end.

Almost.

Because his love—it was there. It was real. It was everything.

But it wasn't enough.

2

I squint against the rain as it glides across my windshield, the early June downpour painting a blue tint over the city as I drive across the West Seattle Bridge. The skyline looms in the distance, the gray and black shades of the buildings no more than a blur through the foggy mist. In another life, the skyline used to be one of my favorite views.

Now, I don't spare it a second glance as it disappears in my rearview mirror.

The streetlights glare across the water as I get off the highway, trying to ignore the pit of dread forming in my stomach, one that has been steadily increasing in depth since the second I woke up this morning.

It's been three years, exactly. To the day.

Three years since the night that changed everything.

I swallow against the lump in my throat, willing myself not to think about it, about that night, about *him*. I slow to a stop in the rush hour traffic, fumbling with the buttons on my dashboard as music begins to hum quietly through the speakers. I stare through the windshield dazedly, seeing nothing and everything all at once. My phone starts ringing, magnified by the Bluetooth in my car and jolting me out of my reverie.

I suck in a breath, and for a split second, my body freezes when I wonder what would've happened that night if he'd answered the phone. But I'll never know because he didn't.

I hadn't wanted him to.

Maybe it's the date or the way my mind hasn't stopped replaying that final goodbye over and over since the moment I woke up this morning—but I wonder if I will ever get a phone call in a car and not think of him.

For a split second, I consider abiding by his "no answering phones while driving" rule that used to make us laugh when we were teenagers, but I am at a red light, and it was a stupid rule anyway, so I steel my nerves and press the green button.

"Hey, Mom."

"Stella, are you almost home?"

No, *"Hey, how was class?"* If she hadn't been so worked up about me being "behind" a semester, I wouldn't even be taking summer classes anyway. Pursing my lips, I try to refrain from snorting at the bluntness in her tone.

But then again, one word I'd never use to describe my mother is *warm.*

I release a short exhale. "I just got off the exit. I'm about ten minutes away."

"Since you're already running late, can you stop by the grocery store and grab some ranch dressing?"

My eyebrows furrow. "Ranch? I thought we were having Chicken Alfredo."

"We are."

I pause, my mouth pressing into a firm line as I wait for further explanation. But, of course, I get none. Glancing at the clock, I note there are still twenty minutes until the time she put in the family group text (which I double-checked today).

"I thought you said dinner was at six. It's always at six."

She exhales, and I hear the sound of bowls rattling and silverware clanking. "It was. We had to move it up an hour because Daniel has to be somewhere at six-thirty. You know how busy he and Dahlia have been lately."

The light finally turns green, and I sigh as I roll through the intersection. "Yeah, I do. No one told me."

She's silent for a moment, and I wonder if it's out of guilt or annoyance. I can only guess it's the latter when she says nothing.

A few seconds later, she huffs, "So, can you swing by the store?"

I'm used to the dismissal, and it's all I can do not to roll down my window and chuck my phone into the Puget Sound. I muster, "Yep, see you soon" and hang up.

I try to shake off my mom's contempt because, after all this time, I should just expect it. I don't know if I'm more annoyed at the fact that nothing has changed or at the fact that I expected it to. Because, of course, they didn't think to tell me we were eating earlier. Why would they? It's never been important to them to make sure I'm included.

I've been an afterthought my entire life.

# 3

After circling the parking lot for a second time, I give up on trying to get a spot near the front and pull into the first one I can find. I turn off the ignition and fling my car door open, unceremoniously throwing my purse over my head and hurrying into the store. I sidestep a man on the phone ("I told you they don't *have* organic, Tiffany.") and a thin woman in a matching Lululemon workout set talking to the baby on her hip like he's her best friend at book club ("Can you believe that, Knox? It's like she was practically telling me I could hit the gym more as if she hadn't already seen me there three times this week . . .") and finally locate the ranch dressing.

I successfully make it through the rest of my impromptu shopping trip without any further human interaction (thank you, self-checkout) and make my way through the glass sliding doors.

It's raining harder now because, of course, it is. I don't bother trying to shield myself this time as I cross the parking lot and run toward my car. I'm almost to the driver's side door when I awkwardly leap to the left in an attempt to avoid the massive puddle in front of me—and collide with someone *hard*.

I stagger backward as a hand immediately reaches out to steady me. I begin mumbling an embarrassed apology, but then I look up, and the words get caught in my throat. My entire body goes rigid, and I feel all the color drain from my face as my gaze locks on an achingly familiar pair of dark brown eyes.

I register that his mouth is moving just in time to catch him saying, ". . . are you okay? I'm so sorry, I wasn't looking . . ." But he trails off as his eyes finally meet mine, and I see the shock register across his features. His eyes widen as his hand drops from my arm, his lips parting in surprise.

"Stella?" he breathes so quietly I almost think I dreamt it.

My mouth opens, closes, and then opens again as I feel tears start to burn. He's here.

He is standing in front of me with his brown hair that I've run my hands through a hundred times before soaked and plastered to his forehead, cheeks that I've cupped in the palm of my hands pink and flushed from the wind, and that same green jacket I can still feel wrapped around me clinging to his skin. I stare at him, and it's just like the first time.

My heart hammers in my chest as I take him in, the reality of the past three years suffocating the air between us. My body is frozen, stuck somewhere between wanting to laugh, cry, throw myself into his arms, or run away.

The familiar scent of him drifts past me with the breeze. My lungs constrict, my eyes blur, and my chest aches. For a second, it's him and me and nothing else, and my heart feels like it's turning the key into the lock of my house after being away for too long—the quiet hum of relief, the familiar feeling of home.

But then he takes a step toward me, and I break from my daze and realize I haven't had a home in three years because I haven't had him.

Spurring into action, I stumble backward again, splashing through the puddle I miserably failed at trying to avoid the first time.

"Stella! Stel, wait—"

But the rest of what he says is lost to the rain as I slide into my car and shut the door. Without another glance at him, I hurriedly pull through the parking space and drive up the row, only noticing his silhouette still frozen in place in my rearview mirror as I pull out of the lot.

Bridger. *My* Bridger.

He's back.

$$4$$

The only words running through my mind over and over the entire drive home are these.

*Bridger is back.*

I pull up to the house and park on the street, wondering how the hell I managed to get here in one piece. I stay in my car, attempting to even out my breath and calm my still racing heart, not caring that I'm officially going to be "late" to dinner.

I'm not sure why my mom even cares about keeping up these family dinners so much. It's not like we never see each other. My brother Daniel and his wife Dahlia stop by all the time, and I, against my better judgment, still live here. But I guess the happy family facade has to be kept up one way or another.

I steel myself, shakily getting out of my car and grabbing the stupid ranch from the passenger seat. I make my way to the house, passing the perfectly trimmed green hedges as I walk along the curved stone path to the front steps. Stepping onto the porch, I pause in front of the door, a different kind of pain taking root in my gut. The heart-racing anxiety I felt when I saw Bridger again drops low in my stomach, morphing into a churning, heavy pit of nerves. Now, my heart is racing for an entirely different reason as I brace myself for the dinner ahead.

I don't want to sit through another meal of simple platitudes, watching everyone walk on eggshells and stick to the deemed "safe" topics. And that's just on any random weeknight, let alone today.

June fourth.

I don't know what I'm so worried about—it's not like we'll talk about it or even acknowledge it.

We never have.

My parents will ask each other how work is going. Daniel will use any excuse to turn the conversation back to him and Dahlia—and I know they'll have plenty to talk about, with the baby and all. As long as I make sure to nod and smile at the appropriate times, no one will think twice. So, really, it's just another night.

Shifting the grocery bag into my left hand, I clumsily open the front door and trudge into the entryway.

"Stella! Is that you?" Mom shouts from the kitchen.

I huff out a laugh. "Do you know anyone else with a house key?"

"Your brother," she shouts back, and I hear footsteps approaching as her voice gets louder.

"Well, yeah, but he's—"

"Not here yet," she interrupts, appearing in front of me.

My eyebrows pinch together when I realize their SUV wasn't in the driveway. Confused, I slip off my wet shoes and shrug out of my jacket. "Are they running late? I thought we moved this dinner up so they could make it."

Her hands are on her hips, defenses already raised. I'm not sure how I managed to reach the hands-on-hips level of annoyance by asking one question. But, as always, leave it up to me.

"We did. They had an ultrasound and got stuck in rush hour traffic leaving the hospital." Her short brown hair is a few shades darker than mine, and she has it pulled back into a low, messy bun. She looks at me through narrowed eyes, the *"My favorite people call me Mom"* apron she's wearing a subtle oxymoron I try to ignore. Her hazel eyes are always primed, and tonight, I need to be extra cautious not to poke the bear.

She reaches a hand toward me, raising her eyebrows. "Did you get the ranch dressing?"

I reach down and pick the bag up off the floor, holding it out to her. "Why do we need this, anyway? Who likes ranch all of a sudden?"

She takes it, saying, "Dahlia requested it. Pregnancy craving." She pats me on the arm as she turns on her heel and hurries back into the kitchen.

"You're welcome," I mutter under my breath, following her through the archway that opens up into the large, bright living room.

Our house is all high ceilings and ornamental rugs, the long dining table the only thing dividing the kitchen wall from the living room. A plush L-shaped couch fills the space with one of those fancy looks-like-a-picture-frame flatscreen TVs mounted to the wall. Another archway leads into the kitchen from the hall-way, all dark oak cabinets with granite countertops and mixed marble accents that somehow just work together.

It all seems cozy and hospitable at first glance, and I guess that would be expected due to Mom's third and most loved child —her interior design company, The Abode.

As aesthetically pleasing as it may be, the house doesn't feel *lived* in. All the family vacation photos and school pictures have slowly been replaced over the years with dark framed mirrors, random artwork, and funky-shaped candlesticks.

It has been a really long time since this house felt like home.

Dad looks up from his perch on the recliner in the corner of the room. "Wow. You're drenched," he says.

I shrug and half-heartedly reply, "Seattle."

Dad smiles knowingly, turning his attention back to the crossword in his lap. I don't expect him to say anything else, but sometimes, I still hope he will. I wish conversation came as easily as it used to for us, that we could regain some small semblance of how things were.

My parents and I have never been super close by any means, but the air never used to feel awkward. Mom, as expected, is still usually her abrupt and to-the-point self, perhaps a little sharper than before, but it feels like my dad is just a little more distant.

Which, to be fair, he always has been . . . but never usually with me.

He is more reserved, quiet, and matter-of-fact by nature, but even I can tell how he's hardened around the edges over the past few years. It pains me to think of how far apart we've all grown, how time loosens threads and blurs images. But it's inevitable, I guess. Nothing can stay the same for long.

I'm about to go to the bathroom and towel off my hair when the front door opens behind me. I turn in time to see Daniel closing the umbrella behind Dahlia, her sweet laugh carried in with the rain. They step through the door, and my mom bursts out of the kitchen.

"Oh, you made it!" She claps, bringing them in for a hug.

"Sorry, we were running behind. That traffic was *insane*," Dahlia says, running her hands through her damp hair.

Mom waves her hand around in the air. "Don't you worry about it. I'm just glad you guys were careful."

"Hey, I was just driving in the rain, too, and all I got was a 'Did you get the ranch'?" I tease.

Mom doesn't bat an eyelash as she points at me and says seriously, "You're twenty-one. I'd expect you can manage driving just fine—and besides, you're not carrying my first grandchild."

The smile melts from my face. "Yeah. And thank God for that, right?"

She sighs, squeezing the bridge of her nose. "Stella, I don't know why you have to act like everything I say is—"

"You got the ranch?" Dahlia interrupts quickly.

Mom turns to her, and the sweet smile is back in place. "Of course, I did! Let me go finish getting it all ready . . ." Her voice trails off as she heads back to the kitchen.

With a grimace, Daniel follows behind her.

Already exhausted, my gaze drops to the floor. "Thanks," I mutter.

Dahlia reaches over and gives my arm a light squeeze, adding with a small, almost sad smile, "I got you." Placing her hands on her small bump, she walks into the living room.

Taking a deep breath, I trail behind her.

# 5

"Can you pass the green beans?" Daniel asks, gesturing to my dad.

As promised, Mom made Chicken Alfredo with steamed vegetables, dinner rolls, and salad. We dig into the plates of steaming food set intentionally around the table, and we're so hungry that the first few minutes of the meal are spent in silence.

"So, how was the appointment? Did you get a new picture? Did they tell you the gender?" Mom starts rapid-firing questions, eager to hear any news about the baby.

Daniel replies, "Great, yes, and no," around a mouthful of food.

Mom rolls her eyes at him as Dahlia reaches down into her purse, pulling out the new ultrasound photo.

As she hands it over to my mom, she says, "I'm twenty-eight weeks today, the baby is perfectly healthy and measuring right on time, and we are *still* not finding out the gender until birth." The smile in her voice is evident, the love she has for this little life radiating through her.

They hunch over the photo, Dad's reading glasses already perched on his nose.

"Oh, look, the baby is sucking its thumb!" Mom exclaims, leaning in closer to the picture.

Dad takes the ultrasound from her, squinting and holding it up to the light. "Here?" he says, pointing at the image.

"No, Justin, that's a foot," she chastises, snatching the ultrasound back and showing him again.

I pick up my glass to take a sip of water, knowing it's going to be a while before I get a chance to look at my niece or nephew.

"Hey, Stella, did you know Bridger is back in town?" my brother says casually, piling more green beans onto his plate.

I choke on my water the second the words leave his mouth, sputtering and coughing as I register what he just said. Dahlia starts patting me on the back incessantly and shooting daggers at Daniel. "How—" my voice comes out raspy and weak, so I clear my throat and try again. "How do you know that?"

"We saw him and his dad leaving the hospital as we were walking in for our appointment today."

"Yeah, but I wasn't going to mention it," Dahlia whisper-hisses at Daniel.

My parents stop ogling the picture still in their hands, and Mom leans forward with curiosity as Dad nervously flicks his eyes between me and Daniel.

Daniel shrugs, saying, "I mean, it's been a while. For all I know, she may not have even remembered who I was talking about."

My mind instantly flicks back through the mental images of Bridger in the parking lot a mere hour ago, and I almost laugh at the thought of not remembering him. His honest eyes, his steady hands, and his kind heart.

As if I could ever forget.

Dahlia sighs. Before she can reply, I hurriedly interject, "Guys—it's uh, it's fine. Let's just forget it."

Ignoring me, Mom starts thinking out loud. "Well, he is Stella's age, right? So technically, he should just be finishing up his third year at . . . where did he go again?"

"UNC," I reply quietly, eyes lowered to the table, not surprised at the fact that she conveniently couldn't remember the college I was supposed to go to.

"Oh, that's right, I knew it was somewhere on the East Coast. He went there on a soccer scholarship, right?"

I nod, trying to act like the very mention of his name isn't causing me to burst into flames.

"So, why is he back? Do you think he's home for the summer?"

I shrug my shoulders, letting out a small puff of air. "I don't know."

"I mean, he could've dropped out," Daniel joins back in.

I pinch my lips together, turning to look at my brother. "He wouldn't. Not after how hard he worked for everything." A dull pain throbs in my chest as I say the words.

He gives me a look, tilting his head slightly and lowering his eyebrows. "And you would know that how?" I take a steadying breath as he shrugs casually. "I'm just saying. She hasn't talked to the guy in, like, what, three years now? Who can say what he's gotten up to at college?"

My hands are gripping the edges of my chair so tightly that I can feel my knuckles turning white under the table. "He's not like that."

Dahlia is rubbing her temples, and Mom still has a contemplative look on her face like she's not really hearing what we're saying.

"Hey, how *is* school going, Stella? Summer semester started last week, yeah? I haven't heard much from you about it—you're either at class or holed up in your room," Dad interjects with a tight smile. He's always the first one to redirect the conversation whenever the past is concerned. Trying to keep the peace while simultaneously keeping to himself.

I'm just thankful that there's at least someone here who can read a room. He's looking at me expectantly, and I shoot him a quick, thankful glance before clearing my throat and taking the out he offered. "Yeah, it's going good so far. I have eleven credit hours, so it shouldn't be too bad."

He nods along, but Mom speaks up again before he can add anything else. "Why was Bridger at the hospital? Is he okay?" she says, voicing the question I was too afraid to even think about.

*Is he okay?*

"We didn't really get to chat. I mean, he looked fine, though," Daniel says matter-of-factly.

I don't understand how he can talk about all of this so easily, like he's not single-handedly ripping back open the tear in my heart that I wasn't sure I'd ever be able to fully mend.

"I'm sure he's fine, Stel. He's probably just home for the summer," Dahlia assures me before changing the subject yet again.

I don't hear another word of the conversation as everything that happened today whirls around in my mind, the implications hitting me all at once: Bridger, home from school, seeing him in the parking lot, hearing his voice, his hand touching my arm, he and his dad leaving the hospital . . .

"I don't feel very good," I say suddenly, cutting off my own thoughts. I abruptly stand from the table, my remaining food untouched. "I think I'm just going to head up to my room." I turn and leave the dining room before anyone has a chance to say anything else. Tears burn my eyes as I race up the stairs, the afternoon weighing heavily on my chest.

I shut my door and slump to the ground against it, covering my face with my hands to muffle my sobs. There's so much about him now that I don't know, years of his life that I haven't been part of. Moments and memories I've missed out on, pockets of joy and hurt that have nothing to do with me. I can feel that divide like a palpable thing—a slow pull, a subtle ache, all these years between us and the map that led us here.

I wish I could say I would've done something differently if I could go back now. After everything, I'd like to think I've come that far, at least.

But one glance at those deep brown eyes, and I knew.

This is how it has to be.

# 6

## THEN

September, Sophomore Year

I walked across the school grounds to the soccer fields, glaring at the grass, irritated that today, of all days, was the one that I decided to wear my white Converse. I silently cursed Mr. O'Neal for giving us this assignment and pulled my jacket tighter around myself, clutching my notebook to my chest.

We were working on promotional essays in creative writing this week, which I was trying not to be annoyed about but failing miserably. If I was honest, I couldn't even blame Mr. O'Neal for the fact that I was walking to the varsity boys' soccer practice after school because he'd said our principal had asked him directly to have his students help *liven the atmosphere of extracurricular activities and embolden students to join* with a promotional essay. When he fed us that line in class today, his tone was flat, and he was using air quotes, which led me to believe that he also wanted us to be doing, quite literally, anything else.

If Mr. O'Neal hadn't told us that our principal had sent out an email to the staff and coaches, letting them know students would be sitting in on the extracurriculars—and to expect us—I would've just googled some stuff about soccer and called it a day. But instead, I trudged the rest of the way to the benches on the sidelines in the early autumn chill.

The remnants of summer were almost nonexistent by then, auburn-brown leaves crunching under my feet as an early September breeze blew through my hair. The sun was just starting to peek out of the clouds following the midday down-pour, a soft hue painting the afternoon gold. I tucked my light brown hair into the claw clip I found in my bag and sat down on the bench.

The coach blew his whistle, followed by a gruff, "On the line!" So, I stayed and watched in the cold for another half an hour, wondering why I couldn't have been assigned something indoors like basketball or theater. I would've even settled for chess club if it meant I got to keep my white shoes white.

Glancing at what I'd written since I sat down, I was honestly impressed at the fact that I'd almost filled an entire page. Of course, it was mostly just things like, *"The guys are all laughing and joking around,"* and *"The players seem to be in good spirits despite the rain,"* which was better than nothing. At least, that was what I told myself by the time the coach called them all in for a post-practice huddle.

I started gathering my stuff to head to the warmth of my car when I heard that same gruff voice call, "Miss Reynolds?" Star-tled, I turned to see the coach heading my way. I managed a small nod and wave before he stopped in front of me and extended his hand.

"Coach Doug," he said with a smile. Then, without missing a beat, he continued, "So, what did you think?"

I swallowed, unprepared to discuss the "notes" I had been taking. "Uh . . ." I glanced down, panicking as I skimmed the length of them. "It looked . . . fun."

Coach Doug smiled and nodded, eyebrows raised as if he was

waiting for me to go on. So, I stammered, "Yeah, it looked like everyone was, you know, having a good time." I tried to smile, which I was sure looked more like a grimace, but he continued nodding nonetheless.

"So, did you gather enough information for your paper?"

"Yep!" I said brightly—*too* brightly?—as more of the players began walking by. I recognized a few of them from my grade, some smiling or giving me a head nod as they passed.

I looked back to Coach Doug, hoping for a dismissal, but instead, he smiled and said, "Well, we've got a great group of guys this season." His face brightened, and he followed up with, "Hey, how about a player interview?"

My heart started racing. "Oh, no, that's really okay. Mr. O'Neal said tha—" I began, but he wasn't listening as he started waving someone over.

"Wells! Wells, hang on a sec!"

I blew out an anxious breath, shivering as it started drizzling again. I looked over toward the group of guys as Coach Doug gestured with his hand. One of them slapped another on the back, pulled down the hood of his dark green rain jacket, and started in our direction. He approached with furrowed brows and shifted his equipment bag on his shoulder.

"What's up?"

"Bridger! Stella here," Coach jerked a thumb in my direction, "is working on a soccer project for her English class."

I frown. "Well, it's creative writing—"

"And she needs to do an interview—"

"I don't, actually. That's not—"

"And I told her you're the guy for the job!" he finished.

Bridger looked between me and his coach, nodding slowly. When he glanced at me again, I squinted and mouthed, *"He didn't say that."* The corner of his mouth lifted slightly in response, a small smile briefly flicking across his features before he looked back at Coach Doug.

"Sure thing, Coach."

"Perfect." Looking at me, Coach Doug continued, "Bridger made varsity his freshman year and didn't let an ACL injury slow him down. He knows just about everything about this sport you'd want to know. Team captain this year too. Only a sophomore!" He beamed at Bridger, who coughed and shifted on his feet uncomfortably. Coach Doug leaned over and slapped him on the back before walking away.

I turned to Bridger, who let out a small laugh as he awkwardly rubbed the back of his neck. "He's, uh . . ."

"Enthusiastic?" I supplied, and Bridger smiled, nodding slightly.

Clearing his throat, he said, "So, an interview?" He looked about as uncomfortable as I felt.

It was my turn to laugh awkwardly as I brushed a loose strand of hair out of my face. "Oh, we don't actually have to do that. The assignment doesn't say anything about interviews. That was your coach's idea . . ." I trailed off.

He huffed out another laugh as he ran a hand through his messy brown hair. "Okay, good." He took a small step toward me, glancing back over his shoulder before his eyes met mine again. The breeze drew out his warm, musky scent, and I found myself noticing his rain-damp hair and the way the floppy curls rested against his forehead.

Close up, I could see the depth of his amber-flecked, dark brown eyes. His pink, flushed cheeks were a warm contrast to his lightly tanned skin, and I silently wondered how someone could pull off the post-practice soaked and sweaty look so . . . well? And also—how could someone still smell that good after playing soccer for an hour in the rain?

I snapped back to reality when he started speaking again. "Between you and me, he seems like a total softie in any normal context, but on the field . . ." He shook his head again, that same glint of amusement crossing his features. "He's the toughest coach I've ever had."

I forced myself to look over his shoulder at his coach, if for no other reason than to get myself to stop staring at *him*.

I shifted my bag on my shoulder. "At least he's passionate about what he does, right? I feel like you don't see that a lot nowadays."

He tilted his head as he looked at me, brows drawn together and lips turned slightly upward. He studied me for a moment like he was trying to see the words on the page of a book without cracking the spine.

I looked away and cleared my throat, feeling like I just shared too much too soon and made it weird. "Well, I should probably go. I think I got everything I needed," I said, waving the notebook around lamely in the space between us. "Nice to meet you, Bridger," I mumbled as I turned around and began the long walk to my car. The rain had started to pick up again, and I had only made it about ten steps before his voice rang out from behind me.

"Stella, right?"

I turned back around. "Yeah." I nodded.

He smiled that same half-smile, and at the sight of the small dimple hidden in the hollow of his cheek, I could feel a faint blush rising up my neck. Suddenly, I was glad of the distance between us because I'd already embarrassed myself enough over our five-minute interaction.

"I can't wait to read your paper."

Then, I was glad for the distance *and* the Seattle weather because if it wasn't for the misty rain creating a veil between us, I'm sure he would have been able to see the fact that my face was on fire against my pale skin.

I brought a hand above my head in an attempt to block the rain. "It's not going to be anything to write home about," I said, backing away toward the parking lot as the drizzle quickly progressed into a downpour.

"Coach Doug might disagree," he said with a smile as he started backing away too.

I laughed, shaking my head as I stuffed my notebook into my bag.

"See you around, Stella!" he shouted over his shoulder as he jogged in the direction of the locker rooms.

I finally made it to my car, my wild heartbeat the only sound against the sudden, silent warmth. I turned the key in the ignition and shuffled my playlist, but I didn't even register the music playing through the car speakers. The only thing floating around my mind the entire ride home was the way he'd said my name.

And I didn't know it then.

*If only I had known it then.*

That was the beginning of everything.

# 7

I stepped into the house and was greeted by the smell of garlic bread and Mom's homemade pasta sauce. Clinking silverware and soft laughter sounded from the dining room, and I wasn't surprised they had started eating without me. Mom liked routine and schedule, and on weeknights, dinner always started at six. Glancing at the clock over the fireplace, I was ten minutes late.

Hurrying up the stairs to my room, I threw my bag on the floor and quickly changed into dry clothes, attempting to finger comb my hair as I made my way back downstairs into the hallway. I was about to round the corner into the dining room, but my steps slowed and then halted completely when I heard a voice talking amongst the others that I didn't recognize.

I surely would've remembered if we were going to have guests over, and Mom definitely wouldn't have let me be late. Cautiously, I crossed the threshold into the dining room and stopped short, not even trying to mask the confusion etched into my features.

My parents sat in their usual spots, with Mom at the head of the table and Dad just to her left. Across from my mom on the other end sat my brother, and to his left, in my usual seat, sat a girl I did not recognize. She had gorgeous, deeply tanned skin and beautiful wavy hair so black it almost looked iridescent. Everyone was laughing at whatever she had said as she animatedly told a story. The conversation continued, and it took a minute for Mom to finally notice me.

"Stella, there you are! Here, come sit," she said, gesturing to the barstool hastily pulled up to the corner of the table between Dad and Daniel. I walked toward it, awkwardly perching on the seat about two feet higher than everyone else, knees knocking into the plate in front of me. The silence was loud as I attempted to get comfortable in the less-than-ideal seating arrangement. I waited for someone to say something, and when I knocked my knees into the table for the second time, Mom finally spoke.

"Why don't you introduce yourself?" she said brightly, but as I looked up to tell my name to the dark-haired goddess sitting diagonally from me, I glanced at my mom again and realized she wasn't talking to me.

"Hi! I'm Dahlia," she smiled.

"Hi." I smiled back, hoping it looked genuine as I silently begged someone to tell me what the hell I'd missed.

Daniel reached over and grabbed Dahlia's hand, lightly squeezing it before adding, "My girlfriend."

Oh. *Oh.* The pieces fell into place as Dahlia looked over at Daniel and winked at him—she actually *winked* at him—and somehow, on her, it worked. Daniel had mentioned a few weeks ago that he was seeing someone he'd met during freshman orientation at the University of California, Berkeley, but I didn't know we were already at the meet-the-parents phase.

"It's so nice to meet you," she added brightly, pushing her shiny hair behind her shoulder.

"You too," I said, wishing I didn't feel like I was watching from the outskirts of my own life. I looked around the table and couldn't help but feel behind. Not because I'd walked through the door late but because no one had even told me she was coming over. I felt like an idiot trying to make up ground I hadn't even known I'd lost.

Mom somehow managed to find my foot underneath the table and nudged it. She grimaced at me and tried to subtly incline her head toward our apparent guest of honor.

"I'm Stella," I mustered, slapping on that same pinched smile.

"Of course, you are. I've heard so much about you!" Dahlia exclaimed, still beaming.

One glance at Daniel's averted gaze, and I could tell that she probably had not, in fact, heard so much about me. I was about to say something along the lines of *"Right back at ya!"* But that would have been a lie. So instead, I cleared my throat and looked at my dad. "Can you pass the garlic bread?"

At that, everyone started eating again, and Mom picked up the conversation. "Stella, you didn't tell me you were doing anything after school today. I expected you would be home on time."

*And yet you didn't text me when I wasn't.*

I traced the condensation on my water glass to avoid her gaze. "I was at the varsity boys' soccer practice, remember? I told you about it earlier this week."

She twirled some more spaghetti onto her fork, and I could see the wheels turning in her brain right before she looked up and said, "Oh yes, I remember. For English?"

"Creative writing," I said for the second time that day.

"Right, that report on school sports." She waved her hand around in the air as if to say, *"You know what I mean."*

"For the school newspaper?" Dad chimed in.

Before I could get in a word to actually explain what the assignment was again, Daniel asked, "That's why you're all wet? You were at soccer practice?" He chuckled, adding with air quotations, "For research?"

I met his gaze fully, my annoyance brimming. "Yes."

Daniel dropped his smile and scoffed. "Oh, come on, Stella. You really sat through an entire practice? I'm sure everyone bull-shitted that assignment except for you."

"Language, Dan," Mom chided.

He raised his hands in mock surrender, and I closed my eyes, inhaling a deep breath through my nose.

"I mean, come on. That's like actually doing the assigned summer reading. No one does."

"I did." My eyes snapped open when I heard the unfamiliar voice coming to my defense. "And I would've gone to practice too. Just because you scraped by doing the bare minimum doesn't mean everyone else does," Dahlia said, poking Daniel lightly on the arm.

We sat there for a moment in stunned silence. Then, a smile cracked across my features. "I like her," I said, staring at Daniel.

She laughed at that, and despite the dig, Daniel still looked at her like she had hung the moon.

Dahlia turned to me and said, "I think that's really cool. You're into creative writing?"

"Yeah," I said. At her open, earnest expression, something in me gave way, and I blurted out, "I want to be an author."

"Oh! How fun!" she exclaimed, sounding like she genuinely meant it.

I was about to tell her more when I looked over in time to catch my parents giving each other *"the look."* The same one they shared every time I talked about what I wanted to do in the future. That *"just wait until she gets to the real world"* look. Like I was naive.

Looking back over at Dahlia, I cleared my throat. "What do you want to do?"

I was glad when she smiled broadly again, moving along gracefully when the conversation flipped back to her. "I'm a business student," she said, and I caught my mom giving her a different look, the look a mother gives her child after they'd just won the first-grade spelling bee.

A look she'd never given me.

Dahlia continued, "I'm an intern at The Abode. On the digital marketing side, of course, since I have to do it virtually from school in California. I'm actually from Seattle, though. It's like taking a little piece of home to school with me." Her smile lit up her whole face.

I almost wanted to roll my eyes at my mom's matching expression. "And she is doing a fantastic job," Mom says as she reaches over and pats her hand. "Isn't it crazy that Dahlia is from Seattle, too, but she and Daniel didn't meet until they were both at school in California?"

Dahlia looked at my brother, gaze softening as she played with the dainty threaded gold bracelet around her wrist. She grinned at him, and he grinned right back.

Then he laced his fingers through hers and said, "It makes fall break super convenient. We're hanging out with her family tomorrow."

I tried to smile, nodding along as Mom pulled the conversation back her way. But all I could think about was Dahlia's previous statement about interning at The Abode, the place Mom had always hoped I would work one day. And all at once, the hearts in my mother's eyes when she looked at Dahlia made sense.

It was times like that when it almost hurt to think about how different my mom and I were, how far apart we'd ended up. Or maybe . . . how far apart we'd begun. I would never fit the mold of who she wanted me to be because I had never been like her.

I wasn't the daughter she thought she was getting. The one she hoped she would have. The one who was supposed to grow up and want to go to a fancy business school and co-own her company one day. The one who would happily attend countless work dinner parties and avoid wrinkles in her blouse. The one who would care more about how her life looked than how it felt.

But I had never been that girl.

I was the one in the shadows of the nice dinner party, writing a story on the back of my napkin, losing myself in other worlds and places and daydreams, grasping onto the words that took me there. She'd always scolded me for not paying attention or being caught up in my head, but I couldn't help it. It was like I was programmed from the start to exist somewhere inside of myself entirely, somewhere different than the world around me in this glow of hope and possibility that only I could see.

She had tried to smother that glow, always thought it was a waste of my time. I had constantly disappointed her, again and again, and over the past few years, it seemed like she'd given up trying with me. Like she had given up *on* me entirely.

It almost hurt. But not quite.

Because I couldn't say I never saw it coming.

I'd never be who she wanted me to be, but I wasn't sure that mattered anymore.

One look at Dahlia, and I realized that my mom was about to get everything she'd ever wanted.

It was a sort of simultaneous pang of relief and trepidation, as if there was some intrinsic part of me that still hoped we could get there someday. To a place where it didn't matter who exactly I was, just that I was hers.

But she'd always been the one to tell me not to waste my time on fantasies.

I slid off my stool and said, "I'm tired. I think I'm just going to head up for the night." I walked out of the dining room, not having eaten a bite. Either no one noticed or no one cared as I walked down the hallway and up the stairs to my room.

# 8
## THEN

<br>

October, Sophomore Year

"You have got to be kidding me." I threw my keys into the passenger seat and dropped my head into my hands, blowing out a breath. I should have been happy the school week was finally done, but the ease I usually felt on a Friday afternoon was replaced with a sharp annoyance that was growing hotter by the second. I should've been home by then, but I was still in the parking lot because my car wouldn't start.

It had been one of those days where I wondered why I even bothered getting up in the first place. I had fallen asleep the night before slumped against my desk, and my alarm didn't go off because I hadn't set one. By the time I had finally startled awake, I'd missed my first class entirely.

When I'd hurried down the stairs and grabbed my lunch from the kitchen, Mom was there, sipping her coffee casually and asking me why I wasn't responsible enough to set an alarm. I didn't bother asking her why she didn't wake me up after she realized I'd overslept. Instead, I said I obviously hadn't meant to fall asleep at my desk, and when she'd asked me what I could have possibly been doing that was so important I couldn't walk the five feet to my bed, I replied, "writing."

At the look she gave me after that, I should've just turned around right then and there and called it a day.

I grabbed my phone out of the cup holder, hesitating as I hovered over my contacts. My dad was at work, my brother was back at the University of California, and Mom usually had tons of afternoon meetings on Fridays. I realized with a small laugh that felt as humorless as it sounded that there was no one.

I could list on one hand how many people I had in my life that I was supposed to be able to count on, and apparently, when it came down to it, those people didn't actually count.

With another sigh, I opened Google instead, but before I could type anything into the search bar, the phone died in my hand. Of course, it wasn't charged because I didn't miraculously plug it in before I accidentally fell asleep. I blinked at it in disbelief, my resigned face the only thing I could see in the reflection of the black screen. I closed my eyes, let it drop into my lap, and pressed the heels of my hands to my face.

Releasing another breath, I dropped my hands and flung the door open, the air in the car suddenly feeling too stuffy. The breeze was a relief, and I relished the feeling of the cool air on my skin. I sat there for a second and decided against my better judgment to try one more time. I grabbed the keys and shoved them into the ignition, hoping against all hope that it would work.

And, of course, it didn't. The same broken wheeze sounded over and over as if the car was painfully attempting to hold in a sneeze.

I huffed out a breath as I got out, annoyed that I was going to have to go into the school to find a teacher, or a lunch lady, or Coach Doug, or someone, *anyone*, to ask if they had jumper cables when a voice cut through the noise in my brain and broke off my train of thought.

"Do you need a hand?" The boy from the soccer field—Bridger, I reminded myself quickly—was standing a few feet away with his practice bag slung over his shoulder, unruly brown hair blowing gently in the breeze.

"Oh. Uh yeah, I just—my car," I finished lamely. "It won't start."

He nodded in understanding, and amusement glinted in his eyes as he said, "I heard."

I laughed, slightly embarrassed when I realized how loud my car must've been, considering how many attempts it took before I gave up. My cheeks heated, and I looked away.

"It's my brother's old car. My parents gave it to me for my sixteenth birthday last month. I think the battery is dead, and I was about to Google how to jump-start a car, but my phone died, and I don't even have jumper cables or another . . . car, so—" I cut myself off, my confidence waning with every word as I rambled.

He got his keys out of his pocket and started walking toward a dark blue sedan a few spots over. "So, I do happen to have a car, but as for the jumper cables, if we just link arms and touch our car batteries, I think there should be enough kinetic energy to . . ." He looked over at me again, and I'm not sure what expression was painted on my face, but it caused him to stop with his trunk half open and say, as he tried to hold back a smile, "I'm kidding."

I abruptly let out an overly breathy laugh (that I immediately wanted to kick myself for) as he reached down into his trunk and held up the cables for me to see. "My dad owns an auto shop, so I have too many, actually. You can just keep these when we're done."

I instantly stuttered, "Oh no, that's okay. I'll just—"

"Seriously. Take them," he said, backing away, opening his car door, and sliding into the front seat. "It's like free marketing. Just make sure you go to Adam's Auto Repairs for your next oil change," he joked, and then I was the one trying to suppress a smile.

He drove his car directly in front of mine. Parking, he got out and popped his hood, so I took that as my sign to do the same.

"So, do you just hang around in the parking lot after school, hoping to find business then?" I teased.

He smiled, and when that dimple just barely showed around the corner of his mouth it suddenly became my life mission to get it to appear again. "What, I see a pretty girl with a dead car battery, and I'm just supposed to walk away and *not* offer her my perfectly useful jumper cables?"

My lips parted in surprise. His eyes widened slightly, his cheeks immediately turning pink as if he had just then registered what he'd said. He looked down and coughed, ran a quick hand through his hair, and thrust the cables out in front of him. "Here, you take these. I can walk you through it," he said, still diverting his gaze. I reached out and took them, trying not to react when my fingers lightly brushed against his. "You know, just in case this ever happens again," he finished, still looking anywhere but at me.

"What, you mean if my battery dies, and there aren't any auto-mechanic heirs loitering around?" I said, attempting to clear any awkwardness from the air and bring back the light atmosphere that we had moments before.

He looked up at me again, and I swore I saw something like relief flash across his face, but it was gone before I had the chance to think it meant something. He gestured to the empty lot around us. "I'd hardly call walking to my car in the high school parking lot after meeting with my soccer coach *loitering*," he said.

"Kind of odd that you felt the need to have an alibi. Should I go ask Coach Doug what time you left his office, or . . . ?"

He laughed full out, and the dimple reappeared, along with a sudden warmth blooming brightly in my chest. My heart picked up speed as if it already knew all that laugh would mean to me, as if it had heard it before.

"You know, Coach Doug asked about you again," he said as he started to show me where to attach the different colored cables.

I attached the red clamp to the place he pointed to on my battery and choked on a laugh. "Why?"

"He wanted to hear all about the interview."

"No way." I shook my head in disbelief.

"He did. I told him not to worry and that I gave you great material to work with."

The smile on my face started to slip away as I said, "It's not like he'll read it, though, right? I mean, people act like they care because they have to, but when it comes down to it . . ." I paused when I looked up and realized he'd stopped what he was doing, his hand resting on the open hood, watching me.

He lowered his hand from the hood and faced me completely. "He'd better have. I left an extra copy of the article on his desk before I left."

A few of the essays from the creative writing assignment had been printed in last week's edition of the school newspaper. Mine happened to be one of the ones that was selected for the "Sports and Spectators" section. "You read the school newspaper?" I asked him, surprised.

"No." My brows furrowed at his response, confused, and he continued, "Well, I mean—I hadn't. Not until last week, at least."

Then it was my turn to stop, my hand slipping from the second cable I had just attached. "You read my article?"

He met my gaze, and the warmth in my chest dropped lower into my stomach, heating me from the inside out. "Of course. I told you I would."

I managed, "Oh. Cool," because I wasn't really sure what else to say. I tried to tell myself that it wasn't a big deal, but the sad thing was . . . it actually was. No one had ever acknowledged my writing, and even though it was just some dumb short article in a school newspaper—it mattered.

"It was really good. I especially liked the part about the color of our new jerseys being totally in this fall."

My heart stuttered as my face fell, realizing maybe he just said he read my article because it was the nice thing to do, or worse—he was mocking me. It was as if a cold bucket of water had been dumped over me, and I suddenly realized how pathetic it was that I cared so much.

"Stella," he said. I looked back at him again to see a serious expression painted across his soft features, accompanied by an intense stare. "Sorry. That was a dumb attempt at a joke. Your article—it was good. Really."

My brows dipped, and I couldn't help the tilt of my head that followed, saying that I didn't believe him without telling him.

He turned back to the car to attach the final cable. "Honestly," he said. "I mean that."

A faint smile spread across my lips. "Thanks. Let's hope Coach Doug thinks the same," I replied.

He laughed again, a deep chuckle that I felt reverberate through every bone in my body. He exhaled before looking at me with those dark, kind eyes. "Okay. So," he walked around his car, "you have to start the car with a working battery and let it run for a couple of minutes . . ."

I knew I should've been listening, but all I could think about was how a cute boy was being patient and sweet and understanding, and how he stayed to help me, and that he read my article. The next thing I knew, he was standing in front of me again, and I realized too late that his mouth was still moving and I still wasn't listening.

"Sorry—what?" I cleared my throat in an attempt to divert some embarrassment, but all I think it did was make it more obvious that I didn't hear him.

"I said you can go ahead and start your car now."

"Oh. Right, of course." I dug my keys out of my hoodie pocket and opened my car door again. I leaned over and turned the key in the ignition, breathing out a deep sigh of relief when it hummed to life. I fist-pumped the air and mouthed, *"Woo-hoo!"* at him through the windshield. He looked at me with that same amused, almost shy expression he had before.

I jumped out of the car and held up my hand in the air in front of him before I realized I was doing it. That full, dimpled smile broke out across his face again as he gave me a high five. "Thank you so much, really," I told him as he stepped back toward the hood of the car.

He shrugged with a small shake of his head. "It's no problem." He motioned to the cables and told me which ones I should remove first, telling me to make sure they didn't touch as I did. Bridger insisted once again that I kept them and handed me the bag to put them in.

I tried not to react as our hands brushed again, tried not to watch as he ran his hand through the hair that kept flopping across his forehead, and tried not to admit to myself that this meant anything more than it did.

"Keep it running for a few minutes after you get home, yeah? Maybe drive a couple extra laps through your neighborhood before turning it off again."

I nodded, placing the bag in the trunk. "Sounds easy enough."

He nodded along with me and said, "You've got this next time. You know, if it ever happens again."

"Yeah, because I totally pulled a ton of weight there." I laughed, meeting his eyes.

He shrugged. "I believe in you."

And even though I knew it was dumb, and even though I knew it shouldn't have, those four words pulled and tugged at the threads of my mind and buried themselves in the corners of my heart because I knew he was talking about a car battery, but it felt like more. To me, with him, I'd quickly learn—it was always more.

Pulling my gaze away from his, I said quickly, "Hopefully it won't come to that!" and started to open my car door.

"Wait—" he said.

I stopped, my hand resting on the window frame. He looked as though he was contemplating something, and it made me uneasy.

"Would you want to . . ." He trailed off, and my heart started pounding incessantly in my chest. "I thought maybe—" He started again, cutting himself off with a slight shake of his head. Bridger looked away as he cleared his throat. "I was just thinking that if, uh, that if your car gives you any more trouble, just bring it into the shop. My dad will look at it. For a good price," he added, and a slight pink tint rose on his cheeks again.

"Oh. Yeah, okay. That sounds good, thanks," I stammered back. I wasn't sure what shifted in the air, but there was a subtle intensity that wasn't there before, something taking up residence in the space between us.

"Cool," he replied and nodded at the ground with pursed lips. It still felt like there was something he hadn't said, but I didn't want to push.

"Well, thanks again for staying after school and helping me. Seriously—you're a lifesaver."

He looked up from the ground and met my eyes again. A small smile pulled at the corner of his mouth. "I'm happy to help."

Then his eyebrows shot up quickly as he said, "Oh—hang on a sec." He pulled out his wallet and began rummaging through it. Just as I began to panic that he was going to—*pay me?*—he handed me a small white card with *Adam's Auto Repairs* printed on the front in bold blue letters with a phone number underneath. "He just got a bunch of those made, and he's really proud of how they turned out, so . . ."

He trailed off again, and my heartstrings pulled at how obvious it was that his dad meant a lot to him. I turned the card over in my hands, a small smile tugging at my lips. "I appreciate it."

He smiled at me, and I smiled back, trying to ignore my still-racing heart, not allowing myself any time to read into it. I opened my car door fully, and before any silence could stretch on, I said, "Thanks." I could feel myself blush as I added dumbly, "Again."

He laughed and said, "You're welcome." A brief pause, and then he added with a smile, "Again."

I smiled back at him as if I could resist when he was looking at me the way he was. Clearing my throat, I said, "See you around."

He nodded, that same soft, half-crooked grin back in place. I got in my car and drove away, not realizing I was still smiling until I was halfway home.

<br>

# 9

## NOW

Monday comes as uneventfully as it always seems to, and I watch as morning light sifts through the blinds and lands across my bed in slanted yellow rows. I haven't really left my room over the past three days after retreating here in the middle of our family dinner.

After seeing Bridger.

Dahlia came up to say goodbye before they left on Friday night, telling me not to worry about what they saw at the hospital and reiterating that maybe Bridger was just visiting his dad for the summer. I agreed half-heartedly, but even after everything, I still know him well enough. If he's back, he's back for a reason.

This knowledge followed me everywhere over the past seventy-two hours. Everything I did to keep myself busy was clouded by the relentless hum in the back of my mind. No matter how hard I tried, I couldn't shake it.

I couldn't shake him.

And so, I stopped trying. I gave up and gave in, letting my mind wander, walking through all the possibilities, all the whys and what-ifs it could think of. My therapist would probably say that's not a good idea, and I would probably agree. But I already knew I was going to be thinking about it anyway, so I decided I might as well just let it consume my mind in one go and hopefully move on with my life quicker rather than ruminating for weeks. Again, my therapist would say that's a lame excuse, and once again, I would probably agree.

It's not uncommon for me to stay holed up in my own little world for days at a time, and if my parents were worried that I only left my room to eat and shower this weekend, they made no mention of it.

On Monday morning, I jog down the stairs and head for the front door.

"Oh, look! She does still live here." Mom's voice rings out from the kitchen, and I sigh as I peek my head around the arched doorway. Dad is sitting at the breakfast table doing the morning crossword before going into the office, and Mom is making her coffee before she heads out.

"Good morning to you too!" I reply with false enthusiasm.

"Where are you off to?" Dad cuts in, peering at me over the top of his mug before Mom has a chance to reply.

"UW."

"Campus? I thought all your summer courses were online," Mom says.

"Not all. But I'm not going to class, anyway. There's a course I think I need to drop, so I'm going to go talk to a guidance counselor."

Mom turns, hand on her hip, primed and ready at eight in the morning. "Drop a class already? Really, Stella?"

"Yes," I reply, not offering anything else, knowing there is nothing I can say that will placate her.

Living at home during the past three years when I should've been away at UNC has been challenging, to say the least. After I deferred the first semester and transferred to UW, it was too late to get a dorm for freshman year.

Not that I really cared, of course, because that year, I had trouble caring about anything at all. So, in my first semester, I commuted from home. When I saw how much money I would save by not getting a dorm . . . I just never did.

Days like today are when I regret that decision.

But now, as I spend my third college summer in a row within the walls of my childhood home, I wish I had gone to UNC like I'd planned.

Mom takes a deep breath, pinching the bridge of her nose. "Your dad and I were very understanding when you decided to defer the first semester, but I don't think it's smart to get any further off track—"

"Understanding?" I cut her off. "That's how we're remembering it?"

She drops her hand, rings smacking against the counter. "*Yes,* Stella, because maybe if you hadn't—" She cuts herself off, and all the air immediately leaves the room.

No one says anything. When I finally speak, my voice comes out shaky. "If I hadn't what, Mom?" I say, voice low, a question and a challenge all in one.

She's rubbing her temples now, and I cannot believe that after all this time, we still can't even *talk* about it.

Dad cuts in. "The important thing is that she's sticking with it. Right?" He raises his eyebrows at me in question.

I sigh, conceding. "I'm only dropping this class because I can't take it until I finish the prerequisite, which I'm enrolled in right now. I don't know how it got onto my course schedule. I'm going to see if I can replace it with another class, so don't worry, Mom. I'm staying on track just fine."

But she'll believe what she wants, and I'll pretend like I don't care, and we'll continue to do this dance, and maybe one day it won't hurt. For now, I turn on my heel and trudge out the door, not even hesitating as I reach for the handle because I know they have nothing to say.

# 10

I walk up the long pathway to the Office of Admissions, the early morning dew still clinging to the grass along the edge of the sidewalk. It feels weird seeing the campus so quiet, but there's also a sort of peace hidden in the solitude. There are only a few other cars parked near the building, so I hope this will get sorted out quickly so I can get back to the preferred peaceful solitude of my room.

I open the door and am instantly met with the smell of pencil shavings and printer ink. An older woman sits behind the desk, glasses halfway down her nose, gray-flecked hair pulled back into a low bun.

She smiles as I enter, taking her glasses off and letting them hang from the beaded strap around her neck. "How can I help you?" she says.

"I need to drop a class and maybe add a new one," I say.

She nods, typing something into her computer and asking for my student ID. "If you just have a seat in the chairs around the corner, someone will be with you shortly."

"Thank you," I reply, making my way to the sitting area. I round the corner to see six plastic chairs lining the walls of the tight space, with a small coffee cart tucked into the corner. The only other person in the area is a guy at the cart, dumping a packet of sugar into a cup of steaming coffee. I sit down, taking in the gray-and-purple-flecked carpet and off-white walls, then settle into my chair and really look at the coffee guy for the first time. His back is to me, but as I watch him, I can feel my pulse start to slow as my mind catches up to my eyes.

No. *No.*

It can't be him.

My breathing stops as he slightly turns his head, his profile visible as he throws the empty sugar packet in the trash. As if I even needed to see his features to recognize him. It's obvious now, the blatant pull of him, every fiber of my being screaming from just being five feet away from him. I'm frozen to the spot, running through my options, knowing I have about two seconds before he turns around and notices me. He grabs a lid and picks up the cup, and I decide to run a second too late as he turns to face me when I'm halfway out of my seat.

He startles, and I realize he probably didn't hear anyone else come in. His eyes widen, and I silently hope it's from surprise rather than recognition. I quickly duck my head and stand up fully, grabbing my bag and hurrying around the corner. And, of course, my hope is short-lived when I hear that voice.

"Stella?"

I pass the main desk, the office lady's eyebrows shooting up in surprise as I hurry past. "I'll come back another time," I offer weakly over my shoulder as I burst through the double doors and into the morning sun. The fresh air is a welcome contrast to my too-hot skin. I take the side stairs toward the parking lot two at a time, sucking in a breath as I hear the door open behind me again.

"Stella, wait—"

I hear footsteps behind me and gasp as I feel a hand lightly touch my forearm. I come to a halt, breathing heavily. I wish I could blame it on the fact that I was moving fast, but we only made it about twenty steps away from the building.

Bridger lets go of my arm, and I can hear him breathing just as hard as me. Emotion wells in my chest, and I swallow against the burning in the back of my throat. I knew I couldn't outrun this forever. Even though I've tried—literally—twice now in the past week. I, of all people, should know that everything always catches up. I just thought I had more time.

Steeling myself, I slowly turn to face him. Whatever I had been able to catch of my breath is lost in a second, the same way I lost him. My eyes follow the path my hand has traced a million times before—the prominent line of his cheekbone, the soft angle of his nose, the sharp curve of his jaw. He has a new scar just above his right eyebrow, and it kills me that I don't know how it got there. It kills me to think that there are so many little things I don't know about him anymore, that his life has gone on just as mine.

Time moved on without me. And I wonder if he has, too.

We stay that way for a few heartbeats, taking each other in, nothing but air and breath and all the things we should've said spanning the distance between us. He looks at me, and I wonder what he sees. I wonder how I look to him now, wonder if he can see the last three years weighing on me as if they're a barbell laying across my shoulders.

His eyes pool with an emotion I can't quite name as he wears an expression I can't quite distinguish. I blink rapidly, painfully, as I realize all at once that I don't know how to read him anymore and at one point he was my favorite book. He runs a hand across his face as if waking from a dream, and I meet those dark brown eyes once again.

"It's—I . . ." he starts, dropping his hand to his side. "It's you," he finishes quietly.

"What are you—" I break off, unsurprised at how wobbly my voice sounds. I swallow, willing my breath to stay even. I look up at him again, not quite meeting his eyes but not looking away. I clear my throat, trying again. "What are you doing here?"

He scratches the back of his neck, meeting my eyes once again. He gestures back to the building we just came from and says, "I was trying to get my course schedule for the summer semester worked out. I'm . . . I'm transferring here. To UW."

All the breath rushes from my lungs again because this means he's here to stay.

"Why?" is all I can manage.

He blows a puff of air out of his cheeks, rubbing his hand along his jaw before letting it drop to his side again. "Tore my ACL and meniscus last season."

My mouth falls open as my heart sinks.

He tries to placate me with a smile, but it looks more like a wince before he continues, "Long story short, I lost my athletic scholarship."

My blood runs cold, and my mind races with more questions as he runs a hand over the back of his neck.

He hesitates before continuing, "And now there's everything with Dad . . ." He trails off again, shrugging slightly. "I had to move home."

My eyes immediately drop to the new, prominent scar on his knee. I remember Daniel saying he saw Bridger and his dad leaving the hospital, and the familiar pang of worry settles in my chest as heavily as the expanse of the years between us.

There's so much I want to know, and that's exactly why I can't ask. I don't get to be that person for him anymore. I haven't been for a long time.

"So . . . what are you doing here?" he asks tentatively.

I bite the inside of my lip, thinking of how to give him enough of an answer that he won't ask any more questions. "I go here. I deferred the first semester, so . . . I'm taking some summer classes to help make up for it."

He nods slowly. "Oh." Gingerly, he takes a step toward me. "Stella . . ." he breathes, his eyes searching, pleading.

"Bridger, I—" I exhale, cutting myself off sharply and shaking my head. I wipe my eyes quickly, backing away, unable to withstand this closeness any longer. "I have to go." My voice comes out just barely above a whisper as I turn away from him.

"Wait. Please."

I stop at the slight tremor in his voice, a sort of heaviness I haven't heard before.

"Please. Just—" He exhales shakily again. "Just hold on."

I turn back around, looking into his glassy eyes that mirror my own.

"Can we talk?"

I look at my shoes, knowing I won't be able to say what I need to if I'm watching him. I squeeze my eyes shut, hating myself for what I have to do. "I don't think that's a good idea."

"Why not?"

"Bridger . . ."

"Stel."

I freeze at the sudden closeness of his voice, my eyes opening to find him right in front of me.

"What happened to us?" he whispers.

And that's the final blow. There's no stopping the tears as they flow freely down my cheeks. I choke back a sob, bringing my hands to my face and, almost instantly, he's there. He's there like he always would've been if I had let him.

I instinctively step toward him, and he wraps his arms around me. Sinking into him, I bring my hands from my face to his chest and feel his rapid heartbeat underneath my fingertips. I'm soaking his shirt, embarrassed for me and sad for him, yet somehow, curling closer into him with each inhale because right now, he's him, and I'm me, and for a second, we're us again.

I give up and give in, feeling something give way inside of

me, something that always knew it would be him. Somehow, it would be him.

I bury my head in his shoulder, and he pulls me tighter, one hand anchored to the small of my back and the other rubbing circles up and down my spine. I let out a shaky breath and wrap my arms around his torso as his hand moves up to my hair, cupping the back of my head, holding me steady against him.

And we stay like that. He holds on to me like he used to, like he said he always would. Like I never thought he would again.

After minutes or hours or decades, when I'm certain I won't fall into a million tiny pieces if he lets go, and when I finally come to my senses, I pull back. He lets me go, and I turn away, wiping my eyes and sniffing into my sleeve. "God, I'm so—I don't know what just . . . I'm sorry."

He's shaking his head, his t-shirt stained with my tears. "For what?"

I shrug helplessly, my voice coming out scratchy and raw as I reply, "For all of it."

He releases a wobbly exhale, and I swear I can hear my heart fissuring. "Don't do this. Don't run away again."

"You're the one who left." It's a cheap dig, and I know it.

His face twists in pain. "You're the one who told me to go."

I sigh, exhausted, already feeling the post-sob headache coming on. "I know."

We're quiet then, nothing but the sound of distant cars honking and birds chirping filling the silence around us.

Finally, I say, "I think I should go."

He lets out a breath, eyelids heavy. "Give me a minute." Then, running a hand over his face, he adds, "Please."

I press my lips together and wait, knowing that standing with him in the silence he asked for is the least I can do right now. I try not to count the seconds that pass before he speaks again.

"Do you hate me?"

The question catches me so off guard that I actually take a

step backward. "Do I— What? No, I could never . . . no. I don't hate you."

He exhales again, nodding, and I know I'm not imagining the relief I see flitting across his features. A whole new wave of guilt washes over me when I think of all the weight he's been carrying these past three years, the way the burden hasn't been all mine. And my heart breaks all over again because one look at the way he's looking at me right now, and I know. I know he doesn't know what happened that night, and I can't tell him the truth because I'm afraid the truth will be the final blow.

I'm afraid the truth will crush him.

"I'm sorry, Bridger," I say, turning to leave. I don't even make it a step before he speaks again.

"Did you change your number?"

I purse my lips, angling my head back to look at him. "Yes," is all I offer.

He nods slowly. "Okay."

I add, "I had to."

His eyes narrow, concern marring his features. "Okay?" He draws out the word slowly, a question in his tone.

"It wasn't a big deal." I try to backtrack, but he doesn't take the bait.

"It was to me," he says quietly, the words feeling like a sharp edge in my gut. He sighs, and I can see the moment the fight leaves him. Then, quietly, he says, "Are you okay?"

My brows furrow. That's not at all what I was expecting him to ask. "Yeah." I nod, unsure whether I'm trying to convince him or myself. "I'm good."

"Okay. Good," he replies. I can tell he doesn't quite believe me, but I am thankful he leaves it at that.

"Are you?" I ask without thinking.

He stills before dipping his head slightly. "Been better."

"Right," I whisper, hoping he can't see the shame that claws at my insides. I'm about to turn away again before I can make anything worse, but there is a part of me—an unnamable thing—a small piece that somehow survived all this time that doesn't want to leave him again.

He clears his throat. "Um. Well, it was . . . good to see you again." He grimaces after the words leave his mouth, and my heart flips at the familiar expression.

I suddenly feel a surge of panic, a frantic rush that pulls at my heart and the tether between us. I don't want to watch him walk away again. I can't. I know it's selfish, and I know I shouldn't, but I step forward before I think better of it—before I think at all—and hold out my hand. "Can I see your phone?"

His brows pull together. A small, questioning smile tugs at the corner of his mouth as he slowly reaches into his back pocket, hesitates, and hands it to me.

I put my new number in and hand it back to him, trying to ignore the small glimmer of hope I know will be in his eyes if I look. He stares down at the new contact I added with a frown.

"Stella Reynolds."

"Yes . . . ?"

"Why did you put Reynolds?" he says, pointing to the glowing screen in front of him.

Now, it's my turn to be confused. "Because . . . it's my name?"

He gives me a pointed look. "Stella. I'm still me."

I hesitate, the weight of his words thickening the air between us. "Yeah, well. I don't know how many Stellas you know now."

He smiles, but it's sad. "Just the one."

I think of the years he spent on the other side of the country in a completely different state with entirely new people. "I find that hard to believe."

He shrugs. "It's true, but—even so. You're the only Stella who matters."

My breath catches in my throat again, unsure of what else to say. There are too many words, but they're still not enough, and my thoughts are tangled together like the history between us.

"I've missed you," I blurt out. Immediately, I clamp my mouth shut, watching as his cheeks turn a light shade of pink. I feel mine turning the same shade, shocked that I still have that effect on him and that he still has the same one on me.

Seeing him here, having him here, knowing he'll be here indefinitely—it's a lot to take in. I can feel myself wavering, wondering what it would be like to know him now. Wondering if, after everything, he still wants to know me.

I get my answer as he slides his phone back into his pocket and says, voice low and tentative, "Would you maybe want to . . . I don't know, catch up sometime?" He huffs out a laugh after he says it, shaking his head. "God. I sound ridiculous. I just . . ." He shrugs, averting my gaze. "I've missed you too," he all but whispers.

And hearing those four words awakens something that's been dormant inside of me for three years, a gentle nudge, a subtle pull.

"Okay," I hear myself say. A small smile breaks across his face, and I can't help the one that breaks across my own.

"Okay."

I let out a quiet breath. "Okay. Um, I should probably go," I say.

He nods as he starts to back away. "Maybe I'll see you around?"

I give him a small nod. "Maybe."

And with that, Bridger offers a small wave before turning toward the opposite parking lot. I start walking to my own car, my mind whirling in disbelief at what just happened. I'm still unable to even comprehend that I saw him here, let alone the fact that I practically agreed to see him again.

I told him I miss him.

He said he's missed me too.

*Selfish, selfish, selfish.* The words echo in my head, timed to the pounding of my heart. I slide into the driver's seat and let them fill the space. At some point on the drive home, my heart beats a normal rhythm again, and I realize the words have changed.

*What if, what if, what if?*

Later that night, my phone buzzes against my nightstand. All the breath rushes from my lungs as I see those seven numbers I still know by heart.

Maybe: Bridger

10:07 p.m.

UW is a lot bigger of a campus than I remembered . . . I'll probably need a tour sometime. Just saying.

(This is Bridger, btw)

You think I have a lot of people texting me asking for campus tours?

You're funny, you know that?

Glad you still think so!

And sure, I'm happy to

# 11

## THEN

October, Sophomore Year

"Mom, seriously. I wasn't even planning to go."

"And that's exactly the problem." She gave me a stern look from across the living room.

I was instantly annoyed with myself for letting it slip that the fall bonfire was tonight. Earlier this week, I heard people talking in class about the annual school event on Saturday, and I honestly had no intention of going—until Laynie from my biology class personally asked me if I was attending. Laynie and I weren't super close by any means, but I'd known her since middle school, and we had shared a lot of the same classes over the years.

I'd acted as if I was thinking about it, all the while knowing dang well I was going to be curled up in my room with a good book on Saturday night. She said she would text me the details, and I told her I'd think about it—but school events had never really been my thing.

Until yesterday, when, on a rare occasion, Mom asked me what my plans were for the weekend and, dumbly, I'd made a joke about the bonfire. For some reason, she decided then that it was her sole job to make sure I attended. So, there we were on Saturday evening, and she still hadn't let it go.

"Why do you want me to go so badly? You've never cared what I do on the weekends." (Which was nothing, usually.)

She pursed her lips. "I just think you need to leave the house every once in a while, go enjoy high school, make some friends."

I looked at her skeptically because I didn't understand why any of this mattered so much to her all of a sudden—and then almost laughed to myself because, according to her, even when I was doing nothing, I was still doing it wrong.

I tried to reason with her. "Mom, you're looking at this all wrong. I'm a good student. I don't get into trouble. And honestly, you never even notice when I am here, so what difference does it make whether I'm here tonight or not?"

She sighed and gave me a look that almost resembled pity. "It's just—Daniel was so social in high school. And look at him now! A freshman at the University of California, already a part of a few extracurriculars, nice friends, a wonderful girlfriend . . ."

And that was when I stopped paying attention because that was how it always went. My brother and I couldn't have been more different, yet all my parents ever did was compare us. He was the golden boy who could never do wrong in their eyes, and I was the lost one who never said the right thing.

I tuned back in as she finished with ". . . and he's heading down a great career path."

I meant to sigh, but it ended up sounding more like an exasperated huff because it *always* came back to this. "What does going to a dumb high school *bonfire* have to do with a career path?"

Her eyes narrowed. "Because I'd rather you go actually *try* to make friends for once instead of never leaving the house and wasting all your time making up stories."

The second the words were out, the air around us shifted.

She had taken it too far, and we both knew it. The only thing was, she would never admit that. And I know now that something in me shifted then, too. I bit the inside of my cheek to keep the emotions at bay and, nodding wordlessly, walked to the front hallway. I stopped by the front door, hesitating before I grabbed the handle. It was a subconscious split-second pause as if some helpless part of my heart was hoping she might say something.

Of course, she didn't. So, I didn't look back before I opened the door and walked out of the house.

# 12

I was still reeling as I pulled off the main road and onto the unpaved side street that led to the bonfire. I tried not to replay my mom's words over and over in my head the whole drive and failed completely. Things were always weird and tense with her about this kind of stuff, so I typically just tried to avoid it.

I was hoping that the drive over would help me cool off, but my annoyance just gave way to nerves as I parked behind a banged-up Subaru in the grass off the edge of the road and truly realized, for the first time, what I had gotten myself into. Right before I left the house, I texted Laynie, asking if she could meet me outside and walk in with me. Showing up at all was already a huge feat, but walking in alone was a whole different beast. So, I was relieved when she texted back almost immediately, saying she would.

I sighed, knowing how pathetic it would look for me to back out. A new message popped up on my phone from Laynie, saying she was waiting for me by the yellow pole. Immediately, I looked up and found her standing near a break in the tree line.

After taking a deep breath, I got out of my car, trying to

remind myself I'd rather be anywhere but home as I walked down the gravel road lined with cars. As I neared the trees, I started to hear voices and the subtle hum of music. My stomach was laced with dread, and I quickly wondered if I could make it back to my car before she noticed me.

But, of course, that was the exact moment she looked up and waved excitedly. "There you are!" she exclaimed, strawberry blonde hair bouncing around her shoulders as she beckoned me with her hand. "It's just through here," she said as she turned on her heel and started through the trees.

There was a small dirt trail that led between the towering Douglas firs. As I followed her, I noted how thankful I was that she came out to meet me because there was no way I would've found it easily on my own. After winding through the trees for what seemed like forever, they gave way to a clearing bigger than I expected, packed with more people than I had hoped for.

My eyes widened as I took in the scene before me. In the middle of the space sat a large fire pit stacked with wood, people sitting on logs and random folding chairs scattered around it. Off to the side was a boulder set up as a makeshift table where people were milling about, taking turns filling the red cups in their hands. A few coolers sat on the ground at the base of it, and a small speaker sat on top of another, playing a song I didn't recognize. To the right, I noticed a pathway through the trees to another clearing. People leaned against the surrounding trunks, laughing and talking, and it struck me as odd for a moment how normal it all seemed for them.

It felt almost as if I was behind it all, watching my life unfold in front of me from a different vantage point. For some reason, I'd always felt separated, as if life was there and happening ahead of me—but I had never known quite how to reach it.

I blinked away the things that I would rather not think about and instead focused on Laynie, who had begun walking toward the center of the clearing. I hurried to catch up, wrapping my arms around myself as the breeze rustled the trees around us and raised the hair on my arms. Of course, I didn't think to grab a hoodie before I threw my shoes on and walked straight out the door.

"There's no fire." I voiced my observation to Laynie when I caught up with her after noticing the absence of warmth that one would usually provide.

"Yeah, there never is." Her brows furrowed, her shiny lips forming a slight frown. "I don't know why they call it that, honestly. I've never thought about it." She shrugged, turning toward the crowd of people over by the rocks, smoothing her features over with a smile. "I'm going to go get a drink. Do you want one?"

"Oh no, that's okay—" I started to say as I turned back toward her, but my voice faltered when I realized she was already gone. "I . . . don't really drink," I finished anyway, releasing a breath as I scanned the people around me. I could slowly feel my heartbeat increasing as I stood in the middle of the crowd, completely alone. A light panic started to set in as I realized, with a quick glance around, that I didn't really recognize anyone.

By then, the sun was setting gently over the top of the trees, its final light softly shining through the breaks in the leaves and casting the rest of the area in shadow. It was a nice ambiance in theory, but just made it that much more difficult to find someone I knew. If I wasn't regretting my decision to show up before, I really was then.

I started walking toward the outer edge of the clearing, deciding I would probably look less stupid not standing by myself in the middle of everything. I wandered toward the drinks, hoping to find Laynie again, but, of course, she was already gone. I continued walking and passed a group of guys howling with laughter, slapping each other on the back and sloshing their drinks around, then passed a bunch of girls giggling, huddled around a phone. As I got to the outskirts of the fireless bonfire, the groups of people lessened, two or three bunched together— couples paired off, and friends talking.

The farther I got from the music, the quieter the night became. I sat down on a stump just beyond the tree line. Trying to ignore the nagging feeling of not belonging anywhere, I raked my gaze across the crowd of people again. The sun had made its way behind the trees completely, and from there, everyone just melded together in a blurry haze.

My eyes continued past the crowd, landing on the opening I'd noticed earlier. I took one last glance around and decided I had nothing to lose.

The path was slightly overgrown and denser than I expected. Carefully, I made my way around the questionable plants and twigs. Ahead, the Puget Sound came into view as I stepped into the early autumn evening past the tree line. The air instantly felt cooler so close to the water, and I took a full breath for the first time since I'd arrived.

The view in front of me was stunning. The sun that was long gone behind the trees of the forest was still barely shining over the silhouette of Bainbridge Island, visible in the distance on the other side of the Puget Sound. The half circle of light shone brighter than ever as it reflected across the water, coloring it orange and gold.

I blinked away from the setting sun and moved farther into the open air. About ten steps ahead of me, the long grass met a small drop-off that gave way to the rocky shoreline. A small concrete wall had been built up against it to bridge the small drop from the grass to the sand.

To the right was an expanse of dense trees running parallel to the water as far as I could see. When I stepped fully into the clearing, I peered to my left and was startled when I realized I wasn't alone.

Someone was sitting on the concrete wall, staring at the

sunset like I had just been. He was the only one out there, and for some reason, it felt like I was intruding on something private. The atmosphere back here caused a different sort of peace, and I didn't want to bother him. Thankfully, he hadn't noticed me yet, and I took one last look at the island before I turned to go. I had only made it a few steps when, of course, I stepped on the loudest twig known to man.

"Stella?"

I whirled around in surprise before exhaling heavily as I recognized the voice that rang out among the stillness. The sun was almost completely below the horizon, dusk overtaking the air around us. I squinted against the lack of light as if that would help me see him better.

"Bridger," I said back, no question in my voice. I tried to hide the relief that was loosening the tightness in my chest because it didn't quite make sense to me as to why I felt that way. "How did you know it was me?" I said, walking over to meet him where he sat. There were only about ten feet between us, and I felt lighter with every step I took toward him. The sliver of remaining light highlighted the angles of his face and jaw just enough that I could see the corner of his mouth quirk up as I approached him.

"Lucky guess," he said, patting the spot next to him. I sat down and narrowed my eyes. A full smile broke out across his face, crinkling the corners of his eyes. He shrugged, and I swore I could see a tinge of pink on his cheeks in the dying light. "I thought I saw you across the field earlier. You're pretty easy to recognize."

"Is that an insult, or . . . ?" I said, trying to ignore the way I felt my own cheeks heating after noticing his.

That shy smile was back in place, my heart doing flips as he looked at me. "Definitely not."

I laughed softly, turning my attention back to the water. The sun disappeared behind the island completely, and the air felt like it had dropped ten degrees. When the breeze picked up again, I shivered involuntarily.

"Are you cold?" he said, immediately reaching to his left and grabbing a light gray hoodie.

"Oh no, that's okay," I started to say as I wrapped my arms tighter around myself.

"Stella, you'll freeze. Here." He held it out to me. A moment passed before I thanked him and took the hoodie from his outstretched hand, trying to think about anything other than the way he said my name.

"Man, first it's the jumper cables, and now it's this. I promise, Bridger, I'm not usually this needy," I said as I pulled his sweatshirt over my head, thankful to be enveloped in its sudden warmth.

He laughed, nudging me with his elbow. "I don't mind."

The goosebumps I felt breaking out across my skin weren't from the cold at all. I pulled the sleeves of the hoodie over my hands and burrowed deeper into the soft fabric.

"So, what are you doing out here on this side of the bonfire?" I said, trying to deflect the odd wave of comfort those three words brought me.

"Considering it's not much of a bonfire, I decided I'd prefer to sit out here by the water rather than watch Matt Reilly try to prove he can shoot beer out of his nose."

My nose scrunched in response, eyebrows pulling together in disgust. "Fair enough." I laughed as I shook my head, trying to clear my mind of that image. "So, you're here with the soccer guys?"

"Yep. It's supposed to be a team bonding thing every year, but most of the guys usually just end up getting wasted or making fools of themselves trying." He looked down at the sand, fiddling with his hands.

"But not you?"

He shook his head, meeting my eyes again. "Not me." Something passed between us in that moment, something that was felt rather than spoken in the weight of his gaze. In the short time I had known him, I could already tell there was something different about him. Something honest . . . something sure.

He made me want to know him.

"What about you?" he said, his words breaking me from my thoughts.

"Here with the soccer guys? No," I said lightly, feeling oddly satisfied when he smiled again.

"With *a* soccer guy, maybe?" he joked with raised eyebrows.

"Maybe." I shrugged, crossing my arms in front of me, fighting the smile tugging at my lips. One look at his earnest expression and my smile slightly faded. I felt the sudden urge to give him more, to grant him some sliver of the truth.

I sighed. "I don't really know why I'm here, honestly. Just . . . something to do, I guess." I shrugged again, adding as an afterthought, "I'd rather be here than at my house."

I tensed as he stilled, the words out of my mouth before I registered the weight of them. At the shift in his gaze, I realized how bad it sounded. Not wanting him to get the wrong idea, I hurried to add, "Speaking of, I should probably head back soon."

I stood, wiping the dirt off the back of my jeans. He got up beside me, and I was silently thankful that he didn't say anything about the words that thickened the air between us as we turned toward the trees.

I began walking down the dense path through the tall pines, Bridger following behind me. We stopped at the edge of the clearing, our classmates in view once again. The sudden chorus of voices and steady beat of the music were a stark contrast to the peaceful lapping water from just moments earlier.

Bridger fell into step beside me as we followed the tree line, the moonlight shining against the outline of the forest surrounding us. String lights I hadn't noticed in the daylight were hung through the trees, connecting back together at the rock where people still stood and held their drinks.

"Did you drive here yourself?" Bridger asked, leaning slightly closer to me, dipping his head so I could hear him over the noise.

I looked over at him, hoping he couldn't tell how affected I was by his sudden closeness, his body mere inches from mine. "Why, you don't think my car could handle it?"

He laughed softly, putting his hands in his pockets before saying, "No, I was actually just wondering if I could offer to drive you home."

My hands fell to my sides, surprise overtaking my features. My stomach swooped, and I found myself wishing I didn't even have my license. "I did, actually. But . . . you could walk me to my car?" I replied, not expecting the words to feel so vulnerable. "If you want, of course. It's just—I'm not sure I could make it back out of here on my own," I added.

He nodded. "I'd love to." He didn't try to hide his smile this time, and neither did I.

We continued walking in the direction we had entered, finally coming across the slight break in the trees. I let Bridger lead the way, the sounds of the party becoming nothing more than a distant hum behind us, growing fainter the deeper we ventured along the barely visible path. We made our way through the woods mostly in silence, my gaze trained solely on the ground in front of me as I tried to avoid loose branches and rocks.

I wasn't looking out for tree stumps, apparently, as I tripped over a small one in front of me and stumbled right into Bridger's back. He let out a quiet *oomph* and then somehow managed to catch us both, and I gripped his arm to steady myself.

"Crap, I'm so sorry, I didn't see that there, and—"

"Hey, it's okay." He cut me off, shaking his head at my apology. "Is your foot all right?"

I laughed quietly. "Yeah, I think the only thing wounded is

my dignity." I then became acutely aware of the way I was still gripping his arm when I felt his laugh from my fingertips down to my toes. I let go and took a slight step backward, not wanting to make anything awkward.

I squinted at the trail ahead, headlights barely visible in the distance. "Do you think we're even halfway there?"

Laughing again, he shook his head. "Not even close."

He turned back toward me and held out his hand, a reassurance and an offering all in one. I barely even hesitated before linking my fingers through his, savoring the feeling of his warm palm against my own. I tried not to think about how natural it felt as we hurried along the path ahead of us.

We broke apart when we reached the gravel road, the walk shorter than I'd hoped. As we approached my car, I turned to him, wishing I'd parked on the other side of the country.

"Thanks for walking me out," I said, pulling the sleeves of his hoodie over my hands again and looking down at my feet.

"Happy to," he replied. A contented silence fell between us in the chilly October air.

I couldn't bring myself to get into my car just yet, wanting to stay in this quiet moment for as long as he'd let me.

After a few more heartbeats of silence, he cleared his throat. "Would you maybe want to . . . hang out sometime? Like, for real?"

Hope bloomed in my chest, heavy and warm. I tucked my hair behind my ear as he added, "I mean, like—on purpose. Not just running into you in the school parking lot or at a bonfire."

He ran a hand through his hair, and it struck me then that he was nervous too.

An easy smile rose to my lips as I said, "Yes, Bridger. I would love to hang out with you on purpose."

His laugh rang out in the crisp night air, and I felt like I'd just discovered my new favorite song. We exchanged numbers, and he waved goodbye as I got in my car.

I didn't know how much that night would mean to me or how it would weave itself into the fabric of who I was. I didn't know how well I would remember it or how often in the years to come, I would wonder if that was when it had started.

Only now I know that by that night—it had already begun.

As I fell asleep that night, I thought of him.

I thought of the way he looked staring out across the water, the way he had braced my fall, and the way we ran through the woods together, hand in hand. I thought of how easy things felt when I was with him and the way his laughter still ricocheted around in my heart hours later. It was Bridger that I thought of then, and it was Bridger that I would think of for all my nights after.

Eventually, I would think of him even when I wished I didn't.

But for that night, I thought of him—truly thought of him—for the first time. The warmth of him surrounded my thoughts and my senses as I slowly let sleep take me.

The next day, I woke up and realized I was still wearing his hoodie.

# 13

## NOW

It's been a week since I saw Bridger on campus, and today, we decided to meet for his unofficial tour.

And by we, I mean him and my complete lack of self-preservation.

Our loose plans have been nagging at the back of my mind for the last seven days. I knew if I didn't give him the tour soon, my anxiousness was going to eat me alive. Some things never change, I guess.

I texted him last night, thankful when he said he would be free today. I've been keeping myself busy at my desk all morning —writing, reading, and getting ahead on assignments. Needless to say, I've only gone downstairs twice. Once to get coffee and then again to refill my mug.

Now, it's almost three, and we agreed to meet at four.

I close my laptop, resting my head on my interlocked fingers and trying to remind myself to take deep breaths. I still can't believe I agreed to this, but . . . that's the thing about Bridger. When it comes to him, I lose all resolve.

I always have.

There's been a growing pit in my stomach all morning, and it hits me all over again how much has changed since we last spoke. It hurts to think about how much I don't know about him anymore, and that pit in my gut grows deeper still when I think in turn about how much he doesn't know about me.

And how it's better for both of us if it stays that way.

I glance at the clock one last time before heading downstairs, thankful my parents have been at work all day, and I've had the house to myself. It's easier to avoid questions you don't want to answer when no one is asking them.

My phone starts ringing as I grab my keys off the hook. I hurry to fish it out of my back pocket and then almost drop it when I see the name flashing across the screen.

My stomach bottoms out as I stare at his contact name. Heartbeat suddenly frantic, I wonder how on earth I thought I was ready to face him again when this is my body's reaction to just seeing his *name.* I lean back against the edge of the couch to steady myself as I shakily press the green button and lift the phone to my ear.

"Hello?"

"Hey." Bridger breathes down the line, sending a fresh wave of nerves to my stomach. "I just . . . I guess I just wanted to make sure you still wanted to do this. Because we don't—we don't have to." He sounds nervous, a slight shake in his voice that he's probably hoping I don't notice. But, of course, I do.

I notice everything about him.

Something about this comforts me—that I still know some of his tells after all this time. And against my better judgment, against every reason I shouldn't see him again, the part of me wins out that always will where he's involved. The part of me that's been longing to hear his voice for the past three years, the part of me that knows that knowing him is the one thing that will matter more to me than anything else for the rest of my life. That small part of me sends a spark of hope down to my chest, one I know I can't afford. I know I can't afford it, and yet I hear myself saying, "I want to, Bridge."

He breathes out. "Good, because I'm already on the way."

I let out a breath of laughter despite myself, and it's only then that I take stock of the distant noise on the other end of the line —the sound of a turn signal blinking and the hum of an engine. My heart stops.

"Are you—" I swallow and attempt to clear my throat, my voice coming out thick. "Are you driving?"

A heavy silence follows, everything he is not saying louder than anything he could. "Yes."

And all at once, the spark dies out, and a weight settles against my ribcage, and reality is a kick in the chest when I remember he's not that person anymore. But can I blame him? Neither am I.

"Okay. Um, be safe." I cringe right as the words leave my mouth.

"You too, Stel. I'll see you soon."

"Bye."

He hangs up, and my keys suddenly feel like lead in my hand. I can't just pretend he doesn't exist, and I can't pretend like we didn't either. I've been avoiding this for so long, and it's gotten me absolutely nowhere.

But what other choice have I had?

I'm trying to move as fast as I can, trying to get as far away as possible from the girl I used to be, but my heart is on a carousel that keeps bringing me right back to where I started every time.

I know we'll never be what we were—we can't be what we were. But that doesn't mean I can't walk around with him for an afternoon. That's all it has to be.

All it *can* be.

It's just him. It's just me.

*And that,* says the quiet voice in the back of my head, *that's exactly the problem.*

# 14

Arriving on campus, I park in the same visitor parking lot as last week. When I see that same little blue Toyota pull into the spot next to me, I get hit with a wave of nostalgia so sharp it physically takes my breath away.

I turn away from the window and act like I'm looking for something in my center console, blinking away the stinging in my eyes. Since when did I become such an emotional mess?

I refuse to let myself fall apart in front of him again.

After searching for nothing for a few more seconds, I look up and see him getting out of his car. I blow air from my cheeks and step out of mine. I plaster on a smile that I hope he can't see right through and greet him with what I hope is convincing enthusiasm.

I notice the way his smile doesn't quite reach his eyes after taking in my expression, but thankfully, he doesn't comment on it. Instead, he takes one look at my car and raises his eyebrows.

"No way that thing is still running," he says by way of greeting.

His lighthearted tone causes me to crack a real smile, some of the tension uncoiling in my chest as I feel my shoulders relax.

I reach out my hand and pat the hood twice. "Yeah, well, I happen to know a pretty good auto repair shop."

His smile falters for a split second, so fast I almost miss it. But then it quickly turns back into one that reaches his eyes, and I try not to notice how they soften ever so slightly when they meet my own.

He turns toward the buildings, rubs his hands together, and says, "So, where should we start?"

I squint. "Well, there's a huge 'W' on the other side of campus, and having your picture taken in front of it is, like, the thing to do when you start here, apparently," I try to say with a straight face.

An amused smirk pulls at his mouth, and he says, "Do you have a picture in front of this 'W' from when you started?"

I frown. "No."

"Then I think I'll pass."

"Fair enough." I nod, pursing my lips.

We head toward the sidewalk, falling into step easily with each other as we start along the path. The leaves rustle through the trees overhead as a warm breeze brushes past my shoulders, the sun muted behind a passing cloud. I take in the serene campus around us, hoping the quietness around me will help suppress the noise inside my head. We continue to walk side by side, the ghosts of who we once were trailing behind our every step.

After another minute or so, Bridger says, "You're one quiet tour guide. At this rate, I won't be able to tell the cafeteria from the library."

My brows scrunch together. "You really don't remember any of this? We literally got a tour junior and senior year. High school wasn't *that* long ago," I tease, unaware of the weight those words carry until I glimpse Bridger's face.

"No, it wasn't."

The air around us goes heavy. I avoid his gaze and look at the ground, not wanting him to see how easily those words affect me. How it has only been three years, and somehow, that feels like an eternity and a millisecond all at once. Both that and the dawning realization that I don't know how to be around him anymore. There are so many words that I want to say, but none that could change anything.

I clear my throat, still not meeting his gaze. "Feels like a lifetime, though."

He's quiet, and when I finally look over at him, he's staring at me with that same question in his eyes, that same expression that makes me feel like he can see right through me. I don't want to give him time to respond and open any unwanted doors, so I pick up the pace.

"Anyway! Back to the tour. Sorry, I'm a terrible guide." I attempt to laugh, but it comes out strained.

"No, you're not." I only make it a few steps before he's beside me again. "I didn't really even expect a tour, honestly. I've been here plenty of times." He smiles softly. "I just . . . I wanted an excuse to see you."

His words are quiet, as if he contemplated even saying them. I hate that we've lost the openness we had before, that used to come as naturally as air, and it's as if I'm noticing the depth of the chasm between us for the first time like I'm not the one who started the earthquake that caused it. My chest constricts as I look into his eyes and see him try to blink away all the pain that I've caused.

I want to tell him everything . . . which is exactly why I can't.

Instead, I just settle for, "Are you here for good?"

"Seems that way." He nods at the ground as if reassuring himself. He hesitates, then adds, "Are you?"

My steps begin to slow at his words, and all I can offer is a sad half-shrug. "I never left."

He stops dead in his tracks, and I don't even have to look at him to know exactly what expression he is wearing, but I have a track record of self-deprecation, so I look anyway.

"That's not fair," he says so, so quietly. His eyebrows have the slightest crease between them, the one he always gets when he's trying not to show his hurt. If we were seventeen, I would reach over and smooth it out with my thumb like I always did, but we're not seventeen anymore, and I'm the one who put it there.

"I know."

We stare at each other, and I wonder then if I made the right choice. I wonder if things could've been different if he'd answered the phone that night. I wonder how things would've ended up, wonder if we'd still be standing here with our hearts all bruised.

He studies me, bites the inside of his cheek, and then nods his head over toward a bench a few feet away.

We sit down beside each other in silence, leaning back against the cold metal. I glance over at him, noticing the curls at the nape of his neck and the slight curve of his lip that means he's thinking. He's right beside me, but he still feels so far away, and how much I've missed him gets stuck in my throat because I'm afraid I'm just going to find more ways that I'm capable of hurting him.

I can't find the words to tell him that I miss him, that there was nothing he could've done, or that the way I need him is the reason I can't have him.

I can't find the words, so I don't say any.

We sit there silently, not quite uncomfortable but not really content.

"If I ask you something, will you promise to answer it honestly?" He shifts so that he's facing me, and despite my suddenly sweaty palms and the alarm bells ringing in my head, I don't turn away.

I can't bear the thought of letting him down any more than I already have, so I say, "I don't want to make you any more promises I can't keep."

"Can you try?" The honesty in his voice surprises me, and with one look into his eyes, I nod.

He takes a deep breath. "Were you ever going to speak to me again?"

I had braced myself internally because I knew his question was going to hurt, but nothing prepared me for hearing his voice form the words. At my silence, he continues, "After senior year, you just . . . disappeared. With just a voicemail. So . . . was that going to be it? After everything, was that going to be it for us?"

"That was three questions," I say under my breath, then startle when he abruptly stands from the bench and runs a frustrated hand through his hair.

"Why do you keep *doing* that?" He shifts on his feet and paces a few steps like he can't bear to stand still. "Dodging everything with a joke, or some vague answer, or another question?"

The outline of him blurs through the tears I desperately try to will away. I know he deserves more than I could ever offer him. The shame rips me wide open, and I look down at my hands, unable to hold his gaze any longer.

"Stella." He says my name like a desperate plea, enough sorrow for the both of us laced between those two syllables. "Stella, look at me." A silent pause and then a broken whisper. "Please."

I slowly lift my head, my eyes meeting his. He squats down in front of me, resting his hands on the bench on either side of my legs. The world around me is still fuzzy, and as I blink away a stray tear, he reaches one hand up and wipes it away with his thumb. I shiver at the contact, and his hand lingers before he drops it back down to the bench.

His features have softened, his dark eyes shining in the soft afternoon light. He's looking at me so earnestly and openly that I can't seem to look away, his closeness covering me in a familiar warmth that causes my sight to blur again.

Against all my better judgment and against the rational part of my brain begging me to stop, I reach my hand up and brush the stray strand of hair that's fallen across his forehead. He closes his eyes briefly against the touch, and now I'm the one letting my hand linger before I bring it back to my lap, lacing my fingers together.

"Bridger, I'm sorry. I really am. I just . . . I can't give you the answers that you want. You wouldn't—" I inhale a deep breath, my voice wobbling. "I couldn't even begin to make you understand." It's a lame answer, and I know it, but it's also the truth.

"Try me," he all but whispers.

"I don't know how." My face crumples again, and I shake my head, hating myself for not being able to tell him what he wants to hear but certain that it's something he can never know.

And even if I wanted to tell him . . . it's true. I don't know how. I don't know how to talk about it because I haven't talked with anyone. Not Dahlia, not my brother, definitely not my parents—I can still barely even broach the subject with my therapist, let alone face it myself. That shame still covers me like a blanket in the heat of summer, and it's heavy and suffocating and blocking out the light.

He nods, and his throat bobs as he continues to kneel in front of me. "Then just tell me this." He moves his hands from where they rest on either side of my legs and gently grabs my hands, still clasped in my lap.

I lace my fingers through his like I instinctively know he's the anchor my heart has been searching for after three years at sea.

"If I had stayed in North Carolina, would we ever have spoken again?"

My silence says enough.

He exhales shakily and squeezes my hands before letting

them go and moving to sit next to me again on the bench. He's not looking at me anymore, and I'm afraid I've lost him again, even though I never really got him back. My heartbeat picks up, and I hurriedly try to give him some piece of the truth. The words tumble out of me in a rush, like if I don't say them right now, he may never know.

"I don't know, but what I do know is that I miss you. I miss you, and I've missed you, and there hasn't been a day that has gone by that I haven't thought about you. It's not fair, and I don't know what it means, but you have to know that." I inhale a ragged breath. "It's just so much more complicated."

He's quiet for a moment, and I swear I can hear my heart pounding in my chest. I expect his voice to be full of contempt when he speaks next, but it is anything but. "Why didn't you say something that night? Why did you let me get on that plane and fly to UNC that summer and let me think you were joining me in the fall?" His voice comes out quiet, hollow, and sadder than I've ever heard it. "Why didn't you join me in the fall?"

I don't know what to say. There's a lump in my throat the size of Jupiter, and I'm drowning in the hurt I know that I've caused him.

"After I heard that voicemail, I was worried sick, and no one would tell me anything. I was across the country and had no clue what the hell was happening. Then all of a sudden, you just *weren't there.* You weren't anywhere."

My heart breaks as his chin quivers, and the rawness in his voice makes me want to shield him from this pain, to hide him from it—and then I remember. I tried.

And look where it got us.

He takes a deep breath, looks up at the sky, and blinks twice before looking at me again. "That was the longest week of my life."

I sit there silently, once again at a loss for words. That week was the longest of my life, too. One that I've spent the years since trying to forget.

Every emotion weighs heavily on my heart, the frustration and sadness soon giving way to defeat. "Why are you even talking to me? How can you even stand to be around me?" I huff out a broken laugh, saying under my breath, "I can barely stand to be around myself."

"Stel . . ." He instinctively shifts closer to me, and his leg presses lightly against mine. "Don't say that."

I lean away from him, releasing an anguished laugh. "It's true. I mean . . . I ruin everything." I look at the ground, blinking away more tears. Not wanting him to see me fall apart again, I stand up from the bench and turn away from him. I shake my head, my guilt as obvious as the wetness on my cheeks.

And then he's beside me again. "No, Stella, I just—" He sighs. "I'm just trying to understand."

When I look up again, he's in front of me, hands shoved in his pockets like he's trying to refrain from reaching out and touching me.

"Let me try to understand."

But I can't. I can't ask that of him. I can't risk bringing him down with me again. And yet, as I stand before him, I'm hit with so many conflicting emotions—hurt and want and warmth and longing and fear. We've been an enigma from the beginning, as if the same force that's keeping us together is the one trying to push us apart.

"Bridger." I take a deep breath, finally meeting his eyes again. "I'm not the person I was three years ago."

His features soften in the way they always have when it comes to me. I look up at the sky, then down at the ground, then at my hands, anywhere but him.

"Neither am I." He takes the smallest step closer before continuing. "I know things are different now, and I know it's not my place anymore. I know you probably don't want anything to do with me, and I've spent all this time trying to make peace with that."

His hand finds the back of his neck, and he looks at the sky briefly before continuing, "I'm not going to stand here and pretend to know what these years have been like for you or act like these past few years have been easy for me. But I'm *also* not going to stand here and watch you walk away again without trying when I've already lost you once.

"So, if there's some small part of you that feels the same way, Stella—any small part that wants to let me back into your life— just . . . just give me a chance." He blows out a breath through his mouth, cheeks slightly pink and eyes heavy. I chew on the inside of my cheek, willing myself to keep the tears at bay.

He looks at me and hesitates, like even after admitting what he just did, he's still afraid to add this final truth. "I want to know who you are now."

I rub the back of my arm, shaking my head when I finally look at him again. "I want more for you than that."

He shakes his head in response. "There isn't more for me than this."

Tentatively, he takes a step toward me, swallowing thickly. Something like hope flares in his eyes, and that same small hope flares in my chest because maybe he still wants this, and maybe I do, too, and maybe I hate myself for it. But I can't lose myself in the fantasy of my own selfishness. I can't lose him again.

And I can't lose him if he's not mine.

"I don't think I can be what you need me to be anymore," I say softly, hating the words as soon as they leave my mouth.

That crease appears on his forehead again, the same look after all these years. "All I've ever needed you to be is exactly who you are." He shrugs, dropping his gaze to the ground. "I know a lot has changed, Stel. But that hasn't."

He releases a breath, and I do too. I realize then that even though we're not the same anymore, maybe some small part of him still is, and maybe that part still lives in me too.

And maybe that's all we need.

But still, there's one question I need to ask him before I lose my resolve, and I know if I don't ask now, then I never will. "You got to ask a question with an honest answer, so . . . can I?" The second the question is out of my mouth, it feels wrong, almost selfish, but he immediately nods.

"Anything."

I take a breath. "Would you have ever tried to come find me?"

He stills, then takes a breath of his own. He meets my eyes and then says with an equally quiet tone, "You made it pretty obvious you didn't want to be found."

The wind curls around us like our past, twisting and winding and slipping away.

"And now?"

"And now . . . here you are."

I look at him again, into those dark brown eyes that I know better than anything. His lips tug upward, and so do mine, and maybe even after all this time, we still know each other better than we think. He sticks out his hand, his boyish grin taking over his whole face, and I see those dimples I've loved since I was sixteen for the first time in forever. My heart swells, and my stomach flips, and I don't know much, but I do know him.

"So, friends?" He raises his eyebrows, hand still outstretched in front of him.

I laugh, rolling my eyes and bringing my hand to his, accepting whatever version of a fresh start we can offer each other. "Friends."

# 15

## THEN

December, Sophomore Year

I glared at the check engine light glowing red on my dashboard as if it personally offended me.

At that point, I felt like it had.

On the way home from school, a rattling noise started sounding from the front of my car. I almost wanted to just ignore it and get home to my bed, but the more I tried to pretend I didn't hear it, the louder it seemed to get, so I pulled over into the first parking lot I saw.

After trying to look up what the issue might be on my phone, I was simultaneously convinced the light was a fluke and that my car could possibly explode at any given minute.

I rummaged through my bag to make sure I had a charger because even though my phone still had almost a full battery, I didn't want to risk it dying on me in a crisis (again). A few random things tumbled out of my bag as I located the charger— ChapStick, a few pieces of gum, and a small white card. I picked up the items, pausing when I realized that I was holding the auto shop card Bridger had given me when he helped me jump-start my car in the school parking lot.

I breathed out a sigh of relief, thankful that one small thing might actually go right today.

On the second ring, the line connected.

"Thanks for calling Adam's Auto Repairs. How can I help you today?" A familiar voice carried through the speaker. I froze on the spot, surprised to hear his voice and even more surprised at the way I felt myself instantly relaxing. My heart fluttered, and I sank down into my seat as if I hadn't just seen him yesterday.

In the few moments that my silence stretched on, he said hesitantly, "Hello?"

I quickly cleared my throat, sitting up straighter in my seat. "Bridger? It's Stella." Biting my thumb, I hoped he couldn't hear the smile in my voice.

A light laugh flitted down the line, and my face instantly warmed. "Of course, it is. How's the old Clunker?"

I laughed at his use of the name I so affectionately gave my car a few weeks ago after an especially cold morning when it took a few tries to start. Bridger and I were able to hang out over fall break once his soccer season finally slowed down, and I was heading out to get coffee with him the Saturday after Thanksgiving when it happened. I told him about the incident, saying that the car was a "hand me down clunker from my brother," and the name had stuck ever since.

"Well, that's the thing," I began.

"Everything okay?"

I swallowed, trying not to fixate on the way his tone had changed, becoming more serious all of a sudden. He sounded like someone who cared.

"Yes! Yeah, it's fine, it's just . . ." I trailed off, because why would I call the repair shop if my car was fine? Shaking my head slightly, I continued. "My car's just making a weird noise, and the check engine light is on."

"Where are you? I'll tell my dad to get the tow truck—"

"No!" I cut him off, then felt immediately stupid for doing so. I just imagined my parents seeing what a hassle I had caused, not to mention the unnecessary cost of bringing out a truck. I quickly continued, "I just mean, I can drive it to the shop. It's not a big deal."

"It is to me. I don't want anything to happen to you if the car—"

"I'll be fine! Don't worry. See you soon!" I said.

Pulling the receiver away from my ear, I faintly heard "Stella —" before I hung up. I felt terrible for being so abrupt, but I knew that when word got around to my parents that my engine failed, it would somehow be my fault, so I decided to prolong the inevitable.

I typed in the address of the repair shop, paling slightly when the noise sounded again. Putting the car in reverse, I said a quick prayer and started toward the shop.

When I pulled into the small auto repair shop parking lot, I saw Bridger's form immediately through the open garage door that took up almost the entire front of the building. When he heard my car, his head snapped up from the papers he was holding, and he quickly set them on the small work table behind him. He made his way toward me, and I turned off the ignition and opened my car door. I glanced up just in time to see him giving me a look.

"I could hear you coming from a mile away."

Grimacing, I got out of the car and met his eyes. "That bad?"

He nodded solemnly, peering around my shoulder to look at the clunker in question. "That bad."

I sighed, running my hands through my hair, hoping my embarrassment wasn't written all over my face.

Bridger nodded his head toward the shop and motioned with his hand for me to follow. "Dad is just inside. It's been a pretty slow day, so he should be able to get right to work on your car."

"Okay, perfect." I started to follow him, adding a quiet, "Thanks."

He smiled at me over his shoulder, and the sight of that singular dimple made me wish my car would break down every day.

We walked into the small shop, and the scent of rubber and metal filled my nostrils as we passed through the open garage. Stepping through a doorway in the back, we entered another, smaller room that I could only assume was the office. There was a desk covered in scattered papers with two seats in front of it, and a window to the left overlooked the garage. Random picture frames lined the walls, consisting mostly of models of older cars and a couple of award certificates.

There was one photo in particular that caught my eye from where it hung right behind the desk. It was a photo of a younger Bridger holding up a soccer trophy in a little blue jersey, grinning up at the camera with a toothless smile. I was about to say something about it to Bridger, but just then, his dad walked through the open door.

"Stella, this is my dad. Dad, Stella." Bridger motioned between us, and his dad stepped forward with a warm smile and extended a hand for me to shake.

He was slightly taller than Bridger, but the resemblance was shocking all the same. Younger than I expected, his hair was a light brown shade with gray flecks peppered throughout. He and Bridger shared the same kind eyes, his face crinkling warmly as he smiled at me. His jeans were oil-streaked, and he wore a light blue collared shirt with the company logo emblazoned on the front and the name *Adam Wells* embroidered underneath.

"It's so nice to finally meet you," he grinned, looking from Bridger to me.

Bridger coughed, and I didn't miss the way his neck reddened slightly.

"It's so nice to meet you too, Mr. Wells," I replied, smiling back at him.

"Oh, please, call me Adam," he said kindly.

Before he had a chance to say anything else, Bridger jumped in and said, "Stella has been having some issues with her car, so I told her to bring it here so you could check it out for her."

"Of course!" Adam headed for the door. "Let me get some paperwork together, and then I'll get your keys." He smiled brightly again before leaving the room.

Bridger blew a puff of air out of his mouth before turning back to me with a sheepish smile.

"Your dad seems great," I said, looking back toward the picture of a toothless Bridger, thinking that his dad was probably smiling just as big behind the camera.

He followed my gaze, his smile softening slightly as he said quietly, "Yeah. He's the best."

Before I could ask him anything else, his dad came back into the room. I filled out some paperwork and then handed over my keys as we returned to the main portion of the shop. His dad walked out and turned on my car, and I winced because Bridger was right—it was *loud*.

We watched as he drove the little silver Honda through the garage doors, and I only realized then that I didn't have a way to get home. "How long do you think it'll take?" I asked Bridger.

"Depends," he replied, turning back to me. "If it's just the muffler, it should be pretty quick, but if it's something like the catalytic converter . . . that could take a minute." He hesitated, then added, "And that is if he has the parts."

"Oh. Okay," I said, exhaling as I rocked back on my feet.

We stood there for a few moments before Bridger said, "Do you need a ride anywhere? I could drive you home if you need."

"No! No, that's okay. I wouldn't want to pull you away when

you're working," I said as I gestured vaguely back in the direction of the shop.

He shrugged before saying, "I'm not actually working right now. I just like to hang out at the shop after school now that soccer is done." He hesitated before adding, "It beats sitting at home in an empty house."

My brows furrowed, but before I could ask what he meant, his dad emerged from the doors again.

"You good here if I drive Stella home?" Bridger asked him.

I was about to protest, but his dad said, "Absolutely. This will probably take a few days, so I was coming out here to tell you to drive her home if you hadn't already offered." He slapped Bridger on the back before looking at me and saying, "I'll call you when it's ready to be picked up."

"Thank you so much, again."

"It's not a problem at all," he smiled, turning back toward the shop.

Bridger walked over to his car and opened the passenger door. "Your carriage awaits," he said.

I rolled my eyes with a laugh, walking over to the car. "You're too good to me," I said jokingly as I stepped into the car.

He looked down at me from where he still stood at my side, holding the door frame. "You deserve nothing but the best." His voice still held a joking lilt, but his expression was earnest.

As he walked around to the driver's side, I had to remind myself to breathe as the weight of those words settled in my chest and took on a whole new meaning in my heart because no one had ever said them to me before.

Sinking into the passenger seat, I turned my phone over in my hand, checking it for the fifth time.

And once again, no new messages.

I sighed, trying not to let it bother me as Bridger pulled out onto the main road toward the direction of my house.

"Everything okay?"

I offered him a closed-mouth smile and said, "Yep. All good."

He tilted his head at me, unconvinced. I dropped my phone again.

Letting out a breath, I continued, "It's just . . . I was supposed to be home almost two hours ago, and no one has asked me where I am. And I know my parents are home from work now, so I don't know. I guess I was hoping at least one of them would check up on me." I huffed out a sad laugh and turned my eyes down to my black Chelsea rain boots. "Isn't that pathetic?"

Embarrassed, I kept my eyes down and tried to ignore the heaviness in my chest. I felt him slow down, the red light reflecting through the windshield.

"It's not pathetic."

I shook my head as I blinked rapidly, feeling dumb and defeated. "No, it's fine, they probably haven't even—"

"Stella." His hand landed on my shoulder, the weight heavy and warm. He squeezed gently as I finally looked over at him. "It's not fine. It's okay to be upset about that." His eyes were so warm and so tender with an emotion that I felt like I didn't deserve that I had to look away.

The light turned green, and he pulled onto the road. When he moved his hand from my shoulder, I instantly missed the comfort of it, the surety it held.

"Can we, um," I started, sniffling and feeling like an idiot. "Can you actually not take me home? I don't really want to be there right now," I said quietly.

He didn't even hesitate. "Of course." He looked at me briefly before flicking his eyes back to the road. "Where do you want to go?"

I took a deep breath. "Anywhere."

## 16

Fifteen minutes later, we were pulling off the interstate, the towering green trees blurring past the window. The only sound was the rhythmic swish of the windshield wipers as they worked to clear out the afternoon rain, and for once, the quiet was peaceful.

I rested my head back against the seat, slowly realizing how comfortable I was with him. I glanced over at the driver's seat, taking him in.

The way his brows furrowed in concentration, the way he leaned his elbow against the center console, the way his thumb lightly tapped along the steering wheel to the song playing gently through the speakers. The way he was there, how he'd been there, holding space for me whenever I needed it.

His eyes flicked over to mine and narrowed slightly in time with the slight upward tug of his lips when he noticed I was already staring.

"Where'd you go just now?" he asked, a smile in his voice.

I shrugged as I looked through the window again, fighting a smile of my own. "Just thinking about this guy that I know." I looked back over at him as a full-fledged smile broke across his face. My heart leaped into my throat, the previous feelings about my parents gone in an instant.

He laughed through his nose, eyes trained on the road again as the rain started picking up. "Oh yeah? What's he like?"

I shifted in my seat and angled my body toward him as I fought the smile that dared to flit across my own features. I sighed dramatically before saying, "Oh, you know. Pretty tall, all right at soccer, decent with cars." I lifted my eyebrows, that same smile pursing my lips as he laughed. "Pretty nice guy, all things considered."

He scrunched his nose, squinting at me, and I thought it might be the most adorable thing I'd ever seen to date. "All things considered?"

"Yeah. Always driving me around, saving the day over and over, being there for me. He takes it like a champ."

His face softened, and I knew that subtle smile was just for me as the rain sprinkled the windows. I wondered then how much of what was between us had been left up to chance. I could write some of it off as pure coincidence, I was sure—but how many choices had we made to actually be around each other? To enter each other's orbit, to let one another into our lives?

It wasn't until then that I realized how much he had infiltrated mine. And it startled me, suddenly, to realize how glad I was that he had.

His smooth voice broke through the silence again. "He seems all right."

I leaned back against my seat again, comfortable and happy and at ease. "You could say that."

His phone started ringing, cutting off the music and, subsequently, my thoughts. He glanced at the dashboard, the screen lighting up with *Mom*. He pushed a button on the steering wheel, and the music picked up again.

"You're not going to get that?"

"No."

I felt my forehead crease, and my curiosity won out. "Why not?"

"I'm driving," he stated matter-of-factly.

I opened my mouth and closed it again, only coming up with, "Right . . ."

Bridger kept his eyes on the road as he started tapping his fingers along the steering wheel again. This time, he wasn't tapping to the beat, and I thought it had to do with something more than the music.

"I know it seems stupid, or dumb, or whatever, but it's just this rule my mom drilled in my head right when I got my license." He huffed out a bitter laugh before adding, "Hell, I think if I answered her call, and she could just *hear* the sound of the engine, she'd fly up here herself and personally rip the phone from my hands." He shook his head, his grip on the steering wheel tightening.

"Fly?"

He exhaled. "She lives in California. She has all my life." He pulled onto a side street, the rain from before quieting to a light drizzle, the sun just barely poking through the clouds. He cleared his throat. "She tries to still be involved, though, in the ways she knows how. Rules, phone calls." He pursed his lips. "Stuff like that."

I couldn't read his expression or the tone of his voice. "Do you miss her?"

He only shrugged. "It's all I've ever known."

I nodded again, not really knowing what to say. He'd never talked about his mom before, and as much as I wanted to know more, I didn't want to pry.

He parked on the side of the road. I took one look around and recognized the houses around me, and a smile overtook my face as he turned off the car. "Kerry Park?"

"You've been here before?" he joked as he smiled back.

My laughter was carried with the breeze as we got out of the car. "Never." I feigned surprise as we walked down the sidewalk toward the staircase leading to the lookout ledge.

Once we got to the top, we walked over to the balcony, leaning up against it as the wind whipped through our hair. "Did you know that Meredith Grey's house is just up that hill?" I said, pointing behind us.

He laughed, giving me a look that sent butterflies down to my toes. "I think everyone in the state of Washington knows that Meredith Grey's house is just up that hill."

We laughed again, the sound in warm contrast to the gloomy winter chill. The park was empty—probably due to the cold— and I stood close to the railing, biting back a shiver. The shadow of a grin still on his face as he shifted closer to me, setting his hand on the railing around me. The nearness of him hit me all at once, and I thought that maybe it should scare me how natural it felt to be wrapped up in him, but it didn't. Tucked under his arm, I attempted to turn to look at him and ended up meeting his shoulder instead.

I laughed. He must have felt the vibration because, with an amused note in his voice, he said, "Something funny?"

"I don't think I realized how tall you were until right now."

He chuckled, turning toward me and resting his chin on the top of my head. His warm breath fanned my hair, and I could hear the smile in his voice. "It's never mattered until right now."

I pulled back, the cold air whooshing through the two inches of space between us. "That can't be true."

He raised his eyebrows before saying matter-of-factly, "I play soccer."

I grinned, facing him fully, aware of the closeness of his face to mine for the first time. His gaze softened, and my smile did, too. I lifted my eyes to his as he lowered his head to mine, and I wondered if he wanted to kiss me. I imagined what it would be like to close the distance separating us still, wondered what his lips would feel like.

I didn't have to wonder long.

His throat bobbed and my breath hitched, and I watched as his eyes slowly dropped to my mouth. His hand reached up to cup the side of my face.

And then his lips were on mine.

Slowly at first, tentatively, a sort of question that I answered without saying anything at all. I wrapped my arms around his shoulders, pulling him closer, his body a warm weight against my own. His mouth moved against mine like that was what it was always made to do, and I shivered into the kiss as his fingers slid from my cheek to my hair. His other hand rested on the small of my back, steady and sure, and I relished the way it felt to be held by him like this, to have him in this way. With one final brush of his lips, he pulled away, leaning his forehead against mine, flushed and giddy and breathless.

He moved his hand back to my cheek, his thumb slowly tracing the curve of my bottom lip. His face broke out into a smile, and so did mine. My cheeks started to heat up, and I knew that he saw because his smile grew wider as I buried my face into his shoulder again.

I let the moment settle in my chest, wondering how this could be real, wondering if it always felt like *this*. I could feel the racing of his heart through his jacket as my head rested against his chest. Shifting in his arms, we huddled together and stared out over the horizon.

Breathing in the frigid December air, I pulled my coat tighter around me. I looked out at the reflection of the lights from the buildings on the icy surface of the Puget Sound, festive lights strung about the city.

"I think this will always be my favorite view," I said, the breath from my words forming a small cloud in front of my face.

A few moments passed before he replied quietly, "Me too."

But when I looked back at him, he wasn't looking at the skyline ahead of us, or the vibrant city below us, or the last dying light of the evening around us.

He was looking at me.

# 17
## NOW

Today is Dahlia's birthday, and Mom's only goal is to make sure everybody knows it. She coupled the occasion with a baby shower—a two-in-one, all-day event.

She spent yesterday setting everything up—pink and blue balloons are tied to every post, matching streamers line the deck out back, and a white tablecloth and a small cake shaped as a onesie sit on top of the porch table.

And *that* cake, of course, is not to be confused with the birthday cake, which sits inside on the dining room table along with cupcakes, table toppers, and even more streamers and balloons.

I almost fell down the stairs this morning when I saw everything put together for the first time because Mom said she was going all out, but this is *full* out, even for her.

But honestly, I wouldn't expect anything less for the perfect, more favored daughter (in-law, but not that anyone acts like it). For my mom, anything goes when it comes to Dahlia.

The party goes smoothly, with family and friends filling every corner of the house and patio. Dahlia glows, as per usual. The one thing I've learned over the past five years she's been in my life is that her bright radiance is simply contagious; you can't *help* but be drawn to her. And her personality is just the icing on the cake because she's as genuine as it gets. You truly, honestly, can't help but love her.

I used to resent her for that.

But now, as time has passed and she has stuck by my side time and time again, she is the one person I can truly consider a friend. I'm eternally grateful to have her in my life, even if it took us a while to get here.

The weather must love Dahlia the way my mom does because it was sunny all afternoon, and only now are the clouds starting to cover the early evening sky as we sit on the back deck, organizing all her gifts.

"Mom really wants the baby to be a girl, huh?" I say, holding up a light pink onesie with a matching tulle skirt that reads, "Grandma's Princess."

Dahlia snorts, lowering herself into the wicker chair to start gathering more gifts from the table. "She told me she also bought the matching boy ones, but those are still in the bag with the tags on them, just in case," she laughs.

I continue folding the baby clothes, and Dahlia asks, "You haven't told me what your guess is yet. Boy or girl?"

I sit back on my heels, releasing a breath. "Honestly, I haven't really thought too much about it. I'd rather not get my hopes up one way or another, you know?" I shrug. "Besides, it doesn't matter anyway. I'll love him or her all the same." And I really mean it.

"I know you will." Her voice comes out wobbly.

Immediately, I look over at her and see that her eyes are glassy. "Dahlia, don't cry," I laugh, walking over and sitting down in the wicker chair beside hers.

She reaches over and clasps one hand in mine, using the other to wipe a fallen tear. "I know, I know, I just—" She takes a deep breath, cutting herself off and tightening her grip on my hand. "You are going to make an amazing aunt, Stella. And I want you to know—no, I *need* you to know—that I am so proud of you."

Now, her glassy eyes mirror my own, and I don't know what to say, so instead, I lean over and give her the best hug I can muster with her growing bump. That is, until I feel a light tap against my midsection and jerk back instantly.

"She kicked me!" I exclaim as we burst into laughter.

"She?" Dahlia raises her eyebrows.

I sigh, rolling my eyes and fighting the smile I feel tugging at my lips. "It's a habit. I still live with Mom, remember? Oh, speaking of—" I pull out my phone to check the time. "It's almost four. Don't want to be late to therapy."

She purses her lips before saying, "Nice segue."

I grin, replying, "I knew you'd think so." I turn to head back into the house, needing to change and grab my keys.

"Stella?"

I stop, looking over my shoulder. "Yeah?"

"Thank you."

I furrow my eyebrows. "For what?"

She smiles softly, resting a hand on her belly. "For being here." She turns away, wiping her eyes and directing her attention back to the pile of baby clothes in front of her.

My vision blurs again, and I cross the deck, wrapping her in another hug. She laughs through her tears, squeezing me tighter. "Happy Birthday," I say quietly, and she squeezes me tighter one last time before letting me go.

I hurry into the house, heading up to my room and quickly changing into a pair of sweatpants and a hoodie, because if I'm going to be anything for therapy—it's comfortable. As I descend the stairs, I hear hushed voices and slow to a stop on the landing. I know I shouldn't listen, but my curiosity always wins out. I hold my breath as my mother's voice carries over the banister.

". . . I'm just so thankful for Dahlia. If she hadn't come into our lives, I wouldn't have gotten to throw bridal and baby showers. Do you think she liked the party today? I know she . . ."

But I can't hear the rest of the sentence through the pounding in my ears. Once again, it's Dahlia, the perfect daughter, and me, not even in the equation. I'm sick of pretending like I don't care, like it hasn't always bothered me, like it isn't happening. I step off the remaining stairs and turn the corner into the living room where my parents stand.

My mom startles, reflexively bringing up a hand to her chest. "Goodness, Stella, you scared me." My dad stands next to her, frozen, no doubt wondering how much I heard. But Mom, of course, is indifferent to the matter, never in the wrong. She raises her eyebrows at me as if to say, *What do you need?*

"What am I to you, Mom?"

Her forehead creases, and she sets her hands on her hips. "I don't know what you mean."

I shake my head. "You know *exactly* what I mean." They just stare at me, and a bemused laugh falls from my lips. "Right. Well, I'm leaving. The perfect daughter you always wanted is out on the back porch, and I'm sure she needs help packing away all the shit you got her today. I'd hate for her to lift a finger, you know, since she's carrying your precious grandchild and all."

I'm being unfair to Dahlia, and I hate myself for it, but right now, I also cannot bring myself to care. I look out the back window to see that Daniel has joined her on the porch, laughing and talking and eating another slice of cake.

On a roll, I continue, "Some things never change. Go be the little family you so desperately wish you were."

Mom's face has paled a shade, no doubt from shock or anger —but never guilt. Her usual stony expression cracks, and I turn before she has the chance to point a finger.

"Stella, let's talk about this," my dad tries.

I pause, turning back to look at them. Raising my eyebrows

at my mom, I repeat my earlier question. Quieter this time. "What am I?"

She lets out a short breath. "Well, right now, you're being immature."

I purse my lips, nodding slowly, wondering why I thought I'd ever get a real answer out of her. I've always known she is disappointed in who I'm becoming, but instead of trying to get to know me, she took Dahlia under her wing and has been content to let her be everything I'm not.

I'll never get through to her. I don't know why I still try.

"I'm headed to therapy. Clearly, I have a lot to discuss," I say and continue toward the door.

I hear her muffled voice behind me, no doubt about to start rambling off to my dad about how ridiculous I'm being. But I wouldn't know because, by the time she speaks, I'm already gone.

# 18

I hurry through the hospital hallway after my appointment, the bright light reflecting off the stark white walls as I weave through this particular wing that I've come to know like the back of my hand. I make sure not to linger, wanting to move faster than the memories from this place can catch me.

The sterile smell and rhythmic beeping follow me all the way down the corridors leading to the main entry. I pass by the front desk, approaching tinted glass double doors with distinct black letters printed just at eye level that read, *Dr. Carol M. Dilton, Psychiatry.*

Pushing them open, I finally make it into the main lobby for this section of the hospital and breeze through the sliding glass doors.

The early evening sun drops below the trees, the air cooler than I expect it to be for Seattle in late June. I'm about to start the long walk to my car when my phone buzzes in my hand. I glance down, thinking maybe it could be Dahlia asking how my session went because she always asks how my sessions go. But instead, my heart leaps into my throat, and I almost drop the phone onto the pavement.

*Bridger Wells* flashes across the screen.

We haven't spoken since that day at UW when we decided to be friends. Granted, that was only a week ago, but still. I didn't know what that meant for us. And quite frankly, I still don't.

With a shaky hand, I slowly slide the bar across the screen and suck in a breath before answering, "Hello?"

"Hey, Stella."

I try to ignore the way my body instantly seems to relax at the sound of his voice. At the way he still says my name, as if it was his for the taking all along, like those six letters have always been meant for him to keep.

"What's up?" I wince at the slight tremble in my voice and silently smack myself on the head, taking a seat on a nearby bench. The line is quiet for a moment, and I pull the phone away from my ear quickly to make sure the call didn't disconnect.

"What are you doing right now?"

I hesitate, then say, "I'm just leaving therapy."

A brief pause. Then, "You're in therapy now?"

I exhale at the tender confusion in his voice. All I can muster is a simple, "Yes."

"What changed?"

Despite myself, I laugh. "Everything."

But right after I say it, I'm uncomfortable with how honest it felt, so I barrel forward with, "Was there a reason you called?" I pale, hearing how rude that sounded. "That's not what I meant. I mean, not that you have to have a reason to call, but we don't really call anymore, so I just figured that since you did, then you probably had a reason, and so if you did, I was jus—"

"Stel," he laughs, "breathe."

I do, thankful he can't see my flushed pink cheeks or feel my sweaty palms.

"Sorry," I huff out a short laugh. "I'm not used to not knowing how to talk to you."

I hear a slow, sad sigh on the other end of the line. "Don't apologize," he says quietly.

We just sit there for a moment, listening to each other breathe, and I almost want to close my eyes and imagine him next to me, but then he speaks again.

"So, there actually is a reason I called, though."

I can hear the smile in his voice again, and I wonder now if this is normal, how acutely aware you can become of a person, how every look, every lilt of tone, every calloused touch can be imprinted on your brain so clearly, so vividly, as if you're seeing your favorite painting for the first time and the hundredth time all at once.

"I was wondering if . . ." he trails off, and my pulse speeds up. He starts again. "I'm at the hospital, and I was wondering if—"

I'm immediately on my feet, turning back toward the main entrance. "The hospital? Which one? Are you okay? Do you need me to—"

"No! No, God, no, sorry. That was a terrible way to start out. I'm fine. It's nothing like that."

I exhale a heavy breath.

"I was at therapy too, actually. Well, *physical* therapy, if you want to get technical. But I mean, I do still see a real therapist too. Well, I guess all therapists are *real*, so to speak, but what I meant is—"

"Bridger." I'm laughing now, the previous embarrassment evaporating into dust. "Breathe," I tease.

I hear him chuckle lowly on the other end of the line. "You're right. That was weird."

My brows furrow, and I run my free hand over a loose thread on the hem of my hoodie. "What was?"

"Not knowing how to talk to you."

I squeeze my eyes shut, knowing he's right, knowing I'm the one who just said it first, but feeling the weight of it all the same.

Clearing my throat, I manage to say softly, "Right, so, physical therapy?"

"Yeah, so, we started some new exercises today, and my knee hasn't felt this crappy in a long time . . . and I just don't—I don't really feel comfortable driving, I guess. And I'd rather not worry my dad, you know? He has enough going on."

*No*, I think. *I don't know.*

But I take a deep breath, knowing how difficult it is for him to ask for help. I feel a surge of pride and then a pang of sadness as I think of all that he has been going through without me, but then I think of all that I've gone through without him, and I realize that we're probably even.

But I don't want to keep score. So, I say, "Of course, I can. I'm already at the hospital, so just send me your location, and I'll drive the car around to you."

He breathes out a sigh of what I can only assume is relief. "Thank you, seriously. I owe you one."

I smile sadly. "We both know you don't."

# 19

"So, how often do you have physical therapy?" I glance at Bridger in the passenger seat.

After picking him up from the physical rehabilitation unit, I tried not to notice how he favored his left knee when he climbed in and winced as he tried to get his leg comfortable in my too-small car. I don't like not knowing anything about how this happened to him or the severity of it, so I test the waters, not wanting him to feel like I'm trying to pry.

"It's still once a week. I thought I'd be down to every other week now, at least, but . . . I don't really have a track record of things working out the way I'd like them to."

I feel his words like a sting in my gut, but I ask another question anyway. "How did it happen?"

He runs a hand over his jaw as he stares out the window, and with one look at his solemn expression, I wonder if I've pushed too far. I try to backtrack by saying quickly, "Never mind, you don't have to tell me."

Out of the corner of my eye, I see him shrug. "It's okay. I don't mind talking about it."

He pauses, the passing cars and steady hum of the streetlights the only sound. "It was post-season earlier this year—back in January—and we were doing this running drill, sprinting full force to the marked cone and then stopping almost just as fast. It was a super early practice, so the grass on the field was cold and wet . . ." He grimaces, face faltering. "I tried to cut around the cone, but I slipped, and my body went one way, and my leg went the other." He pauses, sighing. "And then I passed out." He drops his hands to his lap, leaning his head against the seat.

My stomach bottoms out. "I'm sorry, Bridge. That's . . ." I start lamely. I sigh, my arms feeling like heavy weights against the steering wheel. "That must've really sucked," is all I can manage.

"It really did," he nods, a sad expression flashing briefly across his features. He exhales slowly. "So, anyway, I woke up in the hospital, had no clue what was going on, felt like my leg had fallen off. Found out I had torn my ACL and meniscus all in one go."

My chest tightens, and I will my eyes not to fill with tears. I flip on my turn signal to turn into Bridger's neighborhood, my chest tightening in a different sort of way when I realize I drove here on autopilot, subconsciously, like I could've done it with my eyes closed.

"I needed to have surgery a few weeks later, and it just made more sense for me to have it here, in Seattle, instead of across the country alone. That night, at the hospital, when it all happened, the one thing all my doctors kept telling me was how much support I was going to need over the next few months as I recovered. And at UNC . . . I had none."

I swear I can feel the small fissure that was starting to split my heart down the middle finally crack in two.

"So, right then, before I even knew I had lost my scholarship, before my dad even found out what happened, I had already decided I was moving back home. To finish out junior year and do my rehab here over the summer."

I'm glad it is at this moment that I pull into his familiar gravel driveway because the world around me is starting to blur as my eyes fill up. Parking, I clear my throat and finally look at him. "But—why did you lose your scholarship?"

He looks at the floor as if he's still processing. January wasn't that long ago, after all. "I fully intended on going back. I was going to finish out rehab here, keep training, and be back for my final season. It was going to be fine. That's what I thought I wanted. So I had the surgery, started physical therapy, and I was so intent on getting back to one hundred percent that I think I pushed myself too hard . . . and I ended up with a fractured patella. It basically just didn't heal right, I guess. So, I had to have another surgery."

My face falls. "Bridger," I whisper.

I knew he'd gotten injured again, and I knew it had to have been pretty serious if he stopped playing—not to mention the fact that he moved back *home*—but hearing it out loud like this makes me nauseous. I swallow the lump in my throat and focus on the hum of the engine.

"I mean, we both knew my knee was already bad anyway. I should've listened to you in high school," he jokes, offering me a sad smile with a small shrug.

I shake my head slowly, unable to form any words.

"After my second surgery, the recovery process basically started all over, and there was no way I was going to be able to be ready to play in the fall. I talked to the coaching staff, and they basically told me the athletic department at UNC deemed me ineligible. Said that since my ACL had already been torn once before, I was a liability." He laughs again, but it sounds pained, maybe even a little bitter.

My heart sinks for him, knowing how much that word must have meant. How much it still obviously does—how he's felt like a liability his whole life.

"So, anyway. I really didn't have a choice but to transfer to

UW after that. When the scholarship was revoked, there was no way I could afford UNC on my own. Dad offered to help, but I couldn't ask that of him. Not with all my medical bills, all the complications, the extended hospital stays . . ." He trails off with a slight shake of his head.

"Bridger." I can feel the pain radiating off him, and it kills me that he feels even a little guilty, like any of this could have possibly been his fault. I reach out and grab his hand, and his fingers instantly grasp onto mine as he looks at the floor. "You're not a liability."

He drops his head lower, closing his eyes.

"Hey," I speak gently. "Look at me."

Slowly, he does. He opens his eyes and lifts his face to mine, and his battered expression is the saddest I've ever seen. For the first time, I notice how worn down he looks, and I wonder how much of that same look is reflected in me. I know I can't offer him much, but I can at least offer him this.

I repeat myself. "You are not a liability. I hate that you've ever felt that way, but I need you to know this. You're not, okay?"

He squeezes my hand and lowers his gaze again, leaning back against the seat. He doesn't speak for a moment, and neither do I, letting my words hang in the air between us. After another moment, his raw voice breaks the silence.

"See, this is just it." He gently releases my hand and runs his fingers through his hair. "College soccer was hard, and exhausting, and way more taxing than I thought it would be. It was nice, though, being able to throw myself so completely into something, to be so busy with practices and scrimmages and games that I didn't have time to be alone with my thoughts. To think. And I don't think I realized how much I relied on that distraction until I didn't have it anymore."

"A distraction from what?"

"You."

My body tenses, and I'm afraid to move, to breathe, to lean

into the opening he is giving me. He sighs softly, and out of the corner of my eye. I can see him start to rub his knee.

"You, us, that summer, my mom, my grades, all I left behind —everything," he continues.

I exhale a wobbling breath, unsure of what to say. The last thing I wanted after he left was to add to his pain or to make things worse for him. In letting him go, I thought I was doing him a favor. "I'm so sorry, Bridger. I just—God. I'm so sorry," I say, the words barely more than a whisper as the tears cloud my vision.

"Stel, don't cry. Please," he says sadly, reaching back across the seat and squeezing my shoulder, his thumb slowly moving back and forth against my collarbone. "It happened, and it sucks, but it is what it is. And looking back now, after everything, I can honestly say I'm kind of glad for it."

I look over at him, confusion and curiosity rippling across my features. "What? How?"

He squeezes my shoulder once before pulling away. Shrugging, the hint of a smile plays at his lips. "If things hadn't panned out this way, would we be sitting here together like this?"

I sniff, turning away and wiping at my eyes. "I guess not," I say quietly.

He doesn't say anything else, and when I look back at him, there's a weight in his expression I can't quite explain. Leaning against the seat, he clears his throat and blinks a few times. "So, anyway. Enough about me. What's been going on in your life over these past few years?"

Thrumming my fingers over my thighs, I purse my lips. I think about all the time that has passed, everything that's different, and all the ways that our lives have changed. And then I think of us here, in this car, and I can't help but think that, somehow, some things still seem the same. I think about last year and the past few months and him moving away and coming back, and then it hits me all at once, and words tumble out of my mouth before I can stop them.

"Wait. You've been back since *January?*"

He nods. "I mean, back here, technically, yes. But I wasn't really out and about for the majority of that time."

"Oh, right. Sorry." I wince.

"You have nothing to apologize for."

Under my breath, I exhale, "You'd be surprised." I can't tell if he heard my quiet admission or not, but thankfully, he doesn't say anything about it.

When I look back over at him, I can tell his mind is elsewhere again. I want to say something to bring him back to me, but I know he's not mine to have. So, I let the silence grow between us, resting in the solemn familiarity of his presence.

The night is now completely cloaked in darkness, the silver moon barely illuminating the street below. In the stillness, I can hear the breeze gently rustling the leaves, and I can't help but think of the nights we used to spend just like this. And when I finally glance back over at him, he's already looking at me.

"Where'd you go just now?" he says softly, breaking through the quiet.

The ghost of a smile pulls at my lips. "I wanted to ask you the same thing."

"Why didn't you?"

"It's not my place anymore." And whatever small flame was starting to reignite itself between us is gone in an instant, and I can't even allow myself to feel the loss of it because I'm the one who blew it out.

Hurt flashes through his eyes before he faces forward again, reminding me of all the reasons we can't do this. Why I can't do this to him.

Not again.

He puffs out his cheeks as he blows a long breath out of his mouth. "Stella, that's not fair." He sighs again. "I'm not the one shutting you out."

He leans forward before I have a chance to register the weight of his words. He drops his face into his palms, and I resist the urge to reach over and rub my hand across his back like I used to do without a second thought. His voice is muffled through his hands, and I can't make out what he's saying.

"What?" I ask softly.

He lifts his gaze back to mine and repeats so quietly I almost ask him to say it a third time, "Tell me something real. Please." He sits up straighter, running a hand through his hair. "Anything."

*What's been going on in your life over the past few years?*

"Dahlia is pregnant," I blurt out, trying to give him some form of the truth, some semblance of the time I've spent without him.

His eyebrows shoot up, lips parting in surprise. "I—wow. That's . . . that's great. Tell them I say congratulations."

I can only nod, and he clears his throat before looking back over at me. "Your parents are thrilled, I assume."

"Oh, you have no idea." I choke out a laugh that would've gone unnoticed by anyone else, but, of course, he sees right through me.

"Were you not?"

"No! Well, I mean, yes. I was. I *am*. It's not that. It's just . . ." I trail off, ending the sentence with a shrug. "I mean. You know my mom." I think back to the shower earlier today, what I heard her admit from the living room. "Dahlia is everything she ever wanted in a daughter, so I'm happy for them."

His face falls again, and I hate that for the second time tonight, I'm the reason.

"Stel," he starts but gets cut off by his ringtone coming from the center console. He glances down, then sighs. "That's my dad. I bet he's on his way home."

I look at the clock on the dashboard for the first time, and my eyes widen when I realize we've been sitting here for almost an hour. "Oh, it's getting late. I should probably head home anyway, so . . ."

He swallows. "Right. Okay." Opening the car door, he steps out slowly and turns back to face me, one hand resting on the doorframe. "Thanks again for the ride." He drops his hand, taking a step back.

"Of course," I manage.

He smiles, but it's sad, weighted. "Goodnight, Stella."

Shutting the car door, he turns and starts up the driveway. I wait until he's inside before putting my car in reverse. I pull onto the road, everything he told me swirling through my thoughts and weighing down my heart. I drive the familiar roads from his house to mine that I've taken a thousand times before, and I cry the whole way home.

# 20

## THEN

December, Sophomore Year

"Who was that boy you were hanging out with on Thursday?" Daniel said as he flopped down onto a barstool at the kitchen island. I stilled, the bowl I was rinsing from dinner slipping from my hands and clattering into the sink.

He'd just gotten home for Christmas break a few days ago and, as my parents so affectionately said, "It's like he never left." With the way they'd been acting, you'd think we were hosting the Prince of Wales in our house for the next three weeks.

It had only been a couple of months since he was home for fall break, and it wasn't like he'd be gone for that long after he went back the next semester. As ridiculous as my parents were being, it made me wonder how they'd act if I was the one away at school. It almost made me want to leave just to see if they'd care when I came back.

The house had definitely become quieter since he'd left for college, but all things considered, things hadn't been that different. Four years older than me, it wasn't that Daniel and I had never gotten along necessarily, but it never quite seemed like we were on the same page either. We had always been in each other's orbit, but we'd always kind of just . . . missed each other. Like two parallel lines moving through the world side by side but never really crossing paths.

So, for him to ask questions about who I was spending time with was new. And weird. He'd never cared to ask before, and I wondered what had pushed him to start. I flicked my eyes over my shoulder to try and gauge his expression, but he wasn't even looking at me as he typed on his phone.

I shrugged, wondering how he was going to play this. "His name is Bridger."

He set his phone down on the countertop. "Oh, is it?" he said, the smirk present in his voice.

I rolled my eyes, not bothering to turn around and look at him. "How do you even know about that?" I asked, wondering when he'd seen us together.

"I saw him drop you off."

My face scrunched, and I looked over at him. "It was dark." I turned back to the sink as I felt a blush creeping up my neck, thinking about that day. How Bridger had kissed me at the park and how he had kissed me again before I got out of the car. He had offered to walk me to the front door, but I said he didn't have to because I knew Daniel was home and I wanted to avoid . . . this.

"I mean, I didn't actually see him, but it's not like you have any friends you typically hang out with."

I rolled my lips inward as I started scrubbing the now spotless bowl with more force. "Good one."

The steam cloud from the hot water warmed my face, and I winced as a scalding droplet landed on my wrist. I wiped it off quickly, marveling at how my twenty-year-old brother had the sense of humor of a ten-year-old.

And still, he continued, "I mean, Mom told me she practically had to *beg* you to go to that school bonfire a few months ago. The annual bonfire! That thing was always so lame." He laughed to himself. "There's never even an actual fire."

I turned the water off and whirled around, pinning him with a glare. "Not everyone can be the prom king, class president, and voted most likely to succeed, okay?" I seethed, annoyed at our mom because, *of course,* she would have mentioned that to him.

I closed my eyes and took a deep breath, white-knuckling the counter. I dropped my gaze, staring at the reflection of the lights on the floor. We stayed like that for a few moments, neither one of us breaking the silence that weighed between us. I heard him shifting and looked up to see him get off the barstool and lean against the counter next to me.

"I'm just kidding around. You know that, right?"

"Yeah," I nodded, exhaling through my nose. "You always are."

Nudging my arm with his, he said matter-of-factly, "Just . . . try not to take everything so personally, okay? I wasn't trying to make you feel bad or anything."

"It's fine," I replied tersely.

Because with him, it would always be a losing battle. He'd say whatever he wanted and be surprised when I got offended, and then I would be the one in the wrong for having a reaction. I needed to lighten up, learn to take a joke, not be so sensitive. It was all I'd ever heard from him and my parents, so I'd learned to keep quiet.

"Besides," he pushed off the counter and turned around to face me, "you have a boyfriend now!" And, of course, his voice echoed through the kitchen just as I heard Mom and Dad walk through the front door.

"Who has a boyfriend?" Mom called from the hallway.

"No one!" I turned around to whack him on the arm as he laughed.

Just then, my parents rounded the corner into the kitchen, and Dad moved straight over to the fridge to put away whatever leftovers they'd brought home from Mom's work Christmas party.

"What's all this about?" Mom set down her purse and looked at me with raised eyebrows.

I weighed my options, knowing I could either tell her it was nothing and have Daniel make me out to be a liar, or I could give them just enough to shut down the conversation.

"I've just been hanging out with a friend from school," I shrugged, feeling guilty as soon as the words left my mouth. *I knew he meant so much more to me than that, but that didn't mean my family needed to.*

"A friend or a *friend*?" Daniel teased.

"A . . . friend," I repeated flatly, trying and failing to give him a look over Mom's shoulder.

"Okay, well, I'd love to meet this *friend*," Mom said, putting emphasis on the word like Daniel did. Before I could begin to object, she added, "You should invite him over for dinner next weekend."

Panicked, I sputtered a response. "No, it's fine, I don't think he'd want—"

"And you should invite Dahlia!" She beamed at my brother. "You're both home for Christmas break. It's perfect!"

For once, my dad actually spoke up. "I think it's a great idea. I'd love to get to know the people my kids are spending their time with."

My eyebrows lowered, and I wondered when he had become so diplomatic all of a sudden.

Mom clapped her hands, loving any reason to make a big meal and show off the house to someone new. "Then it's settled. Friday night at six."

She and my dad left the kitchen, and I turned to Daniel slowly. "I. Am going. To kill you," I breathed as he laughed and walked toward the hallway.

"Relax, I'm doing you a favor. Trust me."

I let out an exasperated huff as he sauntered out of the room. I vowed right then and there to enjoy what I thought would be my last week with Bridger because I was sure that after Friday, he'd never want to be around me again.

If only it had been that simple.

# 21

My heart skipped a beat and my stomach bottomed out the second I heard a knock on the front door that Friday night.

When I told Bridger that my mom wanted to have him over for dinner, I expected him to (and hoped he would) refuse. But he was Bridger. So, of course, he was more than happy to, saying it was only fair since I'd met his dad. I tried to argue that it was different, but he simply said my name, put his hands on either side of my face, kissed me gently, and said, "I want to come."

Tell me, honestly, how was I supposed to argue?

And so, there we were, sitting around the dining room table with Dahlia and Bridger in tow. The flowers Bridger brought my mom sat proudly in the center of the dining room table, Mom already displaying them in her most favorite vase.

"Nice touch." I gave him a look after Mom hurried away, and all he did was wink at me. The fool actually winked at me.

And I hadn't been able to wipe the smile off my face since.

Dad sat at the head of the table on my left, Mom at the other head on my right. Bridger sat to my left, Daniel across from him, and Dahlia across from me. And thankfully, we had enough seats this time, so I didn't have to sit on a stool two heads taller than everyone else.

I reached across the table to grab another dinner roll, my plate of pasta already almost gone. Bridger, Daniel, and my dad were all bonding over the Seattle Seahawks as Mom and Dahlia laughed on the other side of the table. For a moment, I sat back and enjoyed the scene before me, in disbelief at how smoothly the night seemed to be going.

But I should've known then that if something was going well —that meant it wouldn't last. And on that particular night, of course, I'd had the thought too soon.

"So, Bridger, what do you want to do after you finish school?" Mom said.

He finished the sip of water he was taking and cleared his throat. "I'm hoping to go to college somewhere that I can get a good soccer scholarship. I've had my sights set on UNC for a while, but I tore my ACL toward the beginning of freshman year, so last season was a little rough. And it's probably a long shot anyway."

"Well, from what I hear, you're really good," Mom said.

"Thank you," Bridger replied, glancing at me briefly, amusement alight in his eyes.

I didn't tell my family a *ton* about Bridger beforehand, but I did mention that he played soccer. And that he'd been on varsity both years so far. And served as a captain last season. And that he'd played club in the spring. And was really good. So. Anyway.

"That's really cool," Daniel cut in. "You know, I'm surprised you and Stella have anything in common since she doesn't have an athletic bone in her body."

Bridger frowned, and I felt my face grow hot from embarrassment. Dahlia smacked him on the arm and gave him an exasperated look.

"I mean, I'm just saying—"

"Can you please try to act your age for five seconds?" I

snapped at him, cutting him off before he could say anything else.

"Stella, please watch your tone," my mom said with a slight shake of her head.

I clasped my hands together in my lap, taking a measured breath through my nose. I only relaxed slightly when I felt Bridger press his leg against mine under the table.

"I don't have an athletic bone in my body, and you still like me," Dahlia said, looking at my brother with a pointed stare.

My parents laughed, and Daniel tossed his napkin at her face, laughing too. I wondered how she could do that, how she could lighten the mood and simultaneously take some of the attention off me so easily. I felt the tension in my shoulders start to ease at her words, and I made a mental note to thank her later.

I liked Dahlia, and I thought she was good for Daniel—I just wasn't sure how she put up with him. I was biased, of course, because I would always see him as the immature pain in my side I knew him to be. But, for the first time, I wondered how many sides of him I didn't know, what pieces of himself he might not let me see.

"Stella is talented in a lot of ways, though. I mean, more so with a pen than a soccer ball, but—honestly, in the long run, that's way more valuable." A weighted silence settled over the table, but Bridger continued. "Have you guys read her latest short story for her creative writing class? It was amazing." He raised his fork to his mouth, taking another bite.

My eyes closed briefly as I released a breath because I knew this conversation was heading nowhere good.

Mom cleared her throat, and I opened my eyes to see her looking at Bridger. "No, we haven't, actually."

Bridger looked up, read the room, and started chewing slower. Swallowed. "Oh. Well . . . it's really good."

"Yes, well, we all have our hobbies," she said smoothly, folding her hands under her chin.

Bridger squinted a little, confused, looking at me with a question in his eyes. At the slight shake of my head, I hoped he would just drop it.

"So, what are you wanting to study?" My dad's voice cut into the conversation.

Bridger slowly peeled his gaze away from me to look back at my dad. "Architecture."

Dad nodded his approval as Daniel let out a low whistle and said, "Okay, now *that* is legit."

"As opposed to . . . ?" Bridger questioned, but no one heard him above the discussion his answer had started. He looked over at me again with a crease in his brow, and I tried to give him a small smile to let him know it was fine. The crease deepened, and I was grateful when he got pulled back into the conversation because, at that point, I was trying to run away from the English degree topic as fast as I could.

"We just had a big meeting today with the team of architects we're collaborating with for our next project," Mom started. "I co-own an interior design firm, and today . . ."

That was precisely when I started to tune them out as she dove into a lively discussion about interior design, making sure to point out the fact that Dahlia was an intern and was doing so well. Thankfully, the rest of the dinner passed quickly. Mom excitedly hopped out of her chair to grab the dessert she had made, my dad following behind to help her.

Out of the corner of my eye, I could see Daniel and Dahlia talking to each other heatedly in low voices, Dahlia gesticulating with her hands. I looked back down at my plate and could feel Bridger's eyes on me, but I pretended not to as I pushed the remaining pasta around with my fork.

My parents reappeared, Mom holding a plate of strawberry poke cake, Dad trailing behind with a small bowl of whipped cream in one hand and extra napkins in the other. We ate the dessert, and Bridger and my dad made more polite conversation while I ironically poked at the cake on my plate, my appetite gone. A few minutes later, Mom started to gather the plates as everyone began to clear out.

"Here, let me help," Bridger said, standing and grabbing the other dishes and silverware.

"Oh, you don't have to do that. Thank you." Her voice trailed off as she disappeared into the kitchen, Bridger following.

Dad looked at me and said, "Nice boy," with a nod before heading over to his favored recliner in the living room.

I raised my eyebrows as if to say, *"Okay, then."*

"Oh, Dad, did you see that stat I sent you about the Mariners this year?" Daniel's voice trailed off as he followed Dad into the living room.

Dahlia and I stood, and I was about to follow Bridger into the kitchen when she said my name, stopping me. "Hey, Stella?"

"Yeah?"

"Just so you know, I told Daniel that if he ever talked to you like that again, I would break up with him."

I released a startled laugh, it being the last thing I expected her to say.

She grinned at me. "Also . . . I'd love to read your short story sometime," she added, her eyes bright and kind.

"Oh. Um, yeah. Okay," I said and felt a genuine smile break out across my face.

"He seemed really proud of you," she added softly, nudging me on the arm.

I smiled at her again as best I could before moving my eyes back down toward the table, hoping no further emotion showed on my face. Just as I was about to leave the dining room, Bridger's phone started buzzing on the table.

*Mom* flashed on the screen, and despite not wanting to seem like I was being invasive, I hurriedly decided I should bring it to him. I still didn't know much about his mom, but from what I could tell, she didn't seem like the type of person you'd want to miss a phone call from.

I snatched it from the table, Dahlia waving me toward the kitchen. Quickly, I walked through the archway and saw him and my mom over by the sink, the latter laughing at something Bridger said as they dried dishes.

He looked over his shoulder at me and said, "Hey, Stel—oh." He looked down at his phone as I held it up in front of him, then up at me, then back at his phone.

I was honestly surprised it was still ringing.

"Thanks." He took the phone from me and then apologetically looked at my mom. "I should take this," he muttered as he walked out into the hallway.

I turned back toward my mom as she finished drying the last dish. I was about to ask her what she and Bridger were talking about, but before I even started to get the words out, she said, "Hey, can you go grab Dahlia for me real quick? I have a question I want to ask her about the meeting today that I don't want to forget."

I blinked, almost wanting to laugh at the dismissal. Nodding, I walked out of the kitchen, pivoting around the hurt. After telling Dahlia she was wanted, I took a seat at the dining room table again, sitting in a house full of people yet somehow still alone.

Then I thought of Bridger, just around the corner, and a warmth filled me so suddenly it almost felt tangible. Because even across the room, even though I couldn't physically see him, his presence was an all-encompassing thing, like when the sun is behind a cloud, but you're still warm anyway because you know it's there.

I let myself sink into that moment and tried to memorize the way it felt because even then, I knew one day it would be winter again, and I would need to remember what it felt like to sit in the sun.

Just as I had the thought, Bridger came around the corner, and I swore his shoulders sagged in relief when he saw me there at the table.

I was immediately on my feet the second I saw his face. "Is everything okay?"

He nodded and cleared his throat, and whatever previous emotion had lingered there was gone in an instant, replaced by his usual self again. "Yeah, it's all good. I think maybe I should head out, though."

I tried to ignore the sinking feeling in my stomach, praying winter wasn't already here. "Okay."

"Will you come with me?" He paused. "I just mean, like, maybe to the car. We could drive around for a little while? I don't know. Actually, you know what, never mind—"

"Hey," I said, stepping in front of him and placing my hand on his arm. "That sounds fun." I could tell he had something on his mind, and I wondered how much the call from his mom had to do with it.

"Yeah?"

I nodded firmly, then said, "Let's go tell everyone we're heading out."

So, we walked around, and he said his *goodbyes* and *nice to meet yous,* and no one even asked why I was leaving too. By the time we got to the front hallway, any fight left in me had been drained, and I was left feeling disappointed and embarrassed at how the evening had played out.

Defeated, I pulled on my coat as we slipped out the front door. Just as I was about to shut it, Daniel shouted, "Stella! Tell your boyfriend he's welcome anytime!"

I slammed the door at that, squeezing my eyes shut and inhaling a deep breath. In the stillness that followed, I silently cursed my brother because I was afraid he had just ruined everything. But when I finally opened my eyes again, they were met with a huge grin. Exhaling, I smiled back tightly. I hoped he wouldn't say anything about my expression, but he had always been observant, and that smile never fooled him.

His face got serious. "What's wrong?"

I just shrugged. "I feel like that Taylor Swift song."

He looked off into the distance, seemingly lost in thought. "You mean "Gorgeous," right?" he asked seriously.

I laughed a full-out belly laugh for what felt like the first time in weeks, and I hoped he couldn't see the way my face warmed at his words. "How do you know that song?"

Eyes glittering, he gave me a look. "I'm going to pretend not to be offended by that."

I laughed again. "I think "Death By A Thousand Cuts" is what I was going for."

"Oh." He nodded, eyebrows raised. "Well, to be fair, that song does have one of the best bridges in her entire discography."

My mouth fell open again as I stared at him in pure awe.

He grinned and held his hand out, nodding his head toward the street where his car was parked. "Come on. It's freezing."

**22**

"Where'd you go just now?" Bridger said after getting into the car, cheeks flushed and features soft.

My mind had already started wandering to thoughts of the dinner, my family, and what a mess the night had been in the short time it took for us to walk from the house to his car. I didn't know if I was more surprised that he'd noticed or that he'd asked.

Rubbing my hands together, I wished the car would warm up faster. "I'm just thinking about how terrible that went, honestly. I'm sorry about them." I looked out the window, not knowing what else to say.

"You have nothing to apologize for."

"Yeah, well. It feels like I do." I shivered, and I didn't think it was from the cold. "The way they talk to me sometimes . . . I don't know. It's just embarrassing." Shrugging, I put my hands up to the vents. "I didn't want to have to drag you into that."

His lips pulled down. "You didn't drag me into anything. If I can recall correctly, I willingly showed up on your doorstep tonight. With flowers."

I snorted, and a silence fell between us. After a few moments, he spoke again. "And there's nothing you have to be embarrassed about, either. Not with me." The streetlight danced along the side of his face, painting his brown hair gold. "And for the record . . ." he continued, "I know that one day you're going to be an amazing author."

A startled laugh sounded in my throat, and I shook my head. "You don't have to say that."

The silence stretched for a moment, and then Bridger spoke so softly I almost didn't hear him. "If I don't, who will?"

My breath caught in my throat, and eyes burning, I looked away again.

"Do you ever tell them about your writing? Have they ever read any of your work?" He paused, contemplating. His voice softened. "Do they even know you're writing a book?"

I choked out a pained laugh, ignoring his first question because, right then, the wound was too raw. "That's the problem. They do know, and they couldn't care less. They think it's a waste of my time." I shook my head, continuing, "I mean, I want to write fantasy books about kingdoms and dragons and magic. Of course, they'd think it's dumb. Hell, I bet even you think it's dumb." I dropped my face into my hands, the tears scalding my cheeks.

I felt his warm hand fall onto the center of my back, a gentle, soothing touch that made the tears flow faster.

"Stella," he all but whispered, "look at me."

I shook my head, my face still buried in my hands. "It's fine."

"It's not." His hand moved away from my back, and I inhaled a sharp breath as I felt his hands tenderly wrap around my own. He gently pulled them away from my face and dipped his head down into my line of vision. "And it's not dumb."

I let out a shaky breath, and he reached up to wipe away a stray tear as it rolled down my cheek. "Don't let them convince you that you can't do it or that you shouldn't try. Okay?" He swallowed, throat bobbing, and I let my eyes linger there, unable to meet his eyes. I could only bring myself to nod.

"You have so much to offer the world, Stella." He reached out and moved a piece of hair out of my face. "You're not here to exist halfway."

I finally looked up, and the sincerity in his eyes almost took my breath away. I forced myself to hold the weight of his gaze, all the while feeling the ghost of a smile tugging at my lips. "Is that just a cooler way of telling me not to let anyone dull my sparkle?"

His smile overtook his face, and in that moment, I thought to myself that I had never seen anything so bright or so beautiful.

"I'm serious, though," he added, his dark brown eyes searching my own.

"I don't know," I said, looking back out across the wind-shield. "Sometimes I feel like I barely exist at all."

"Don't say that." He reached over and squeezed my arm lightly.

I tried to offer him a weak smile. "Where did you hear that anyway? A Hallmark card?" I said, trying to lighten the mood and redirect the conversation.

He leaned back, his hand dropping to his lap as the corner of his mouth tugged upward. "My dad, actually." He paused, and as his smile grew, I thought my heart did too. "He usually adds 'kiddo' onto the end of it, but—I was trying to read the room."

We burst into laughter again, and the tears that filled my eyes then weren't from sadness at all. I marveled at him, at how easy it all was—to fall apart and let him catch me when I did. I looked at him then, and I couldn't explain it, couldn't put the feeling into words, but I think I just . . . knew. This different type of knowing from deep within myself, this unparalleled certainty that this boy would mean something to me for a long, long time.

I cleared my throat, leaning back against my seat. "So, UNC, huh?" I said, wiping my wet face and wondering how he put up with the hot mess that I was so seamlessly.

He exhaled through a smile, finally regaining composure. "Yeah, it's been my dream school for as long as I can remember."

"That's cool." I pursed my lips, not wanting to sound like an idiot but knowing I was going to anyway. "So, remind me. What does it stand for again?"

He snorted out a laugh, turning down the heat that was blasting through the vents. "The University of North Carolina. At Chapel Hill, if you want to get technical."

"Yeah, that's what I thought," I said, nodding matter-of-factly.

"Right." He nodded along playfully. "But who knows if I'll even get in. I'd need tons of scholarships and stuff to even afford to go, anyway, and soccer will probably be the only shot I have at making it." He let out a breath like he'd been holding it in for a while.

"Bridger, that's really cool. Like, for real."

He shrugged. "I'm trying not to get my hopes up."

"Hey, you're not here to exist halfway, either," I said, reciting his words back to him. "Go show your gifts to the world, become a soccer star," I continued, adding jazz hands and then immediately regretting it.

He looked down at my hands and then back up at my face with his eyebrows raised and an amused expression lighting up his eyes. I felt my cheeks turn pink as I quickly tucked my hands under my thighs, giving him a forced grin. "Anyway! Why UNC? Any reason in particular?" I said, trying to move the conversation along.

"My dad always wanted to go there—he was a soccer player too. So, I kind of just grew up with it, in a way. We always used to watch the games together on live streams, and I used to pretend it was me out there on the field. It sort of became this dream that I always felt I had in me, you know?"

I nodded. "Absolutely."

He continued, "And especially since my dad never did actually get to go, I kind of . . . I don't know. I want to do it for him too."

I tilted my head, curious. "Why didn't he go?"

Bridger pursed his lips, dipped his head a little. "My mom got pregnant."

I pulled my head back in surprise. "Oh."

He nods. "Yeah."

And I could see in that moment the way the responsibility weighed on his shoulders, the slight crease in his forehead that made me feel like he didn't talk about this subject a lot.

"So, he stayed in Seattle to be with your mom?" I asked tentatively.

He scoffed and ran a hand over his mouth before answering. "Kind of the opposite, actually." He dropped his gaze to his lap, and I let the silence envelop us, giving him space to say more if he wanted to. "My mom found out she was pregnant with me halfway through their senior year. I can only assume now that she never really saw herself being a mom, I guess."

He lifted his eyes to mine, and I saw raw emotion shining there that made me instantly like her ten times less, even though that was the first I had really heard about her.

"Shocker, right?" He said it bitterly, sighing before he continued. "I don't know, they were . . . young. Probably thought they could make it work somehow. But her plan was always to go to UCLA. Dad tells me that's all she ever cared about, really. Said her drive was admirable at first but then kind of became . . . consuming. It mattered to her more than anything else." After a weighted pause, he took a deep breath. "Evidently, more than even me."

"Bridger," I whispered, reaching over and grabbing his hand, giving him something real to hold onto.

He shot me a grateful look, his thumb starting to trace

patterns on the back of my hand as he kept talking. "So, she had me in the summer and went away to college in the fall."

My mouth opened in surprise, and I shut it quickly, hoping he hadn't seen. "Oh," I said again, lamely.

"Yeah. So, my dad decided to stay in Washington to be near his parents. It wouldn't have been possible for him to go to UNC then anyway, not with a newborn. My whole life, he has told me it was the greatest decision he ever made, and if he could go back, he'd make the same one in a heartbeat. But it's still hard sometimes, you know? To not feel like I took something from him."

I squeezed his hand harder, wrapping my other hand around his as well. "Bridger, that's not your fault."

He nods slowly. "I know."

"So . . . your mom just stayed in California, then?"

"Yeah. After she graduated, she got a job as an attorney at a huge firm down there. She used to visit a few times a year when I was a kid, but over the years, the visits have become less and less frequent, replaced with a monthly FaceTime call." He ran his free hand over the back of his neck, shaking his head. "She started sending me emails when I turned thirteen." He laughed again, his gaze far off. "Like it's just another business transaction. A colleague she needs to make sure she reaches out to before five on a Wednesday."

I could tell he needed to say this, and I was grateful that I was the one who could be there for him to listen.

"And the funny thing is, when we do talk, she doesn't even ask about *me.* How I'm doing. All she cares about are my grades and soccer. She wants me to get a huge scholarship and become something great." His shoulders dropped, and he blinked a few times. "It's just so ironic if you think about it."

I nodded, letting him sort out his thoughts.

"And it's hard still, sometimes, not to be bitter. But it's weird, though, because . . . I still love her, you know? She's my mom."

I nodded again, his hand still tightly clasped in mine. "Yeah. I get that." Then I paused, thinking back to the reason he wanted to come out to the car. "Was that why you seemed off in there? After the phone call?"

He exhaled, nodding. "I don't know. Talking to her always makes me feel . . .heavier? It's been a lot to process, but I've been going to therapy for a few years now, and it's honestly helped a lot." He shrugged. "It's been good to talk through everything. I mean, I had never really given it much thought because it was always so normal. I've always just been used to her never being around."

He nodded at his lap as if reassuring himself. "So, it's been good to work through things that I didn't even realize were affecting me. You know, attachment issues and all that stuff."

He looked back over at me as if realizing all he'd just admitted. Color rose up his neck to his cheeks, and he cleared his throat. "Sorry. You didn't ask to hear my whole life story."

"Thank you for telling me," I said honestly. He met my eyes, and a moment passed between us then—one of understanding, a different kind of tenderness. A new kind. The kind that I knew I'd never want to let go of, not after having it once.

I sighed as he gave my hands one final squeeze. "I could probably benefit from therapy. But One Direction would get back together before my mom would ever allow that."

"That's . . . quite the analogy," he stated with furrowed brows.

I shrugged. "It's the truth. Anytime I've tried to broach the subject, she tells me that therapy is for people with 'real problems,'" I said with air quotes. "That I have a roof over my head, food on my plate, and a place to lay my head at night. What could I possibly need to talk about?" I shook my head, knowing it would always be the same story every time.

"Damn," Bridger said softly.

"Damn," I agreed.

The front door opened, and we watched Daniel walk Dahlia

out to her car. I realized in that moment how it probably looked, Bridger and I sitting there in a dark car parked on the road.

"I should probably go. I don't want Daniel asking any questions." I started to open the car door, pausing when I felt his gentle touch on my arm again.

"Thank you," he said.

"For what?"

"For . . . being here. For listening. And—" He smiled, and despite the suddenly freezing night air, I was warm all the way down to my toes. "Tell your mom I said thanks for dinner."

I rolled my eyes. "The flowers weren't a thank you enough?"

He smiled. "Goodnight, Stella."

"Goodnight, Bridger."

Then I shut the car door and walked back to the house, smiling to myself as he lingered by the curb until I made it inside.

# 23

NOW

Everything has pretty much gone back to normal since my argument with Mom after the end of the baby shower last week—normal in the sense that we've all just resumed tiptoeing around each other and the things that actually matter, never crossing any lines.

So, I'm surprised when I hear a soft knock on my door as I sit in bed, laptop propped up on my legs in front of me.

"Come in," I call hesitantly. The door opens slowly, and Mom pokes her head in. I try to mask my surprise, fighting to keep my face neutral. "What's up?"

My mom rarely ever comes into my room, except for the days when she decides she needs to deep clean the entire house. She's always liked everything in the house to be a certain way, and my room is no exception with light gray walls, a deep green duvet with white accent pillows, and perfectly spaced picture frames with depictions of Seattle in different seasons fitted within. A small desk sits on the adjacent wall, and aside from the framed photo of me and my grandma sitting in the corner, this could be any random guest room. The only other indications that this room belongs to me are the matching white bookshelves on either side of my window and a small white reading chair in the corner.

Mom steps into my room, taking a quick look around as if to make sure everything is in order. "I just wanted to check in." She wears a tight smile, smoothing her perfectly manicured fingers down the front of her shirt.

My repressed facial expression wins out, my eyebrows creasing and my lips turning down at the corners. "Oh. Okay?"

She sighs, moving to the corner and gingerly lowering herself onto my reading chair. I sit up straighter, setting my laptop down on the side of the bed. "You know we're trying, right?"

My frown deepens, and I give her a questioning look. "Sorry?"

She rubs her fingers against her temples, already making me feel like I'm being difficult when she's the one who came in here and decided to be cryptic. "After the baby shower last week, what you heard in the living room?"

I nod, unsure of where this is going.

"Dahlia has always just had such a good head on her shoulders, and from the moment I met her, I could kind of just . . . see it."

I hold my breath, trying to steel myself against whatever she is going to say next. "See what?" I ask, even though I'm pretty sure I'd rather not know.

"The bright future she had ahead of her. *Has,*" she corrects. "She's always been headed down such a solid, steady path, and, honestly, honey," she shrugs, almost matter-of-factly, "I could never really say the same about you."

And there it is.

"She's always known what she wanted and did whatever she could to go for it. I could just see myself in her. That's all I meant. I know you would never want the type of baby shower I threw for her if you ever do have one. There's just one part of me that felt like . . ." She rolls her shoulders and lifts her chin up slightly higher as if cementing her words. "Like this is my one chance."

I roll my lips inward, taking a calming breath through my nose before saying anything, trying to gain some semblance of composure. "I've always known what I wanted, Mom. You just didn't agree."

"Stella." She practically rolls her eyes.

"No, no, I get it, Mom. I do. Dahlia is in interior design like you, working at your company like you always hoped I would, and is everything you wanted me to be. It'll always be her—you've proven that time and time again." I release a breath before more words tumble out of my mouth. "And, you know what? I've come to accept that, Mom. You're really lucky that I'm stronger than I used to be because I don't know if I—"

"Stella." My mom gives me a seething glare, and I slump backward, leaning against my headboard.

That line I mentioned never crossing? I almost did. But Mom would never let me get there. I suck in a breath, blinking heavily. I hear her release a deep breath, and I look over to see the moment all the fight leaves her eyes. She looks tired.

After rubbing her temples again, she drops her hands into her lap. She swallows before continuing. "There isn't a handbook for something like this. It's just . . . it's all been a little out of left field for us, okay? These past few years, especially." She shakes her head, pursing her lips slightly. "We're all just doing our best," she finishes quietly.

I want to say, *"No, there's not a handbook, but there are probably resources,"* but the weight of the past feels too heavy to bear, and I almost want to sink down into the mattress and let the darkness take me.

I shake the thought as quickly as it comes, making a mental note to maybe bring that up at my next session with Carol.

I look at my mom, the fight leaving me too. I just say, "Right," instead because, of course, she'll never say sorry. This is as close as it comes. Acting as though my pain is inconvenient to her, diminishing and twisting the truth into something she can believe, and acting like she's doing me a favor because of it. That she's doing something right by me by ignoring every real problem.

She gets up then, lingering for only a second before moving toward the door. She pauses with her hand on the handle, and for a second, I stupidly think she might apologize. But all she does is look down at the floor and say, "Would you mind putting those shoes away?"

I just blink. "Yeah."

She offers a tight smile before she walks out and shuts the door. I stand up, glance at the shoes on the floor, turn off my light, and go to sleep.

# 24

Semester B for the summer term started last week, and unfortunately for me, that means I have to actually go to campus for one class every Tuesday and Thursday. I've only had two classes so far, and as I head to the school this morning for the third, looking down at the empty coffee cup in my hand, I wish I had stopped for another.

Making my way across campus, the midmorning sun casts shadows across the sidewalk, the breeze rustling through the trees the only sound. Today is July first, but I have to keep reminding myself that it is summer because, lately, it feels like anything but. Not outside, of course—today especially, it being unusually sunny and bright for Seattle—but aside from that, it just feels like any other Tuesday. Summer hasn't meant anything to me for a while, though.

Not since sophomore year. Not since him.

I shake away the thought as I swing open the door to the English Department building. Opting to take the stairs to the second floor, I walk across the lobby, throwing away my empty cup on the way up. I take my typical seat in the middle of the classroom, waiting for the lecture to start. Other students begin to file in around me, but this being a summer elective class, there are only about fifteen of us total—which is completely fine by me because this means all the fewer people to have the possibility of interacting with.

I have the thought almost right as I look up at the board and see, in big black letters amongst the other words, *group project.* I groan inwardly, hoping we won't have to dedicate out-of-classroom time to it. Just then, our instructor, Professor Linden, walks in and announces what I had already gleaned for myself.

Just as I begin looking around, sizing up my classmates and potential project partners, she continues on to say that she has already selected our groups for us, and we can talk with them at the end of class to discuss when to meet.

I almost laugh at the absurdity of the fact that my inner dialogue quite literally seems to be working against me. I lean back, feeling the anxious tremor of my knee as it bounces repeatedly. Fumbling through the rest of the lesson, I breathe a sigh of relief once the hour is up. Professor Linden starts reading off the names she is assigning to work together, and to my relief, we're only working in partnerships.

"Stella Reynolds and Magdalene Townsend," she calls out, and I look around the room to find a girl sitting a couple of seats in front of me, twisting around to look at the same time. She has shoulder-length blonde hair and striking blue eyes that I can see brightly from all the way back here. Our eyes meet, and she offers a small wave. I smile back, starting to gather my things as Professor Linden continues explaining the assignment.

"This project is to be completed by the end of the term, and should you choose to present it, I will count that as your final exam grade. If you forgo the presentation, you will still be expected to take the final exam on the last day of term," she says. My stomach immediately goes heavy at the thought of presenting, and it doesn't feel any better at the thought of taking the final exam instead.

"Sounds kind of like a lose-lose to me."

I startle, lost in my head already after getting stressed about the end of term. The same girl who was smiling at me before is standing before my desk now, smiling still. A soft laugh escapes my mouth, and I finish gathering my things as I stand up too. "That's exactly what I was just thinking," I sigh, hoisting my bag over my shoulder.

"Magdalene. But—call me Maggie, please," she says with a slight shake of her head, extending her hand out to me.

"Stella," I say in reply, reaching out and shaking her hand in return.

"I hope you're better at this than I am," she says, gesturing a thumb back toward the whiteboard, "because this project might be a little difficult otherwise," she laughs.

I laugh, too, saying, "I was just hoping the same about you."

"So, are you majoring in English?" she asks as we step into the hallway.

I shake my head. "No. Education, actually." I can still feel the pang in my chest as I say it, shaking away the notion that things could've ended up any differently.

"Oh," she says with raised eyebrows.

"I do want to be an English teacher, though, if that counts for anything," I say back almost self-consciously. I'm still not really used to the feeling of saying that to other people yet.

"What? Oh, no, I wasn't trying to imply anything. I think that's really cool," she says intently. "Sorry, I just—I'm not great at meeting new people."

I smile. "Trust me, neither am I."

She smiles again. "Okay, good. I mean not *good*, necessarily, but—" She cuts herself off, shaking her head. "What I mean is, now that we both know that we aren't great at first impressions, we can agree to not take anything personally."

Laughing again, we round the corner, heading down the stairs to the lobby. "So, are you an English major, then?" I ask.

She nods. "And I'm not entirely sure what I want to do with that degree yet, so I'll save you the trouble of asking."

"I wasn't going to. Trust me, I know the feeling."

As we reach the main doors, she points to the other side of the building and says, "My car is over there, but—here's my number. Maybe we can set up a time soon to meet for the project?"

"Sure," I say, typing her number into my phone.

We say goodbye, and I walk back to the parking lot, thinking of how nice it was to talk to someone who doesn't already know everything about me and all the reasons she should stay away.

# 25

## THEN


March, Sophomore Year

"**A**re you sure this is fine?"

Bridger looked over his shoulder at me with a questioning smile as we walked up to his front porch. "Yes, Stella. For the fourth time—you're allowed in my house."

I followed him up the two remaining steps, staring down at my Birkenstocks as I reached the landing.

When I looked up at him again, he was facing me with a slight tilt of his head. "Is everything okay?"

I breathed out through my nose and pursed my lips into what I hoped would pass as a smile. "Yeah, everything's fine." I shrugged, taking in the cute, cozy bungalow behind him.

Dark blue siding, white shutters, and a matching front door. The wooden front porch was small but big enough to fit two chairs and a round glass table between them. With a gravel driveway tucked in behind plump bushes and tall pine trees, his house already felt more inviting than mine ever had.

He raised his eyebrows.

"I just . . ." I sighed again. "I just don't want to feel like a bother. Or like I'm intruding. Or—or make your mom mad," I finished with a grimace, finally admitting *most* of the truth.

"You do know that she doesn't live here, right?" he said, mouth twisted into a half smile. But, at that point, I knew him well enough to see the concern swimming in his eyes.

I met Bridger's mom on his monthly FaceTime with her last week. We happened to be together at the time she called, and while I insisted that I didn't want to interfere, Bridger was more than happy to introduce me to her. Honestly, I think the whole thing would've been a lot scarier if I hadn't been so amused by the sight of him and I squished together in a tiny box in the corner of the phone.

I tried to meet his smile with a half one of my own, but his shoulders slumped slightly as he released a breath, the earlier amusement fading away instantly. He reached out and put his hands on my shoulders, angling his head down toward me. "Stella—no." He winced. "You're not going to make her mad. I don't want you to ever worry about that, okay?"

I nodded, trying to force another smile. "Okay."

I took in his still slightly worried expression, and my heart squeezed as the distance between us suddenly felt too large. I barreled toward him, wrapping my arms around his torso and pressing my face against his neck. He huffed out a surprised laugh, moving his hands from my shoulders to my back, pulling me closer. His hands moved gently back and forth in the space between my shoulder blades, and I wondered then if I'd ever get used to being held by him like this.

I squeezed him tightly, my words muffled by his shirt as they came out. "I know. But you remember what she said. The last thing I want to be for you is a distraction."

*"You need to focus on what's important, Bridger. I don't want anything or* anyone *pulling you away from performing your best on the field."*

At that point, I had already left the conversation, but she was speaking loudly enough that I knew she was aware I could still hear her. She wanted me to hear.

And I knew that routine well because my family practically invented it.

Holding my breath, I acted as though those words hadn't been bugging me every day since the phone call as I waited for his response.

His breath fanned the top of my head as his chest rose and fell. "Yeah, well. We know how much she cares about any other aspect of my life. She said the same thing about my dad last week," he laughed, but I could tell it was strained. "Not wanting me to be putting in too many hours at the shop so I'm not worn out for practice."

I pulled back just enough to see his faraway stare and said softly, "That's stupid."

An abrupt laugh escaped his lips, and he blinked, looking down at me. "Yeah. It is."

I released my hold on him, checking my imaginary watch. "Speaking of which, don't you have practice soon?"

His club season officially started back in February, and he'd started conditioning with the team not long after the school season ended in the fall. I'd be worried about him burning himself out if it wasn't so obvious how much he loved it.

He shrugged. "Not for a few hours. You hungry?" He turned to the front door, unlocking it and holding it open for me.

I said, "Very," and walked past him into the house.

I wasn't sure what I expected as I walked in, but it wasn't what I saw. Dark hardwood floors lined the main living space we entered, running down a hallway off to the left. A brown leather recliner was positioned in the corner of the room facing the TV, and a matching couch ran along the far wall. A wooden coffee table that looked like it was made by hand sat in the center of the room, complete with matching end tables on either side of the couch. The place had character, the afternoon light cutting across the built-in bookshelves on either side of a wood-burning fireplace.

"Wow," was all I could manage as we walked through the entryway. I heard Bridger shut the door as he chuckled from behind me. I turned around to face him and said with raised eyebrows, "This is so . . . cute. My mom would love the way this is decorated. It literally looks like something from one of her magazines."

Bridger nodded, smiling. "Dad would actually love that you said that." The smile faltered slightly before he continued, "On one of Mom's first visits to this house after we moved in when I was younger, she made a comment about how it felt too much like a 'bachelor pad,'" he said, using air quotes. "So, alas." He spread his arms out to his sides, turning toward the living room. "Crown molding was born." I laughed full out, and he turned back toward me, cheeky grin in place once again.

I followed him into the kitchen as he patted a barstool on the opposite side of the center island. Sitting down, I took in the simple wooden cabinets and granite countertops, the bowl of fruit on the counter, and the cutting board next to the sink—and that's when my eyes landed on the fridge.

I gasped, and Bridger whirled around to me, his face crinkled in worry. I jumped off the stool and hurried around the counter, stopping in front of the cutest pictures I had ever seen in my entire life.

Pictures of tiny Bridger holding ice cream, at the zoo, splashing in a pool, and playing soccer, much like the one his dad had hanging at the auto shop. In almost all of them, he was grinning so big his eyes looked squeezed shut, and in almost all of them, his dad was standing right there next to him, beaming just the same.

It hit me again then, just how close they were and how much they truly meant to each other—it having been just the two of them for Bridger's entire life. I blinked rapidly to get my emotions in check because the love that was so evident through every single photo was enough to make my heart burst.

"Bridger," I breathed.

He followed my line of vision, letting out a dramatic sigh. "I meant to hide those before you ever stepped foot into this place."

I gave him the dirtiest look I could muster, trying to convey, *"Now, why on earth would you have done that?"* with my eyes.

I took a step toward the fridge, looking closer at the pictures in question. And when I looked again and saw just how young his dad seemed, too, I realized that if Adam had Bridger when he was around eighteen, he couldn't be more than in his mid-thirties now. Which hit me hard, considering my parents were in their mid-thirties when they had *me.* I swallowed, the reality of it all landing like a weight right on my chest.

"What's that look for?" he asked, his face a mixture of confusion and concern.

I swallowed the emotion back down. "I just"—I sighed, gesturing to the fridge behind him—"these pictures are so sweet. And I guess . . . I just can't believe that your mom didn't want to be a part of it." I finished quietly, hesitant about broaching the subject but not wanting to lie to him.

He stilled, and I immediately regretted the words as soon as I said them—until he gave me a sad smile and said, "Me too."

He leaned back against the counter next to me, staring at the pictures. "She's made her priorities clear over the years, though. She made her choice," he said flatly as if it wasn't her own son in question. But he was right. After he introduced us over the phone call, for the next fifteen minutes, all she did was ask him about soccer. About conditioning, what the club team looks like this year, what he needed to work on after the scrimmage last weekend, if he was ready for his first game, and reminding him that you never know where college scouts will show up.

It was a lot of nodding on Bridger's end, filled with variations of "Yes. Yep. Okay. Good." And "Yeah, Mom. I got it." Not once did she ask him anything about *him* or about anything that wasn't directly related to the sport. He acted like he didn't care, that it didn't bother him. But after his mom's calls, the few times I'd seen, he'd gotten this kind of faraway look about him, and his knee started bouncing, or he started wringing his hands.

Bridger continued, breaking me from my thoughts. "I'm just glad my dad made his choice, too."

"So am I," I agreed softly. "Where is your dad?" I said, realizing I hadn't heard anyone else around the house.

"He's probably still at the shop," he said casually, stepping forward to open the fridge. "Sandwich?" He looked at me over his shoulder, and I nodded, hoping he couldn't tell that my mind was completely elsewhere upon realizing that we were the only ones home.

I blinked quickly and cleared my throat, fighting the rising blush. I walked back around the island, hopping up onto the stool. "So, got any big plans this weekend?" I said mindlessly, needing to start thinking about anything else.

He shrugged, his back still to me as he grabbed plates from the cupboard above him. "Just the first game. What about you? Any raging parties I should know about? That I should be offended that I wasn't invited to?" He wiggled his eyebrows as he glanced at me over his shoulder.

"Yes, because we all know I'm exactly the type," I joked back, tucking my hair behind my ears.

I watched his shoulders lift again as he said, "Hey, you know what they say. It's always the quiet ones."

I laughed despite myself. "Do you remember the bonfire last fall? I literally walked out to the water alone because I had no one to talk to."

He twisted around to face me. "Right. And you've somehow seemed to forget that I was already out by the water for the exact same reason."

I huffed out a laugh. "Yeah, but you had your soccer guys. You were practically just . . . getting some fresh air."

"Mm-hmm. Yes, and that's why I immediately left with you five minutes later," he laughed, turning back around to the cabinets, getting a knife out of a drawer for the peanut butter.

I smiled down at my hands, thinking back to the memory. But when I remembered how awkward and out of place I felt before I'd found him that night, the smile faltered.

"You okay?"

I nodded, clearing my throat. "Yeah, I just . . . It feels kind of weird sometimes. Like, I feel like I'm missing out on some fundamental high school experience because I don't really hang out with people or have some huge group of friends. Or any friends, for that matter." Looking back down at my hands, I finished my thought in a breathy ramble. "And it's not for lack of trying, but I've always struggled to have that *best* friend. That one person, you know? I mean, I try to be nice to everyone, and I get along with the people in class, but . . ." Sighing, I looked up at the ceiling, avoiding his gaze. "I've just never really stayed in touch with anybody outside of school. I've never really been that person for anyone."

I shook my head, trying to backtrack out of it, not giving him a chance to reply. "Gosh, sorry, didn't mean to get all serious. All I meant is"—I looked down to where the peanut butter and jelly still sat out on the counter, the loaf of bread sitting beside it—"It just feels like, in the bread of life . . . I'm an end slice."

He exploded into laughter, throwing his head back with his eyes shut tight. I laughed along with him, only then realizing how dumb that sounded. He lowered his gaze to mine, shaking his head as his laughter died out. "Stella, I hope you know that's not true. Not even close."

"It is!" I argued, still laughing. "It just feels like no one would willingly *choose* me."

His laughter faded, face going serious. "I did."

My whole body heated instantly, my mouth opening slightly in shock. Or awe, maybe. His eyes traveled up my neck, which I knew was one thousand different shades of red by then, and he smirked because he could see it too. Turning back to the counter, he grabbed the bread again, and I hurriedly fanned myself, willing my face to return to normal color by the time he turned back around.

But, as if he knew, he put everything away slowly, then grabbed one of the plates and turned back to face me. He slid it across the counter. "For you," he said, looking awfully pleased with himself. I reached out to touch the plate, eyeing him warily.

"And for me," he grinned, grabbing his sandwich from his own plate on the counter behind him. My breath caught in my throat as he brought the sandwich up to his mouth—two end slices, smushed together—took a huge bite, and winked.

# 26

Summer arrived quickly after that, the remainder of the school year passing by in a blur of final exams and crowded hallways. We were finally upperclassmen; Bridger had reminded me as we walked out of our sophomore year hand in hand.

We'd been official for some time by then, and every time I looked at him, I still couldn't believe he was mine. Soccer season finally ended in mid-May, and then he really was just that.

All mine.

We spent countless summer days together, split between the auto shop and the pool where I had gotten a lifeguarding job. When Bridger wasn't working on cars with his dad, he was with me, floating in the deep end of the pool, keeping me company until my shift was over.

Then we would spend our nights driving around the city, frequenting local ice cream shops and meandering through bookstores to get out of the heat. Kerry Park became our favorite place, and we wasted hours sitting on the benches people-watching, creating entire stories for those who walked by and happened to exist in the same time and place as us.

I told him more about what I was writing, and he told me

about his soccer conditioning, and even though I was still learning all the rules of the sport—I held on to every word as if they were the answers to the crossword puzzle my heart had spent my whole life trying to figure out.

We explored each other's bodies and minds, becoming familiar with each other in ways we had never been with anyone else. We spent as much time in each other's daydreams as we did in each other's arms, sharing the things we had tucked away in the deepest parts of who we were, warm whispers across pillowcases in the middle of the night.

Learning what it meant to love someone with such reckless abandon and to be loved exactly that same way in return was like someone had finally turned on the light in my room after the sun had set, and I hadn't realized how dark it had become until then.

I finally had a soft place to land.

And for those three months, my life was what I had always hoped it would be, how I always wished it would stay.

It was the best summer of my life.

It was the summer of us.

# 27

## THEN

August, Junior Year

The second the final bell started ringing, I was out of my seat and through the classroom door before anyone else had even begun to pack up their things.

It was the third week of our junior year, and so far, it was off to a rocky start. Between classes that had already proven to be even more difficult than last year and the looming deadline for college applications, my stress levels seemed to be at an all-time high.

And, on that day, to add to those stress levels, I was going to watch Bridger's first home game of the season. It wasn't that I was worried for him or his team, even though it was supposed to be a close game. I was more nervous about the fact that I was going to a sporting event for the first time in my entire high school career.

By myself.

Social situations and big crowds tended to make me anxious in the first place, but the thought of all my peers watching me sit there alone was making me sweat. But I knew that was ridiculous, even as I had the thought—because they weren't even going to be looking at me.

No one cared about me *that* much.

But, the idea of it was still enough to cause me to have a minor panic attack last weekend when I told Bridger I wanted to go. He told me that he would understand if I couldn't, but the way his face lit up when I mentioned wanting to made me even more determined to attend.

And that determination became set in stone as I walked quickly through the hallways, hurrying down the main corridor for one reason, my heart leaping into my throat as I rounded the corner to see that reason already leaning against my locker.

His face lit up in the same way it did over the weekend as he looked at me then, and I almost wanted to stop and take a picture of him. To remember him this way—North Crest High Soccer t-shirt, athletic shorts that hung just right on his hips, soccer bag loosely slung over his shoulder, and his hair flopping lazily across his forehead. It felt like I was standing in a museum, staring at a new artist's painting that had been commissioned just for me.

As I approached, someone stepped in front of Bridger, blocking my view. The kid was slightly shorter than him, so I could still barely see his face as they started talking. I didn't recognize him, but whenever this happened, I usually didn't.

Soccer was what our school was good at. Some school's athletic departments were fueled by the football or basketball teams, but at North Crest High, soccer was the sport that won state championships. And it was because of this that I'd realized people were interested in who was on the team.

In Bridger's case, especially—a (hot, objectively) upperclassman who'd scored a hat trick in the opening game—was bound to turn heads. When I'd asked him if a hat trick was the same thing as a buzzer-beater, he'd just laughed and kissed me, and I had forgotten what I even asked as I melted into him like I always did. I looked it up later, and needless to say, three goals in one game was definitely something to brag about.

I was still getting used to school Bridger, the one people wanted to talk to, the one who got stopped in the hallway, the one who had friends. The one I had to share.

He was still himself, though. This was obvious to me once again as he finished his conversation, and the kid in question strolled away, leaving nothing between us. He eyed me with that look I loved, warm and questioning and inviting all at the same time. I closed the remaining space between us, and he pushed off my locker to allow me access.

"Are you excited?" I asked him, grinning as I put in my combination.

"What do you think? I haven't seen you all day," he said, and I glanced at him to see that he was serious.

I squinted and gave him a look. "I meant about the game tonight."

He threw his head back and laughed. I soaked it in, letting it warm every part of me. That laugh had become the soundtrack in the movie of my life, playing quietly in the background, unknowingly making everything brighter, better.

"Oh, yeah. That. Sure." He shrugged, a rare mischievousness cast over his expression making my insides into jelly. I shook my head, trying to conceal my smile as he grinned again.

I closed my locker, and we started down the hallway.

"Are you?" he asked, looking at me sideways. "Because you know that I want you there more than anything, but I don't want you to go if it's going to make you anxious—"

I cut him off before he could finish his sentence. Putting a hand on his arm to stop him, I said, "Bridge. I'll be there." He nodded once, and I swore something like relief passed through him. "And, of course, I'm excited! I mean, come on. How could you honestly expect me to pass up an opportunity to see *the* Bridger Wells at work? Making hat tricks and all?"

He laughed again, and, of course, I did too. As we walked out of the double doors and into the sunlight, our laughter was carried away with the wind, drifting and floating the way I hoped our love always would. We started veering toward the athletic wing, and I knew we didn't have a lot of time before he needed to be with his team—he was Varsity Captain, after all. But these stolen seconds after school were my favorite of the day.

"How's your knee?" I asked him seriously.

"Fine," he said with a shrug. "How's yours?"

I narrowed my gaze at him, and he smiled, tucking me into his side. "Honestly. It feels fine, and if it gets sore again, I'll just ice it after the game."

Since tearing his ACL freshman year, his knee had been his weak spot—mentally as much as physically. Last year, it was fine, but he said it had been sorer than usual after games lately, and when I asked him if the athletic trainer said it was normal, he said he wasn't going to ask.

So, as it was, I nodded into him as we rounded the corner, the student-athlete entrance in sight.

He moved his hand down my arm and squeezed my fingers once before pulling away and turning to face me. "I love you."

I didn't think I'd ever get used to the sound of those words coming off his lips, knowing they were meant for me.

"I love you too," I beamed at him, lifting up my hand for a high five.

He stared at my hand, a slow smile breaking across his face. He shook his head, amused. "What's this for?" He laughed but still slapped my hand anyway.

"It felt right. Go crush it."

He started to head toward the building, walking slowly,

looking at me over his shoulder. "You're not going to wish me luck?"

It was my turn to shake my head. "You don't need it," I said, attempting a wink.

His full laugh sounded again, and I swore the sun burned brighter.

## 28

And I was right.

Luck was the last thing he needed as he maneuvered down the field, me and the rest of the people in the stands watching in awe. I was mesmerized as I watched him doing what he did best, and my pulse raced every time he had the ball. He had it at that moment, running down the field at a speed no one should be able to run while keeping a ball at their feet. He cut back across the last defender, planted his foot, and shot the ball.

It hit the goalpost.

I released an anxious breath, and we all clapped anyway. A teammate slapped him on the back as he started jogging back across the field. He got subbed out shortly after, grabbing a water and listening intently to Coach Doug, nodding along as he talked to him with a hand on his shoulder. Coach slapped his arm once, turning back to the field.

Bridger walked over to the bench, pausing at the end of it. He looked up into the stands, his eyes scanning the crowd quickly, and I felt my own start to do the same, trying to guess the person he was looking for. *Maybe his dad?* I thought, and I looked back toward Bridger. His eyes scanned the area just to my left for another second before landing right on me. He visibly relaxed, grinning. He lifted his hand to wave, looking at me as if he hadn't just seen me a few hours ago.

My chest warmed and my stomach flipped when I realized that he was looking for *me.* I quickly waved back and gave him an enthusiastic double thumbs up. His shoulders shook in laughter, and he raised his water bottle to me before turning back to the field and sitting on the edge of the bench.

I glanced down at my hands, unable to wipe off the stupid lovesick smile I knew had taken over my entire face. I fidgeted with my phone in my lap for a few seconds, taking a deep breath. But when I looked back up, that smile quickly faded as I realized that a group of girls to my right were staring at me.

Clearing my throat, I tried to focus on the game as Bridger got subbed back in. I told myself it was a coincidence, not needing a reason to get any more paranoid than I already was. The minutes went by, and I could still feel their eyes on me, stealing glances every so often.

It was then that I became acutely aware of how I must've looked sitting alone in the stands. Any previous pride I had for walking in and picking a seat by myself dissipated in an instant, that familiar anxiety coiling tightly in my chest.

The crowd cheered, and I focused back on the field again, not realizing I had zoned out. My heart sank as I watched Bridger's teammates sprinting over and slapping him on the back, jostling him around and messing up his hair with grins on their faces.

The announcer's voice boomed through the speakers, "Goal by number four, Junior Captain Bridger Wells!" And the crowd cheered louder. I joined in, whooping and hollering for the boy I loved, simultaneously feeling like shit that I missed it because I was too worked up in my own damn head.

The clapping died down as they set up for another kickoff. The score was two-to-one, and I tried my hardest to focus back in on the game, not wanting to miss anything else. I crossed my arms, the stadium lights turning on as the last bit of sunlight disappeared behind the bleachers. A breeze blew past, and goosebumps gathered on my arms that I wasn't sure were entirely from the cold. My knee started bouncing, and I curled deeper into myself.

I glanced at the clock to see there was about five minutes left until halftime. Swallowing, I kept my eyes on the field. On Bridger.

Then, out of the corner of my eye, I saw the group of girls begin to stand up. I felt a moment of relief as they started to slide off the bleachers, but that relief was instantly replaced with dread when I realized they were walking toward me.

My heart was pounding as they climbed the final few steps between us. I recognized one of them, the girl in the front with freckled skin and an auburn ponytail that swished behind her, a few loose strands somehow framing her face perfectly.

"Hi!" she said brightly.

"Hi," I replied warily as they sat down one row below me. They all sat with their backs to the field, facing me.

"I'm Gracie. We have history together?" She phrased it as a question before continuing, "And this is Sarah and Morgan."

"Oh, right," I smiled back, trying to seem friendly when my tight chest felt anything but.

"Pretty good game, huh?" Gracie said.

I nodded, wondering what had propelled them to come and sit by me as I briefly flicked my eyes back to the clock. Just under four minutes.

Another voice cut through the brisk evening air. "So, that was you waving at Bridger, right?" I looked back at the girls to see Morgan watching me expectantly.

"Oh," I cleared my throat. "Yeah," was all I offered, nodding again while trying (and probably failing) to mask my confusion.

Sarah jabbed Morgan's side sharply, giving her a look as they all burst into laughter. I rubbed my chest out of instinct, feeling awkward and out of place.

"Sorry, we were just—we were just wondering. Do you know him well? Are you two friends?"

I opened my mouth to respond, but there was no time to say anything before they started talking over each other again.

Sarah started. "He's really cute. Morgan was hoping you could introduce her—"

She was quickly cut off by Gracie, who said, "Oh please, let's not act like you weren't the one who wanted to come over here in the first place so you could meet him—"

And Morgan chimed back in with, "Oh, says the one who has had a crush on him since *freshman* year," she gasped, and they all laughed, turning back to me with hopeful expressions on their faces.

If I thought I felt awkward before, there was truly not a word that existed to describe how I felt then. I cleared my throat again as my knee resumed its bouncing. "We're together."

Then, as a result of their pinched brows, I added, "He's my boyfriend." It still came out with less conviction than I'd hoped for.

My cheeks burned at the collection of raised eyebrows and surprised faces. "Oh, we—I didn't—we didn't know. Sorry," Gracie said.

"Oh, don't worry about it. Seriously, it's fine," I said emphatically with a swish of my hand through the air.

Then, it was a sea of awkward smiles and mumbled apologies until Sarah cleared her throat. "Well, enjoy the game!" she said before they hurriedly got up and walked away.

The referees blew their whistles, signaling halftime, and I nearly jumped a foot off the bench. My heart hadn't stopped pounding, and after that encounter, I felt like everyone had their eyes on me, like everyone was realizing how strange it was that Bridger would be dating someone like me.

Or maybe I was just realizing it for the first time.

It was almost like the inside of my skin was itchy, like I was hyper-aware of the space I took up in the world. The spectators around me were loud and silent all at once, muffled by the roaring in my ears.

I watched as the teams jogged off the field toward the locker rooms, and I took that as my opportunity to run to the bathrooms. I hurried down the ramp leading out of the stadium, cutting through the crowd of people heading to the concession stands, ducking into the women's bathroom, and shutting myself into a stall.

I felt like such an idiot.

Not only was I embarrassed about the interaction with Gracie, Sarah, and Morgan—but I was even more embarrassed that I couldn't even watch the guy I love doing what he loved without somehow having a panic attack. I couldn't do this one normal thing for him.

I shut my eyes as the shameful tears escaped down my face, and I wiped my cheeks with the sleeves of my hoodie—Bridger's hoodie. Sighing, I made a mental note to make sure the tears were completely dried before giving it back to him. I didn't want him to know about my . . . whatever this was.

I stayed there in the bathroom, taking deep breaths and trying to remember the "Calm Breathing for Anxiety" technique videos I'd watched on YouTube.

I was unsure how much time had passed, but after I felt like I'd calmed enough, I took one final inhale through my nose and left the stall. I washed my hands, dabbed some cold water under my eyes, and pushed the door open, savoring the cold air on my skin.

## 29

The game was over.

My stomach dropped as I walked back toward the stadium, hearing the roar of the cheering crowd as the trill of the final whistle echoed through the air.

*The game was over.*

I stopped, standing there, frozen like an idiot, watching all the people who actually *saw* the game heading down the ramp to leave the stadium. I quickly stepped to the side, the reality of it all settling in.

How was I in the bathroom that whole time?

I watched as everyone walked past me, talking and laughing with their friends or family, feeling so ashamed I was afraid that it would swallow me whole.

I still had a decent enough view of the field that I could see the teams heading down into the locker rooms. I knew Bridger would soon be on his way home, and, having agreed to meet at his house after the game, I needed to head out.

Not that I wanted to stay any longer, anyway.

So, with my head hung low, I joined in with the crowd,

walking through the gates and out into the parking lot, hoping Bridger hadn't noticed I missed the entire second half.

Twenty minutes later, I was sitting in Bridger's driveway, waiting for him to get back after his debrief with the team. I considered texting him that I didn't feel well and was just going to head home, but I couldn't bring myself to lie to him. As I sat there in his driveway, my mind raced with all the things I could possibly say, searching for any explanation as to why I spent the last half of the game practically hiding—and I came up short.

I knew him well enough to know that he would never be angry or upset, but I also knew how much he cared about the sport and how passionate he was about this thing that meant so much to him. And I also knew what it was like to have the people that you love treat your passion like a child's toy, waiting for you to grow out of it or move on to something "real."

I didn't want Bridger to think that I didn't believe in him or that I didn't care.

So I sat there, spiraling, every thought making my heart race faster than the last as I came up with more reasons as to why I was a terrible girlfriend.

Living with an anxious mind was already enough of a burden, but trying to explain that anxiety to someone else was like trying to keep a damp fire lit in the pouring rain. Especially when that seemingly small kindling had been so easily smothered away and dismissed my whole life by the people who were supposed to understand. All I'd ever been told was to "not let it bother me" or to just "not get so worked up about things."

Time had worn me down and hollowed me out, and I was just starting to feel the effects of it at the ripe old age of seventeen.

*Now* I know that just because I was young didn't mean my struggle didn't exist.

I didn't know that then.

Sitting there, I ruminated over every possible way he could react when headlights passed across my windshield, snapping me back to the present moment. Straightening in my seat and turning off the ignition, I was no closer to figuring out what I wanted to say to him.

I should've known I wouldn't have to say anything at all.

He bounded over to my car, smiling huge, arms stretched wide. I stepped out to meet him and an unbridled grin broke across my face at the sight of him. He wrapped his arms around me, burrowing his face into my shoulder. He started talking, his words muffled against my sweatshirt.

"Did you see that goal? I thought it was going to hit the post because that corner kick was so high, but the ball curved in! Was it windy, do you think? That's the only explanation I can think of because Stel—I honestly don't think I could replicate that kick if I tried."

His excitement made my heart want to burst, and I loved it when he was like this. Describing the game so ardently he could barely get in a breath, rambling off the plays and the goals. Usually, I'd have gotten this debrief in the form of a phone call on the bus ride home from an away game, but feeling them spoken against my skin—I felt a new type of adoration for him, warmed by the awe in his voice that couldn't be translated through a speaker.

"It kind of sucks that my dad had to miss it, but—" He pulled back, his hands falling down to my arms and squeezing once before continuing, "—I'm just glad you were there."

I felt my composure crack as I looked at him, as tears that I hadn't even realized had formed blurred my vision. I inhaled a shaky breath, not wanting to put any sort of damper on his joy, willing the rain that seemed to follow me everywhere to stay as far away from his parade as possible. But the second his eyes met mine, his face fell, concern immediately creasing his forehead and etching his features.

"Hey," he breathed, rubbing his hands up and down my arms. "What's wrong?"

The mood instantly shifted, and I hated that I was always the one who brought it down. Lip wobbling, I sniffed and forced myself to meet his gaze. "I missed it."

"What?" he said, voice gentle.

"I missed it—your goal. I . . . I didn't see."

His shoulders dropped, and some of the tension left him. His brows dipped, the concern still palpable but less, somehow. A confused smile turned his lips upward as he spoke. "Stella, it's okay." He shook his head softly and pulled me back into his chest. Resting a hand on the nape of my neck, he ran his fingers through my hair. "Please don't cry."

He sounded worried, and I pulled back again to look at him, my arms still wrapped around his waist. "No, it's not. You were doing so good, and I was so excited to watch, but I got stressed sitting there alone, and I think maybe I zoned out because I was overthinking everything, and then the crowd started cheering, and some girls came by to ask me about you, and I spent the entire second half in the bathroom somehow, and I—"

"Breathe." He cut me off, the concern in his eyes back in full force as he put both hands on my face. "Stella—*breathe.*" He wiped away the tears that were rapidly falling down my cheeks.

I hadn't even realized I'd started crying again. I tried to inhale, but it ended up sounding more like a wheeze than a complete breath. "I'm sorry," I choked out.

He shook his head slightly as he dropped his hands, one resting along my back and the other sitting just below my ribcage. He didn't continue speaking until I took a few more breaths, his hands staying firmly in place as if making sure my lungs were expanding and contracting at an even rate.

"It's okay, Stel, really. It doesn't even matter. It was one stupid goal in one stupid game. I just want to make sure that you're okay—"

"Don't do that."

He squinted. "Do what?"

"Make yourself or your accomplishments any smaller to try to make me feel better."

He exhaled, dropping his gaze and frowning at the ground, seemingly lost in thought. I placed my hands over his, gently removing them from where they still rested on my waist and soaking in their warmth for a split second before letting them go.

"It's just . . . I feel terrible. I'm a shitty girlfriend, I know that. And I'm sorry."

His head jerked back, and his expression looked almost as if I had slapped him. "*What?*" He stepped closer to me, the confusion replaced with hurt. He paused and then, quietly said, "Stella. What happened tonight?"

I sighed, conceding, trying to give him the brief version. "When I was sitting there, these three girls I have a class or two with walked over." I hesitated, knowing it was stupid but needing to get it out anyway. "And they basically said they saw you wave at me, figured we were friends, and asked if I could introduce you to them."

He raised his eyebrows, waiting for me to continue. "And so, I told them that we're together, and they seemed really surprised. And then they left."

With a slightly amused glint in his eye, he tilted his head. "Clearly, they haven't been paying much attention."

"Not a lot of people usually do. To me, anyway," I shrugged.

"That's not true."

I gave him a look. "You're an anomaly."

"Stella—"

"I just get so annoyed at myself. Like, who am I to be sitting there, not even able to cheer you on like a normal person, all because my brain hates me? It's so pathetic. You deserve someone who—"

"Hey. *No.*" Any trace of amusement on his face was gone as he shook his head at me. "You don't get to do that."

"Do what?"

"You and I both know damn well that you are the one thing in this life that I *don't* deserve."

"Bridger—"

"I'm serious." He closed the remaining distance between us, put his hands on my shoulders, and bent down until his eyes were even with mine. "You are too good for me, Stel. You're too good for this world. And you're the only one who doesn't believe that."

I knew anything I said to argue would make him want to prove me wrong, so I didn't say anything at all. I only looked at his earnest expression and amber-flecked eyes. I could get lost in those. And I let myself, for a second.

"You're too hard on yourself." His voice broke the silence again, and I released a deep breath, feeling tired, worn out, and defeated. "I hate that you've been made to feel like you need to be. I just . . ." He pulled me close again, resting his chin on the top of my head. "I wish you could see yourself the way I do."

I brought my arms back around him, holding on, trying to soak in his words and feel some semblance of truth in them. The night wrapped around us as we stood there, intertwined, the same way that we had so many nights before. I let his words hang in the air, tried to grab onto them, put them somewhere I could easily find them for when I knew I would need to remember them again. I stored them tightly and put them in the drawer that belonged to him, that filing cabinet in the corner of my mind that he had built for me.

He pulled back again, slowly, searching my eyes. "My dad should be at every home game from here on out. You could sit with him if you wanted."

I nodded, the ghost of a smile flickering between us. I'd spent a lot of time at Bridger's house over the past few months, and I thought his dad was more up-to-date on my life than my own father had *ever* been. For no reason other than the fact that he'd always cared enough to ask.

"I'd love that." I stood up on my toes and kissed him, saying *thank you* and *I'm sorry* and *I love you* all at the same time, and he kissed me back like he understood every word I didn't say.

"Now, let's go inside. Dad is probably on his way home, and I can think of a couple of ways we could celebrate before he gets back."

I gasped as I pulled back, whacking him on the arm, a smile taking over my expression as a blush crept up my neck.

He smiled back, planting a soft kiss on my forehead as he murmured, "There you are."

# 30

## NOW

The Fourth of July has always been Mom's favorite. The holiday serves as another excuse to throw a huge party, and that's exactly what she does—*has* done, every year—for as long as I can remember.

When Daniel and I were younger, we were allowed to invite friends from school and sports, which Daniel took complete advantage of. I, on the other hand, never really had anyone to invite. The other attendees were mostly people from Mom and Dad's circle of friends—coworkers, colleagues, neighbors, and anyone else deemed important enough to invite.

I usually spent the party over by the food table, watching everyone playing games and enjoying each other's company. I gave up attempting to socialize a few years back when my Aunt May spilled her (definitely not spiked, she promised) red punch all over my favorite white shirt as she performed an enthusiastic rendition of Mamma Mia.

So, I've formed my own tradition over the years, slipping away from the party unnoticed into the cool, quiet house and heading up to my room to watch the fireworks from my window by myself. There was one year that Bridger was able to come, and

I was thankful to actually have someone to spend the day with for once—but we still snuck up to my room before the fireworks went off anyway.

Quickly shaking the memory away, I return to the task at hand. I secure the final streamer in place with one last piece of tape, step back, and admire my handiwork.

"Stella, are you going to go get changed? People will be arriving soon," Mom says as she rushes out of the house, hurrying down the back porch steps.

I frown, looking down at my cutoff jean shorts, blue cropped shirt, and white Converse. "This is what I was planning to wear?" I say, the words sounding more like a question as I look back up at her. But by then, she's already halfway across the yard.

Sighing, I walk into the house, already deciding I'm not changing. She won't pay me any more attention for the duration of the party anyway. I could come back out here in my pajamas, and she wouldn't notice a difference.

I pass by the kitchen where my dad is filling up buckets of ice, thinking I'll just get out of everyone's way and head up to my room until the party starts. But just as I get to the first stair, the sliding glass door sounds behind me again.

"Stella, I meant to tell you." Mom's voice rings out. "I invited Bridger and Adam to the party."

I freeze on the spot. Blinking slowly, I turn to face her. "You—what? When?" I say, barely able to get the words out.

"I ran into Adam at the post office last week. Small world, huh?" She smiles at me with that same smile she used to use when I was five years old, trying to get me to go and make friends on the playground.

I swallow. "Are they coming?"

"I think so. Bridger hasn't mentioned anything to you?"

Shaking my head, I grip the staircase railing so hard my

knuckles turn white. "No, Mom. You do remember we haven't exactly been on the best terms in recent years, yes?"

She rolls her eyes, already on her way back out the door. "And whose fault is that?" she mutters to herself as she disappears into the yard once again.

Dad just sighs over the sink, and I remain standing right where I am, trying to remind myself to breathe. I curse the angry tears as they prick my eyes, and the burning sensation behind my nose is finally what spurs me into action. I turn for the hallway, practically diving into the main floor bathroom. Locking the door behind me, I grip the edge of the sink and will myself not to have a panic attack.

The only person who has ever successfully helped calm me down is Bridger—but the thought of him right now is too painful, and I'd rather not reach around and twist the knife in my own back.

You would think that at this point, after everything that's happened, my family would be a little easier on me. But, as today has proven, it's been the exact opposite. I stare at myself in the mirror, taking deep breaths and focusing on the sounds of my beating heart and the feeling of my lungs expanding with every inhale.

Eventually, my heart slows, and my breathing evens. I almost forget about the party that has begun on the other side of the wall—but then someone knocks on the door, and I realize with a jolt that the party actually has started, and I can't hide in here forever.

Smoothing out my hair, I splash some cold water under my eyes and pray that these next few hours will go by quickly.

Taking one final deep breath, I swing the door open to reveal a woman I don't recognize, who takes one look at me and offers what I can only describe as a pitying smile. Muttering, "Excuse me," I hurry past her into the hallway and duck back into the kitchen. Walking silently over to the sink, I glance out the window that overlooks the backyard, wondering how much time I actually spent in the bathroom when I see the sheer amount of people who have already arrived.

I head out the door to the back porch and scan the growing crowd quickly, instantly feeling relief flood my veins when I spot Dahlia standing at the food table.

One hand rests on her round belly, and her flowing, burgundy, flounce-sleeved dress hugs her frame perfectly. She looks almost ethereal in the dying amber light.

"Hello, Lady Liberty," I say, dragging out the first word as I sidle up next to her.

She laughs, shooting me a disbelieving look. "Don't let the dress fool you. I'm only wearing it because I can't fit into pants anymore." She sighs, grabbing a cupcake off the table. "I feel more like a Founding Father."

Choking on a laugh, I shoot the same look of disbelief right back at her. "You are quite *literally* glowing," I say seriously.

She hums appreciatively, peeling back the cupcake lining. "George Washington was a beautiful man."

I laugh harder than I feel I have in years, unable to help the blank looks and curious stares as Dahlia and I double over. After Dahlia wipes the tears from her eyes and I finally catch my breath, I reach out and grab a cookie from the table. I not-so-subtly scan the people around us again, my body still thrumming with the possibility of him being here.

"Your mom didn't tell you she invited Bridger and Adam, did she?" she says quietly. I shake my head, thinking about her earlier comment in the kitchen.

"Not until about an hour ago."

Dahlia nods. "Would it have made a difference if she did?"

I sigh again. "It never does." Picking at the cookie, I add, "They probably won't come, anyway."

She rests a hand on my shoulder. "And why wouldn't they?" she asks, and I'm about to give her about a thousand reasons why, but then I look up to see her gaze locked on a point over my shoulder.

My eyes widen as I feel the blood drain from my face. And then, to my utter disbelief, Dahlia lifts up her hand, grins, and waves.

"Dahlia," I hiss, glaring daggers.

"He's looking over here. Turn around and wave," she manages through gritted teeth, smile still firmly in place.

I exhale slowly, realizing it will look weird if I don't acknowledge him after he obviously knows that I know that he's here. Turning my head over my shoulder, I don't even have to try to locate him—my eyes instantly lock onto his as if they've been waiting for him to come into view. I lift my hand, and with a dip of his head, he waves back.

I turn back around to face Dahlia. "Are you happy now?" I blink repeatedly at her, the smile that crossed my features moments ago dropping instantly.

She sighs, dropping her gaze to the ground. "Listen, Stella. I don't know all of the specifics that went down between you guys, and you can totally ignore me if I'm completely off the mark here." She pauses, lifting her eyes back to mine. "But I do know how awful high school felt for you and that you've always been really hard on yourself. I *also* know that throughout everything, amidst it all . . . he was your one good thing." She shrugs, the wind rustling her wavy hair as she gathers it over one shoulder. "I'd never seen you happier than the days that you were with him."

I bite my cheek, trying to keep my emotions at bay. "I know," I whisper because she's right. He was my one good thing.

"You deserve good things. You know that, right?"

All I can do is nod, not trusting my voice.

"Okay. Good." She straightens, giving me a once-over. "And now," she grins, her eyes bright and sparkling as she says, "It's showtime." I barely have time to question what she's talking about before she spins me around, smacks me on the butt, and scurries away.

I spot Bridger immediately, weaving through the people between us. I almost want to turn around and run after Dahlia, knowing she can't be far because these days she doesn't move that fast.

Bridger's dark blue t-shirt hugs him in all the right places, and I try not to ogle his biceps as he approaches. "Happy Fourth," he smiles, stopping a few feet in front of me.

"It is now," I joke, reaching out and playfully punching his arm. I cringe as he starts laughing, but shortly after, I'm laughing too. "Sorry. I don't know who I become when you're around me anymore."

His laughter fades into a boyish, lazy grin. "I know the feeling."

Ignoring the way my stomach still flips at the sight of him, I try to conceal my own smile, watching as the wind ruffles his shirt and the sun catches the light in his hair.

"I never thought I'd be at another one of these infamous Reynolds' Fourth of July parties," he says, surveying the yard around him.

"Me, either," I tell him.

In more ways than one.

I follow his gaze, trying to see everything from his point of view. The wide expanse of green lawn mowed to perfection, the plants surrounding the fence line tall and blooming, the red, white, and blue balloon arch leading out from the back door, the streamers that are (very expertly spaced, might I add) twisted around the rungs of the porch, the drink table just to the right of the steps, and the various games scattered throughout. Some people I don't recognize are throwing a football around, and the whole thing looks so . . . normal. Friendly. Like the opening scene in any classic suburban romcom.

If only we were guaranteed a happy ending.

As my eyes continue to scan the yard, I realize there is one familiar face I've yet to see. Clearing my throat, I turn back to face Bridger. "Is your dad here?"

Nodding, his eyes start roaming the space behind me. "Somewhere."

He tensed slightly when I mentioned his dad, a sort of protectiveness creasing his features that I'm not used to.

That familiar pang of worry settles in my stomach again, and I think back to when Daniel said he and Dahlia ran into them at the hospital and then again to when Bridger said his dad was one of the reasons why he couldn't go back to North Carolina. Swallowing that fear, I search his face, wondering how to broach the subject without seeming nosy.

I'm cautious around him now in ways I never have been before, in ways that I never had to be, and I hate it. It feels unnatural in a way I can't really describe, and every time I'm with him now, that feeling deepens when I learn something new, something more, something else that I've missed.

I drop my gaze, staring down at my shoes. "How is your dad?" I say, testing the waters.

He stuffs his hands in his pockets, shifting on his feet. "He's all right. Doing better, now."

I look up at him again, the worry deepening as I take in his expression, his mouth slightly downturned at the corners and that same crease between his brows that seems to be there more often than not nowadays. I wait for him to continue, allowing him the space to offer up what he wants to, if that's anything at all.

"He was in a car accident."

My stomach bottoms out, and I feel my whole body stiffen.

He quickly follows up with, "He's okay. Well, he's getting there." He clears his throat. "He will be."

"What happened?" I all but whisper.

He scratches his arm mindlessly, and I can tell his mind is far away. "A truck blasted through a red light and T-boned him. He dislocated his shoulder pretty badly, broke his fibula and a bunch of ribs . . . ended up needing to have emergency surgery. I was actually at physical therapy at the hospital when they called me, though. So, that was nice, I guess." He flinches slightly, chewing on his cheek.

"Bridger, I'm so sorry. I . . . I had no idea." I breathe out, voice wobbling.

He nods, straightening slightly and giving me a half smile. "He's making really good progress, though. The surgery went well, which was great news after everything that happened with mine."

I suck in a breath, turning away and bracing my hand on the dessert table we're still standing next to. I feel a weird surge of anger, words bubbling out of me before I can consider them. "This sucks. Life just . . . *sucks* sometimes. I hate that this happened, and I hate that you've been going through this, and I hate that it has brought us here. These past few years, I just . . . I feel like all of my problems have been the only thing consuming the lives of everyone around me, that it's easy to forget that other people are going through things that are just as hard, you know?" I breathe out.

"No, I get that." He nods, looking up at the sky thoughtfully. "I feel like after something so drastic or life-changing happens to you, it's kind of all you know for a while. After blowing out my knee and moving home and all that has happened with Dad, I feel the same. To be so wrapped up in the shit that's smeared on your own wall, you forget other people are trying to wipe up shit too."

A hint of a smile plays across my lips, and I look over at him to see the same one reflected on his. "It just feels like after what happened senior year, my world has been confined to the four walls of that house that my family is tiptoeing around in, and I —" I sigh, dropping my head. "I've just been so selfish."

He tilts his head and leans against the table. "I know we haven't been around each other much these past few years, but that doesn't erase the years that we did have together. Stella . . ." he pauses, stepping closer to me. "Selfish is the last word I would use to describe you."

I blow a sharp breath out of my nose. "Right, just after weak, helpless, and fragile," I say with a slight shake of my head, scoffing out a laugh.

"Stella." The roughness of his voice startles me, and I look up to see the lines of his face, hard and unmoving. "How could you possibly think so lowly of yourself? This self-deprecating talk, the things you say about yourself—it pisses me off."

I stare at him, unable to utter a word.

"You are the strongest person I know. You're smart, talented, independent, capable, creative, determined—" He stops himself, his cheeks heating slightly. He sighs, his gaze softening. "I just wish you could see yourself the way I do. The way I always have," he finishes quietly.

My face is hot, shame eating away at my insides. "Bridger, I'm sorry. I'm really not trying to drag you into any of this. You have so much going on, more than I could've ever imagined, and I don't—"

"Hey." He stops me, placing a hand on my arm. "It's never too much. Not for you, okay?" He rolls his lips, taking a breath before continuing. "Don't pull away from me because you're worried I have too much on my plate. I don't want to go down that road with you. Not again."

I nod, taking a breath. Trying. "It's just . . . those are all of the things I've been made to feel like I am. It's all that I've felt like, ever since I almost—" I stop myself quickly, blanching at the words I didn't say.

He steps even closer now, dropping his hand to rest next to mine. "Ever since you almost what?" he says softly.

I step back, straightening instantly and wiping my sweaty hands on my shorts. "Nothing."

Someone walks up next to us then, reaching around me for a brownie. Remembering where we are, I feel dumb for having what felt like such an intimate conversation in the middle of a party. "Oh, sorry," I mumble, inching away from the table.

Bridger indicates toward the yard with his head, leading me toward the fence line. We walk for a few moments in silence, and I'm unsure of where to pick back up. I can feel the words we said floating in the air between us, the ones I didn't say making it hard to breathe. It's a few more steps before he speaks again.

"Are you ever going to be able to tell me?"

My chest aches, and I forget how to breathe. Voice hollow, I whisper, "I don't know."

His throat bobs as he swallows, staring at the ground.

I don't want him to think it's a dismissal, even though it feels like one. So, I say, "It's just, I'm still working through a lot, and I think . . . I think I just need time."

Nodding, he works his jaw and runs a hand through his hair. "Okay."

I sense him pulling away, and I scramble to find more to say, something, anything to save whatever this is. "That doesn't mean I don't want you in my life, though. Earlier, you said you wanted to know who I am now, and I want that too. I want to know who *you* are now. And I don't know if you really meant that, and I don't know what anything means for us, and I don't know how to just be your friend, but I want to try."

I stop walking, and he only takes one more step before he does the same, the corner of his mouth tugging upward. "I did mean it."

I exhale heavily. "Okay. Good."

At some point in the conversation, we turned to face each other, and now only a few inches separate his body from mine.

He reaches up, tucking a stray piece of hair behind my ear. I nearly shudder at the contact, my eyes never leaving his.

"I've missed you. I know I've already said that a million times at this point, but *fuck*, Stella. I've missed you."

And then, before I can consider it or realize what I'm doing, I'm in his arms, wrapping myself around him, tucking him close, breathing him in. "I've missed you so much," I say into his shirt, the words coming out muffled.

And as he holds me like he used to, I feel lighter than I have in a long time. I squeeze him tighter, and his laughter vibrates against my head as it rests against his chest. After a few more seconds of standing with him like that, he gently pulls away and brushes my hair off my forehead.

Sheepishly, I look away and say, "I think I'm going to need some practice with this whole friend thing."

He smiles, shrugging lightly. "We've got time."

I fight the smile growing across my face and turn back to face the party. "So, what do we do now?"

He grins, and I want to bottle up the sight of him and keep it hidden away in the deepest part of my heart so I can pull it out when I need to be reminded of the good in the world.

"Now," he says, extending his hand out to me, "we go show Daniel how it's done in Ladder Golf."

I laugh as I take his hand in mine. "We're still undefeated, aren't we?"

He gives me an *"Are you kidding?"* look. "Let's go defend our honor." And as I let him pull me along, I realize that somehow, even now . . . he's still defending mine.

# 31

"**S**tella?"

I spin on my heel, accidentally yanking Bridger to a stop. He lets out an *oomph* sound. I wince. "Sorry." I'm about to tell him I thought I heard my name when I hear it again.

"Stella! It is you." I look over to see someone waving at me by the drinks table. It takes a split second, but then recognition dawns on me.

"Maggie?" I smile at her, confused.

"What are you doing here?" she asks.

I laugh. Gesturing to the house, I say, "I live here."

Her eyebrows lift in surprise. "Oh! Well, shoot," she says, surveying the area around her. "You really know how to throw a party."

I shrug. "Trust me. It's all my mom," I say, because it's the truth. "What about you?"

"I guess my mom is a frequent client at The Abode, so she got a family invite. My brother, sister, and I all tagged along with her."

I nod. Maggie's eyes flick to my right, and I'm reminded that Bridger is still standing beside me, undoubtedly confused.

"Oh! Maggie, this is my—this is Bridger," I say, clearing my throat and stumbling over my words. "Bridger, this is Maggie. She's in one of my summer classes this semester."

He reaches out with the hand not currently holding mine to shake hers. "It's nice to meet you," he says.

She smiles, letting go of his hand. "You too."

I stand there trying to think of something else to say when Bridger's eyes catch briefly on mine, and I'm thankful at this moment that only one of us is socially inept in this pairing as he speaks again.

"We were just about to head over to Ladder Golf if you want to come over there with us?"

Her eyes light up. "Sure! I love that game."

I squeeze Bridger's hand once, trying to tell him *thanks*, and he squeezes back twice. The previous game is just ending as we walk up, right as Daniel and Dahlia approach from the other side of the yard.

"Just who we were looking for," Bridger jokes as Daniel walks up and claps him on the back. Dahlia walks up and greets him with a hug as well. "Your husband had better be ready to lose," Bridger tells her, eyebrows raised.

"Trust me, he's used to it." She grins and pats him on the shoulder.

Bridger laughs, turning to face me. "You ready?"

I nod, and Maggie says, "Good luck!" before sitting in the grass a few feet away.

Daniel groans. "C'mon, that's not fair. I lost my partner," he says, gesturing to Dahlia.

"Sorry. I'm out of commission this year." She sighs dramatically, placing both hands on her belly.

"You can still play, babe. Your arms work just fine," Daniel argues, and Dahlia gives him a knowing look.

"I could," she nods, glancing over my way. "But Stella's throws can get a little wild sometimes. I'm not risking anything."

"Hey!" I say, looking over to Bridger to defend me, but his lips are pursed as he tries not to laugh. I gape at him, offended.

"Sorry, but . . . she's not wrong."

I roll my eyes, laughing along with everyone else. It feels good, this ease that seems to follow Bridger, lingering whenever he's near. That's how it has always felt between us, though. He brings the peace, and I bring the storm. And sometimes, that storm knocks out all the power and desolates the town until there's nothing left. Ever since he walked back into my life, I've been so afraid of that storm raging again and destroying everything once more. But being near him is like realizing a foundation still exists under the rubble—like I could brush away the debris and start building a new town right where I am.

Bridger speaks, "Well, you could always forfeit this year and—"

"No." Daniel cuts him off, and somehow I'm the only one who notices the laugh Bridger tries to mask with a cough. "Do you happen to know anyone else who is *not* pregnant and would be willing to play with me?" Daniel asks, and I almost want to laugh again at the seriousness in his tone.

"I could play?" Maggie offers from the ground. "And I'm definitely not pregnant," she adds.

Dahlia bursts out laughing before clapping her hands together and saying, "Perfect!"

I reach out a hand to help Maggie stand, introducing the three of them. She walks over to the ladder closest to us and starts gathering the bolas.

Daniel shouts, "Bridger, you're down here!"

Bridger leans down to me. "I'd wish us luck, but we won't need it." His warm breath tickles my ear as he turns and walks away. "I remember how to play, Daniel. It hasn't been that long." His voice trails off.

I turn back to Maggie, who is staring at me, open-mouthed.

"You didn't tell me that you have a boyfriend!" she exclaims, and my face instantly heats.

"Oh, he's not—we're not—" I cut myself off with a quick shake of my head. "We're friends."

She nods slowly, giving me a disbelieving look. "Right, because all of my good friends lean down to whisper sweet nothings into *my* ear before a game too."

"What—that's—" I stutter, my face becoming even more red, causing her to laugh harder. I start laughing too. Thankfully, just then, Daniel's voice cuts across the way.

"You guys ready?"

I respond by chucking the first bola at his head.

He lunges out of the way, the bola hitting the fence behind him as Bridger doubles over with laughter.

"I call the next game." A familiar deep voice rings out against the early evening. I take in a sharp breath, looking over and seeing Bridger's dad for the first time in over three years.

At a glance, he looks pretty much the same—save for the fact that his hair has much more gray throughout. Well, that, and the sling holding his left arm and the slight limp he is sporting.

Swallowing my surprise, I attempt to smooth out my features as he starts to walk my way. "Hi, Mr. Wells," I say. The arm that is *not* currently in a sling stretches out to meet me, and I gingerly step into the side hug he offers.

"Oh, don't start that now. It's still Adam to you."

I smile weakly, a sudden onslaught of emotions threatening to swallow me whole. I blink quickly, looking away.

"I know you're pretty good at this game, Dad, but you kind of need an arm to, you know, throw the bola," Bridger teases.

"I always find a way. You know that better than anyone." Adam laughs as he steps off to the side to let us continue.

I swallow, trying to ignore the implications of that sentence and try to focus as the game carries on. Maggie actually is really good, and Dahlia still stands on the sidelines, whooping and hollering for Daniel.

It's Bridger's turn, and as he shifts the bola in his hand, readying his throw, he looks up at the ladder I'm standing next to. I watch as his eyes go wide, and he yells in a rush, "*Stel watch ou—*"

But I don't register his words before a blinding pain shoots through the back of my head, and I'm sent crashing to the ground, face-planting into the green earth. The world blurs, and I blink against the setting sun that has suddenly become way too bright. I can feel Bridger next to me instantly. I turn my head, noticing the football resting next to his foot. I blink up at him, seeing that his lips are moving, but I'm unable to hear any of the words coming out of them beyond the ringing in my ears.

There are three of him, anyway.

I blink again as the world spins. There are four of him now. The sky is where the ground should be, and the ringing is somehow even louder. I roll back to my stomach, managing to get myself up onto my elbows—just before vomiting all over my mother's perfectly manicured lawn.

32

Bridger quickly grabs my hair and holds it gently away from my face, and his other hand rests on my back. He positions himself between me and the growing crowd that I can see slowly gathering behind him. The feeling of his hand anchors me back to reality as I start to regain the feeling of the ground beneath me. The world slows, and the ringing lessens. I cough, trying to catch my breath.

"Stel—*shit*. Stella, can you hear me?"

I nod and croak out, "Yeah." My throat feels raw, and when I glance at Bridger again, I let out a quick sigh of relief when I see there's just the one. I try to push up onto my hands, and Bridger helps me move into a sitting position. Maggie appears in front of me with a napkin, and I look at her gratefully before wiping my mouth with it.

"Oh, Justin, grab the hose." My mom's voice rings out from somewhere in the throng of people, and Bridger tenses next to me.

I try to shrug at him in an attempt to tell him that, of course, she would care more about the lawn I just ruined than me and that he shouldn't be surprised. But the motion disorients me, and I start swaying to the left involuntarily. He swiftly wraps one arm around my shoulder, gently pulling me to him, and I lean back against his chest, thankful for the stability. My head rests in the crook of his neck, and Dahlia appears in front of me again with a glass of water.

"Thanks," I say, voice still weak.

"She's awake, though. That's good, right?" I hear Daniel saying.

I feel Bridger nod against my head, and then he says, "Can someone check the size of her pupils?"

Maggie squats back down in front of me. I blink slowly at her, hoping I'll pass her test.

"They look okay to me," she says, still kneeling. Then Dahlia starts asking me all sorts of questions, and, confused, I answer all of them fine.

"Guys, I'm okay. I think I should maybe just go lie down."

Maggie grimaces, Dahlia starts rapidly shaking her head, and Daniel, looking down at his phone, says, "It says vomiting after head trauma is a sure sign of a concussion."

"What? No, I don't have a concussion. I just get motion sickness sometimes. That was a lot of . . . motion," I say, more alert than before and gesturing vaguely with my hand.

"I think you should take her to the hospital," Dahlia says, and I start to shake my head and then immediately stop, already regretting the movement.

"Stella," Bridger says, shifting slightly so that I can see his face, "I'm going to take you to the hospital, okay?"

"I don't need to go—"

"I've had concussions before, and they're not a joke. I'm not taking any chances with you," he finishes. The unsettled expression and utter concern etched across his features make me give in. I've never seen him look scared for me like this before, and it sends me down a mental path I'd rather not travel down.

"Okay," I concede. Just then, Dad rounds the corner with the hose in hand, my mom following close behind.

"Right here, Mom," I say, pointing near the spot in the grass. "Sorry I ruined your perfect party," I slur, suddenly feeling way more tired. "Who threw that football, anyway?" I mumble as Bridger and Daniel help bring me to my feet. Bridger wraps an arm around me, and I lean against him as we slowly make our way across the yard.

"Do you want to take her car?" I hear Dahlia ask, and I feel Bridger nod.

"Dad, you good to drive home?"

Adam replies, "Yeah, Bridge, absolutely. You take her. Don't worry about me."

Dahlia reappears a second later, holding out my keys. "Keep us updated," she says, biting her nail and returning to Daniel's side.

Bridger replies, "Of course."

Somehow, we've made it to the car, and he's helping to lower me in, and even though I know I shouldn't, I relish the feeling of his hands on my body. He hurries around to the driver's side and continues asking me questions the whole way. I try not to wince every time he hits a bump because I don't want to worry him anymore.

A few hours later, we leave the hospital. They confirm that I have a moderate concussion, telling me to rest and do pretty much nothing for the next forty-eight hours, which is more than fine with me. I only got annoyed when they told me that reading doesn't count as doing nothing. Avoiding bright lights, TV, and crowds will be easy. Although, I realize as we get back in the car that right now, my house most assuredly has all three. In abundance.

"Can we go back to your house? Mine doesn't seem like the best option right now for someone with a concussion," I ask Bridger, getting comfortable in the passenger seat of my own car.

"Of course," he replies, carefully starting to make his way out of the parking lot.

He's still tense, and I reach over to put my hand on his shoulder as he turns onto the main road. "Are you okay?" I ask him softly.

He gives me an incredulous look. "You just got smacked in the head by a football, and you're asking me if I'm okay?"

When I don't reply, and he sees that I'm serious, some sort of fight leaves him. He exhales. "You scared the shit out of me, Stel. I don't—I didn't—"

"Hey," I cut him off gently, moving my hand from his shoulder and grabbing his hand from where it drums anxiously on his leg. "I'm fine."

He laces our fingers together. "That was a *really* hard hit."

"Trust me, I know. It was my head," I say, trying to lighten the mood. His eyes stay firmly on the road, the same crease that seems permanently fixed into place lately when it comes to me still set between his brows. "I'm sorry," I say quietly, not having anything else to offer.

He chances a quick look at me, disbelief written across his features. "Let me repeat myself. You just got smacked in the *head* by a *football*. You are the last person who needs to apologize."

I smile softly and look down at our intertwined hands, his familiar calloused fingertips brushing over my knuckles.

We drive a few more minutes in silence before he speaks again. "I almost flipped on your mom when she asked for the hose."

I laugh and immediately regret it, wincing as I rub my head with my free hand. Bridger glances over at me, worried, but I try to give him a small smile. "Remember in high school, when you would say that your mom had made her priorities clear?"

He blinks once, twice, and nods slowly.

"Well. My mom has obviously made hers clear too." I huff lightly, tears stinging my eyes and making my headache a million times worse. "I bet she hasn't even texted to check in."

"Maybe she's waiting for a call," he offers quietly, even though we both know she isn't.

"Or maybe she just knows that I'm safe with you." I speak the words so softly that I wonder if he even heard them until he squeezes my fingers that are still wrapped in his. He brings our hands up to his mouth, pressing a featherlight kiss to the back of my hand, lingering there for a moment before lowering our hands back down to his leg.

"I'm just glad you're okay."

I smile, tears blurring my vision as I look out the window, blinking them away. "Me too."

## 33

All the lights are off when we enter Bridger's house. He leaves them off, slowly guiding us to the couch. I plop down harder than I intend to and lower my head into my hands against the relentless pressure in my skull.

I hear Bridger's dad in the kitchen, and he appears a moment later through the archway holding a glass of water. They talk in hushed voices, and I don't even bother trying to decipher what they're saying.

"How are you doing, Stella?" Adam asks quietly.

I offer him a measly thumbs up, lamely attempting a smile. "Never better."

He laughs low, his lips falling into a sad sort of smile. "You've always been tough, kiddo."

He leaves the room then, and Bridger sets the glass of water down in front of me on the coffee table.

"Is it fine if I stay the night here? I don't know how long the party will go on back at mine, and I bet the fireworks haven't even gone off yet . . ." I trail off.

"Stel. You don't even have to ask," he says, pulling the blanket off the back of the couch. I feel the cushions dip under

Bridger's weight as he sits next to me, and I automatically start to lean toward him. You know. Muscle memory and all that.

"Will you stay with me?" I ask quietly.

"Always."

Laying the blanket across our laps, he opens his arm for me. I curl into his side, breathing a sigh of contentment as he brushes my hair out of my face with his free hand. His other arm wraps tightly around my waist, and I sink into the feeling of being here like this with him.

"I'd get whacked in the head a million more times if it meant I'd get to go home with you."

He laughs softly, the vibration of his chest warm under my cheek. "If you wanted me to take you home, all you had to do was ask," he says.

I smile against him, letting out a sigh. "Maybe I'll do that next time. Try to make things a little less complicated."

He sighs now, too, my words hanging in the air between us. One hand gently moves up and down my back, his other one resting on my knee. Something begins to settle heavily on my chest, and I get this sinking feeling somewhere deep in my heart, pulling me down, fast. The one question that has been lingering in the back of my mind over the past month creeps to the surface. Maybe I can blame it on the fact that I'm slightly delirious, and maybe the concussion is the white flag letting down my natural defenses . . . Or maybe I could blame it on the fact that I am just. So. *Tired.*

I'm tired of running, tired of being treated like I'm about to break, tired of not actually existing in my own life. And I know I shouldn't, and I probably don't even want to know the answer, but I blame it on the exhaustion and ask anyway.

"How can you still stand to be near me? After everything?" It comes out in a whisper, so quiet I wonder if he even heard me. But then he stills, so I continue, needing to get the thought out and put it away before it consumes me. "I—I've only made your life miserable. Even when we were together, even in high school, I just made everything so much more difficult."

He takes one slow, even, measured breath. "That's not true," he whispers quietly, the palpable hurt emanating from his entire being.

"If I were you, I would've moved on by now." The words cut through me as they leave my mouth, but I have to say them. I need to hear him agree, to tell me to go, to prove to me that three years ago, I did the right thing.

"Stella. I haven't. I couldn't, I—" He takes a deep breath. "I've always known I could never live without you. I just . . . I didn't think I'd have to try."

A shuddering breath escapes me as I cling tighter to him, tears forming. "Why haven't you given up on me already?" I choke out, my voice trembling in disbelief. "Why haven't you just given up on me like everybody else?"

He's quiet for a moment, and for that aching second, I think he might not say anything at all. Honestly, it would serve me right. I wouldn't reply to me, either. But just as I have the thought, a soft, broken whisper cuts through the darkness.

"Why haven't you given up believing that I will?"

Silence falls, the words we laid bare sitting between us like heavy rain on a battered window, loud and relentless yet somehow comforting all the same. The exhaustion of it all hits me with full force, and minutes pass as we hold each other, my mind catching up with my body. But as my eyelids grow heavy, he speaks again, so quietly I wonder if I'm already dreaming.

"When will you understand that I'm not going anywhere?"

I feel him lean down, pressing a kiss to my forehead before he relaxes into the couch, pulling me deeper into his embrace.

I am dreaming, I realize.

I have to be.

I wake to darkness, struggling to gather my bearings as I slowly regain consciousness. My head hurts, my throat is dry, and the full memory of yesterday comes rushing over me like a tidal wave as I register the heavy arm draped over my back.

*When will you understand that I'm not going anywhere?*

At first, I think last night must have been some sort of fever dream, but when I start to remember the way he cared for me, how gentle he was with me . . . I know it had to be real. And I think that scares me more than anything because as I rest here in his arms, I realize it's the only place I ever want to be.

Shifting slightly, I try to make sense of where we ended up. Over the course of the night our bodies melded to each other, and I'm pressed against him with our legs tangled together, wrapped up in him in a way that I'd never even let myself begin to hope I'd get to be again.

Deciding to try to reach for the water on the coffee table in front of me, I gently start to move his arm from where it rests along my side, but he only exhales a breath and adjusts his grip, wrapping his arm tighter. He pulls me closer to him, one hand resting around the ridge of my hip and his other hand falling along the back of my thigh.

I freeze, and then, conceding almost immediately, I sink back into him, letting him hold me the way he used to, shutting my eyes and allowing myself to imagine we're seventeen again and there isn't so much distance and time and layered hurt between us.

Though I know I need the rest and should try to fall back asleep, I feel wide awake, hyper-aware of every point where my body touches his. He is still asleep, his breathing steady and even. I find comfort in the rhythmic rise and fall of his chest as I lay there, my hand tucked under his side, face pressed into the hollow space where his shoulder meets his neck.

I don't know how much time passes, but I find myself

wishing that time would actually stop so I can stay with him here forever like this.

But time is never so kind.

He stirs, and I already miss this moment, already long for the warmth of him even though he hasn't yet moved.

He shifts again, bringing both hands to the small of my back before lifting one to gently move my hair off my neck. I suck in a breath, remembering how he used to move my hair that same way. Such a subtle movement, a simple gesture that somehow says a thousand words as our bodies act of their own accord, responding to each other in ways they haven't been able to during all these years apart.

I glance up to find him already looking at me, blinking blearily as a slow smile spreads across his face.

"How's your head?"

Only then am I reminded of the dull throb that seems to surround my skull, the pressing hum behind my eyebrows. "Been better."

I look at him and see those tired, amber eyes assessing me head to toe. I don't want him to be worried. I want to show him that I'm fine, that I can leave as soon as he needs me to—and so I start to push up on either side of him, making it about two inches off his chest before the pain thickens behind my eyes, and I hiss a breath.

"Easy," he says gently, helping me up. He hands me the water I lamely attempted to grab earlier, and I shoot him a quick smile in thanks as he stands. He lingers near me, and I realize he's nervous to walk away. I smile again.

"You can go to the bathroom, you know. You're allowed to leave me—I'm not going to combust." I try to joke.

He gives me a soft, sad smile. "Yeah, well. I know what it's like to lose you. I'd rather not feel that again."

I swallow as he turns and heads down the hallway. Leaning

back against the couch, I close my eyes, pulling the blanket tighter around myself again.

He reemerges a minute later. I open one eye, peering over at him. "Do you think I should head home soon?"

Slowing his steps, he stops in front of the coffee table. "Do you want to go home soon?"

"No," I say without hesitation.

"Then no." His lips pull into that half smile.

"I won't be in the way? I don't want to infringe on your plans or whatever you need to do today—"

"Stel." He stops me. "First off, it's Saturday, so we aren't doing anything. And second, you are the last person who needs to worry about being in the way here."

I release a breath. "Okay." I gnaw on my lip, staring at my phone where it rests on the table. "Can you check and see if there's anything from my parents since I'm not allowed to look at screens? I should probably let them know I'll be here for a little while," I say.

He nods, grabbing my phone, not even having to ask before putting in the passcode that is still the same. He sits back down on the couch next to me, and I watch his face as he looks at the device in his hands. His brows crease slightly, but he quickly smooths his expression when he sees I'm watching him.

My stomach falls, and I don't know why I even bothered asking him to look. It's just embarrassing proving time and time again that nobody actually cares about me.

"Nothing, right? It was stupid to ask. I knew they wouldn't check in anyway," I say quietly, attempting to mask the obvious hurt in my voice.

"No, there's not, but . . . that doesn't mean nobody cares," he says, tossing my phone on the adjacent recliner. "I texted Daniel an update last night, so he probably just filled everyone in."

"Yeah. Probably," I say, unconvinced.

Frowning slightly, a few moments pass as he glances in the

direction of my phone. "So, I've been meaning to ask. Why'd you get a new number, anyway?"

I tense. "Um," I begin, clearing my throat and scratching an invisible itch on my arm. "It was something my therapist suggested I do at the time."

He purses his lips. I can tell he's forming another question—just as his dad appears from the hallway. The mood immediately shifts, and I feel some of the tension uncoil from my chest.

"Good morning, Stella."

"Good morning," I reply as he heads into the kitchen.

Bridger stands. "Do you need anything?" he says, returning his attention to me, probably sensing I am thankful for the interruption and change of topic.

I shrug. "I feel like I need to lie back down." A sudden wave of tiredness hits me again, and my head is a welcome excuse to stay in this little cocoon of safety that is his house.

Yesterday's events roll back through my mind like a film reel, and all I can see over and over is my mom, caring more about her lawn than me.

Bridger nods, helping me to avoid hitting my head as I ease down onto my side. "Can you believe she asked for the fucking hose?" I murmur, the exhaustion taking away any filter.

He sighs, laying the blanket across from me again. "There isn't a lot that surprises me anymore."

"Right? You think I'd be used to it now," I mumble bitterly, wincing at the sudden movement.

He scratches the back of his neck, his hand falling to my ankle. Squeezing once, he looks me in the eyes again, and I'm surprised to see the emotion welling up in his own. "I just don't get it, Stel," he says quietly, lowly, sadly.

"Why she doesn't seem to care about me?"

"Why you stayed." I freeze as he continues. "We were supposed to go to North Carolina together. I thought . . ." He clears his throat, blinks, and looks at the ground. "I thought we were going to go together," he all but whispers. He looks heart-broken still, and something twists low in my gut.

I spent all this time praying he hated me enough that I would never have to see this look on his face.

"I only left early for soccer conditioning that summer because I knew that eventually, you were coming too. And I've spent these last few years trying to come up with any reason why you didn't, why you would just cut me out of your life, and I come up short every time." His eyes go heavy. "Why didn't you go? Why didn't you meet me there?" His voice cracks and my heart does too.

Pressure builds in my chest. I will myself not to cry, knowing it would just make my headache worse. "Believe me, I did," I say, the tears welling anyway. "More than anything. But . . ." I hesitate.

I have his full attention now, his body turning toward me from where he sits on the end of the couch.

"It wasn't that simple," I offer lamely, watching as his expression closes off.

He nods. "Right."

I don't want to lose this, whatever it is, so I continue to try to climb back out of the hole I fell into all those years ago, trying to follow the one sliver of light and losing it every time. "It was just smarter to stay here. It was a time in my life when I knew I shouldn't be alone. I was *told* I shouldn't be alone."

He looks at me, hurt and confusion and anguish rippling off him in waves. "You had *me*," he says brokenly.

I wipe my face, pressing a hand against the building pressure in my forehead. "I know—I *know*. That was the problem. I couldn't put that much weight on you. That wouldn't have been fair."

Eyes glassy, he meets my gaze again. I force myself to hold his stare. "You didn't get to decide that for me."

I blow out a puff of air, frantically grasping at anything, any semblance of truth I can offer. Anything to make him stop looking at me the way he is right now. "I had to. Plus, do you know how pathetic it looks to follow your high school boyfriend across the country for college?"

His hand falls off my ankle, and he rubs his face before exhaling a pained, rattled breath. "So that's what it was to you? Just some high school thing?"

I pale. "Bridger, no, that's not—"

"Three years, Stella. Almost three years, over in a matter of days. A *day*," he chokes out. "All I did for those three years was fight for you. But . . . but when it came down to it, you didn't fight for me." His voice breaks as if he is just realizing this for the first time. "You didn't even fight for yourself."

I'm silent, knowing that there aren't any words that can change this, knowing there's nothing I can say that will make a difference. Staring at the ground, I'm not surprised when I hear the shift on the couch, knowing he is going to leave. Knowing I would leave me too.

But then I inhale sharply when his arms wrap around me, covering me, holding me the way only he can. "We shouldn't be talking about this now, Stel. I was . . ." He sighs. "I'm sorry. Here," he says, releasing me and readjusting the pillow underneath me. "Get some rest, okay?"

He says it and walks away, but there's something off, something new, something I don't like in his expression. I think I ripped a new rift wide open between us, pushing him away the second I let him get close again.

It's exhausting to know me, I realize.

And I let this realization carry me back into unconsciousness, staying on the couch all day, feigning sleep whenever he or his dad walks into the room, pretending not to notice the way Bridger adjusts my blanket every now and then or when he places a new glass of water on the coffee table. I even pretend to ignore the light kiss he presses into my forehead that night before he settles into the recliner across from me.

I lie there, hoping he can't hear the sound of my chest caving in, breaths coming short as I think of all the ways I've hurt him and all the ways we've come undone.

*He's better off not knowing me,* I think to myself. That one familiar, recurring thought, the one that has plagued my mind all this time. I immediately shut the thought out, knowing that following it would mean opening the door to a winding, dark path I don't want to go down again. A path I'm terrified I'll go down again.

So, I stay there, listening to Bridger breathe. And I do, too.

I take one breath.

And another, and another, and another.

# 34

Bridger is gone when I wake. I start my usual morning routine—which consists of staring at the ceiling—when Adam emerges from the hallway.

He smiles at me, undeserved. "Morning, kid."

I offer a weak smile back. "Morning."

He walks into the living room, perching on the arm of the chair across from me, wincing slightly as he does.

I clear my throat and ask him what I've been intending to ask since the party. "How are you doing?"

He smiles again, genuinely, eyes crinkling at the corners. "I'm all right. Only one more week until I can get rid of this thing," he says, gesturing to the sling that still holds his left arm. "I was pretty beat up, but I've been handling it."

"I'm glad you're okay," I say, meaning it.

"Me too." He points a finger down the hallway. "For that kid's sake, if nothing else."

My heart clenches, and I swallow heavily. "How are things at the shop?"

A tight-lipped smile this time, and I brace myself. "It's okay. Been tricky to get everything done with, you know." He holds up his sling again. "So, business has slowed a little. But it's all part of the trade, I suppose."

I nod again, dropping his gaze, letting the silence sit between us before he speaks again.

"With Bridger in summer classes and physical therapy, he's not able to help out around the shop as much as usual. You know you're always more than welcome to swing by and sort paperwork like you used to. I wouldn't mind one bit."

I look back up at him, surprised. "You'd want me to do that?"

"I'd never turn down an extra hand. When you're up for it, of course," he adds.

"I would love to, but I don't know if Bridger would want that." I have to restrain myself from visibly wincing as I remember our conversation from last night.

Adam stands, head slightly tilted, assessing me. "Trust me," he says, starting to head toward the front door, "he would."

He grabs his keys off the hook, turns, and says, "You going to be okay here for a little while longer?"

"Of course," I say, even though I'm not sure it's entirely true.

He nods and smiles, then hesitates near the door, almost like he wants to say something else. Instead, he looks back at me, waves with his good hand, and leaves.

Slinking back down on the couch, I resume staring at the ceiling. A few minutes pass, and my eyes start wandering around the room, finally taking in my surroundings for the first time since I've been here. I think of all the time I used to spend here, how this room has seen it all, and realize it hasn't changed a bit since the last time I was in it.

I admire the familiarity and let it surround me like a warm blanket—the same dents and scratches lining the floors and the walls, the soft morning light breaking through the gap in the curtains, the subtle hum of the ceiling fan as it whirs overhead.

Every creak and groan of this house are like the beginning notes of my favorite symphony, as familiar and comforting as a sheet of music that I've heard a thousand times before. I know the notes of these rooms like the back of my hand, and could play the songs of this home with my eyes closed.

I'm not sure how much time passes before I hear footsteps sounding down the hallway. A few moments later, Bridger emerges, freshly showered.

I think he's trying to kill me.

He's wearing light gray sweatpants that sit just below his hips and a light blue t-shirt that does wonders for his form as he musses his damp hair with a towel. He enters the living room, and I try to look away from the sliver of golden skin showing where his shirt is slightly raised. My eyes land on the waistband of his sweatpants, and I feel my cheeks go hot, so I look at the ceiling again because the ceiling is safe. Out of my peripheral, I see him drop his hands, throwing the towel over the back of the recliner.

"Hey," he says.

"Hi," I reply, not trusting myself to let my gaze trail anywhere else but the plaster above me.

He clears his throat. "So, listen—"

"I'm sorry," I blurt out. "I'm so sorry. For everything. And I understand if you want me to leave. Actually, it's probably better if I do, so maybe I'll just head home now. Do you think you could take me? Or if you're busy, I can probably drive—"

"What? Stella, no," he cuts me off, and I finally look at him. "No, I . . . I wanted to say that *I'm* sorry. For last night. I shouldn't have pushed you, especially after the week you've had." He shakes his head, running a hand through his wet hair again before clearing his throat, then saying quietly, "Some friend, right?"

Smiling back weakly, I say, "You're a better friend than me."

I try not to notice the way his shoulders slump slightly as he drops my gaze. One day, he'll finally realize it's probably better off this way, despite our conversation last night.

It has to be.

"Your dad just left a little while ago," I say, trying to think of something else to say.

He nods slowly. "Did he say where he was going?"

"Uh . . . no."

He nods again, looking confused but trying not to be. I think of the way Adam hesitated before he left, wondering if he could sense we needed to work something out, alone.

Moving past those thoughts, I gasp. "Oh, gosh, what if he did and I already forgot. Is memory loss a symptom of a concussion?" I say, turning on my side and throwing the back of my hand over my forehead dramatically.

He narrows his eyes at me. "Not funny."

I raise my hand in front of my eye, pinching my thumb and pointer finger together as if to say, *"A little bit funny?"* He just continues staring, his gaze unflinching. I deflate, letting my hand drop to the couch. "You're no fun."

He snorts. "Maybe I'd be a little more fun if your head wasn't broken."

"My head isn't—" But then I cut myself off, pondering. I nod. "Valid."

He cracks a smile, and my chest floods with warmth. I wonder if he ever won't have that effect on me, wonder if when he smiles at me, it'll always feel like the first time. My phone pings loudly with an incoming text, and I'm surprised it still has a charge after sitting on the chair untouched for two days. My eyebrows shoot up, and I look at Bridger. He walks over, picks it up, and looks at me with a question in his eyes. I nod.

He flips it over in his hand. "There are three from Dahlia, two from Maggie, and two from your mom."

"Okay. Um, read the ones from my mom first. Just rip the band-aid off."

He clears his throat, and I watch his eyebrows knit together as he opens the messages. "You shouldn't have wasted money going to the emergency room. It was obviously a concussion, and we all knew they were just going to tell you to rest."

I ignore the sinking feeling in my gut as he runs a hand down his face. "Stella," he starts, but I cut him off.

"What does the next one say?"

He sighs, giving me a long look. I don't know what he sees on my face, but I must look desperate because he relents, eyes lingering for another second before returning to the phone. "Do you think you'll still be up for The Abode's charity gala on the twenty-first? You know how important it is that my entire family is there. It would be terrible if you missed it again."

I shut my eyes, slowly inhaling a breath through my nose and letting it out slowly through my mouth.

"And also, you should definitely invite Bridger this year. I bet it would be a lot less agonizing with him there."

My eyes fly open, and he's still looking at the phone. "She didn't add that last part," I say, amused.

He looks up at me, the same amusement mirrored in his own eyes. "No. She didn't."

I smile, but it melts from my face almost as quickly as it appears. "You don't have to go. I'd love for you to, but it's always so boring."

He shrugs. "Right. It's *boring* because you've never been there with *me*."

I huff out a laugh. "Fair enough."

He smiles, looking back down at the phone. His eyebrows knit together, and he reads the message again. "Why did she say she didn't want you to miss it *again*?" he asks, adding emphasis to the last word.

I drop his gaze, staring at a loose string on the rug. "I didn't go a few years back. The summer after senior year." Sighing, I say, "She'll never let me forget it."

"She'd never let you miss before," he says, remembering the

few times in high school over the summer that I'd go on and on to him about how much I didn't want to go.

"Yeah, well. Unforeseen circumstances and everything." He doesn't say anything else, and I don't give him a chance to before saying, "Don't reply. Just read Maggie's. Please."

Another moment of silence passes, and I worry he'll press the previous statement further, but thankfully, he continues. "Hey, I know you probably won't see this, but I just wanted to check in and see if you're doing okay. Oh, and also, I just found out it was my brother who threw the football, so . . . Sorry about that."

I laugh, and the corners of Bridger's lips tug upward as he goes on to read the last message.

"Dahlia said, 'Hi sis. Hope you're doing better and—'" he cuts himself off, choking on a laugh. Oh God.

I groan, covering my hands with my face. "Do I even want to know?"

He's silent, and when I peek through my fingers, I find that a full-on grin has taken over his entire face. He holds the phone back up and says, "Hope you're doing better and are enjoying your stay with the boy toy."

I drop my hands, mortified. "She didn't." She knew he'd have to read me the text. I make a mental note to never speak to her again.

"Oh, I'm not done," he says teasingly, a mischievous glint in his eyes.

"Oh, yes, you are." I stand and make like I'm going to take the phone from him, but his eyes grow wide.

"Hey, hey, whoa," he says, reaching an arm out to steady me. I've only gotten up over the past two days to go to the bathroom, and the sudden movement dizzies me a little.

"I'm fine. I can walk. I'm not on bed rest." I shake my arm from his grip, and he narrows his eyes at me. "I'm hungry."

He sighs, still assessing me. Then, he looks down at the

phone again, smirks, tosses it onto the chair, and starts walking to the kitchen. I glance at the chair, hoping to read the message quickly, but then Bridger shouts over his shoulder, "No screens. Doctor's orders."

I close my eyes and release a breath. Glaring at my phone again, I turn, slowly stalking after him into the kitchen.

# 35

## THEN

November, Junior Year

When Bridger's soccer season was officially over, we spent more time together than not, either at my house, his house, the park, or his dad's shop. The rest of his season was amazing, and even though they got second place in the state championship, *they made it to the state championship.* Bridger had already been scouted by countless colleges, and I felt honored to even know him, let alone be loved by him.

The newfound popularity he'd gained from soccer had only gotten more prominent as the season progressed. I sat with his dad at all of the remaining games and tried not to let the odd looks from girls in my classes or in the hallways get to me. I mean, his captain's armband was still hanging from my bedpost, after all.

I looked at it now as Bridger and I lay sprawled across my bed, laptop open across my lap as I tried to come up with ideas for a new project I was working on, burrowing farther into his hoodie that I still hadn't given back from sophomore year. He lay beside me, a book he had picked off my shelf open in his lap, his hand resting against the inch of bare skin showing between my hoodie and the waistband of my pajama pants.

"Your hand is so cold," I said, trying to hide the smile on my face as he traced lazy circles above my hip.

"I like giving you goosebumps," he said playfully, and I didn't even have to look at him to know he was smiling, I could hear it on his lips. I rolled my eyes, laughing, and swatted his hand away.

Glancing at the book, I snorted another laugh as I clocked his page number. "Bridge, you've been on that page for fifteen minutes."

He groaned and rolled over, burying his head into my side and tossing the book to the edge of the bed. "You're distracting me," he mumbled, words muffled against the fabric.

"You're joking, right?" I said in disbelief. "I've been trying to work on this for the past thirty minutes with *you* lying in my bed."

He lifted his head, raising his eyebrows as if to say, "*And?*"

I narrowed my eyes at him and felt my chest expand as a slow smile spread across his face. He looked up at my laptop, squinting against the bright light cast from the screen.

"When can I read your book?" he asked like he always did.

And I gave him the same answer as always. "When it's finished."

He sighed dramatically, head falling back against my pillows.

"And besides, that's not even what I'm working on right now."

"What are you working on?"

"Well . . ." I swallowed, hesitating, my finger hovering over the minimize button.

He noticed the shift in my expression and sat up straighter on my bed, leaning against my headboard. Bridger always had this sort of natural attentiveness toward me, and when he gave me his full attention, I knew that I *had* it. That he wasn't only listening but was actually hearing what I was trying to say, some-times when I didn't even know what I was trying to say.

That attentiveness had always been one of my favorite qual-ities about him, but I think that's the thing about knowing someone like you know your favorite song. At first, you love the chords, the melody, the way the lyrics flow throughout—but then the song gets overplayed like it always seems to, and one day when it comes on shuffle, you sigh and finally hit next.

I just didn't know, then, that eventually, that song would become too painful to hear, and the one skipping it would be me.

"I actually wanted to talk to you about something," I said warily. He shifted his body fully toward me, eyebrows knitting.

"Everything okay?"

"Yeah. Yeah, I just . . ." I trailed off, instantly wanting to back-track, already wanting to drop it. "Never mind. It's stupid."

"Try me," he said, voice soft as he tucked his hands behind his head.

I released a breath, closing my laptop and setting it by our feet. "So, there's this writing competition." I paused, waiting for him to scoff, for some hint of reproach to pass across his features. But, of course, none did. His eyebrows rose slightly, curious, waiting for me to continue.

"It's through North Seattle Community College. Mr. Whit told me about it—it's a short story competition, so that means no more than thirty pages. There are different categories and age groups, of course, but . . . I was thinking about entering." I stared at my hands as I continued talking. "The prizes are really cool. Third place gets five hundred dollars, second gets the same and their work published in the local paper, and first place gets all that, plus a recommendation letter sent to anywhere of their choosing . . ."

I trailed off when I finally glanced over at him to see him grinning at me. My stomach dropped. "You think it's stupid, don't you." I didn't even ask it as a question, and I could feel the defeat already turning my cheeks pink.

"What? Stella, no," he said, smile faltering, confusion shifting his expression. "Why would I think that? This is a great opportunity to get your work out there, and you should take it. Your work is *good.*"

"You're biased."

He shrugged. "Maybe so, but even in some alternate universe where you weren't my hot author girlfriend, when I read your story—because in any universe, I'd read your story—I'd still be like, 'Damn. That girl can *write.*'"

I laughed, shaking my head and tucking my legs into my chest. "I'm not an author."

"Yet," he said, nudging my shoulder and leaning in to press a kiss to my temple.

I chewed on my lip, feeling the doubt simmering. I paused, then said, "How can you be so sure?"

He leaned back again, grabbed my hand, and started to trace mindless circles on my palm. "It's the same as playing a soccer game."

"Oh?" I say, laughter bubbling in my chest.

"Hear me out. Before I go onto the field to play a game, I'm not wondering how well I'll do, if I'll get injured, if we'll win. I just go out there with the mentality that we've already won." He shrugs like it's the easiest equation in the world.

And, in that moment, more than anything, I wished it were. After hearing for years and years that writing was a "good hobby," a "fun pastime," or "something I'd grow out of," that hope had been worn down.

For as long as I could remember, I had always been the only one to take my writing seriously because when you're a kid, they tell you that you don't know any better. That one day, once you grew up and got to the real world—wherever the hell that was—you'd realize that you need a "real job" after all.

That deeply rooted insecurity took hold of my thoughts and forced the question out of my mouth. "And what if you have that mindset and still lose?"

A grin took over his whole face. "Then I still have a hot author girlfriend to come home to, regardless."

I laughed again and went to swat him on the arm, but he caught my hand, and I let him pull me onto his lap.

I nestled into him as he leaned against the headboard again and moved my hair off my neck, tracing the exposed skin there. I played with the hem of his t-shirt, savoring the sureness of him, wishing some of it would bleed into me.

"So, let's say I do enter," I started, not moving my head from where it rested on his chest.

"Mm-hmm," he hummed softly.

"What should my story be about?"

He let out a breath, the warm air tickling the top of my head. "You could always write one about a cool guy who helped a cool girl jump her car in the school parking lot?"

I tried to suppress my laugh. "I'm not sure how well that would place."

He huffed. "Fine. Or how about one where two star-crossed lovers share a firework-worthy first kiss at Kerry Park?"

I shook my head, laughing more. "You do know star-crossed means their love is doomed, right?" I said, pulling back from him to look at his face.

"Oh," he frowned. "Okay, yeah. Scratch that."

I laughed again. We spent the next twenty minutes throwing around ideas and coming up with different plot twists, each one more ridiculous than the next. Eventually, I laid my head on his chest again, marveling at how easy it was to talk about this, about *anything* with him.

He was the only one who had ever talked about my writing, or my book, or my dreams without a hint of mockery or spitefulness. He always told me how important he thought my writing was, whether it be another piece printed in the school newspaper, a poem written for class, or a random story idea I'd tell him about. He would even proofread my essays for spelling mistakes (even though he would say, "*Me* proofreading *your* essay is as unnecessary as *you* teaching *me* how to kick a soccer ball." And yet he still proofread them, every time). And last weekend, when I was at his house, I realized that the first article I wrote sophomore year was still taped up on his wall.

He was the first one to believe in me and to spur that belief in myself. Looking back now, I wish I could have bottled that belief up somehow and kept it with me over the next few years as I tried to navigate life without him.

I wished I'd known how badly I would need it.

# 36

"Can I talk to you guys about something?"

Yesterday, I decided I was going to enter the competition. The idea for my short story came loosely to me as I was falling asleep, and now I could see the glittering outlines floating around in my head, urging me to form them into something tangible.

My parents turned to me as I entered the living room. My mom sat with her blouse still perfectly tucked, her maxi skirt flowing over the edge of the couch as she crossed her legs in front of her. My dad sat across from her in his favorite recliner, UC Berkeley hoodie on, with his cabin sock-clad feet kicked up on the coffee table.

I cleared my throat as I moved to rest against the arm of the couch. Mom folded her hands in her lap, looking at me with slightly raised brows as Dad removed his reading glasses.

Swallowing, I looked between them both. I let the words out in a rush before I lost my nerve. "So, there's this writing competition that's being held through the local community college. It's a really great opportunity, and I think I'm—no, I *am*—going to enter." I paused, waiting for something, unsure of what, but they both just kept looking at me, so I just kept talking.

"I'll basically just have to write a short story, and if I win or place at all even, there's prize money, and I could get it printed! And there's also the letter of recommendation, which would be helpful for anything, really. Not to mention how good it would look on college applications, so I—"

"Stella." My mom interrupted with a long sigh.

My stomach dropped as she gave my dad that look, the one that I'd learned to associate with the subtle crushing of my dreams.

"Honey." Mom tried again, and I almost flinched at the forced sweetness in her tone, the same one you'd use to speak to a stray dog you'd just found and were trying not to spook. "We know how much you love making up stories. You've always been very . . . imaginative."

My eyes drifted back up to their faces, wondering how she'd already managed to belittle me within the first two sentences.

"And we know it's important to you and that you're passionate about it. But . . ." Dad began, but it was Mom who drove the nail home.

"Passion won't pay the bills."

I pursed my lips, already regretting the conversation before it had truly even begun. I knew I should've just entered without telling them and let the win speak for itself after the fact. It was stupid of me to think the conversation would've gone any other way.

"Hobbies are important, Stella. I know you know that." A weighted pause, and I braced myself. "I love playing tennis on the weekends, but you don't see me trying to make it to the Olympics."

I frowned. "Right. But what does that have to do with—"

"It's your junior year, Stella." She cut me off again. "You're seventeen now, and things are starting to get more and more important. We just . . ." She glanced briefly at my dad, and I hated the unspoken words that passed between them. "We just think it's time you started thinking realistically about your future."

It took everything in me to stay rooted in place, to not get up and walk away from this like every ounce of self-preservation was screaming at me to do. For once, I wanted to see it through. Prove to *them* that I could see something through. "This is really important to me." My voice came out quieter than I'd hoped it would, lacking the conviction I knew I needed.

Dad leaned forward slightly. "I know—*we* know," he started, eyes flicking between me and my mom. "We're your parents. We're just trying to help set you on a path where you can be successful."

"We must have different versions of success," I replied flatly before thinking. At the sight of Mom's expression gone sour, I hurriedly tried to save the conversation before it was too late. "No, that's not—what I *meant* is that . . . success can look different for everybody. I don't have to have a pantsuit and an office job like you in order to make a living."

"No," my mother sighed, "you don't. But what you do have to have is the surety *of* making a living. Some sense of security, a steady income."

I rolled my lips, that familiar burn starting at the back of my throat. "I know that Mom, and I could have that as an author. It'll take time, I get that, but I want to—"

She held up her hand, and I stopped, feeling like I was five years old. "I don't want you to base your entire future on a what-if. You can't spend your life floating along, relying on dreams and chance."

That burning sadness immediately turned to frustration, and I let out an exasperated breath. "No, Mom, you're right. I can't. But what if I relied on hard work and talent? I'm *good* at this, guys. I'm good at this, but neither of you would even know that because you haven't ever bothered to read a single thing I've written." My breath became heavy, my eyes stung. Through my blurry vision, I could see my mom rubbing her temples and starting to stand.

"Justin, I told you she'd be like this . . ." Her voice faded away as she walked out of the room.

I looked toward my dad and threw my hands out to my sides hopelessly. He stood, ran a hand over his hair, and regarded me slowly.

Sighing, he said, "We'll talk about this later," and left the room.

I sat there, unmoving, taken aback at how quickly I was shut down. I didn't understand any of it. At all. Why did I have to try to become someone else entirely to appease them? I'd spent the last seventeen years trying to find the balance between "too much" and "not enough" to make the people around me more comfortable. But that night, I realized how much of myself I had compromised and lost in the process.

I'd always been the sensitive child, the emotional one, the dramatic one, the one with her head in the clouds and her heart on her sleeve. The dreamer, the believer, the one who'd *hoped*. Who knew there had to be more.

But, on that night, I realized—maybe there wasn't.

Something cracked in me then, a subtle feeling that had been gnawing at me quietly, almost unknowingly, sitting just under the surface for far too long. It wasn't until then, as I sat there in the living room that night until my tears finally dried, and I walked to my bedroom in silence. It wasn't until then that I realized I didn't have that hope anymore.

It had been gone for a long time.

～

My phone lit up next to my pillow that night, illuminating the pitch-black room where I'd been laying in silence for I wasn't sure how long. I grabbed it, already knowing who the text came from. The same person all my texts ever came from.

Bridger <3

9:34 p.m.

How'd it go?

. . .

How do you think?

I dropped my phone onto my bed and let my head flop back onto the pillow. Not even three seconds later, my phone vibrated with an incoming call, a picture of Bridger flashing across the screen and lighting up the darkness. I felt my lip start to tremble as pressure began to build behind my eyes, almost laughing at the metaphor. Me, a broken mess, retreating into my darkness, and him, the one beacon of light glowing through it.

I couldn't bring myself to lift my hand or answer the call, and so I let it ring soundlessly on the sheets as the first tears dripped down my nose. I laid there, thinking of matches and stars and fireworks and things that burn brightly until they're blown out, smothered, or spent.

I thought of him, that shining bright light, and how I didn't want my darkness to snuff him out.

# 37
## NOW

I spent a few more days camped out in the Wells' living room, despite the fact that Bridger insisted I take his bed because I shouldn't be sleeping on the couch with a concussion. I refused simply for the fact that it was painful enough being back in his house, let alone in his *bed.*

I didn't tell him as much, of course, instead saying I was fine where I was, so Bridger stayed with me in the living room every night, sleeping on the recliner. When I told him he didn't have to do that, he just said that if I wasn't sleeping in his bed, then no one was . . . and it took me the entire next day just to shake off all that sentence implied.

Bridger and I settled into a quiet sort of companionship, as familiar as it was new. He was gone a lot at class or the shop, so I spent a lot of time staring at nothing and taking naps. He let me borrow a t-shirt and sweats, and I'd forgotten how good it felt to be wrapped up in someone's presence even when they weren't around.

Since Bridger always insisted on "cooking" for me, my diet consisted mostly of cereal and sandwiches—and the one time Bridger made himself a sandwich of his own, he used the end slices. He said they were still his favorite, which made me wonder if that meant I was still his favorite, but then I realized that was stupid because it was a piece of bread. I ended up having to chalk it up to the fact that after doing that for the better part of three years, it was probably just a habit.

It's been almost two weeks since I got my concussion. I went back to my house a couple of days ago—much to my dismay, might I add—but I had to face reality again eventually. Bridger told me I still need to take it easy, but I also have a presentation due this week that I completely left Maggie hanging on, so I'm venturing out for the first time since the injury to a coffee shop to meet her.

I sit at a small table in the back corner of the shop after opting to get here early. I wanted to avoid stressing myself out further by having to try to find her upon entering, but now I just feel stupid sitting here alone. I try to remind myself no one is looking at me and no one really cares, but it's hard to train your mind to put down its defenses after they've been raised so high for your entire life.

My vanilla latte warms my hands as it rests on the table between my fingertips, and I take in the details of the coffee shop around me. It's newly opened in Seattle, converted from an old, closed-down auto repair garage. Concrete floors, whitewashed cinder block walls, and exposed beams above tall ceilings are coupled with an industrial smell, which might be a little off-putting if not for the warm lighting and plants housed in every corner. The entire right wall is covered in garage doors, and one of them is open now to let in a cool breeze.

As I look at the open garage doors, I think of Adam's repair shop and wonder if Bridger would think this place is cool or tacky. Then I'm wondering why I'm wondering what he would think at all, and I'm thankful when I spot Maggie walking through the door. Her face lights up when she sees me, and she waves as she steps up to the counter.

Her blonde hair is pulled up into a messy bun, and I wonder how many tries it took to get it so perfectly unkempt. Wearing an oversized t-shirt paired with black biker shorts and one of those crossbody belt bags, she looks effortlessly cute.

I've only known Maggie for a few weeks, but even in that short time, I've noticed the way she carries herself and the way the world seems to move around her. It's almost as if she's never wondered about her place in it before. For a moment, I wonder what that would be like.

She approaches the table with ease, balancing papers in one hand and her drink in the other with a huge grin on her face. She sets the papers down, taking a sip of her matcha latte. "So, how's your head?" she asks with a cringe.

I shrug. "Pretty much fine now. Sorry about leaving you with all this," I say, gesturing to the papers strewn around the table as I pull out my laptop. "I wish I could've helped. I didn't mean to make you do it all."

She looks at me in disbelief. "Yeah, I really blame you for getting whacked in the head and practically knocked unconscious. Which—by the way—Miles never heard the end of it from me on the way home. And pretty much every day since. He felt really bad, but he's only fifteen, so not bad enough."

"Miles?"

"My brother. The football assailant."

"Ah," I say, nodding my head once, shrugging again as if to say, *"It's fine."*

"And anyway, I saw that hit. It was brutal. Honestly, I'm just glad you're still alive." She laughs, joking, of course.

I freeze, blink, clear my throat quickly, and hope she didn't notice. "Yeah," I say, opening my laptop. "So, what can I help with?"

We spend the next forty minutes pouring over the material coursework, trying to gather enough information to pull together a mock lesson plan for a pretend class.

Leaning back in her chair and blowing a stray hair out of her face, Maggie groans. "This is so stupid. Why am I making a lesson plan when I don't even want to be a teacher?"

Snorting, I say, "That's what I was about to ask myself."

She tilts her head at me, a slight smile on her lips and an inquisitive look in her eyes. "Aren't you majoring in education?"

"Oh. Well, um, yeah." I stammer, my eyes finding a ring from a coffee mug on the table between us very interesting all of a sudden. "I'm going for high school English, though, so still not really relevant to this assignment," I finish quickly.

She takes a sip of her drink, nodding as she swallows. "How long have you known you wanted to be a teacher?"

My least favorite question. "Uhhh . . ." I hesitate, wishing my latte wasn't already gone so I could buy a few seconds by taking a drink. "I guess just this past year."

Her eyebrows rise slightly, but she does a good job of hiding her surprise.

Before she can ask anything else, I turn it back to her. "What about you? Are you a writer?"

"Yeah, poems, mostly. But it's just for fun. And anyway, apparently, you can't just write poems for a living." She says, laughing humorlessly.

"I mean," I say, shrugging my shoulders, "you could."

A hair falls from her bun in front of her face, and she tucks it behind her ear. "You think so?" She looks almost shy as she says it, and I wonder where the boisterous girl who walked in here without a second glance just an hour ago went.

I guess maybe that's what happens when you share your dreams with someone. It feels like the equivalent of holding a piece of your heart out on a silver platter in front of them, hoping they don't drop it and watch it shatter into a million pieces.

"Yeah, I honestly think so. That's really cool," I say, and I mean it.

Her shoulders drop slightly, a soft smile playing on her lips. "I think you're the first person that's ever said that to me," she laughs lightly. "Usually, I get a much less excited reaction. Kind of dampens the fun a little."

"I totally get that. It's always the eyebrow raise, *'Oh, sure you will,'* pat on the shoulder kind of dismissal."

"Yes!" she exclaims, drawing the attention of the couple sitting at the adjacent table. She pays them no attention, continuing, "I know it's not, like, the cut and dry, straight and narrow path I'm supposed to go on," She speaks indignantly, putting quotation marks around the word, "but it's something. Or even if I want to become an editor, or a freelance writer, or a journalist in the end, I just—" She cuts herself off, taking a breath. "I don't understand why people can't just cheer each other on regardless. What I decide to do with my life is not their concern," she finishes, exhaling through her nose with flushed cheeks.

I love her already.

I'm about to open my mouth to tell her as much when her phone starts ringing against the table. She frowns at it, then her eyes go wide. She stares at it, rolling her teeth over her lips. A few more rings pass, and she continues to stare at it, frozen.

"Do you need to get that, or . . . ?" I trail off, not wanting her to feel like she'd be rude to take it.

"No. Yes. No." Her eyes flick quickly from her phone to me, then she says in a rushed breath, "Sorry, it'll be quick." She picks up her phone. I give her a thumbs up as she hurries away, heading for the bathroom.

I mull over the papers in front of me, trying to organize what we've come up with so far. I try not to let my curiosity get the best of me and decide I shouldn't be nosy right as Maggie returns to the table a few minutes later.

"Sorry about that," she says contritely.

"Oh, seriously, don't worry about it," I say with a wave of my hand.

She breathes a sigh through a smile, but I can tell it's forced. She's tenser than before; her fervor from our previous conversation dissipated. "It's just . . ." She exhales again, tugging at her bun and letting her hair fall down her shoulders. "It was just my dad. He lives in Oregon, so I don't get to see him that much. Or talk to him that much, really."

She gathers her hair up again, mindlessly twisting it around into the messy bun she had moments before. "He doesn't call that often, is all. So, it just catches me off guard when he does, I guess." She sighs loudly, straightening her shoulders and shaking her head. "Sorry, I don't know why I said all that. I just—anyways." She huffs a breath out of her nose and crosses her legs.

"Hey, it's all good. I totally get it," I say because, unfortunately, I do. "My friend's mom lives in California, so it's kind of the same thing. They don't talk all that much, either."

"Yeah. It sucks, but we all just do the best with what we have, right?" she says, offering another tight-lipped smile.

I smile, nodding in return. "Right."

Her eyes fall back down to the papers in front of us, and I focus mine back on my laptop. We finalize the rest of the assignment, delegating individual tasks for the rest of the week and agree to meet again next week after class at the coffee shop.

And it's easy, talking to her, working while simultaneously going on random tangents for minutes on end about whatever's in our minds at that moment. There's a sort of lightheartedness to it that I've never really experienced before, a type of relationship I've always felt like my life has lacked.

We pack our things, and as I get in my car, I feel . . . good. Okay, even. I sit there, thinking that this must be what it feels like to have a friend.

# 38

## THEN

March, Junior Year

The holidays passed in a blur of terribly sung, out-of-tune Christmas songs (courtesy of Bridger), the smell of slightly burnt sugar cookies (courtesy of his dad), and a perfectly decorated house (courtesy of my mom—so perfectly decorated, in fact, that it was professionally photographed and put on the front cover of the December edition of The Abode Magazine).

It was nice to have Daniel and Dahlia home for Christmas break. Since they were in their third year at UC Berkeley, their visits seemed to be getting fewer and farther between as their schedules got busier. They seemed to be doing really well regardless, and as much as I hated to admit it—I would be lying if I said I wasn't surprised that they were still together.

But then again, anyone could take note of the fact that Bridger was still with me and say the same thing, so . . . I tried not to ruminate.

Dahlia and I finished up all of our last-minute Christmas shopping together, and though it was fun getting to know her better, I couldn't help but wonder if she just felt obligated to hang out with me because I was her boyfriend's little sister. I later told Bridger as much, and he then told me that she obviously had just started dating Daniel as an easier way to befriend *me*, and I laughed and told him he was stupid, but dropped it nonetheless. And honestly, I was really starting to enjoy Dahlia's company, so even if that was her intention—I didn't mind.

Before I knew it, we were back at school, the final term of junior year in full swing. The short story for my writing competition took me no time at all over the break. It was almost as if the story was itching to be told, bursting through the forefront of my mind in its entirety, taking shape faster than I could will my fingers to type it.

After a week or two of relentlessly editing it and having Bridger read it (and then read it again . . . and again), I finally submitted it and was anxiously waiting to find out if I had received a spot in the top three.

And so, on a lazy Sunday afternoon at Bridger's house, there I was, still anxiously waiting.

"Okay, but, like, you can't try to tell me that she really never thought the letters would get out. I mean, she literally *addressed* them," Bridger said emphatically.

I looked at him incredulously. "I cannot believe that is the only thing you took away from this movie. You were supposed to be taking notes. Peter Kavinsky is, like, easily top five ultimate fictional boyfriends."

His hands went still against my calves, where my legs were resting haphazardly across his lap. "The ultimate—*what?* You're joking, right? Stella, he didn't even get her scrunchie back. Her *favorite* scrunchie."

I frowned, blinking at him slowly. "That's . . . that's a good point."

"Thank you. And anyway, you want to talk about top fictional boyfriends? That's Mr. Darcy. *Any* day," he said with all the conviction in the world, shaking his head at me as I tried not to laugh.

I was about to ask him how he even knew who that was when his dad shouted from the kitchen just beyond where we sat, "He's right!"

We all dissolved into laughter, and I thought to myself . . . that was the sound I would hear echoing in my heart for the rest of my life. It was in those quiet moments that I could forget about the outside world for a second, forget the noise that constantly felt like it was pressing down on me everywhere I turned. It was in those little pockets of joy—when I was with Bridger, when I was writing, when I was staring at the view of my favorite skyline—that I felt that weight lessen for a short time, as if someone was lifting the boulder an inch off the ground and letting me breathe for a second underneath it.

My phone pinged on the coffee table as our laughter died down, and I dropped my feet to the floor to reach over and grab it. Opening the notification, I gasped and jumped up from the couch.

"What? What is it?" Bridger's frantic voice said next to me, instantly up and at my side. I held up a finger as I scanned the email over again. And again.

The breath rushed from my lungs in a whoosh as I turned to face him and said, "I got it. I'm—I'm in the top three."

"You're that surprised?" He grinned, pulling me into a bone-crushing hug. I was laughing, and so was he, and then he was kissing me and twirling me around before reading the email for himself. Then he was hugging me again, and his dad appeared and started celebrating too, even though he didn't know what for.

Bridger paused, turning to face his dad. "Stella made top three!"

"HEY!" His dad yelled with his arms in the air, and then we were laughing and celebrating again.

I thought of how we must've looked then, imagined what someone walking by on the street would see if they were to glance at the bay window into the living room—a picture frame encased in soft yellow light, radiant silhouettes dancing around carelessly, three hearts in a home.

And, for a second, it was almost as if it were me out on that street, looking in on the moment—there, but not quite all the way.

"Guys, it's not that big of a deal. I didn't even win," I said breathlessly after we'd settled down.

"Yet," Bridger corrected before pulling me back down onto the couch with him.

I sighed, feeling the doubt creep in from the crack in that window. "I mean, it's just through the local community college. It's not a Nobel Prize or anything."

Bridger glared at me with narrowed eyes. "Don't undermine this. Your story was selected top three out of"—he took my phone again, squinting at the email as if he hadn't already read it three times—"over five hundred others. That's *insane.*"

I felt an unfamiliar heat rise up my neck, not used to my writing being celebrated. I'd always felt like it was a part of me to hide, a dream I needed to keep locked away. But maybe this would show my parents. Would prove to them that my writing was actually something worth pursuing.

"So, what day are the awards?" Bridger's dad asked, settling into the recliner across from the couch.

"Um . . ." I trailed off, pulling the email back up again. "Sunday, March twenty-fourth. The weekend after next. Oh, that's spring break, isn't it?" I looked up, the happy expression quickly wiped from my face as I took in the looks on theirs.

Bridger froze on the couch next to me, eyebrows pulled together, as Adam gazed at the floor. "Shit," he muttered under his breath, looking toward his dad.

"What's up?" I asked tentatively.

"That's . . . that's the weekend of the UNC showcase. I'll— *we'll* be in North Carolina."

*Oh.* Right.

Trying not to let them see any flicker of disappointment cross my face, I hurriedly said, "Oh, duh, the Spring Break Showcase. The one you've been looking forward to for months! That's amazing. I'm stoked for you. You're going to have the best time." I was rambling, and we all knew it.

Bridger let out a measured breath, rubbing his hand over his mouth. "Well, maybe I could—"

"No." I cut him off. "Absolutely not. Bridger, this is your future. This . . ." I waved my hand lightly at my phone. "This is nothing. I doubt anything will even come from it. Don't worry about me. I'll just, like, call you after or something," I finished lamely.

"It's your future too, Stel. This could be huge for you." He looked at me helplessly.

"Yeah, but you need to go show those scouts what you're made of. You've already read this story, like, seven times. Nothing new here." I waved him off again.

"Well, wait. What time is it at?" Adam asks.

Glancing at my phone again, I said, "Not until six."

His eyebrows shot up, and he said, "Bridge, we might be able to make it. We have an early flight anyway because I have to be back at the shop on Monday morning. I'm sure we'll be back by then."

Bridger's shoulders relaxed slightly as a soft sigh escaped him. "Okay. Good." He looked at me and laced my fingers through his. "We'll be there."

～

Bridger <3

8:07 a.m.

Our flight is delayed . . . I'm so sorry. We're not
supposed to get in until almost 9 tonight

Aw :( That's okay, don't worry about it

I feel terrible. I wanted to see you win.

Eh. You said it yourself, first of many, right?

That's my girl

I'll call you as soon as we land, okay? I want to
hear all about it. I love you

Love you <3

Wish me luck!

You don't need it, Stel.

That night, I hurried through the crowd, looking for any familiar faces. With a medal around my neck, flowers in one hand, and my short story with a golden embossed stamp that read *First Prize Winner* on the front of it in the other, I wove through the other contestants and their loved ones who came to support them. Many of them congratulated me as I passed, and I smiled and said *thank you* and almost meant it.

I hoped Bridger couldn't read the disappointment radiating through the phone screen from our texts that morning—it wasn't his fault his flight got delayed. I hadn't heard from him since, so hopefully, that meant he was in the air on his way back to me.

I continued to scan the crowd, my hope dwindling with every step I took. When I told my parents that I had made top three, they actually kind of seemed . . . impressed? Or maybe I imagined it. And with Daniel and Dahlia home for their spring break, I thought that maybe, just maybe, they'd come tonight. I hadn't gotten a chance to tell the latter about the competition, though, so hopefully, my parents had. Yet, as I surveyed the people around me one last time, I realized the thought was unlikely.

Blowing a puff of air out of my mouth, I slipped away to the far wall and leaned against it, pulling out my phone to see no new messages, and no missed calls. I sighed as I slid it back into my purse. I hadn't seen my parents much today, as they were at their usual Sunday brunch with their friends, but that was usually over by late afternoon. If I hadn't had to show up to the community college extra early as one of the finalists, I would have reminded them.

I should have reminded them.

The hall around me had started to clear out, so I swept the area one final time, wondering why I even held onto the hope. That hope was heavy now, almost tangible, and I swore I felt it settle over me like a dead weight around my neck, similar to the round, golden piece of metal hanging there now.

They had forgotten.

I didn't know why I was surprised.

Taking a breath, I tried to keep that disappointment at bay as I turned and exited through the double doors to the chilly spring night beyond, with my head hung low.

# 39

I spent the whole drive home wondering where my parents were and what reason they would give as to why they couldn't make it. As my car rolled to a stop in front of my house, I had come up with a myriad of excuses, none of which seemed likely. I turned off the car and picked up my phone, silently willing it to ring in my hands, needing to hear Bridger's voice before I walked in.

I instantly pushed the thought away, hating how pathetic it made me feel. He was the most important thing to me, the most steadying thing in my life, but he couldn't be the only thing. I needed to be okay without him sometimes, do things on my own. The last thing I would ever want to be to him was a burden. A silent chill snaked down my arms at the sharp realization that . . . maybe I already was.

I flung the car door open and practically jumped out, hoping that maybe if I got out of the place where I had those thoughts, they would disappear entirely. Lifting my gaze to the doorway, I took a deep breath. It wasn't until I started to cut across the grass on the front lawn that I realized both cars were in the driveway.

Everyone was home.

My mind started whirling as I slowly approached the door, wondering what I'd find when I opened it.

Entering the house, I kicked off my platform sandals and walked hesitantly into the living room. My breath left me in a rush as I stared at the scene before me.

Daniel and Dahlia were sitting on the couch together, laughing at something on her phone. My mom was still in her Sunday best on the couch adjacent to them, color swatches for a new line she had been working on littering the coffee table in front of her. And my dad, in his recliner in the corner, leaned forward over the book on his lap, reading glasses perched on his nose, like always.

So casual, so calm—serene, even. The perfect picture of a perfect family. But, of course, I wasn't in the image. Never had been.

Dahlia spoke first. "Stella! You look so cute. Where have you been?"

She was smiling, and I couldn't even bring myself to muster any emotion on my face as I looked down at what I was wearing: a long, intricately floral-patterned dress with capped sleeves, hair curled into loose waves, my brown crossbody purse hanging limply at my side.

And I'd never felt more stupid. She didn't know.

"How'd it go?" Mom said before I caught her giving my dad that knowing look, the one burned into my mind, the one I could go the rest of my life without ever seeing again.

My phone almost dropped from my hand, and my bag thumped to the floor as I realized . . . my parents hadn't forgotten.

They chose not to go.

And that stung a thousand times worse.

"Why didn't you come?" I said in barely more than a whisper.

"Stella." My mom said my name through a sigh, the way she always did. "Sit down. Please."

Numbly, I took in my brother and Dahlia's confused expressions as I sank onto the arm of the couch across from the four of them.

"I think it's time we continue this conversation about your future." Mom looked at me pointedly, and all I could do was blink. Daniel stood up from where he sat on the couch, reaching a hand toward Dahlia. She took it, confused.

"Well, Dahl's mom is expecting us for a late dinner tonight, so, uh, we'll—we'll see you guys." He pulled her to her feet.

"We—what? I don't—"

"See you later," he said again before hurrying them out of the room. Dahlia gave my shoulder a quick squeeze as she passed by, that confused expression still clouding her beautiful features. I barely felt it as they bounded past, jingling keys and muffled voices the only sound before the door opened and shut.

My dad moved next to my mom on the couch, abandoning his glasses on the arm of the recliner.

"We know how much you love writing. How you've planned to go to college for a degree in English—"

"Why does this feel like an intervention—" I started, but my mom continued.

"Your father and I just think that it has been getting slightly out of hand lately."

I blink. "Out of hand," I said, lifelessly.

They nodded, and I wondered how many conversations they'd had about me concerning the topic. The thought caused a pit to form in the center of my stomach, swirling and choking and tugging.

"I know we've told you before that writing is a fun hobby. And we love that you enjoy it. But we don't want it to take over your life. Your future."

"Take over my future? Mom, this *is* my future." I tried to argue, but she'd already begun to shake her head.

"That's the kind of talk we're afraid of, Stella. Ever since you joined this contest, it's the only thing you've thought about."

"Well, yeah. Because it's *important* to me—"

"Please. Let me finish." She pinned me with her stare, and I clamped my mouth shut, stuffing my hands under my thighs. "It's been the only thing on your mind at such a crucial time in your high school career. You've got college applications to think about, as well as keeping your GPA up, not to mention the ACT that is in just a couple of weeks. Have you even started studying for it?"

Bridger and I actually had started studying, but I kept my mouth shut because I knew it wouldn't help to say so. Her mind was already made up.

She sighed through her nose, leveling her gaze. "We want what's best for you. And we think you can have so many more opportunities down the road if you try for a degree in something more . . . functional."

"Why does it always come back to this?" I laughed bitterly, finally letting loose the emotion I'd been holding back since I walked through the door. "Why can't you guys admit to yourselves that this is something I could actually be successful in? What will it take? Do I have to show you the first-place medal I got tonight as proof to get you guys to *finally* think pursuing this will be worthwhile? Because I won. I got first place." I ripped the medal out from my purse where it lay at my feet and plopped it onto the couch in front of them.

"And we think that's great." My dad finally spoke. "We really do. But we also just . . . we want you to focus on what's important."

"Why don't you guys get that—"

"You're not going to write the next *Harry Potter.*" Mom's voice cut sharply through the air like broken glass.

I fell silent, mouth agape as tears burned my eyes. "I never said I would." My lips trembled, and my vision blurred. "I just wish you guys would believe in me." The words hung in the air, twisting around us before they dissolved like they never even existed.

"You need to start focusing on your junior year. Then maybe we can talk about this like civilized adults." And with that, Mom stood and left the room. I stared at the place she'd just sat, unmoving, unable to look anywhere else.

My dad followed her out, and I got a sad, heavy sense of déjà vu.

Minutes passed. I started to move through the living room in a numb silence, grabbing my purse off the floor and the medal from the couch. I walked to the stairs, and when I made it to my bedroom, I dropped everything onto the floor and sank onto my bed just as my phone finally lit up in my hand.

I slid the button across the screen, not even bothering to say *hello*.

"How'd it go? First place or what?" The warmth in his tone, the sheer enthusiasm in his voice, caused any restrained emotion I had to vanish. Tears streamed down my face as I tried to muffle my sobs.

"Stella? Hey—Stel, what's wrong?" Bridger's tone instantly changed, and I blubbered out some incoherent words, not even sure what I was trying to say. "If you didn't win, that's okay. I'm still proud of you. It's not—"

"No—no," I croaked out. "I won."

Brief silence from the other end. "Yeah? I knew you would," and then, softer, "so why are you upset?"

I took a shuddering breath, feeling everything and nothing at all. "My parents didn't come. No one did. They didn't even tell Daniel and Dahlia about it because I know Dahlia would've come. They didn't tell her on purpose because they didn't want anyone to be there, and they were trying to prove some stupid point to me that I don't matter to them." I took a breath after I finished, the life gone from my lungs.

"*What?* They—huh? You've got to be kidding me," he said under his breath. I heard his murmured voice on the other end, presumably talking to his dad. "Stella, we just landed in Seattle not too long ago. We're in the car now. I'm having my dad head straight to your house, okay? I'll be there in twenty minutes."

My brows furrowed, and I shook my head even though he couldn't see. "No, Bridge. Don't worry about it. Didn't you hear me? It doesn't matter. I don't matter. None of this"—I glanced around at the books and papers stacked around my room, at the short story sprawled across my bed—"none of this fucking matters. Don't worry about me. Please." I hung up and let my phone drop onto the bed.

Minutes later, I still hadn't moved. I lay there, staring at the ceiling. The cold, circular shape of the medal was still digging into my back from where I'd dropped it on the bed, a constant reminder of what I'd won—and, in turn, had lost.

I immediately felt guilty for hanging up on Bridger, but I had meant what I said. He didn't need to worry about me.

Slowly sitting up, I picked up the medal, weighing it between my hands. I replayed the evening in my mind—how embarrassing it all was. How my parents had known and chosen not to show up for me. How they intentionally didn't tell my brother about it. I thought of how small and stupid they'd made me feel afterward, and all of a sudden, my throat closed up, and my vision went cloudy again, and I stood and chucked the medal on the floor.

After it bounced off the rug with a satisfying thud, I stared down at it before moving over to my desk. Unable to control my breathing, I grabbed all of the previous versions of my story, all stacked in neat piles on top of one another. I stared at the color-coded and marked-up papers, and then they were wet because my tears couldn't stop falling on them, and I couldn't catch my breath, and then I was ripping them, ripping them and tearing them and throwing them behind me, page after page. I whirled to my nightstand, grabbed the award certificate, and ripped that too, and then my eyes landed on the portfolio I had so carefully started to curate, and I started to tear it up as I sobbed there, cocooned in a white blur of falling paper and the smell of spilled ink. I couldn't think straight, couldn't catch my breath, couldn't hear beyond the thundering in my ears, and then there were arms around me, catching mine, stopping me, and I was fighting against them even though I didn't want to, even though they were the arms I'd been waiting for all along. I fell to my knees, sobbing and shaking, the remains of the shredded papers still clutched between my fingertips.

Those strong arms were still around me, holding me, squeezing me, and as my breathing slowed and posture slackened, I started to make out the familiar voice whispering against the roaring in my blood, the pounding in my ears.

"Please, Stel. *Breathe.*" His hand was rubbing up and down my back, his other arm still supporting me. I thought about how many times we'd been here before, me falling apart and him holding my broken pieces together.

"You're okay, I've got you," he said softly, gently, tenderly.

"Bridger," I croaked in barely more than a whisper. My throat felt raw and my lungs felt bruised.

"I'm right here," he said as he moved my hair away from my face.

Any earlier anger I'd felt melted away into pure humiliation and shame, and I lifted my head, surveying the damage around me. I blinked rapidly, trying to push away from him, dropping my head into my hands.

"You should go." The words came out mumbled.

He was silent. After a few moments, I looked up, surprised to find his eyes slightly glassy and red as well, his hair awry, and his expression faintly bewildered. He dropped his head to keep my gaze. "I—no. Stel, I'm not going anywhere."

"I'm sorry," was all I could say, dropping my gaze back to the floor.

He shifted closer to me again, his hand gently resting on my back. "Are you okay?"

I just shook my head, feeling the tears forming yet again.

"Come here," he said, helping me to my feet and moving me over to the bed. I sat down, and he knelt in front of me, gently prying my fingers open and removing the paper still clutched there.

"Can we not talk about it right now?" I whispered, unable to even look at him. I sank back onto the mattress, not waiting for his reply as I eased my feet up underneath me.

"Whatever you need." And he didn't say anything else, just settled down next to me and wrapped me in his arms again before the exhaustion took me under.

When I awoke, Bridger was gone. I watched as the morning light peeked through the blinds, creating soft yellow hues on the hardwood floor—and sat up. I looked at the floor again.

The *clean* floor.

Fighting against the lump in my throat, I stood on shaky legs, not bothering to care that I was still wearing my dress from the night before. I took note of the small trash can that sat by my door and the ripped white pieces of paper piled inside.

Then my eyes roamed to my desk, breath catching in my throat as I saw the one remaining copy of my story sitting intact upon its surface. The ripped certificate had been taped back together, the medal sitting on top of it. I walked over to it and ran my fingers along the scratched surface. Picking the story up, my breath caught in my throat when I realized the crumpled pages had been smoothed out and placed carefully on top of each other —in the correct order. A small, orange Post-it note sat on top, six words scribbled in an achingly familiar scrawl:

*This story deserves to be told.*

My eyes clouded again, my head still throbbing from the night before. I laid the papers down, feeling the weight of yesterday crush me with full force. Sharp, hot embarrassment washed over me, and I couldn't believe the way I had reacted last night, how Bridger came to my house, how he had to clean up after me.

How he'd always cleaned up after me.

It was almost as if yesterday was a different me, like I hadn't been in my body. Last night felt like a scene that I had watched from the outside, one that unfolded in a plane somewhere else that didn't really exist.

I hastily shrugged off my dress, stepping into an oversized t-shirt and grabbing a pair of pajama shorts. I lay back down, letting the exhaustion pour over me once again, unable to face the day. Unable to face anything.

And as the quiet oblivion of sleep threatened to take me under again, I felt that boulder slowly rolling on top of me, crushing me, squeezing the life out of me until there was nothing left, just the shell in which I moved through the world. No one's fingers were there to try to lift the boulder anymore, but even if there had been, it would've been too heavy. It all was.

Bridger <3

3:42 p.m

I am so sorry.

Are you okay?

Yeah. You know I tend to have a flair for the dramatic.

Seriously. You didn't sound like yourself on the phone, and then . . .

Stel. I'm worried

Don't be. It's all good, everyone needs a toddler-level temper tantrum every once in a while, right?

And thanks for cleaning up my room . . . You really didn't have to.

It was the least I could do. I still feel terrible we missed the awards

Seriously, you cannot be blaming yourself for this.

I should've been there.

It's okay!!! I'll just win another one, no biggie

EASY.

Just so you know, I kept one of the copies of your story.

I'm gonna sell it on eBay one day for the big bucks.

Oh, great idea! You'll have just enough for half
a tank of gas if you're lucky.

How'd you get in here last night, anyway?

Your window was open. I scaled the
garden wall

???

We don't have a garden wall.

I know, unfortunately I'm kidding

I knocked.

And here I almost thought my flair for the
dramatic was starting to rub off on you.

;)

I passed off my emotional explosion to Bridger as just that—
an emotional explosion. He called me after his last message, and
I filled him in briefly on the conversation I'd had with my
parents after the competition. He seemed to understand. As best
as he could, anyway.

And after that night, I knew there were layers forming, could
feel them as they did. I thought later maybe I could've stopped
them, but then again, even if I had known how I don't think I
would've cared enough to try. It almost felt like a veil was slowly
casting itself over my life, above my head, covering my heart in
shadow.

I felt it move in like the tide, coming out to meet me and then
receding away. I felt it cover my toes like a wave, slowly burying
my feet in the sand. Every day, the sand got deeper and deeper,

and I should've moved my feet. I should've asked someone to help me move my feet.

But that's the thing about the current.

It comes and it goes, fleeing from the shore almost as fast as it approaches, and you don't realize your feet are buried until you can't see your ankles.

I should have moved my feet.

I should have moved them.

But I never did.

# 40

## NOW

I take Adam up on his offer to help out at the garage, showing up right when the shop opens at eight in the morning the following Saturday.

The nostalgia that hits me as I walk through the door is almost as strong as being in their house again. Everything looks the same, save for the fact that there's only one car sitting in the open garage. I remember Bridger saying business has been slower since the accident because his dad isn't able to take on as much, which makes me all the more inclined to help.

"Hello?" I call tentatively as I make my way toward the back of the shop. Reaching the small alcove where the office is tucked away, I cross the threshold and knock twice on the doorframe. Adam looks up from where he sits at the desk, instantly beaming.

"Stella! What a pleasant surprise." The first thing I notice is that he's wearing the same uniform he was the first day that I met him, and the second thing my eyes catch is that his arm is no longer in a sling.

"Hi. Should I have called first?" *I should've called first.* "You said I was welcome to come and help anytime, so I guess I took that literally," I say, hoping I don't look as stupid as I feel.

"No! No, not a problem at all. I think today is the busiest I've been in a while, so you picked the perfect time. Granted, it's only three oil changes, so I should be done here around eleven . . . but you're more than welcome to stick around. You remember how to sort the paperwork?"

"Yeah, I think so," I say.

"Perfect. You can make camp just like you used to, and I'll go get a couple things ready for you . . ." He trails off, moving back out toward the main garage.

*Just like you used to.*

I try not to let myself think too much about the weight of his words as I sit in the small folding chair that's pulled up to the side of his desk. As I wait for him to return, I take in the office around me.

My breath catches when my eyes land on the familiar photograph still positioned on the wall behind the desk—Bridger in that tiny soccer jersey, that toothless smile grinning at me in the same way it always had. Then I notice the smaller, more recent photograph taped to the wall beside it.

It's Bridger in a hospital bed.

I can only assume the photo is from six months ago, after his ACL tear and surgery. He looks tired and slightly gaunt but is smiling nonetheless with a thumbs-up aimed at the camera. His leg is elevated and wrapped, and there's a singular "Get well soon" balloon on the table next to the bed. My heart collapses in my chest, and I feel a rush of sadness and admiration for him all at the same time, at the way he can still be *him* through everything that this life has thrown at him. The way he's never lost himself.

"He was in a bad way after the injury," Adam's grave voice says from behind me, and I jump, not realizing he had walked back into the room. He sets the stack of papers he brought with him on the table in front of me and follows my gaze to the photos taped on the wall. "I think that was the first time I'd seen him smile since he got back to Washington."

I don't know what to say, so I continue staring at the picture, letting the weight of it soak into my skin until it crushes me.

"This was from a few days after the first surgery when he was told he'd be able to play again." He sighs sadly. "He was stoked."

Emotion burns in the back of my throat, and I want to look away from the picture, but I can't. "It must've been so hard after the second surgery." I can feel my shoulders droop. "When he found out he couldn't play anymore."

I see him nod out of my peripheral vision. "He was crushed. More so at what things could've been, though, I think. Realizing he'd never get to finish out his senior year." He pauses, clearing his throat before continuing. "It's hard when you do something you love for the last time without knowing that it's the last time."

Running a hand over his short hair, he takes a seat in the office chair behind the desk and swivels it to face me. Picking up the coffee cup sitting in front of him, he takes a long sip, probably not really knowing what else to say. Or how to say it.

Lowering my eyes to the floor, feeling like this is still somehow my fault, that it can all be traced back to me, I ask the question I've been wondering since I found out he lost his scholarship. "How'd his mom take it?"

I regret asking almost as soon as the words leave my mouth. His dad's whole demeanor darkens, and he grips the coffee mug in his hands so tightly I worry it'll shatter.

"When he tore his ACL again, she was worried, of course. Called him that night. Once she knew he was okay, they had a long talk about the importance of getting back out there. About how seriously he needed to take rehab and physical therapy. How important it was. To her."

Continuing to stare at my shoes, I take a breath, angry at his mom but knowing I have no right to be because I wasn't there, either.

"When she found out he had to have another surgery, she was . . . livid." He blows a breath out of his mouth, sets the mug down, and drops his hands into his lap. "Made Bridger feel like shit about it. He told her not to call him again unless she wanted an update on how he was doing." He releases a pained laugh. "She hasn't called since."

My eyes blur, my throat tightens, and I almost feel like I know too much—that I shouldn't have pried at all. My heart has never felt this heavy before, and I wonder if this time I can survive the weight of it.

"I'm sorry. I shouldn't have asked. It's not my place," I whisper, wiping my eyes quickly, hoping he won't see the tears that I don't deserve to be crying fall down my cheeks.

"Stella." He smiles at me sadly, grabbing the small box of tissues from the far corner of the desk and handing them to me gingerly. "You'll always have a place here."

The tears come quicker now, and I pull another tissue from the pack. I don't trust my voice, and I have no clue what to say anyway. There are no words to describe the continuous grace that he and Bridger have shown me since I've come back into their lives.

Leaning forward in his desk chair, Adam looks me in the eyes, folding his hands loosely. "Did he ever tell you the reason it took the hospital so long to contact me after he was rushed there this past winter? Why they weren't able to notify me right away?"

Bracing myself, I shake my head, not sure if I want him to finish what he's about to say but knowing I need to listen.

"You were listed as his emergency contact."

The air leaves my lungs, and I'm glad I'm already sitting because my legs go numb beneath me.

"Well, your old number was, anyway. They couldn't get ahold of you—obviously, because that number didn't exist anymore, we know now—but they had to wait until he regained consciousness to ask him for another contact. He was so disoriented that he probably doesn't even remember. But I do. I always will."

The tears keep coming, and the measly pack of tissues in my hands has no chance against them. I feel so stupid, so devastated, so entirely and wholly crushed that I can't seem to get in a proper breath. Adam stands, takes a step toward me, and places a hand on my shoulder.

"I don't tell you this with the intention of upsetting you, Stella. Not even close. I just . . . I thought you should know. Even after the time apart, even after whatever happened between the two of you, it was still you. For him, it was still you."

I stare down at the tissues in my hands, lip quivering, feeling like an idiot. I'm at a complete loss for words, unable to comprehend any of the past five minutes.

On a shaky exhale, I ask, "Why do you still care? About me, I mean? I thought you would hate me. For what I did . . . for what I thought I had to do—" I break off again, voice cracking.

He leans back against the desk, crossing his arms against his chest and lightly massaging his shoulder. It's such a Bridger thing to do that at any other time or any other minute, I would laugh or find comfort in the familiar postures. But right now, I just feel hollowed out and empty.

"I loved you like you were my own. For the entirety of high school, it was the two of you. It was the three of *us*. That whole time . . . I'd never seen Bridger happier, more alive, more himself. You brought that out of him. You did that for him."

"*No*, no, that's not—I didn't—"

"You brought that out in each other. Anyone with two eyes and a beating heart could see that." He smiles softly. "That's not something you can just forget."

I focus on my breath, on the inhale and exhale, the slow

expansion of my lungs. "I'm sorry," I say so quietly that I'm not even sure he hears me.

But then he says, "Me too." He stands and dusts off his faded jeans. "I'll leave you to it, then." He smiles at me with a warmth in his eyes that I do not deserve before patting the doorframe twice. "Let me know if you need anything, okay?"

I nod once before he disappears back into the garage.

Staring at the stack of papers in front of me, I wonder how I let it all go so wrong. I try to get back in that headspace, to feel an ounce of the depth and weight of what I did three years ago, to try to understand why I did what I did. But that day still feels like I floated through it in a daze, the weeks following it a hazy blur that I haven't been able to quite piece together.

I still wear that pain like my favorite sweater, I realize now. Won't take it off, even though it's battered and torn, and there are rips in the seams. I don't even like how it looks on me anymore. I don't think I ever have. I've tried to take it off before, but it's a few sizes too small now, and it gets stuck over my shoulders, and I know I'll never be able to.

I wonder how much longer I can wear it, if I can leave it on forever, or if it'll eventually suffocate me.

Sighing, I look back at the papers.

I begin filing.

# 41

I don't glance up for the entirety of the time I'm sorting through the papers, losing myself in the monotony and repetition of the task. I think that was why I liked helping out in high school, back when Bridger always said he'd rather watch paint dry than sort through the paperwork. I liked the rhythm of it. Still do, I realize. I don't mind the work at all. There's something almost peaceful about knowing exactly where something is supposed to go—organized and in line and set up in a way that my brain is not.

I'm almost to the bottom of the stack when a voice cuts through the small office.

"I'd rather watch paint dry than sort through that paperwork."

My head shoots up from the desk, and I take in a full breath for what feels like the first time in hours. Bridger leans against the doorframe, giving me a relaxed grin, car keys dangling from his finger. His messy chestnut hair flops lazily against his forehead, annoyingly perfect like it's always been. Wearing a loose-fitting black shirt with those light gray sweatpants I've always loved, I almost can't believe he's a real person standing in front of me.

I didn't know it was still possible to feel this way at the mere sight of someone, how knowing someone so deeply can feel like a beginning and an ending all at once.

He straightens, twirling the keys around his finger once before throwing them into his other hand. "I'm taking you to lunch."

I blink. "Hmm?" My cheeks burn because I know I was caught staring, and he knows it too, grinning at me with that Cheshire cat smile that I've loved since I was sixteen.

"*I* am taking *you* to lunch," he says again, slower, as he walks around the desk and holds out a hand to me.

Blinking again, I grab his hand and let him pull me to my feet. His hand is warm and heavy, and I will my features not to deflate when he lets go.

"What time is it?" I say, my voice coming out almost croaky. He smiles at the sound of it.

"Almost twelve."

My eyes widen. "Really? I thought . . . your dad told me he'd be done around eleven."

"That was the old Adam. The Adam with two working arms," he says, and I bite my cheek, knowing he's joking but not wanting him to be. "I came up here about an hour ago to help him wrap up, and we just finished."

I'm not sure what he sees in my expression, but his features soften slightly, and he reaches his hand out, squeezing my elbow once. "He makes jokes like that all the time. I didn't like it at first, either." He shrugs, a muscle working in his jaw. "I think he needed to lighten it somehow, you know? I started doing that, too, a few months after my second surgery."

He scrunches his face at me, pulling his head back slightly. "Hell, you resort to humor all the time. It's your favorite coping mechanism," he says, and I purse my lips to hide my smile, shaking my head.

Forcing my face back to neutral, I shrug. "Humor wasn't always my favorite coping mechanism," I say seriously.

He tilts his head, brows knitting together. "Oh yeah? And what was?"

I stare directly at him, not missing a beat. "You."

His lips part in surprise, and his eyebrows shoot up, color immediately finding his cheeks. I burst into laughter, unable to hold it in anymore, and then he's laughing, too, full-bellied laughter that warms me from the inside out.

I look at him again and see his arm bracing against the desk as he catches his breath, and I start fanning my heated face. "Ah, man. Nope, humor is definitely still my favorite."

He exhales as he shakes his head, still grinning at me. He backs away to the doorway, brows raised once again. "Are you coming or not?"

After getting food from our favorite takeout place, we're back in the car. Bridger drives us to an "undisclosed location," insisting we eat outside. We sit in companionable silence, listening to the music softly playing from the speakers. I squint against the sunlight, and Bridger glances over at me and pulls the visor down to shield my eyes. I don't bother trying to hide my smile.

We pull up to Kerry Park, that smile growing as he parallel parks. Grabbing the bags of food, we begin the ascent up the many concrete stairs.

"Why did we pick this place to be our spot? This is—so much work," I say breathlessly after cresting the top of the hill.

"Because it's iconic," he says easily, voice carrying up from behind me. He appears next to me, and I give him a disbelieving look. "I mean, come on. Did you know that Meredith Grey's house is just up that hill?"

A smile breaks across my face again, narrowing my eyes. "I think everyone in Seattle knows that Meredith Grey's house is just up that hill," I say mockingly, lowering my voice to try to mimic his.

"That is not what I sounded like in high school."

"Yeah, well. We must have a different remembrance of who we were back then." I shrug lightly, but his expression falters for a split second, and his eyes fall to the ground.

"Yeah. I guess so."

Feeling like I got punched in the gut, I turn away and walk to the benches. I focus my attention toward the woman sitting on my left with a small easel in front of her as she paints the sky with pastel blues and whites.

A few seconds later, Bridger joins me, and we stare out at the skyline like we have so many times before. He places the bag between us, but all of a sudden, I'm not hungry. We poke at our food in silence for a few minutes, staring at the city and the water beyond.

The weight of the earlier conversation I had with his dad comes back in full force, and I think of how unfair I've been to him all this time, of all the ways he's deserved better. The ways that he still does.

"Where'd you go just now?" he asks quietly.

I continue staring out at the water, the afternoon sun shimmering brightly against it. I wonder what I should tell him, if he'd even want to know that I know. If he even knows himself.

Taking a slow breath, I decide that, at this point, I have nothing to offer him if not some sliver of the truth. "I was thinking about something your dad told me. When I went in to help this morning."

He stiffens slightly next to me. "What'd he say?"

Tucking my hair behind my ear, I lower my gaze to the

ground. "He said . . . he told me that when you were in North Carolina, and you got hurt, I was still your emergency contact. That they tried to call me first."

I hold my breath, chancing a glance at him. He exhales slowly through his nose, eyes closed. His throat bobs once before he opens his deep brown eyes again, locking them with my own.

"Yeah. I guess you were," he says, looking back toward the water. He runs a hand through his hair, exhaling again. "I mean, as far as I knew, you were going to be the only family I had out there with me. I didn't . . . I must've never gotten around to changing it."

My chest tightens at that one word, the word he threw out so casually, the one that I know means more to the both of us than we'll ever let on. I wonder if he even realizes he said it.

"Honestly, I did think it was weird, though, when they asked me for a parent's phone number after I woke up." He sighs, looking back at me. "But, then again, I had a few more things I was worried about, so . . . I probably didn't linger on it for too long."

A few more moments pass in silence. I'm still thinking about my conversation with Adam earlier, so I say the one thing I know I probably shouldn't. "He also told me about your mom."

He scoffs, a humorless laugh escaping that feels . . . off, coming from him. "What about her?"

"That she hasn't talked to you since your second surgery."

He shrugs, his hand mindlessly dropping to his knee. "It's true. She hasn't." He lifts his gaze back up toward the water, a new emotion reflecting in his eyes. "Not that I'd expect her to, though, you know? I mean, honestly. She has spent my whole life checking in when it was convenient for her, making sure I was still on track to becoming the soccer prodigy she needed me to be. Once that dream failed, once it all came crashing down— what use was I to her? What could she possibly have had to gain from me?"

My mouth falls open, never having heard him speak of her like this before or put it in those terms. "You're her *son*," I say exasperatedly, needing him to remember, to be reminded that this is not how it's supposed to be, that he shouldn't have to *do* or *be* anything to warrant her affection. That he shouldn't have to earn her love.

Then I realize that those words probably wouldn't mean much coming from me.

"Well," he says as he leans back against the bench, hands clasped loosely between his legs, "that has never mattered to her before, has it?"

He says it so pointedly that I have to swallow against the lump in my throat and blink against the confusion that I know is surely marring my face. "You've always given her the benefit of the doubt." It's a question in the form of a statement.

It was something I'd always admired about him, the way he never gave up on people, the way he never turned his back on someone he loved, even when it was more than undeserved.

I look at him and study that faraway expression, trying to read his closed-off emotions. I wonder when that changed in him, when he decided it wasn't worth the fight anymore. Wonder when he started to let go.

Wonder if it had to do with me.

"That's just it. I always did—and for what?"

As I shift on the bench to face him, I'm about to tell him we can drop it and that I'm sorry for bringing it up. But he's not looking at me.

"And besides, it's not the first time someone has cut off all contact without warning. So," he shrugs, cold and unflinching, "who is the common denominator here?"

A lead weight drops into the pit of my stomach. My breath goes shallow, and my body goes numb as my heart pounds in my chest.

"Bridger," I breathe, a quiet broken plea. "Bridger, *no*—" I break off as my blood roars in my ears, unable to stomach the thought of my worst fears being true.

*It's my fault.*

I want to reach for him, to hold him, to touch him, to shake him until he comes back to me. Until he can believe me when I say it had nothing to do with him. But he carries on, continues talking, and I let him because I deserve to hear the words falling from his mouth.

I deserve this.

"And I get why my mom did it. In a weird, backward way, it's almost been a sort of strange relief. But . . . it was never that way with you. There was no explanation, no reason, nothing I could pin it up as or mark it down to. Not one moment I could go back to and say, 'Yes, that, *that* is where it all went wrong.' I could never make it make sense in my head. And believe me, Stel. *Believe* me, I've tried."

He takes a shuddering breath, and I don't think I'm breathing at all. I am weightless, floating, somewhere between him, here, and the me from three years ago that made him this way.

"Bridger. What happened . . . I didn't mean for it to end this way. I thought we'd all be better off if I . . . if—" I break off, unable to finish the words. I feel pathetic. So pathetic and so, so tired. "It wasn't your fault."

His throat bobs out of the corner of my eye. "You keep saying that." He says it so quietly I almost think he didn't mean for me to hear it. But then he turns to face me, and I see the storm of emotion raging in his eyes, in his posture, in his gaze. His eyes are glistening, and I wonder why, lately, we've always ended up this way. Together but not, battered and bruised, wholly broken. I'm bleeding out from the empty space in my heart that he used to take up, from that gaping hole that's shaped like him.

He's bleeding too. I wonder if his wound is shaped like me.

"Stella . . ." He stops himself and quickly lifts his shoulder to wipe away his tears. He swallows again, meeting my gaze. "I keep thinking that I can hang out with you, spend time with you, be around you, and be okay with being your friend because that's what you wanted. That's what you said you could offer me. And I thought I'd rather have you as a friend than not at all. I couldn't let you go again.

"But being *near* you but not being *with* you, it's . . . It almost feels like losing you all over again. Every time." His voice breaks, and so does that final piece of my heart. "Just when things start to feel normal, just when I think that hole in my heart is finally starting to mend, you pull away again. The walls go back up, and I'm on the outside.

"I thought the pain of losing you was the worst I'd ever felt, but now I know—" He cuts himself off, takes a steadying breath, and wipes his eyes again. I can barely see him through the tears in my own as they leave hot trails down my cheeks, my shoulders shaking with silent sobs as I wait for him to continue.

"Now I know that the pain of loving you when I can't be with you is worse. I don't want halfway. I thought I could be friends, but I can't. Not when it's you. So, I guess . . . I'm here when you're ready to talk. When you're ready to tell me what happened. But *please.* Please, Stel, make up your mind. Either let me in, or . . . or let me go."

We sit there, crying, hearts open and bleeding. I can't believe I ever thought he'd be better off this way. I'd say I wish I could go back and change it, but I can't think of any other outcome where he ends up happy. Not if I'm still in the picture.

We stay there in silence for a few more moments, and I grab the takeout napkin he offers me before taking one for himself. We sit there and wipe our eyes in the rubble of what once was. The storm came, just as I feared, and it desolated the town once again.

He crumples the napkin in his hands, leaning forward. I pull my legs to my chest, trying to make myself as small as possible, wishing I could disappear with the west Seattle wind. Dropping my forehead against my knees and shutting my eyes, I lose track of time again, silently hoping that he's left me here. It would serve me right.

Just as I start to convince myself he had, his voice breaks through the afternoon air. "Let me take you home."

I startle, my head snapping up from where it still rests on my knees. "What?" My voice comes out raspy and dry. "No, it's fine, I'll call someone, or—"

"Stella." All the fight has left his voice, and I know it's left mine too. "I didn't bring you out to a park to just leave you here." He stands, grabbing the empty bag and extending his hand to me. "Come on."

I stare at his hand, wondering how—after the conversation we just had, after everything he told me—he could even tolerate being near me, let alone offer me his hand. Taking it slowly, I let him help me to my feet. I let go as soon as I stand, taking the bag from him and hurrying to the trash can just to have something to do. I throw it away, stare into the empty cylinder of plastic, and wonder if now would be a good time to throw up.

"I don't think tossing in a penny will work. Trash cans aren't like fountains, you know."

I jump slightly at the sound of his voice so close to me again, and when I look back at him, he has almost a wistful look in his eyes and something like sorrow painted across his beautiful face. I wonder if it's for him, for us, for me, or for what we might've been.

"Yeah, well. Can't blame a girl for trying, right?" I try to joke, but the words come out flat, all the emotion drained from them.

He inclines his head, and we make our way over to the stone stairway. I can't help but think of this same walk we made the first time we came to this park together over five years ago, hand in hand.

"Do you remember the first time you brought me here?" I ask quietly, trailing the stairs behind him.

He freezes for a split second, and I almost smack into his back—but then he resumes walking. "How could I forget?"

I can't read the emotion in his voice.

We arrive at the flat sidewalk and start walking down West Prospect Street toward his car. I fall into step beside him, wondering why I even brought it up. I'm going to drop it and let us carry on in silence when he says, "I was so nervous that day."

My step falters, breath catching. "You were?"

He turns and looks at me incredulously. "Do you know how long I'd had a crush on you by then?"

I shrug, staring at the ground, heat rising to my cheeks. We walk a few more steps in silence before we approach his car. "Did you know that was my first kiss?" I ask.

He doesn't say anything, and I look up at him to find a slow smile spreading across his lips. My stomach flips, and he says, "Did you know it was mine?"

My eyebrows scrunch, looking to the sky as if I'll find the answer there. He laughs lightly as he makes his way around to the driver's side.

I wait for him to unlock the door, but he freezes with his hand on the keys. "Do you miss it? Who we were then?" he asks as he looks back up at me.

The question catches me off guard, and I hesitate. "I think they had a lot to learn." I meet his stare over the top of his car. "I think they still do."

He smiles softly, sadly, before opening the door and climbing in. I swallow heavily, following suit. We spend the rest of the drive home in silence, two people sharing space, sharing history, sharing breath.

I've shared every part of my life with him, every part of *myself* with him, except for this one thing. This one thing, this black hole, swallowing every part of me and leaving nothing but darkness in the wake of it. The one thing that ruined us, the one thing I haven't been able to talk about in the years since.

He pulls up in front of my house, and I linger in the passenger seat, knowing I can't stay but not wanting to leave. I can feel this strange limbo I've been in with him ever since I saw him in the grocery store parking lot almost two months ago fading away, cracking through, slipping between my fingers.

I don't know how I ever thought we could carry on like this.

My palms start to sweat as my pulse starts to thrum, and I can hear my heart still beating his name.

He puts the car into park, fingers drumming along his leg. "You don't have to say anything now." He runs his hand over his mouth, dropping it back down. "Just—think about it. What I said. Okay?"

Slowly, I open the car door and step out into the sunlight. "Okay."

The ghost of a smile plays on his lips. His dimple flashes, gone as quick as it came, and I shut the door. I walk to my front porch and watch him drive away the same way I did that night.

Maybe this time, we'll have a different ending.

# 42

## THEN

August, Senior Year

The summer before senior year, I kept up my job as a lifeguard and spent most of my free time helping out at the shop with Bridger's dad to make up for the fact that Bridger wasn't there.

He'd gotten scouted to attend the UNC Summer Training Camps, so from mid-June to early August he was in North Carolina, training with his prospective coaches and possible future teammates.

It was huge.

And I didn't mind the extra work—it was easier to busy myself with that than to spend too much time alone with my mind, which I was beginning to learn was a scary place to reside unchecked. So I worked a lot, wrote a little, answered every single one of Bridger's calls, and spent more time with his dad than my own family. Yet, for all I crammed my schedule with, the months went by agonizingly slow.

Things seemed to be moving right along for everyone else, though, as always. My parents' respective businesses were thriving, and The Abode's new blog practically went viral. My mom used this momentum to plan the first annual charity gala hosted by The Abode in July, and it went better than even she had hoped.

Probably because I was assigned to be the doorman, smiling faintly at everyone who arrived and watching over my shoulder as my family sauntered around, making their rounds and welcoming the guests.

Dahlia was practically paraded around the event by my mother, who introduced her to everyone as if she were her own daughter. At least Dahlia had the decency to throw me an apologetic glance every time she caught my eye.

Meanwhile, I stood just outside the doors to the rented ballroom, watching the event unfold from a safe distance. *She'll be less trouble that way,* is what my mom didn't have to say.

A few weeks later, on an evening when I stayed at the shop late to help finish sorting through paperwork, I arrived home to an empty house. After showering and changing into my favorite sweatshirt of Bridger's, I got a text from my brother in a mass group chat to all of the aunts, uncles, and cousins we hadn't seen in years. My stomach dropped the instant I opened the message and saw the photo attached. I looked at the screen, seeing the four faces staring back at me, each one grinning broadly. My mom, my dad, Daniel, and Dahlia were huddled around the phone, Dahlia wiping a tear through her joyous smile and holding up her left hand pointedly to the camera.

I called Bridger, put it on speaker, dropped my phone onto the bed, and stared at the photo. My parents, their son, and the daughter I'd never be.

"Hey! I have about a five-minute break in between sessions. I was just about to call you," he said brightly. His voice was a solid weight through the speaker, something real to hold on to, to steady myself with.

"Stel?" he said again after I hadn't spoken a word.

"Daniel and Dahlia are engaged." The words came out flat, lifeless.

"Oh—wow! Well, congrats to them," he said, meaning it. I didn't reply. "That's . . . good, right?"

"Yes." I swallowed. "Yeah."

He hesitated. "Convincing." Then, softer, "What's going on?"

My eyes stung, and I closed out of the photo, bringing the phone up to my ear as if that would bring him closer somehow. "Apparently, she got engaged tonight. I just found out through a group text with all my distant relatives. Very personal."

He released a breath. "You didn't know it was happening?" My silence said enough. "Shit. Stel, I'm sorry."

I marveled at the whole of it, at how I felt like I was on the outside of everything, separated somehow, like I was no more important than a second cousin and not an immediate member of the family.

I stretched my legs out on the bed in front of me, staring at the ceiling. I sighed. "You know, I don't know why I'm surprised. They've been together for over three years now. They're adults. That's what you do, right? Of course, that's what you do."

"Sure, but it's okay to be—"

"You know what? Forget I even said anything. This is just me overreacting like my mom would say, right? Chalk it up to being an angsty teen. The usual."

"Stel—"

"Actually, I don't even blame them for not telling me. I wouldn't have wanted me there either, honestly—"

"Stella." His rough voice cut through that messy train of thought, my voice halting at the seriousness of his tone.

I stayed silent, practically holding my breath.

"Don't invalidate yourself. You're allowed to be upset about this. If I had a brother and he got engaged and told everyone in my family but me, I'd be pissed too."

I snorted. "Well, when you put it that way."

He sighed quietly. "I wasn't trying to—"

"I know. I know, I'm sorry." I got the nagging feeling that he was sick of me. I tried to push it away.

Muffled voices carried over the line, and a second later, Bridger's voice was clear through the speaker again. "The next session is about to start. I'm sorry, Stel. I'll call you after, and we can talk more about it, okay?"

I nodded, even though he couldn't see me. "Okay."

"I love you."

I fought the growing tidal wave of emotion and refrained from asking him, *"Why?"* Instead, I just whispered, "I love you," and disconnected the call.

Staring at the ceiling again, I traced the shadows as they moved across the plaster, wondering how anyone had put up with me for this long. I always seemed to make everything more difficult for everyone. I took everything personally, or the wrong way, or overreacted.

No wonder I wasn't invited to the engagement party. No wonder they left me out of these things. They were tired of me. And as that single tear rolled down the side of my face, I realized . . . I was tired of myself, too.

# 43

"You're so tan."

Those were the first words out of my mouth when Bridger stood before me for the first time in almost two months. He grinned, pulled me into his house, and wrapped me in a bone-crushing hug. I melted into him, held him tightly, breathed him in. It didn't feel real, having him here again, feeling his weight against me. Being away from him for those two months was like looking away from a lamp when you're in a dark room and noticing the absence of it more heavily—like the darkness just seems darker without it.

I pulled back to look at him before he brought his hands up to my face, smiling softly before he leaned in and kissed me. It was a perfect kiss like they always were with him—slow and unhurried like we had all the time in the world, because then, we thought that we did.

He smiled into the kiss, and I did, too, because for the first time in a long time, I felt like I belonged somewhere.

I knew it was always said that home wasn't a place, but I never knew the weight of that sentiment until I experienced it. No one talked about how scary that could feel—to know that your sense of comfort and security could be gone from you in an instant. Finding your home in a person is a lot like going on a road trip with half a tank of gas. It'll work for a time, could last for a while, even. You might make it, if you're lucky.

But it hadn't taken me long in life to realize that I wasn't.

Breaking apart, I took a mental image of his bright eyes, flushed cheeks, and swollen lips. I nodded my head toward the living room. "Tell me everything."

We walked over to the couch, and I plopped down against him. Instantly, I snuggled under his arm, burrowing into his side like I could build a house and hide forever. I felt his chuckle reverberate through his rib cage as he pressed a light kiss to the top of my head.

"It's all boring, really. You'll fall asleep on me."

I scoffed, leaning back and looking him in the eyes. "You think so little of me."

He rolled his eyes playfully and leveled me with a look as if to say, "*Come on.*" But I narrowed my gaze right back, and he sighed, relenting, and launched into all of it. The scouts, his possible future teammates, the hotel he stayed in, the drills they did, the coaches and staff he met.

It seemed like an amazing opportunity, and I told him as much.

"It was, Stel. I'm so glad that I went."

"Me too." I played with the hem of his t-shirt, focused on the soft fabric underneath my fingers. "I'm really proud of you. You know that, right?" I mumbled against his chest. He huffed out a laugh. Before he could respond, I leaned back to look at his face again. "I know I don't say it enough, but I am. Super proud."

He gave me a bemused smile. "Of course, I know that." He reached up and moved a stray piece of hair away from my face. "Where's this coming from?"

I shrugged, not really knowing myself. "I just had to make sure."

Another one of those slightly confused smiles. I leaned forward and kissed it off his lips. Snuggling into his side again, we fell into the easy silence that we only ever seemed to have with each other. A few minutes passed in that silence as my mind wandered farther and farther away. The fears that I had shoved aside the entire summer were now flashing neon signs in my brain, and I debated on whether or not to bring them up.

But with Bridger, I knew, I never really seemed to have a choice.

"I can hear you thinking. Where'd you go just now?"

I sighed, forgetting how well he could read me. I shifted against him, leaning my head against his chest, unable to look him in the eyes. "So. College."

"Mm-hmm?"

"Do you think it'll be hard for us? To be apart for that long again."

He went still beneath me. "What do you mean?"

I let out a long breath. "If I don't get into UNC and have to stay here and go to school somewhere in Washington, or . . . Oregon, or something. And you went to North Carolina. We'd be apart for, like, months at a time. Double what we just were."

He was silent for a moment. "We wouldn't be if we both got in."

I swallowed. "I know. But I'm also trying to be realistic. I had an average ACT score, my grades aren't, like, phenomenal, and I'm not a soccer prodigy, so . . . the chances are slim."

"Okay, first of all, you need to give yourself more credit. And second of all, I might not get in, either."

"*Pfft.* Come on, Bridge. You *will.* You're amazing. And now, all of the important soccer coach people and scouts know it too."

"It's still not guaranteed."

"I guess not, but—hypothetically."

He exhaled through his nose. "Hypothetically . . . if I went to UNC and you stayed here, we would make it work."

I pulled back and peered up at him again. "You'd want to try?"

His brows furrowed together instantly, and then I watched as that confusion slowly gave way to something closer to sadness. "You . . . wouldn't?"

"No! *No.* I mean, yes! I—I *mean,* that's not what I'm saying."

He nodded slowly. "Okay." He blinked once. Twice. "So, what *are* you saying."

I released myself from his grip slightly, putting distance between us so I could gather my thoughts. "I'm saying that, obviously, we'd try. And we'd probably kill it." A small smile from him. "But . . . four years is a long time."

He shrugged. "Not when we've got the rest of our lives."

A slow smile spread across my face despite the tightness coiled in my chest. I nodded my head in agreement. "We'll figure it out."

He pulled me into him, and I settled back into my spot. "Don't stress yourself out about this now, okay? We still have a whole year. So much can happen in a year."

Though I knew it was meant to be comforting, I couldn't ignore the lead weight that dropped into my gut as his words.

I didn't think either of us knew how right he'd be.

Autumn arrived slowly at first, subtle breezes blowing through the evenings, golden sun reflecting off the orange-tinted leaves. Like a lot of things seemed to for me, it arrived gradually, quietly, and then—all at once.

Crisp air, flannel jackets, football games, and borrowed sweatshirts. I drifted through the season like a ghost, tethered only by the one hand that never let go of mine.

Bridger became close with a few guys on the soccer team that season, and I often found myself hanging around these friend groups—there, but not really.

One of his friends in particular—Ben—had a girlfriend named Katie, and we got along pretty well. She was quiet, too, and never really seemed to know what to do in a group setting either. So, we idled around each other, Bridger and Ben always close by. We talked about school, the weather, college plans, soccer games. And I tried. I was trying.

They tell you that your high school years will be the best of your life—and that terrified me. I felt weighed down under the thought, stuck underneath it, wondering if that really was as good as it got. If those four years were supposed to be the best of my life, if that was supposed to be the end all be all, then I didn't really see the point of anything beyond that. I felt myself starting to lose focus. Lose my grip.

But on those days that I sat there, looking at the friendships around me, at the ease and surety of them, I thought to myself, *Maybe I could be normal. Maybe this could be okay. Maybe I could be okay.*

And then I'd get home to see a new college brochure on my desk, bookmarked and tabbed on different pages, sometimes opened to a business or marketing degree circled in red pen. And then I'd think to myself—*no. No, maybe I won't be.*

But I didn't tell Katie any of those things. I didn't tell Katie, and I didn't tell Dahlia, and I didn't tell Bridger. They were the people who had so much going for them, so much to focus on, so much to look forward to.

Why would I weigh any of them down with that pointless, unnecessary burden?

So, I kept quiet. And I smiled when I should have, laughed when I was supposed to, dodged Bridger's concerned glances, and hoped he couldn't feel my constantly sweaty palms.

But in those moments where he'd squeeze my hand, catch my eye, and give me that small smile I had loved for the better part of my shitty high school existence, it would remind me that there was good in the world.

And I wished I would've centered myself around that feeling, could've breathed in that golden-colored light. But I think there was always a part of me that knew it wouldn't last, that could feel the façade already fading. That feeling was a growing current, and it was heavy.

It was so, so heavy.

So, as I sat there, hanging out with people I knew I'd probably never see again come June, I felt like I was watching the moment slip through my fingers from somewhere else far away —the moment lost before it was even gone.

# 44

## THEN

October, Senior Year

Bridger's senior season was the best he'd had yet. They were undefeated, he was on top of every chart in the Division, and he was getting contacted by scouts left and right. He seemed genuinely surprised every time a new email or phone call came in, and I was just happy to sit by and watch it all unfold from the best seat in the house.

And so, as I sat there on Senior Night, at his final home game ever, a gold, glittery number four painted on my cheek (at Katie's insistence, as she'd painted a number ten on her own), I felt almost as much as I saw his future opening up for him, this wide, glistening road of possibilities and countless days ahead. I was *thrilled* for him.

And yet, when I tried to look into my own future, tried to think of anything beyond the moment I was experiencing, all I saw was a desolate dirt path with tumbleweeds blowing by in a sticky breeze.

The picture was unnerving, so I simply stopped imagining it at all.

I pulled my jacket tighter around myself, still cold despite the fact that I had Bridger's hoodie on underneath it. Scanning the stands around me, I wondered where Katie had gone. It was easy to lose her in the crowd, though, because the stadium was packed to the brim with family, friends, teachers, and loved ones. Times like these made me glad I had never really gotten into any sports because as I looked around the stadium, I thought, *Who would've shown up for me?*

As I had the thought, I looked over at Bridger's dad. I could practically feel him buzzing with nervous and excited energy. I thought to myself, *He would've.*

The game was close, and at halftime, the score was two to zero. The first goal had been scored by Bridger and the second by Ben—which was precisely when I found out where Katie was sitting.

"I'm going to head to the concession stand. You want a hot chocolate or anything?" Adam asked me as he started to stand.

I nodded vigorously, and he chuckled before patting me on the head and walking away. I snuggled deeper into myself, watching as Bridger and his team disappeared into the locker rooms on the far side of the field. I stared at my shoes, those same white Converse I had worn during that first soccer practice I sat and watched sophomore year. I thought of all that had changed since then, and how so much was different. Almost everything was different—except him.

Except us.

I thought about last year when I watched his first game alone and had a panic attack in the bathroom, and I realized for the first time how different it felt to be sitting there then. Not because of some internal growth I'd had or some breakthrough I'd experienced, but because of this dull sort of nothingness that had blanketed over my subconscious that hadn't been there before, a shadowy film that acted as a cover between me and the rest of the world around me.

It wasn't that I didn't feel anxious sitting there alone or that I had gotten used to it somehow, but almost that there was no part of me that seemed to care anymore. This quiet numbness I'd decided to attribute to the cold and didn't care enough to read into.

Later, I knew that I should've.

The players emerged from the locker rooms, taking the field once again. My brows furrowed upon noticing that Bridger's dad still hadn't come back from the concession stand, but with one look at the packed stadium around me, I figured he might not be back for a while.

And I was right.

The game ended in a three-to-zero shutout, and it was Bridger who snuck in one more goal within the last thirty seconds. I'd never seen him smile so big as I watched his teammates circle him, slapping him on the back, jumping and celebrating. The crowd in the stands went wild around me, and yet, I swore I could hear his laughter from the field.

Standing up, I quickly made my way down the stadium stairs to the archway that led to the field where the athletes exited after their games. I shifted on my feet, waiting for Bridger, glancing around for his dad, blowing warm air into my hands and rubbing my arms.

Finally, the team came off the field, and everyone around me started to cheer. Going up on my tiptoes and peering over heads, I finally spotted him at the same moment he spotted me. I felt a grin break across my features, a matching one brightening his as he moved quickly through the crowd, his eyes never leaving mine.

I raced toward him, eager to get my bones moving again but more eager to be wrapped in his arms. And then, finally, I was. He scooped me up and twirled me around, and my laughter rang out around us.

When my feet finally touched the ground again, he pulled

back and kissed me lightly. I didn't even care if we were in a crowd full of people because, at that moment, it was only us.

"You did it."

His face broke into a lopsided smile. "We did it."

I laughed. "Right. Me sitting up in the stands, cheering, and eating a hot dog really changed the tides."

His smile faded into something deeper as he said, "You being here at every game . . . it really did."

My eyes stung, and he kissed me again before tucking me against him. I savored the feel of him, the quiet calm of his presence in the middle of the chaos.

"You know, if confetti was falling around us right now, this would feel a lot like One Tree Hill."

His laugh rumbled through his chest as he murmured against my hair, "This is better."

I squeezed him tightly, then pulled back again just as the roar of the people around us came back in full force. Suddenly, everyone was there, patting him on the back, shaking his hand, and congratulating him on the win. I stood at his side and watched him take it all in, my heart fluttering every time he glanced over at me to make sure I was still there.

When the crowd started to fall away, he turned back to me and let out a deep breath, his eyes still bright. "Where's my dad?"

I frowned. "He went to get hot chocolate for us around half-time but never came back up to the stands . . ." I trailed off, worry overtaking my features.

"I'm sure the lines were really long. Maybe he just picked the wrong one—" he started to say but was cut off by yet another familiar voice.

"Bridger."

His eyes lit up upon hearing his dad, his voice an immediate answer to our unspoken question. But I knew something was wrong the second I watched him look over my shoulder to greet Adam. His face fell, eyes instantly cast into shadow. As I whirled around, Bridger quickly put a hand on my shoulder, steadying me and keeping me close. His dad's expression had evened out, giving away nothing.

I took in the woman standing before us—black pleated pants, crisp white blouse under a pale pink blazer, deep chestnut waves curled to perfection with not one hair out of place. One look at her high cheekbones and amber-colored eyes and my stomach sank to the ground as I realized a second too late who the woman standing before me was. Bridger cleared his throat from behind me, pausing for a second before saying, "Hi, Mom."

# 45

"It'll be okay," were the words his mouth was saying, but his face was saying something completely different. After a brief introduction between me and his mom at the field, Adam announced they were having her over for dinner and that I was more than welcome to come. Bridger had no idea, of course, but, come to find out—his dad had no idea she was planning to show up either. He saw her walk in when he was at the concession stand and wanted to intercept her before Bridger spotted her.

"She hates me," I said.

"She does not."

I gave him a pointed look.

He pursed his lips, trying to hide the smile peeking through. "Okay, well, she's like that with everyone. Even me," he added under his breath. At my silence, he looked over at me and lamely attempted a smile.

I looked ahead at the yellow lines guiding the way home. "Is it weird that we've been together for so long, and I've never met her in person?"

He shook his head. "When she lives in California and hasn't cared to visit me once over the past few years? No. Not at all."

There was a slight bitterness in his voice, and I picked up his hand that was anxiously drumming on his leg and laced his fingers through mine. He held on tightly, and we drove the next few minutes in silence, both of our minds wandering somewhere far away from the confines of the car.

I looked over at him again as I traced the back of his hand with my fingers. "Where'd you go just now?"

He smiled before looking back at me. "That's my line."

I laughed softly with a small shake of my head, watching the smile slowly fade from his face.

He sighed. "I don't know. I guess I'm just wondering why she waited until my Senior Night to show up again. It almost feels like some sort of weird omen?" He shakes his head. "That probably doesn't make sense."

"It does," I said, gently urging him to continue.

"I just feel like I'm on the precipice of the start of my life, of a new sort of freedom, and she just showed up to remind me. To remind me that she has . . . power over me or something?" He took a sharp breath before continuing, "But, at the same time, I'm happy she's here, which feels just as dumb. Why should I care that she finally bothered to show up?"

I squeezed his hand. "Of course, you care, Bridge. You, of all people. Everything you're feeling is valid."

He sighed again, and it sounded more like one of relief. He squeezed my hand tighter, a familiar, grounding anchor between us. "My therapist is going to love this," he said under his breath, and we both laughed as he pulled into the driveway. The gravel crunched under the tires as he slowed to a stop, and we stared at the front door, unsure of what awaited us inside.

And then, we got out of the car.

An hour later, we sat around the dining room table after finishing the fancy carryout from a restaurant I'd never even heard of that Bridger's mom apparently insisted on ordering on the way here.

The dinner had gone by pretty smoothly up to that point, with surface-level talk about school, California, her job (I remember Bridger telling me she's an attorney, hence the business casual attire at a chilly evening soccer game), her flight here (which she got on promptly after a long day in the office, she'd said), and, of course, the game. It wasn't until she brought up college that the familiar weight pressed against my chest, not really wanting to broach the subject with anyone, least of all her.

But what did I say about me and luck?

"So, Stella," she said before taking a long sip of her water. She turned toward me, and for the first time all evening, I had her full attention.

I forced myself to sit up straight and meet her gaze.

"Where do you plan to attend college?"

Steeling myself, I said, "I'm not one hundred percent sure yet. I've applied to UW, of course, The University of Oregon, and a few schools on the East Coast as well. So, I'll just see where I get in and make a decision from there." I wiped my sweaty palms on my legs. Bridger reached under the table and gave my thigh a gentle, reassuring squeeze.

She nodded, her lips slightly pursed. "Do you at least know what you're planning on majoring in?"

"Molly," Bridger's dad said quietly, a soft warning.

She gave him an innocent look, and I willed my heart to slow to a normal pace. It felt like a test, somehow. One that I'd already failed.

It struck me then how completely opposite she and Bridger were. I'd always known that, but seeing it right before my eyes gave me a whole new perspective. I wondered how on earth someone like Bridger could've come from someone like her. But then, I realized Bridger didn't come from her, not really. Not in the ways that counted.

When I thought of Adam, of all he gave up and all he sacrificed to be there for his son—it hit me just how deeply that well of love ran. How lucky Bridger was to have him.

And in that moment, I was thankful. I was thankful Bridger was raised by his dad. A kind, selfless, honest love that I realized his mom had probably never known. And for a second, I almost felt sad for her, but then I remembered she chose this life for herself. As Bridger told me once a couple of years ago, she'd made her choice.

And I couldn't have been prouder of the boy sitting beside me.

Then I looked at him, at his tight jaw and stony expression. I cleared my throat, gathered my strength, and said, "English."

Her eyebrows immediately rose. "Oh? And what do you plan to do with an English degree?"

Any confidence I'd gained within the last five seconds disappeared instantly. I felt the heat creep into my cheeks because that was the exact situation I'd told Bridger about countless times over the years. The second I told anyone I was going for English, they either laughed, raised their eyebrows, or chuckled and said, *"And what are you going to do with an English degree?"*

And every time, it became harder and harder to give them an honest answer and mean it.

My eyes fell to the table, where, out of the corner of my eye, I could see Bridger white-knuckling his water glass. I tried to shoot him a look as if to say, *"Don't worry, I'm used to this,"* but he wasn't looking at me. He was glaring at his mom, who mindlessly dabbed at her mouth with a napkin, waiting for a response.

"I want to be an author," I said with zero conviction.

A tight smile spread across her features. "And do you have a plan B?"

Bridger's fork slammed against the table, and he said, voice low and rough, "And why would she need one?"

"Bridger," I said quietly with a brief shake of my head.

"I mean, I just think it's smart to be pragmatic—"

"Mom." I'd never heard his voice sound so cold. "Stella is an incredibly talented writer, and you don't get to waltz in here and just—"

"*Bridger,*" I pleaded, grabbing onto his arm. He took one glance at the desperate look in my eyes and closed his mouth, still seething, a muscle working in his jaw.

"It's true. She just won a competition last spring with her short story—I've read it. The win was well deserved." Adam's voice cut through the tension, trying to lessen it.

I tried to smile at his dad in thanks but was distracted by Bridger's tense form beside me. "It's okay. It's not worth it," I said so quietly that only he could hear.

"It is to me," he replied.

I cleared my throat and forced myself to meet Molly's unrelenting gaze, the not-so-subtle judgment in her eyes. "I'm actually working on my first novel right now. So, hopefully, throughout college, I'll be able to revise and edit it and make it the best it can be, and when I graduate, I'll start submitting it to agents. That's the plan, for now. And if it's not getting picked up by anyone, then . . ." I shrugged. "I'll just keep writing books until one does."

She nodded, seemingly unconvinced, but apparently decided the conversation was over because she turned to Adam and said, "And how's the shop?"

As I let out a shaky breath, Bridger found my hand under the table. He grabbed it, brought it up to his mouth, and placed a kiss on my knuckles. He didn't look at me for the rest of the dinner, and thankfully, the conversation never fell back to me. After another thirty minutes, his mom announced she had an early flight to catch. We said our goodbyes, and then Bridger and I were finally alone in the car again.

"I'm so sorry," he said quietly.

"You—what? What for?"

He gave me a hopeless look. "My mom. That was so—she shouldn't have—" His shoulders dropped, and he blew out a breath. "She really pissed me off. She had no right to talk to you like that."

"Bridger, it's okay." He opened his mouth, no doubt to say, "*No, it's not*," but I continued before he had the chance. "It's what I've told you every adult says when I tell them what I want to do. I'm used to it."

"You shouldn't have to be."

I shrugged and tried to steady my voice, attempting to make it seem like I was unaffected. "It is what it is. I'll just have to prove 'em all wrong, you know?" I said, lightly punching him on the arm.

He looked at me with a sad smile on his face, almost as if he believed me as much as I believed myself.

Not at all.

But we didn't say anything more on the topic, as if he could sense I'd rather talk about anything else. So, we did.

And when he dropped me off, kissed me goodnight, told me he believed in me, and that he never wanted me to forget that, I told him I never would. And I meant it.

And when I walked up to my room, when I lay down on my bed, and when I cried myself to sleep . . . I wondered if he would always be the only one.

# 46
NOW

"Well, that could've gone worse." Maggie laughs as we sit down at our usual table. The converted coffee shop has quickly become mine and Maggie's go-to place for an iced latte after class.

We just presented our final project for the semester, and I hum in appreciation at the first sip of my iced vanilla chai. "I'm just glad it's over," I reply, moving the ice around with my straw.

Maggie releases a long sigh, taking a long sip of her coffee as well. "I'm kind of going to miss it, if I'm being honest."

I scrunch my nose. "The project?"

She snorts. "Hell no. I meant the fact that it gave us a reason to hang out all the time." She sighs again, quieter this time. "This is going to sound really lame, but I don't have a lot of friends. So, in a way, this has just been . . . nice."

I blink, a foreign warmth spreading through my chest. "That's not lame at all. I barely have any friends, either," I say, smiling. But then my smile slowly fades. "Okay, well, actually, you're my only friend." We burst out laughing, and I'm thankful for the ease between us, the way I don't have to think about what I say around her.

"Trust me when I say this has been the highlight of my college experience so far," she jokes, and I laugh over another sip of my coffee. "And to think, I was so against taking summer classes."

"I felt the same way," I say, shaking my head. I set my drink down, tracing the condensation on the side of the cup. "Are you heading into senior year?"

She nods. "Thought I'd get at least one hard class out of the way. The fewer credit hours I have to take next semester, the better." She takes a sip of her latte. "Same for you?"

"Um . . . kind of. I'm also going to be a senior, technically, but taking summer classes is my way of trying to catch up." I swallow before continuing. "I finally declared a major last year."

She nods, unfazed. "So, are you just a little behind because of that?"

I nod, wondering how much I should say, not wanting to scare her off. "That, and the fact that I deferred my first semester in the fall. There was a lot that happened the summer before, and I just wasn't really in a good place. Mentally." Taking a deep breath, I continue, "I was trying to figure some stuff out and just . . . get better."

Now it's her turn to nod. "Was it serious?"

I hesitate, still not having broached the subject with anyone. But I realize now, maybe that's the problem. I don't know if it's the fact that Maggie had no preconceived knowledge of me before this summer, the fact that she didn't know me in high school, or the way there's no judgment in her eyes. Whatever the reason, it gives me the courage to steel myself and just simply say, "Yes."

She nods again. "Are you doing better now?"

"Honestly?" I move my hands back to the cup, dropping my gaze and tracing the outlines once again. "If you'd asked me a couple of months ago, I probably would've said no. But I think— I think now I'm ready to try."

She smiles, a true, genuine smile, and says, "That's good enough for me." Then her expression goes serious. "I don't know exactly what you've been through, and you don't have to tell me. And I know people think talking about mental health is taboo or whatever," she says with a slight shake of her head. Fiddling with a ring on her right hand, she flicks her eyes toward the ceiling before settling her gaze on me once again.

"And maybe I'm way off the mark, but . . . I see a lot of similarities between us. I think I could see that from the moment we met." Shrugging, she adds, "I could see the weight you carried in your eyes, in the way you spoke about yourself. I'd know because I was the same way a few years ago."

I swallow, not knowing what to say.

"So, just know that whatever it is, whatever it was, you aren't alone. And I'm here if you ever, *ever,* need someone to talk to about it." She offers me a small smile. "Lord knows I could've used a friend back then."

Emotion swells in my chest, and all I can manage is a small "Thank you."

I don't know what to say. Or think. Maggie, this girl I've known for a couple of months now, the girl I would literally describe as sunshine in human form, has faced the same struggles I've dealt with. That I deal with. And what surprises me the most is that after knowing this about her, it just makes me admire her that much more. The fact that she's accepted it as a part of her story, that she can talk about it so openly and honestly—it hits me that I never thought it could be like this. Those words that I wouldn't dare whisper within the walls of my own home, shared across a table at a coffee shop with a new friend. And maybe there's something to be said about that quiet sort of strength.

In the quiet strength that it takes to endure.

I blink, focusing back in on Maggie as she leans across the table and pats my hand twice.

"What are friends for?" She smiles, wiggling her eyebrows. Sighing, she swirls the remains in her cup. "So, we're both about to be seniors, then?"

I laugh, the thought hitting me for the first time. "I guess so."

"Maybe some of our courses will overlap again! Our majors are similar enough, right?"

A small smile tugs across my face. "I hope so." And I really, really do. It's never occurred to me—ever, really—to look ahead at anything anymore. My life since three summers ago has been spent simply trying to get through the day ahead of me, making sure my head got to the pillow at night over and over and over again.

I didn't think I deserved anything else. I'm still not sure that I do. But, as I sit here with Maggie, looking ahead—it feels good. It feels like something I can hold on to.

And an hour later, as we walk out of the coffee shop, I feel a little lighter, some small weight lifted from the ever-present pressure on my chest.

"Oh! I forgot to mention," Maggie says, tossing her keys between her hands. "What's this whole charity gala thing that's happening next weekend? My mom got another invite, and it's all she's been talking about. She's insisting on dragging me and my siblings along again. I told her she should at least have the decency to leave Miles at home, considering what happened last time he was at one of these events, but . . . anyway." She half laughs, rocking back on her heels. "My sister Maisy and I will be joining her, at least."

I rub my temples in memory of the football that struck there, stifling a laugh. Then the laugh turns into a sigh as I'm reminded of the gala. I wonder briefly if this year I'll get to actually be in the venue instead of just at the door. "It's an annual event The Abode puts on. Since my mom is co-owner of the company, she plays a bigger part in putting it all together—hence the personal invitations to her clients."

She nods slowly, contemplating. "Okay. Is it fancy?"

"Very."

"Will there be dessert?"

"Of course."

"Are you going to be there?"

I feel a smile tug at my lips. "Yes."

Another nod, firmer this time. "Then I will be too."

I sigh again. "I'll warn you, though, the last time I was at one of these events, I was the door holder. So, you might not see a whole lot of me."

She frowns. "Is there more than one door?"

"Yes . . . ?"

She grins. "Then we'll be door holders together."

# 47

## THEN

April, Senior Year

I passed through the rest of senior year like a shadow.

The first semester ended almost as quickly as it began, as snowy pine drifts and final exams gave way to warm spring breezes and rain-dampened streets.

Bridger found out he got early admission to UNC back in December, and I thought he was the only one who was genuinely shocked. We celebrated by going out to eat with his dad, who surprised us both with UNC hoodies and proudly acquired a baseball cap for himself. The selfie the three of us took that night is still Bridger's lock screen, and the pure look of joy on his face in the photo was one of my favorite things, which was why that picture quickly became my lock screen, too.

I found out I got waitlisted back in February, and all things considered—I thought I was going to get flat-out rejected—I took it as a win. The only college that had officially accepted me was UW, which was a relief to know that at least one school would have me.

Bridger had been so busy with soccer training camps, conditioning, and workouts during his final spring season with his club team that I had more time to spend on my own. I finally finished the ten-book series I had been reading for the past few months, wrote a few more short stories, tried to rebuild my portfolio, and stared at the untouched document that was my novel.

These things were a welcome distraction from the looming storm cloud that continued to spread itself over my heart, my mind, and my life. I continued to ignore it and act like I didn't notice its impending presence over me every second.

Come March, Daniel and Dahlia's wedding was just barely two months away, and Mom hadn't even cast a glance in my direction in weeks. They were due to graduate at the end of the month, and then they would be back in Seattle for good.

Mom was having the absolute time of her life helping them plan the wedding, and honestly, I couldn't even blame her for it because I had the strange feeling she would never help plan one again.

And as far as fancy events went, Bridger felt terrible that one of the last UNC training camps fell on the same weekend as prom. He insisted he'd make it up to me after I relentlessly thanked him for giving me an excuse to not have to go play the part for an evening. And I think he felt worse because he thought I was playing it down for him, trying to make him feel better, and I didn't know how to tell him that I wasn't. That I just couldn't find it in me to care.

The fact that I was starting to notice scared me more than anything.

Because I knew I should care about missing my senior prom. I knew I should want to pick out the perfect dress with the matching shoes and feel the butterflies in my chest when I walked down the stairs to see Bridger waiting for me, to see him look at me in awe, to dance with him and laugh with him and be with him.

But I didn't care about missing senior prom. Not in the way that I should have.

With all the time I had to myself and all the time I spent in my head, I started to feel like I was a shell. A shell of the girl I once was. A shell of the girl Bridger fell in love with almost three years ago.

I willed myself to quiet that aching feeling, the one slowly freezing my heart and chilling my bones—the feeling that he deserved better than someone like me. Deserved more than what I had to give him.

And I fought that voice in the back of my head every day. But with Bridger gone all the time, my parents preoccupied with the wedding, and Daniel and Dahlia preparing to be married . . . I felt like I was watching from the sidelines. I started to wonder— where did I fit? Where did I belong? And quietly, one day, I realized that I didn't.

I was slowly slipping, slowly fading away, and there was no one around to grab my outstretched hand.

# 48

## THEN

May, Senior Year

The ceremony was beautiful.

In the middle of a lush green garden, a gray stone inlaid path led straight to the altar where an arch stood laced through with different flowers—soft pink roses, white-tipped ranunculus, baby's breath, and, of course, dahlias.

The bride looked ethereal. She was the true embodiment of grace and class as she descended down the aisle in a sleeveless, fitted, white satin gown. Dipped in the back, the dress revealed her perfectly tanned skin, hugging all her curves in ways people dreamed about. The square neckline complemented her perfectly as the pearls on her necklace laid against the hollow of her collarbones.

She was stunning.

As I stood up in front of the crowd, standing last in the line of her bridesmaids, I tried not to fidget under the softly setting sun as she made her way to the front. I looked at the guests sitting before me, immediately finding Bridger in the fourth row, and as we locked eyes, he gave me a reassuring smile and a thumbs up, winking as he mouthed, *"You look hot."* I hoped he couldn't see me blushing from where I stood.

Vows were shared, rings were given, and the new couple was announced.

And that was it. Daniel and Dahlia were married.

At the reception, after finally making it to my family's table, I was nervous when I noticed Bridger and his dad had been seated somewhere else. Then, I exhaled a small breath of relief when I realized that the table in question was the one right behind ours.

I was practically seated at the table alone for the entirety of the meal as my parents went around and said *"hello"* and *"welcome"* and *"thank you"* to the many, many guests who came from all over to celebrate the most special day of *our* lives (as my mother kept putting it).

Relatives I hadn't seen since I was a kid approached the table, commenting on how big I had grown or how I still looked exactly the same (I was never sure whether to take either of those statements as a compliment). By the time the meal was over, I'd lost count of the people who had asked me what I planned to do after high school. When they asked what I was going to major in, their responses went how they always do, and by the fourth person who raised their brows when I said, *"English,"* I'd begun to spare them all and simply started replying, *"I don't know."*

At that point, it felt like the truth.

"Some party, huh?" Bridger said, sliding into one of the empty seats next to me.

"Some party." I glanced at the people around us, some at the open bar, some crowding around the couple I hadn't seen all night, and some already moving onto the dance floor. "I'm glad you're here."

His returning smile was soft and a little sad and didn't quite reach his eyes. "Me too."

He said it with a surety that simultaneously warmed my

chest and dropped a weight into my gut because I think we both knew it wouldn't be like that forever. His hand rested gently over mine on the table. Running his thumb over my knuckles, I savored the feel of it, the quiet intimacy, the innocence of the weight of his hand on my own. The kind of love you didn't have to think about.

The music changed then to a song that had everyone flooding onto the dance floor in a flash of color and laughter. Bridger turned to me with a mischievous grin, and I instantly started shaking my head. He turned my hand over in his and inclined his head over his shoulder to the gathering crowd. I narrowed my eyes at him, trying to glare, but his smile only widened as he stood before me. Grabbing my other hand, I didn't resist as he pulled me to my feet. I couldn't resist as he leaned in and whispered low in my ear, "This can be like the prom we never got to have."

I didn't want to resist as heat crept up my neck, and I tried (and failed) to hold onto my scowl. "I told you I didn't care about that."

"And I told you I'd make it up to you anyway."

And then we were on the dance floor, moving in rhythm to the beat that warmed my veins and rattled my bones. I laughed as he twirled me around, spun me through the breaks in the crowd, and then I wiped the tears from my eyes as he broke it down (his words, absolutely not mine) with the ring bearer in the middle of the dance circle. He was light, and he was joy. A beacon in the dark, a breath of fresh air for all who came near him. He easily chatted with any of my family members who pulled him aside—to compliment his dance moves, to my unparalleled surprise—and made the rest of the night one worth having. I didn't remember the last time I had laughed so much, had felt so at ease within myself.

Being with him like that, free and wild and spinning, almost made the looming decisions of the future seem not as heavy, the incessant questions from earlier not as important.

The music slowed to something slow, soft, and delicate. Bridger extended his arm to me, and I took it gladly, overwhelmed by the weight in his gaze. His hands slid around my waist and mine around his neck, and we swayed slowly to the music, faces close, our hearts in sync.

And as we moved together, as the space slowly closed between us, I looked at his amber-flecked eyes, felt the weight of his hands settled against the small of my back, and breathed him in. I thought to myself, *This is how I will always remember him.*

I knew it then. That in the coming months and even years, this was the moment I would remember. I wanted to take the way he looked at me and paint it across the night sky, blending with the deep blues and fading blacks against the stars that were always there. Those stars that illuminated the darkness by the force of their impenetrable light—not trying to be seen, just shining like they were born to do.

Like he was born to do.

So again, I thought to myself, *This.*

*This is what I will miss.*

# 49

## THEN

June 1st, Senior Year

"**W**ell. That could've gone better," I said as Bridger and I walked up the front porch steps of his house.

"Graduation?"

"High school."

He laughed, pulling me into his chest and kissing my temple. "I don't know. I mean . . ." He trailed off, leaning back to look at me. "I got you out of it."

I gave him a look of disbelief. "Right. And you also got two state championships, a 4.0 GPA, pretty much guaranteed admission to any college in the country, not to mention that everyone loved you . . ." I shrugged. "I couldn't have been the only good thing."

His eyes went soft. "You were the only thing that mattered."

Narrowing my eyes, I fought my growing smile. "So . . . what. You'd give up everything for me if I asked?" I was joking. Entirely.

But to my complete and utter confusion, he didn't even so much as hesitate before saying, "Yes."

I blinked. I didn't know whether to lean into the warmth spreading through my stomach or the dread coiling in my gut as I took in his words and expression. I swallowed, doing the only thing I knew how to, and wrapped my arms around him again. I felt his soft laugh echo through me and buried my head in his chest, trying not to think about the rest of the world as he held me tightly in his arms.

"I would never ask you to do that, you know. Give up everything."

He rubbed a hand along my back, squeezing tighter in earnest. And he said once again without hesitation, "I know."

And I would have stood there like that with him forever if another voice hadn't cut into the silence. I heard the front door open behind us, and then Adam said, "Come on, lovebirds. They're all waiting for you."

I turned around in Bridger's arms, a smile plastered onto my face. Bridger's hands rested upon my shoulders as he gently led me into the house.

Purple and gold streamers lined the ceiling, twisting together as they draped throughout the living room. There were matching colored balloons strewn all over the floor, and the small dining room table to my right was full of dessert. Brownies, banana bread, no-bake cookies, buckeyes, caramel pretzels, lemon squares—and strawberry poke cake, in the same dish Mom always made it in.

I turned to Bridger's dad, trying to smooth out my expression. "Are my parents here?"

His permanently warm expression faltered for a moment, telling me everything I needed to know without uttering a word. With a slight shake of his head, he said them anyway. "She dropped off the cake right after graduation, saying something . . . came up."

I nodded, feeling so stupid as tears burned my eyes. Why had

I thought things would be any different? Why, after everything, did I finally think they'd show up for me?

"Oh. Okay," I mustered, dropping my gaze and suddenly finding the food table very interesting again.

Adam reached out to squeeze my shoulder, saying, "Everyone's out back whenever you guys are ready," before turning and walking out the door.

I inhaled a shaky breath, and Bridger instantly turned me around toward him.

"Hey," he started.

I just shook my head.

He tried to catch my eye, saying more softly, "Stel."

"It's fine," I whispered, feeling that pit I'd tried so hard to keep at bay yawning wide open beneath me. "I mean, they're leaving for their trip tomorrow anyway. They probably have tons to do. I should just be thankful they actually bothered to come to graduation."

He dipped his head to meet my eyes, grabbed my chin softly with his hand, and lifted my gaze to his. "They should be here." He pursed his lips, and his throat bobbed once as he swallowed. "They should've been there. This whole time. The fact that they weren't, that they never have been . . . that says nothing about you, okay? It has nothing to do with you."

In the past, I would've tried to believe him.

But right then, for his sake, I just nodded.

Clearing my throat, I stepped out of his grasp and tried to smile, to reassure him somehow. Of what, I didn't really know. "I'm just going to go to the bathroom really quick." He eyed me warily, so I said, "I'm good. Seriously—I'll meet you out there."

I kissed him on the lips quickly before hurrying down the hallway. Shutting myself in the bathroom, I leaned against the door until I finally heard the sound of his retreating footsteps. I stayed like that for a while, slumped against the wall, eyes shut, reminding myself to breathe.

Eventually, I looked in the mirror and immediately noticed my red-rimmed eyes and the bags beneath them. I rested my hands along my cheeks, wondering if they seemed more hollowed out than usual. I winced at how pale I looked and pinched the skin to try to bring some color back. Sighing, I turned away, knowing nothing I tried to do would help.

Because this type of tired, this sort of bone-deep exhaustion was more than just needing to get a good night's sleep. It was a deep well, stretching beyond and beneath what even I could comprehend.

I was just tired. Of everything.

Straightening and kicking myself out of my own pity party, I braced myself to face everyone in the backyard, all the while knowing most were there for Bridger anyway. It was his dad's idea to have a joint graduation party, and even though I think he only offered because he knew I wouldn't have had one other-wise, I still appreciated the gesture.

Taking yet another deep breath, I walked back through the living room, through the doorway to the kitchen, and out the back door. The backyard was decorated much like the inside of the house—more streamers, balloons tied to the the back deck, and a "Congrats Grad!" banner along the fence line with an "s" drawn onto the end in sharpie.

A small speaker sat on the ground next to the drink table, playing music that could barely be heard over the loud chat-tering of voices—because there were *so* many people. My heart started racing faster as I scanned the crowd quickly for Bridger's mom, who had made another appearance for his graduation.

*"She hasn't visited me twice in a year since I was eleven,"* he'd said to me earlier. *"It's unsettling."*

To which I'd replied, *"You're graduating high school. Of course, your mom is here."* Ironic considering that my own mother wasn't. We were both silent after that.

There was no sign of her yet, but I slipped along the outskirts anyway. I kept toward the side of the house until poster boards leaning against the shed caught my eye, making me pause. There were pictures plastered all over them, and my breath caught in my throat as I approached. Scanning the images, a small smile crept across my face. There were some of my favorites of tiny Bridger—the iconic soccer photo from his fridge—and countless others of him in different colored jerseys. Then, as he got older, the pictures became more sporadic, and I moved my eyes down the board to where I saw some of the two of us.

There was one of him giving me a piggyback ride in his living room, and then another one taken two minutes later of him on *my* back in the living room, me mid-fall—and I could still hear his laugh as I stared at the photo.

Then there was a selfie of the two of us that he took that day in Kerry Park after we'd had our first kiss. My chest warmed at the sight of our flushed cheeks and bright eyes, marveling at how young we looked, even then.

There was another one of me, him, and Adam after one of his soccer games last year. Bridger stood in the middle with an arm wrapped around each of us, grinning broadly for the camera.

I grinned back at the image, but the smile on my face got smaller and smaller as I continued to look at myself in all of the remaining pictures. In one from sophomore year—after he'd had dinner at my house that first night—I was smiling in the photo, but all I could think about at the time was how embarrassed I'd felt by my family.

Then, the one from before his first soccer game I ever went to —where a few hours later, I would miss the entire second half, anxious in the bathroom. And a different one from a few months ago when Bridger found out he'd gotten into UNC. Again, in the photo, I was smiling, but my curved shoulders and the dullness in my eyes told an entirely different story.

All of those moments, captured in memory forever—people

seeing what they wanted to see. You wouldn't know the half of it by glancing at the photos, how much that girl in the pictures carried under those quiet eyes and timid smile. I didn't even think I recognized myself.

Maybe I hadn't for a long time.

I tore my eyes away from the pictures, unable to bear it any longer. The bright and the dark, the sun and his shadow. The beacon of light and the blanket snuffing it out. The shining boy and the lost girl who thought they'd make it in the end.

Rubbing my hands up and down my arms, I tried to regain control of my breathing. Was it always supposed to be like this? Was it always going to end this way? The world blurred around me, and I quickly wiped my tears. Not here. Not now.

I looked up, blinking back the emotion, and took a deep breath.

"Hey Stella," a quiet voice said from behind me.

Spinning around, I managed to smile. "Hi, Katie."

Her face faltered before she glanced behind me at the photos, at the last four years taped to a poster board, realization pulling a knowing, sad smile across her lips. "It's going to be hard to leave it all, isn't it?"

*No, it's not,* I thought.

But I just smiled back, sighing through my nose, simply saying, "Yeah."

She nodded, wrapping her arms around her small frame. "But you and Bridger are both going to North Carolina, right?"

I nodded. I found out that I'd gotten into UNC Charlotte, which offered an amazing English program and happened to be only two hours from the Chapel Hill campus where Bridger would be. I would've gone anyway, I told him, even if he had chosen a different school. He'd said the same.

"That'll be so nice then, having each other out there. I wish I could go with Ben, but—UCLA is so expensive that I didn't even apply."

I stilled. Is that what people thought? That I was following Bridger like some lost puppy, needing to be near him at all times? A chill snaked its way down my spine, my body suddenly cold despite the summer breeze.

"Right," I muttered.

"Well, it's been fun getting to know you this past year. I know you'll do great things."

She smiled at me warmly and honestly, and I suddenly had the unsettled feeling I should've tried harder with her. To be her friend. But the thought left as quickly as it came once I remembered that I was leaving anyway.

"You too, Katie," I told her and meant it. We hugged and said goodbye, and I turned back to the photographs, not really seeing them at all.

"There you are," Bridger's voice broke through my thoughts as he approached from behind. I wasn't sure how long I'd been standing there, but I figured it couldn't have been that long as the party was still in full swing behind me. I turned, spreading my arms as if to say, *"Here I am."*

He pulled me close to him, tucked me under his shoulder how he knew I liked to be. He leaned in and said in my ear, "My mom just got here. Said a work call held her up at the hotel after the ceremony. She's in the house on another call right now."

I pulled back, trying to read his face. Forehead creased, I said, "How does that make you feel?"

A smile broke across his lips, and my frown deepened. He clicked his tongue. "That was a very Phillip-coded question." His therapist.

I scowled through a laugh, swatting him lightly on the arm.

"It is what it is. She's here, so I guess I should be glad for it."

I nodded, the corners of my lips turning downward again.

Pulling me back against his chest, he murmured into my hair, "What about you?"

I didn't have to ask him to clarify. I just echoed his earlier words. "It is what it is."

Pressing a kiss to my temple, he threaded his fingers through mine and led me toward the food tables.

"All these years, and you finally know the way to my heart," I said, joking, trying to get him to see I was here, I was fine, I was me.

Or maybe it was one last attempt at trying to convince myself.

As he held out a plate for me, I took it and slapped him on the butt with it when he turned around. He whirled, pretending to be shocked. A laugh escaped me, and I ducked under his arm before he could retaliate. I heard his laugh ring out behind me, and I thought to myself—*That.* That would be the sound I would always wish for. That I would hear in my dreams, in my heart, in the reverberations that still echoed at the end of the world.

Just that.

Just that sound.

A couple of hours later, people were still trickling in and out of the party. I sat at one of the tables in a white plastic folding chair, swirling the fruit punch in my cup. I glanced around the yard, surveying the people still talking and laughing. I'd recognized some from school or sports, making polite conversation and smiling when I was supposed to.

Daniel and Dahlia were still on their honeymoon, but I liked to think that if they hadn't been, they would have shown up. I told myself they would've if only to make up for the fact that my parents didn't.

As I stood up to try and move away from those thoughts, I accidentally bumped my knee into the table and simultaneously knocked my cup over. I hissed as the red punch hit my shoe, those same damn white Converse that I really, really needed to stop wearing. Hurrying into the house to see if I could salvage them, I paused upon hearing voices drifting from the living room. I wouldn't have cared and might not have paused if not for the clear annoyance coming from the one voice I knew better than my own. Grabbing a paper towel, I squatted down behind the kitchen island and dabbed at my shoe.

"I just don't understand it, Bridger."

"I don't know what there is not to get."

"Of course, you wouldn't. You're only eighteen."

"What does that have to do with anything?"

I flinched at the sharpness in his tone, my heart picking up speed.

"You don't know what love is! You think you do when you're this young, but you *don't*. Not even close."

And then my heart stopped completely.

They were talking about me.

There was silence. Then Bridger's voice came again, quieter. Angrier. "And how would you know, Mom? Let's not forget that you made some super logical decisions when you were eighteen."

A heavy sigh, and I could almost see his mom then, in her pristine lawyer clothes, hand on her hip, a permanent scowl on her face.

"And besides, you're never even *here*."

"I don't have to be to know that."

"To know *what?*"

"That you shouldn't be throwing everything away for some *girl.*"

Silence. Absolute silence.

Then, "Some girl."

It was a question, I knew, but it came out flat. Hard.

"Do you know who came to every soccer game she could,

even when the crowds made her anxious as hell? Who took pictures and videos and screamed louder than anyone else when I scored a goal? Do you know who helped me study for *hours* on end to ensure that I got a good enough score on the ACT? Who stayed up with me on the nights that I felt like I couldn't do it, that I'd never be all you and Dad hoped I'd be, and I'd crash and burn and fail? Do you know who talked me off that ledge every time? Do you know who encouraged me to apply to UNC on those days when I doubted I even had a shot?"

"Bridger—"

"Do you know who helped me through all of my physical therapy exercises and brought my knee brace to practice and games when I'd forgotten it? Who helped Dad out at the shop for *months* while I was away at training camp? Do you know the one person who has seen me for who I am and not for what I can do? The one who has loved me all these years, regardless if I won or lost or even played the damn game?"

His breathing was uneven, ragged intervals between broken breaths. His mother was silent. "Because it was never you."

I had to put a hand over my mouth to stifle my sobs, the tears streaming silently down my face. I didn't dare move, not then. His mom still said nothing.

"I don't know what in hell you think I'm throwing away by being with her, but whatever it is, it's not worth having. Especially not if it matters this much to you, considering what you've proved your priorities to be these past eighteen years."

Seconds stretched on like the longest night in the coldest winter, and I wondered if she'd say anything else.

Then, after a minute, her cold voice cut through the air. "Is she pregnant?"

I was glad I was already on the floor.

"*What?*" Bridger said incredulously, choking on the word. "What—Mom, *no.*"

Another long sigh. "I'm just trying to figure out why you're taking her with you."

"Taking her—what are you talking about?"

"You don't need to bring a girl to college, Bridger."

"I'm not *bringing* her anywhere. She decided to apply to UNC on her own volition because they have an amazing English program."

I was frozen, lost somewhere between the place on the floor and the tired voices on the other side of the wall.

"Even if that's true, you don't need the distraction. Trust me."

"Why should I? Why would I ever trust you?"

Heels clicked on the hardwood floor. "Because I am your mother."

"When it's convenient."

More silence. I needed to get out of there. I needed to leave. I needed to go. I needed to—

"I just don't want you to end up like me." Her voice was quieter now. Calmer. Heavier.

"Trust me. That is the last thing you ever need to worry about."

I didn't hear her reply. I didn't even know if she did. I heard nothing past the roaring in my ears, the pounding in my chest, the cold in my heart. I couldn't see anything around me as I rose on shaky knees, turned to the back door, and walked out of the house.

I didn't look back.

Bridger <3

4:47 p.m.

Where are you?

I left . . . I wasn't feeling very good

Are you okay?

I'll be fine

Do you want me to come over?

It's okay, you should spend some more time with your mom while she's here

I don't want to take away from your time with her . . .

??? What?

Stel

*Missed call*

The back door is unlocked.

# 50
## NOW

The annual charity gala is in full swing. The beautiful banquet hall is decorated in the way only my mom knows how to pull together—flowers and centerpieces and draping linens that are somehow classy and modern at the same time. The ballroom is stunning, complete with exposed brick walls, an arched ceiling, golden accents and flickering candles. It's elegant and tasteful because Meredith Reynolds would simply accept nothing less.

I've come to learn that this gala is mostly just about the exposure. It's an opportunity for my mom to show off her gifts to the world—to show possible future clients what a firm like The Abode could do for their house, business, school, or office.

And it works. Every time.

The hall is bustling already, with guests, laughter, and loud chatter filling the wide space. Somehow, this year, I've gotten upgraded from door holder to seat director. I'm just happy that I'm actually inside this time.

Almost everyone has arrived, except for the one person that I am silently thankful hasn't shown up. Because after last week, after those things he said at the park . . . I'm not sure he'll be speaking to me anytime soon. And, as always, I don't blame him.

I don't even know what I would say to him myself.

Maggie is here, though, which is the only thing currently getting me through the evening.

"Why do I still feel underdressed? I wasn't expecting this to feel like a royal wedding," she says under her breath, sitting beside me at the guest list table.

I snort. "The true American monarchy," I say, glancing over at my parents.

She hums in agreement, smoothing down her dress. She's wearing a dark blue, seemingly iridescent gown that flows gracefully around her legs with sleeves capped in a sheer, glittery material. She looks stunning, the dark blue bringing out that same color in her eyes.

I look at my own dress, the one my mom laid on my bed last week—ensuring that I play the part, no doubt. A muted lavender color with a sweetheart neckline, the material gathers around my waist before flowing over my hips, with a slit rising up to mid-thigh. It's beautiful. Nothing I would've chosen for myself, of course, but at least she knew my size.

The guests are still milling about and slowly starting to file into their seats, the first course about to be served. I look over at my empty seat at my family's table.

"So, I don't want to sound rude, but . . . is this how it always is with your family?"

I glance up to ask her what she means, but then I follow her gaze back to the table toward the front of the venue where my parents and brother are standing. Daniel is shaking hands with someone I've never seen before, and I can't see my dad's face, but my mom is beaming widely.

And here I am, sitting by the entrance against the far wall, checking off boxes next to names as the people more important than me arrive.

"Um. Yeah." I say with a slight laugh because if I don't laugh, I worry I'll cry.

She leans forward, resting her hand on her chin. "Why do you still live at home?"

The question catches me completely off guard, and I blink a few times.

"You don't have to answer if you don't want to. I just . . ." She hurries to follow up, "I just wonder, I guess. Why you've stuck around for so long when they treat you the way they do."

I pause. I think I should be embarrassed at how obvious it is, but instead, I find myself almost relieved. I swallow, thinking for a moment because no one has ever asked me a question like it before. I clear my throat.

"I think . . . maybe it's just been easier this way," I say honestly after a few beats of silence. "We live close enough to campus that I can easily commute, so I'm saving a ton of money. And I haven't really had any other options."

She turns her narrowed eyes to me. "If you'd had an option, would you have left already?"

I blink again. "I don't know."

She nods. "I get it. Trust me, I do." And she looks at me like she really does. Then sighing, she says, "After my parents' divorce, once my mom and us kids moved back home to Washington, and my dad stayed in Oregon—I realized that I could still love him from a distance. Could love him *better* from a distance. Sometimes some breathing room in a relationship, whether that's family, or a relationship, or a friendship . . . sometimes it can be the thing that saves it."

My eyes are still on my family, watching them as her words sink in, and I realize the resentment I've held onto over the past three years. Realizing it's been building for a while.

I don't want to feel like this forever.

I don't want to feel like this at all.

"In my experience, anyway," she continues. "But what do I know?"

Something warm blooms in my chest as I give her a small smile. "More than me."

Her returning smile tells me she understands.

"Remind me to never wear heels. Ever. Again." Dahlia's voice rings out from the other side of me. Slumping into the chair on my left, she attempts to lean over her belly to rub her ankles. "Hey, Maggie," she manages from her hunched-over position.

"Hi, Dahlia. You look beautiful."

Dahlia sits back up then with a doubtful look, but says, "So do you. Both of you." She winks in my direction. Leaning back and resting her hands against her belly, she says, "I made sure to help oversee what dress your mom picked for you. Gently nudged her in this direction." She dips her head my way.

I squint. "You did?"

She nods. "I needed to make sure the dress brought out your eyes. Lavender is definitely your color."

"Needed to?" I laugh.

"Yes." She nods her head resolutely. "You'll see."

"What—"

But then she's already standing and waddling (somehow gracefully, still) over to Daniel. Turning my attention back to Maggie, my brows furrow when I see the playful glint in her eye.

She leans over to me, saying, "I think you're about to find out why Dahlia made sure you looked hot tonight." She wiggles her eyebrows and says, "Have fun!"

"Wait—" I start, but she's already up and moving to join her mom and sister at their table. I'm about to get up and follow her, but then my favorite voice in the whole world speaks from behind me.

"I didn't realize I'd be attending a royal wedding tonight."

A small smile tugs at my lips despite the fact that my heart drops to my stomach. I turn around in my seat, my breath catching in my throat at the sight of him. "You're not the first one to say that tonight."

He smiles. "Your mom really knows how to . . ." He trails off, his eyes roaming the space, hand gesturing around us.

I just follow his gaze and say, "She really does."

As his eyes continue to survey the room, I use those few seconds to survey him. And as my eyes flit over his perfectly messy hair, the slight stubble along his jawline, and those broad shoulders filling out a black suit—I start when I realize that the man is wearing a lavender button-up underneath.

The same exact color as my gown.

I make a mental note to have a talk with Dahlia later about the fact that Bridger and I aren't together, and she needs to stop trying to make it seem like we are. For each other's sake, if nothing else. But I'll admit, the light purple is his color just as much as it is mine, bringing out the varying shades of brown in his hair, the golden flecks in his eyes, the warmth in his cheeks.

He looks like a dream.

Eyebrows rising slightly, he gestures to the empty seat next to me, and I just nod, not trusting my voice. He slides into the chair, and I try not to outwardly and obviously breathe in the scent of him. I distract myself by looking toward the guest list in front of me, grabbing the pen, and checking the box next to the name that reads *Bridger Wells*. The name my eyes have been lingering on all night.

I set the pen down as he clears his throat. I don't know where we stand. I still don't know what to say to him, and I don't know how much longer he can tolerate being in my presence.

"Hey, listen."

I wait for the final blow, bracing myself for the moment when he tells me we're over for good. When he tells me not to bother finding the words to try to explain, that he doesn't want to hear it. But the words out of his mouth are nothing like the contemptuous ones in my head.

"What I said at the park . . ." He scrubs his hand along his jaw and releases a long sigh. "I'm sorry."

My mouth drops open, and I quickly shut it. I swallow, clearing my throat. "Bridger. You have got to stop apologizing to me. It's quite literally the last thing you should be doing."

He releases another long breath through his nose and turns to face me fully. "You're wrong, though."

I raise my eyebrows, and he purses his lips.

"I just mean that I'm not perfect, either. And while I'm not saying that our breakup wasn't your fault . . ." He pauses long enough for me to snort a laugh.

Leaning back in my chair, I raise my eyes to the far wall of windows. "To say the least."

"Stel."

I look back over at him when I feel a gentle hand on my shoulder, electrified at every place his fingers graze my skin. His voice has gone softer, the joking lilt gone.

"I could've tried harder. You stopped talking to me, and I . . . I let you. I know now that there was way more going on back then that I hadn't realized, and I want to understand it. All of it. I know I've said it before, but—you never gave me the chance to."

I suck in a breath, not wanting him to say what I know he will.

"So . . . please. Give me that chance now."

The lights dim, and I'm thankful for it, unable to meet his gaze. My heart starts racing, my hands go clammy, and my breathing goes shallow. "I don't deserve that," I whisper, needing to get up, to get out. My mom walks to the front of the room and onto the stage, and I use the cover as my opportunity to go. "I need some air," I mutter as I jump out of the chair, racing for the back exit.

# 51

## THEN

June 3rd, Senior Year

Bridger's arms held me from behind as I leaned against the railing, overlooking the city one last time.

Tonight, he was going to leave.

And so was I.

I burrowed into his side, his green rain jacket in my peripheral vision as we stood there, arms around each other, fusing together like we always had.

Like we never would again.

I'd only seen him a handful of times since the graduation party, and I hadn't mentioned anything about the conversation I'd overheard with his mom—but neither had he. I wanted to make every last second with him count, to savor the way that we fit together, to memorize the feel of his hands, his lips, his voice. The way he looked at me, the way he saw me, *really* saw me, in a way that no one ever had. The way no one had ever bothered to.

"Where'd you go just now?" Bridger said softly, warm breath fanning my ear.

But how could I tell him? How could I possibly put it into words?

He was going to UNC in the fall, and I couldn't follow. He couldn't pull that weight around with him everywhere. I didn't want that for him.

I needed more for him than that. More for him than me.

No one I'd ever loved had been better off for knowing me. I ruined everything I touched. It was like an invisible poison ran through my veins, drowning out the lives of those who dared to come too close. My family learned that a while ago. I needed him to learn too.

It was better this way. It had to be.

And yet, for some reason, Bridger looked into my dark places. He looked in, and he wasn't afraid, and I think that was what scared me most of all. That he would be willing to dive in there for me, to find me, and ruin himself along the way.

I couldn't keep letting him bleed every time he reached out to touch my jagged edges.

And he would. He would keep bleeding forever if it meant he was with me. And he wouldn't even mind.

But he'd bleed out. One day, he'd bleed out, and it would be too late, and I would have sucked all the life from him just like I had everyone else.

All I'd ever been was a burden. I made everyone's lives harder just by existing in my own. That veil, that void that had been chasing me my whole life . . . I was ready to stop running from it. I was ready to stop fighting it.

I think I had been ready for a long time.

*You're better off without me,* I wanted to say. *Everyone is.*

But instead, I just turned around in his arms. Looked away from the city that made me and broke me. I buried my face into his chest and wrapped my arms around him. "I'm going to miss you."

I felt him breathing under my palms, the sound of his

beating heart pumping blood through his veins, his breath rustling my hair as it left his lungs.

"It's just for the summer, Stel. We've done it before. We've got this." He gently moved his hands up and down my back. "And after summer conditioning, when you come down to North Carolina, then I'll only be two hours away. Just grab a good book, hop on the bus that runs between the Charlotte and Chapel Hill campuses, and boom. Together at last."

*Together at last.*

Was this how Romeo felt when he found Juliet unconscious? Was this the agony that ripped through Achilles when he saw Patroclus in his armor?

Was this the feeling all the poets wrote about?

Bridger continued, "And then when you get that internship set up for next summer with the English department, we'll both be in North Carolina full-time. It'll be the two of us. Always."

Tears burned my eyes, but they didn't fall. I just stayed there and held onto him one last time.

He was holding on, too.

And as we stood there, breathing each other in, holding each other close, I wondered if he knew.

I've always wondered if he knew.

I held onto him tighter, and I swore he did too. And I let that be enough.

I needed it to be.

Because I couldn't bring myself to imagine a future where Bridger's life was better with me in it.

Where anyone's life was better because I was in it.

And so, we stood there, and we held onto each other. The sun set behind us as he kissed my forehead, my temple, my cheek, my eyelids, my nose. He brushed the hair away from my face, looking at me in a way he hadn't ever looked at me before. A look that I knew was reflected in my own eyes too.

He pressed a featherlight kiss to the corner of my mouth.

Then the other. And then, when his lips finally met my own, the kiss was soft. Slow. It was the last dying ember of light, the final flicker of shadow before the flame went out, the concluding note to the last song of the final show.

It was goodbye.

And then we drove home, the horizon fading away, the sky a smattering of blues and purples and golds, as if the sun was taking its final bow before the curtain closed.

We drove in silence, his hand in mine the whole way home.

Pulling up to the house that I grew up in, the house that had seen it all, he walked me to the front door and kissed me again.

One last kiss.

And then I watched him go, and I already missed him. My vision blurred. I choked on a breath and swore I could hear my heart cracking open in my chest. I listened to the low hum of his engine rolling away and watched his taillights disappear down the hill at the end of my street for the last time.

And I knew.

I knew that he'd go to the University of North Carolina and that he'd lead their soccer team to countless victories over the next four years. I knew that he'd go on to study architecture, pursuing all the things that lit him up from within, from that place where his passions intersected with his gifts. I knew that he'd meet people, and he'd change them for the better by just being exactly who he was.

But more than that, I knew that he would become the person he was always meant to be. He would find joy again, he would see the beauty in life again, and he would leave room in his heart for more.

And he would love again.

Oh, he would love again.

This certainty washed over me, wrapped me up like a blanket, and told me it would be okay. *He* would be okay. That it would be better this way, that this was how it had to be. And it was with that certainty that I walked into the house, went into the bathroom, and shut the door.

# 52

June 4th, 3:19 a.m.

I sat on the bathroom floor for five hours.

I was home alone. I didn't know that at the time, but I also didn't care. I didn't know it had been five hours, but I knew it had been long enough.

I knew he was leaving that night. That he had dropped me off and headed straight to the airport. That at 12:49 a.m., he would get on a plane through the night and make his way across the country. He would fly to Raleigh, North Carolina, where he'd land and check his phone and see a missed call and voicemail from me. I knew even if he hadn't been on a flight when I called, he would've been driving to the airport, and he wouldn't have answered anyway.

And so I called. And I left him a voicemail. I told him that I loved him. That he might not understand yet, but it would be better this way. I told him to stay at UNC and do all he had been born to do. I thanked him for all he had taught me, all he had shown me, and all he had done for me. Made sure he knew that he couldn't have loved me better. I told him again that I loved him and that this couldn't have ended any other way. To let me go. And then I hung up.

And I turned to the medicine cabinet. Grabbed the bottle.

I sank to the floor.

And then I was drowning, and then I was floating, and then I was nothing at all.

# 53

June 4th, 3:19 a.m.

*Dispatcher:* 911. What's your emergency?

*Caller:* It's my girlfriend. Her name is Stella Reynolds, but she's in Seattle, and I'm not there, and I think she—I don't—

*Dispatcher:* Take a breath, sir. What is the emergency?

*Caller:* I—I don't know. She left me a weird voicemail, and I haven't heard anything else, a—and I'm really worried—

*Dispatcher:* What's your name, sir?

*Caller:* Bridger Wells, but I'm in North Carolina, and Stella— she's in Washington, so I don't know how to—

*Dispatcher:* I'll have to transfer your call, Bridger. Do you know her exact county and town?

*Caller:* Uh, yeah. She's—it's—King County in Seaview. Please—please hurry. I don't know what happened—

*Dispatcher:* I'm transferring your call right away.

# 54
## NOW

"Stella, wait."

Bridger's voice sounds behind me, but I keep moving until I burst through the back doors and into the cool night air.

"Stella, please."

His voice breaks, and I stop. I can *feel* him behind me, can hear his pain as if it's physical.

"Please, Stella. It is *killing* me not knowing what happened that night. It's killed me every day for the past three years."

"Bridger . . ." I whisper, turning to face him.

"I tried calling. For the next week, I—I didn't sleep, I wasn't eating, I was calling you every day. I was worried out of my mind, and nobody would tell me what was going on. I called my dad to try and find out something, anything. I called Dahlia that first night and then Daniel every day after until he answered, and the day he finally did, he told me you didn't want to talk to me anymore."

Tears spill out of his eyes and drip off his chin. He pays them no attention. "I begged my dad to drive to your house and ask what was going on, to see you, to talk to your parents, to let me know you were okay. I was on the other side of the fucking country—" A sob shuddered through him as he exhaled a shaky breath. "He knocked, and your mom answered, and she said you weren't home. That's it. She said that you weren't home and it would be best if we left you alone.

"So, we did. We did, Stella. Because at least I knew you were out there somewhere, and that you were okay. But there is not one day that has gone by that the voicemail you left me hasn't haunted me. Hasn't left me wondering what the hell happened. So, please. *Please.* Tell me."

He's closer now, and I don't know if he moved or if I did, but we're both crying with our love spilled on the ground between us, and then his hands are on my waist, and my hands are around his neck, and my forehead is against his.

It's just us and our heavy breath and our hurt clouding the night air around us. *Everything has led to this,* I think. *We were always going to end up here.*

I think of Dahlia and all the ways she has tried to help me, of all the ways she has stood up for me. I think of Adam Wells, his kindness and welcoming spirit after all this time. I think of all that Maggie told me about her struggles and her past and her joy despite it all—and the way it's made me appreciate her friendship more. I think of all she said about time, about distance and separation and learning and healing and the love you can still have the capacity to hold.

And with tears in my eyes, I think of Bridger.

And for the first time in three years, I think of that night.

I close my eyes, feeling the lightest brush of his lips on mine, our tears mingling, our hearts on a collision course, heading straight for the other.

"Stella." His voice is barely above a whisper, and it is the most pained I've ever heard him.

The silence stretches on for an eternity. I open my eyes, pulling away. "I needed you to hate me."

"What?" He breathes, his voice distant, aching, somewhere far away.

I step back out of his grip, needing to stand on my own, needing to face this. To face *him*, to let him know this one thing. To give him this final piece that has followed me like a heavy rain cloud, covering everything in shadow, blotting out the faintest sliver of light.

When I finally meet his gaze and see that broken expression cross his beautiful features—I close my eyes again, feeling the hot tears spill down my cheeks. "I was tired of being here."

I can't tell if he's breathing. I can't tell if I am either as I wait for him to speak, to say anything.

"Here? In Seattle?"

A heavy weight drops into my stomach, my insides turning to lead.

"You were coming to North Carolina. We were both going to—"

"No. Bridger. No, not in Seattle. I mean . . ." I trail off, taking a shuddering breath, willing myself to hold his eyes. And then I whisper into the night air, "I was tired of being *here*."

I watch the exact moment it clicks for him, the exact moment the weight of this truth that I've carried with me these past three years hits him like a blow right to the heart. I watch as his face drains of all color, as the tears come faster, and he raises a shaking hand to the hollow of his throat. The pain that contorts his face is almost unbearable to see—and this is it. This is the moment I was trying to avoid all this time. The one that I knew I wouldn't be able to bear, the moment that I knew would kill me even if my mind couldn't.

I almost want to look away as he doubles over, a hand on his knee, the other clutching his stomach, sobs racking his whole body. I step toward him, unable to see clearly through my own tears scalding my cheeks as I reach for him, hold him, rub his back like he's done for me countless times before.

"You . . . you tried to . . ."

He can't finish the words, and I nod, confirming what we both wish wasn't true. He looks up at me, and his face crumbles again. I let him hold me. I let him tuck me under his arm, bury his face in my shoulder, and hold me tighter than he's ever held me before.

"*Stella, Stella, Stella, Stella—*" He whispers my name under his breath like a prayer, like a promise, like a broken plea.

And it's then that I know my answer, the answer to the question I've wondered since that night.

Of course, he didn't know.

My heart shatters more and more with each exhalation, and I murmur into his hair, "I'm okay—I'm okay. I'm still here."

We sit like that, holding onto each other, the heaviest burden I've ever carried splayed across the cheeks of the man I've always loved. The man I tried to save from this.

I don't know how much time passes, but music starts up from inside, the reflection of the lights through the windows tossing shadows onto the grass around us.

He takes a shuddering breath, pulling back from me slightly, and lifts both hands to my face. "So—" His voice breaks again, and he clears his throat, blinking once. "So, that night. I got on the plane, you left that voicemail, and then?" he asks quietly.

I know that the rest of the pieces will hurt him worse, but I also know that he needs me to lay it all out there for him.

Taking a shaky breath of my own, I tell him the words that I don't want to say. "I went to the bathroom and sat on the floor for hours. Then I opened the medicine cabinet . . ."

I trail off, and he squeezes his eyes shut, dropping his head, his hands falling to my arms.

"I threw up all of the pills almost immediately and passed out on the bathroom floor. Dahlia found me, actually. She thought—" I shudder, remembering. I fall silent after that, letting the implication of the words fill the space.

His eyes are far away, and I can tell he's recounting the events as they fall into place. His voice is low and raw when he finally speaks. "I called Daniel. After I heard the voicemail, after I called 911, I called Daniel. I just . . . I just had this feeling. This pit in my gut. I didn't know, I didn't—" He chokes on the words, his hands sliding down to my own. "I called Daniel, and Dahlia answered. I didn't know what was going on. I needed someone to get to you, to make sure you were okay. I'd never felt more helpless."

I sit there with him in the grass, his hands clutching mine like he'll never let go of them again.

"What then?" He looks up at me, emptied out.

I don't bother trying to stop the stream of tears as they continue to cascade down my cheeks. "Dahlia told me everything after. They had just gotten back from their honeymoon the day before. Daniel was still sleeping when his phone rang, and Dahlia saw it was you and panicked. So, she answered and drove straight over. She called my parents on the way, I had forgotten they were out of town at the time. But she called them, and she got to the house, ran inside, and saw that the bathroom door was shut on her way to my room."

Bridger brushes the wetness from my cheeks. Staring, waiting, holding space for me to tell the rest of my story.

"She said the ambulance arrived ten seconds after she did, so that was thanks to you, I guess." Now, it was my turn to wipe the tears from *his* cheeks. "And when I woke up in the hospital, you were my first thought. I knew that once I had . . . failed—"

He bites his cheek as more tears well.

"I knew you couldn't know. I knew I had to shut you out completely, because if I didn't—you would've given it all up for me. I didn't want to burden you with that."

He shuts his eyes, a pained breath shaking through his lungs. "Of course, I would've."

I pull back, looking him in the eyes, putting my hands on his cheeks, and forcing him to look at me. "That was the problem."

He looks at me with bloodshot eyes and tear-stained cheeks. "So, then you told them to tell me to leave you alone."

I nod again. "I had to, Bridge. I had to let you go so that you could live the life you were supposed to. One where I didn't drag you down with me."

He shakes his head, and I drop my hands as his expression turns stony, hardening around the edges. "You didn't get to decide that for me."

"I *had* to. I couldn't let you move back and give everything up—"

"And then I tore my ACL and moved back anyway. No one could've anticipated that happening, but it did, and I dealt with it." He runs a hand down his face, dropping it into his lap. "You could have let me be there for you. We could have dealt with this. All of this . . . together."

"It wouldn't have ended any differently."

"How can you say that?"

My voice breaks. "Because, Bridger, I *had* you. I had you, and it didn't change anything."

He falls silent. I can tell his mind is wandering, no doubt blaming himself, thinking back through everything I've said, the final pieces in the broken mosaic of us. Another tear escapes, and I reach across him to wipe it away.

"How could I not have known?"

"Bridger—"

"How did I miss this? How could I have been so stupid, so ignorant and—"

"Bridger, *no.*" This is the other half of what I was trying to avoid, why it was better for him not to know because I knew he would blame himself. "None of this was your fault. Do you understand me? You couldn't have done anything. *That* is what I'm trying to tell you."

He runs a shaky hand through his hair. "That night, that voicemail . . . your voice had never sounded like that before. I didn't know what to think. I was freaked out, but I didn't . . . I didn't even let my brain go there back then, but I think I should've. I could've noticed or seen the signs, paid more attention, loved you better—"

"Please. Stop." My voice is barely above a whisper, broken and hollow.

He clamps his mouth shut, a muscle working in his jaw. He slowly pushes himself to a stand, hands clasped on top of his head, eyes closed, breathing slowly. I rise next to him, brushing the grass and dirt off my now tarnished lavender gown. I can't bring myself to care as I take in his expression, the grief rippling across him in waves.

"I would have been there for you if you had let me. After everything, Stella." He swallows, his hands falling to his sides. "Why didn't you let me?

I swallow, eyes heavy. "I was in a bad place back then, Bridger. A really, really bad place." My voice breaks, and I cover my mouth with my hand, allowing myself to remember what it felt like for the first time since that night—to feel that kind of hopelessness, that despair, that lack of purpose.

He shakes his head and looks at me incredulously. He reaches for me and grabs onto my face, searching my eyes for answers I know he won't find. "So that voicemail *was* supposed to be the last thing you ever said to me?" he says so, so quietly.

I just nod against his hands. His chin trembles again, and his throat bobs as he swallows heavily. He cups my jaw with one hand, the other moving down to my shoulder.

"It wasn't supposed to be like this. I thought . . . I thought I'd have been long gone by now." Tears run down both of our faces again, but I continue. "When Dahlia came to my hospital room, when she told me you called the ambulance and then called her, I knew you'd be worried out of your mind. I knew you'd try to hop on the first flight back. I knew you wouldn't stop until you knew what happened. And I didn't want you to know.

"I was so embarrassed, Bridge. I was embarrassed, humiliated, and mortified that I couldn't even do that one final thing. I had failed again. I felt unworthy of everything, of breath, of life, and most of all . . . of you. I thought you'd be better off without me."

"Stella." He takes a shuddering breath, shaking his head again.

"And so when I woke up," I continue before he can say anything else, "I made sure Dahlia got Daniel to tell you to stop trying with me. To let me go. I wanted—needed you to be free of that burden. Of the mess I'd made."

I step out of his grip, looking down at the ground and saying again, softly, "I needed you to hate me."

He doesn't say anything, and he's looking at me with such sadness, such disbelief that I almost look away again.

A few more quiet seconds pass. "I could never hate you."

I wrap my arms around myself, tucking away, retreating inward.

"I never have. And I—" His voice breaks, and he scrubs his hand along his jaw again. "After everything, Stella, I was never even mad at you. I was hurt, and heartbroken, and confused but —never mad. It would've been so much easier if I was, and I wanted to be. So badly, I wanted to be, but—it never came. That anger . . . it never came.

"Something was different senior year. I knew that. But I thought it was just the stress, and the changes, and stuff with your family. I could tell you were more muted, quieter. I tried to pull you out, and I thought once we got to North Carolina, things would get better, but—"

"I didn't want to be saved," I whisper.

His breathing turns heavy again. His chest heaves, and he

clutches at the collar of his shirt like he can't get air. I step toward him, but he's not looking at me. Not seeing me.

"I should've turned around. I should've stayed with you, I should've—if I had . . . if I had answered the phone—" He cuts himself off with another ragged breath, and my eyes fill with tears again. "I just drove away," he whispers.

I shrug sadly, everything laying completely bare before him. "I watched you go." I take a breath and repeat my earlier sentiment. "But even if you hadn't, it would've ended the same way."

"You don't know that." He exhales a broken breath.

"I do, Bridger. This . . . this was about more than just us." I take another step toward him, lifting my hand to rest it over his. "This was bigger than you and me. You couldn't have saved me, Bridger. No one could've."

He turns his hand around, lacing it through mine, holding tight. "Stel . . ."

"You were all I had, Bridge. I couldn't put that weight on you. I told you—you couldn't be everything."

"So, you thought it'd be better if I was nothing?"

"*Yes*. You couldn't—that wouldn't have been fair to you. I convinced myself it was better for you that way." I don't remember when I started crying again. Maybe I never stopped.

"And what about for you?" He steps toward me, an emotion shining in his eyes that I've never seen before. "How did pushing everyone in your life away work out better for you? How were you better off leaving yourself to carry this burden, this impossible weight, all alone?"

He's right in front of me now, so close that he reaches up and brushes some hair off my face from where it is stuck to the wetness of my cheeks. His hands linger, moving along my cheekbones and down to the outline of my jaw. He cups the sides of my face, and I lift my hands to his wrists, holding on, anchoring myself to him.

His eyes fill, and he takes a deep breath as he holds my gaze.

"Do you know how destroyed I would've been to live in a world without you in it?

And I lose it. The breath rushes from my lungs in a muffled sob, my knees give out, and I crumple into him, and he catches me, holding me like he would have that night and every night after. The same arms that held me through the worst moments of my life, these strong, steady arms were finally holding me again.

After everything, he's still here.

And so am I.

So, I sob. I sob into his shirt—for me, for him, for the time we had and the time we lost, for the time we were almost never given. I cry for my parents, I cry for my brother, for my sister-in-law, for Bridger's dad, for all the friends who have come and gone, for the empty days and the lonely nights and the path that led me right back here.

Everything I've kept so tightly inside of me for the past three years leaves me in a rush, and I fall apart completely.

And he stays. He doesn't hide from it. He doesn't walk around it, doesn't dodge it, doesn't pull away disgusted. He doesn't look at me like I'm less than.

He doesn't look at me like I'm broken.

He doesn't say anything, but he doesn't need to. He holds me tightly, stroking my hair, my back, and my shoulders, and lets me break apart. I can feel his shoulders shaking, too, and I hold onto him just as tightly because maybe he has to fall apart in this same way. For all he's lost, all he's gained. The time and distance that brought him here.

Back to me.

I pull back, and I wipe his tears, and he wipes mine. I don't know what else to say, what else I have to offer him. I gave him this truth, the full truth, and now he holds my heart in the palm of his hand the way he always has.

"Stella, I need you to know something. I need you to hear

this from me." He takes a steadying breath before continuing. "I need you. I've always needed you. And your family needs you. Dahlia adores you. Your future niece or nephew—they need you. Maggie needs you. The world—the world, Stella, it needs you. Even if after tonight we never speak again, even if we don't end up together, even if you walk away and decide this isn't what you want—you are *needed* here, Stella. Your story isn't over. Not even close. Please never forget that."

Through his anguished words, through the grief weighing on his face, I hear the question underneath.

"Bridger," I breathe slowly. "Do you know what it's like to constantly be at war with your own mind, every waking moment, all the time? I have had to fight to be here. Every day for the past three years, I have been fighting to be here."

Taking a shaky breath, I release my last fear, the final reason this might never work. "Things were dark back then, Bridge. And while I'm doing better now, I can't guarantee that I always will be. This is going to be an ongoing battle for the rest of my life, and I'm scared to let you back in because I don't want to push you away again. I don't want to feel like I have to—to save you from me."

"Stella." He brings me closer, his gaze never wavering. "I'm not afraid of that darkness."

My chin wobbles again, and I swallow past the growing lump in my throat. "You can't fix me."

He pulls back gently, just enough to see my face. "I know, Stel. I know that. But I also know that you don't have to go through this alone. I won't let you, not again. I'm not going to stand by and watch you disappear." On a shaky inhale, he finishes, "I know I can't fix this for you or take it away. But I can *be* here. Please, Stella, let me be here for you. Let me hold your hand."

I shake my head, full of disbelief and awe of the man standing in front of me. "After everything I've put you through?"

He laughs softly through his tears. "After everything."

I swallow past the lump in my throat. "I don't deserve you. I never have."

He's shaking his head, eyes going serious. I drop my gaze, but he moves his hand under my chin, gently lifting my face back up to his. "There is no part of you that you could show me that would make me turn away. Your darkest corners, Stella, they don't scare me."

My chin trembles, the words I never dreamed I'd hear from anyone filling me, lighting me.

"I love you, Stella. All of you." Exhaling, as if he's been waiting to say those words since he got off that plane, he says, "I never stopped."

Closing the distance between us, he kisses the tears that fall from my cheeks. Then he kisses my forehead, my temples, my cheeks, my eyelids, my nose. I bring my arms around his neck, forehead resting against his.

"I love you, Bridger."

And that was all he needed. He presses his lips to mine, softly at first, tentatively. I sigh as the relief of him, of this, of *us* washes over me and I grab onto his shoulders, and he threads his fingers through my hair, my body on fire in every place he's touching and everywhere he's not. Our tears fall and bleed together as our mouths move in the rhythm they've always known, and the kiss turns feverish, hungry. It's like the first time and the last time all at once, every moment colliding together like the sun cresting over the horizon after the darkest winter, and I'm burning in the heat of him. This feeling, this daylight, this love . . . it's golden.

He starts to pull away, but I don't want to let him go, so I bring his face back to mine, and he smiles into the kiss, laughs into it, and then I'm laughing too. He pulls back gently.

"Hey, hey, slow down, take a breath," he says, moving his hands up and down my arms. "I'm not going anywhere." I lean into him, bury my face in his chest as he rests his chin on top of my head. "There's no rush. We've got the rest of our lives, okay?"

My lips part, and I pull back to look at him. The night breeze hits my face again, and I take in his bright eyes and flushed cheeks.

"You think so?" I whisper.

Smiling, he says, "Don't you?"

And for the first time, I do. I see it.

He kisses me again, and for the first time in three years, I can breathe.

# 55

I wake to a heavy weight draped across my stomach, warm breath tickling my neck. I smile to myself, try to wiggle deeper under the comforter and stay here with him like this forever.

My parents always get a hotel close to the venue after the gala because it's usually a late night, so when Bridger drove me home, I told him I didn't want to be alone.

He said I'd never be again.

And so, he came inside with me. And we stumbled through the house like teenagers after sneaking out, kissing and laughing and touching and talking. And when we made it to my room, we collapsed onto my bed, exhausted and winded and bleary-eyed— but *alive.*

So, so alive.

And he stayed with me, and we laid there together, and I kept waiting to wake up and realize it was all just a dream, but the fear never settled, and the shoe never dropped, and I never woke up because it was real.

And he proved that to me over and over as he whispered all

the ways he missed me across every inch of my skin and wrote them across my heart with the loving caress of his hand.

At some point, we fell asleep, and now his arm is draped across me, and my legs are tangled up with his, and when I try to look at him over my shoulder, he tightens his grip around me and buries his face into the back of my neck. I laugh into the sheets, twisting around in his arms so I'm facing him. His sleepy eyes and messy hair stir something low in my stomach, and his raspy morning voice sounds like someone opening the gates of heaven.

"Good morning."

His smile warms my cheeks, and my returning smile does the same to his. "Morning."

"Not good?"

I lean in, pressing a kiss to his mouth. "Now it is."

He laughs as he rolls onto his back, pulling me with him. He traces circles across my hip, and I swear I'm almost asleep again, but then he says, "We should probably get up before your parents get back."

Sighing, I press a kiss into his bare shoulder before rolling off of him. Bracing myself for the cold, I throw the covers off, not wanting to leave this cocoon of warmth that Bridger has created for me.

Finally, I slide out of bed. "I'll go make coffee."

I have two steaming mugs sitting on the counter and am plopped down onto a barstool by the time Bridger pads into the kitchen wearing only his dress pants from last night. I narrow my eyes. "If you're so worried about my parents seeing us, maybe you should at least put your shirt back on."

He pauses in the doorway, a smile tugging at the corner of his lips, that mischievous glint in his eyes. "Says the one who's wearing it."

I glance down at myself, cheeks instantly on fire when I realize I am still, in fact, wearing his button-down from the night before. His laugh trails me up the stairs, and after I reemerge a minute later in my own sweatpants and a t-shirt, he's still laughing over the rim of his coffee cup as I chuck his shirt at his face.

He manages to catch it somehow and not spill a drop, and I scowl into my own mug. We sit there in silence for a few minutes, enjoying the easy comfort of each other's company, knowing each other in the ways we always have and all the new ways that we're beginning to learn.

Another few minutes pass before either of us speaks. Bridger breaks the silence first. "Your room looks exactly the same."

I snort out a laugh, swirling the remaining coffee in my mug. "You'd be surprised at how much shit hasn't changed."

He goes still next to me, and I instantly want to take back the words the second they're out of my mouth. Leave it up to me to ruin a perfectly good morning.

"Can I ask you a question?"

Exhaling a long breath through my nose, I just nod.

"When did you decide to switch your major to education? Before or after you deferred that first fall semester at UW?"

Tangled up together last night, in the comfort of his arms and the darkness of the room, I told him everything. He stayed there with me, and he listened, and he didn't flinch. Even when I told him with tears in my eyes that what scares me the most is that sometimes, since that night, I wish I hadn't failed. And he held me as I told him I never want to feel that way again, and he assured me that even if I did, he would still be there.

He's not going anywhere. And neither am I.

Setting the mug down, I keep my eyes on the table. "It was after. Not long after I got home from the hospital, Mom asked what I planned to do for college since the doctors recommended that I stay local during my recovery."

Luckily, I had applied to UW as my safety school just in case, and upon explaining my situation, they granted me acceptance even though it was after the deadline.

"I didn't declare a major initially, and at first, she didn't push. And then, when she did . . . there was no fight left. So, when Mom told me becoming an English teacher would be the smartest option for me, I said 'okay.'" I shrug, trying to act like it affected me as little now as it did then.

I should've remembered that nothing gets past him. Never, when it comes to me.

"Is that what you want to do, though? Teach English?"

"I think it's the smartest option."

"That's not what I asked."

I sigh, picking at a loose thread in my sweatpants. "One thing you'll learn about every aspect of my life now is that *nothing* is that simple. If I can't write, then I guess . . . I can teach other people the tools instead."

I look over at him finally, after a few seconds pass of him not saying anything at all. His brows are furrowed, his eyes are downcast, and I can tell he's thinking. I almost want to try to say something to change the subject, to move the conversation along. But I let the words hang between us, letting them be what they are, not running from them. A few more moments pass, and surprisingly, it's Bridger who changes the subject.

"How long were you in the hospital?"

I sigh again, giving him a look that I hope says, *"Oh, so we're doing this?"*

And he gives me one in return that says, *"We should've done this a long time ago."*

"I was admitted for a total of five days. They recommended a week, but somehow, my mom convinced them I was all good. She got them to do their examinations and tests a couple of days early. I got the all clear to go home under a guardian's direct supervision, along with the mandatory six weeks of psychiatric therapy that my mom also tried to convince them I didn't need."

His fingers hold the edge of the countertop in a vise-like grip, knuckles turning white. I reach over and gently grab his hand, lacing his fingers through mine. He closes his eyes at the touch.

I say softly, "Hey. Look at me."

He does, slowly. The anguish in his eyes is something I feel like I don't deserve, something I never even bothered to feel for myself.

"It's okay. I mean, I went to the required therapy, and it definitely helped. And as far as school goes . . . it's fine. I think I'll like teaching."

He nods, unconvinced. "Do you still want to be an author?"

I hesitate, then nod.

"Do you still write?"

With a slight shake of my head, I say, "No. Not since . . . before."

He releases a breath through his nose, running his thumb over the back of our joined hands. "Do you still see your therapist regularly?"

"Regularly is . . . probably a stretch."

He squeezes my hand a little tighter. "When was the last time you went?"

I look up, thinking. "Remember when you called me to pick you up from the hospital last month, and I was already there?"

He nods.

"That's why. I was at a session. I haven't been since because it's honestly just exhausting, not to mention expensive . . ." I trail off at the look on his face.

"Please don't make excuses for that, Stella. It's important."

It catches me off guard, the earnest tone in his voice, the concern in his eyes. And for the first time, I realize that maybe I need to try.

For him. Maybe I need to try for him, but also, more than that . . . for me.

"I know, Bridger, I do. But—you have to realize that I'm not used to talking about this. With anyone. Last night was the first time I've even thought about that night since it happened. Everyone in my family walks around on eggshells, afraid to speak or do anything that'll set me off as if I'll break apart at any given moment. I think everyone just thinks . . . maybe it's easier this way? If none of us face it, the implications of it and all that it means.

"And, plus, around that same time was when The Abode's blog started going crazy. Mom was so worried about the company and her image that she didn't want it getting out, what I'd tried to do. So, we didn't mention it. We still don't. Honestly, I think telling them it was over between me and you made things easier for them. Daniel didn't know why I wanted him to tell you to stop talking to me, but no one really questioned it. One less person to try to explain away, I guess.

"I don't think my parents ever really tried to understand. They still haven't. In the end, it weirdly seemed like they were almost . . . angry at me for it? I don't know if they just thought I'd done it for attention, or if it was some kind of subconscious guilt thing . . . I still don't know."

His jaw is tight, and he's glaring daggers at the table, so I quickly finish my thought.

"So, what I'm trying to say is that I don't know—I'm not sure how to talk about it. It feels wrong to, almost. I think . . . I think I've kept all this pain locked up for so long because I was made to feel like I had to. But I want to try, Bridge. I do. So, be patient with me. Okay?"

He brings my hand up to his mouth and presses a long kiss to my knuckles. He gently tugs on my arm and pulls me over to him. I fall into his lap, and he wraps his arms around my waist as I sling mine around his neck.

"That really pisses me off, Stel. You didn't deserve any of this. You *don't* deserve any of this."

I run a hand through his hair, smoothing it down where it's

still wild from sleep. "Thank you," I say softly because no other words come.

I don't think I realized until now how complacent I've become with everything. With life. How I've just let it happen to me, not taking any sort of initiative, or trying to step out of the path I've been set on, or standing up for myself or what I believe in.

I look around at the kitchen, at this house, at this place I've found myself.

Exhaling a deep breath, I look at Bridger, and I say the words that I've been thinking since the day I realized I wasn't going to UNC anymore. "I think I need to move out."

# 56

I try not to grin as I look at my texts the next morning.

Dahlia :)

9:56 a.m.

You took him HOME???

LOL.

. . . It was the lavender, wasn't it?

Right. Maybe you could try being a tad more subtle next time, no??

No <3

You're welcome.

<3

"Just be nice, okay?" I say when I answer the door. It's been a little over a week since the gala, and once Dahlia mentioned to my parents that Bridger and I were back together—much to my dismay—they insisted he come over for dinner.

So, he follows me into the house, muttering from behind me, "My mom might not have taught me much in life, but the one thing she did teach me is that if I don't have anything nice to say, then not to say anything at all."

I try to give him my best glare over my shoulder. After I turn back, he smacks me on the butt, and I immediately whip around to shoot him another look. Neither is convincing, of course, and we're both smiling by the time we make it into the dining room.

"Bridger!" Dahlia hops up (yes, at eight months pregnant, she literally *hops* out of her chair to greet him) and attempts to give him a hug around her stomach.

My dad stands next, offering a handshake, and Daniel leans in to clap him on the back.

My mother just gives him a curt nod, saying, "Hello, Bridger."

I try not to grimace as he gives her the same nod in return with a polite, "Hi, Mrs. Reynolds."

I plop down in my seat, knowing this was a terrible, terrible idea.

I'm immediately brought back to the first (and only) time Bridger ever had a meal with my family, and I'm immediately reminded of all the reasons I made sure he never came over for dinner again. Bridger and I don't talk for most of the meal, letting the others fill the silence—mostly talking about the baby, due in just over a month now.

We're eating pizza tonight, per Dahlia's request, which is more than fine with me. And with Bridger, if the fourth slice he's on has anything to say about it. It wasn't until then that the conversation inevitably got directed to us, and I set down my napkin, bracing myself.

"So, Bridger," my mom starts. "You're back in Seattle."

"I am."

"What do you do now?"

His expression remains smooth and even. "I'm at UW now, like Stella. Studying architecture."

"Ah, I see. I take it you didn't love the East Coast? UNC, was it?"

"Mom." I all but snap at the judgment in her tone. I receive a seething glare in return before she focuses her attention back on Bridger.

"Actually, yeah. It was kind of terrible. As much as I love the game, it was taking up all of my time, and it was really hard to keep up with my coursework each season. Being a student-athlete was no joke."

A little over a week ago, when I filled in the rest of the blanks in the middle of the night . . . He did, too. He told me what it was like in North Carolina, how his dad went to visit in the summers, his classes, his days, his nights . . . all of it. We talked about the pressure he'd felt from soccer, the conversation I'd overheard with his mom in their kitchen at our graduation party, and his surgeries. Everything from then and now and the time in between.

In in his honesty, in the truth we both shared, I didn't think I could love him any more. And yet, every day since then . . . somehow, I do.

She raises her eyebrows, almost wearing an *I told you so* expression. I don't know what ground she thinks she has to stand on in regard to him, but I can immediately feel my defenses going up. I clasp my hands together tightly in my lap.

Bridger notices, setting his hand on top of mine under the table, steadying me with a reassuring squeeze that says, *"I've got this."*

"And your dad? Is he still running the shop?"

Bridger's eyes light up at the mention of Adam, and my heart leaps in my chest. When Bridger and I had walked into his house hand in hand last week, Adam had just smiled and said, "All in good time, yeah?" Then, the three of us watched *Pride and Prejudice* together for the fiftieth time.

"He is. Business slowed a little over the past few months during his recovery time. He was in a car accident back in April," he adds, noticing their puzzled faces. "But physical therapy has been going great, and he's almost back to it. He's doing really well."

"That's so good to hear. Honestly." Dahlia smiles genuinely, and I love her for it.

"I bet your old man missed you while you were away," my dad says.

Bridger smiles, but it doesn't quite reach his eyes. "Oh, yeah. Yeah, for sure," he says, his easy countenance faltering slightly.

"How'd the seasons go that you did play?" Daniel cuts in for the first time all evening. For once, I'm thankful for it.

"They went alright. The team itself was doing pretty well, but I didn't get a ton of playing time at first. Underclassmen usually don't, so." He nods lightly, taking a sip of his water.

"Something to be said about that high school glory, huh?" My mom laughs, but no one else does. She doesn't notice.

My blood was simmering before, but it's boiling now.

"I always tried to tell you kids, just wait until you get to the real world—"

And at that, I unleash it all.

"I am so sick of hearing people say that. What the fuck does that even mean? What about his life hasn't been real, Mom? Did you know that he didn't move back home because it was too hard for him to handle? He had to move back because he tore his ACL for the *second* time and had to have *multiple* surgeries. And yes, his dad is still in Seattle, so he moved back home to recover in a safe and supportive environment, but you wouldn't know much about that, would you?"

"Stella—" Bridger starts to speak. He tries to cut me off before I can say anything I'll regret, but I already know that I mean every word coming out of my mouth.

"What about any of that wasn't real? And what about *my* life hasn't been real, Mom? I'm so sick of you acting like no one is allowed to have real problems until they are twenty-five. What about my junior year when I won that writing competition, and none of you came? Was that not real?

"Or, how about when I had my first heartbreak three years ago when I cut the one person I loved more than anything out of my life to save him from myself? Did that not count, either? Or, Mom, what about the depression that has plagued me since I was seventeen? What about the time that I tried to take my own life? Was none of *that* real enough for you?"

Dahlia has tears streaming down her cheeks, her eyes closed, and Daniel's face is drained of all color. My dad is staring glassy-eyed into his water, and my mother blanches, immediately glancing at Bridger as if gauging his reaction to the last piece of information I just let out.

Bridger is staring at me, shock evident on his face.

"He knows, Mom. He knows. So does his dad; so does Maggie. I told them all. I told them all because it's important. It's important to let the people you love know you. To give them that chance to—not in addition to, but *regardless of.* So, he knows, Mom. They all do. You don't have to pretend around him. We can stop acting like everything has been normal for the past three years. Because I can't. Not anymore.

"So, when you're ready to talk about it, we can. Whether that's today, in a week, or in ten years. But we can't keep running from this, Mom. You don't get to invalidate my pain just because you don't understand it."

I stand, throwing the napkin onto my plate and heading for the stairs, Bridger right on my heels. When we're in my room, I think I'm going to get an earful about how much better I could have handled that, but instead, the second my door closes, he's kissing me. Surprised, I kiss him back with just as much eagerness as my back digs into the door handle.

He pulls back, panting. "That was the hottest thing I've ever seen."

I burst into laughter, looking at him incredulously. "I . . . that is the last thing I expected you to say."

He steps toward me, grabbing onto my shoulder and dipping his chin to look me in the eye. "I'm proud of you. For standing up for yourself. For fighting for something."

A small smile tugs at the corner of my mouth. "Thank you for reminding me I have something worth fighting for."

Bridger left about an hour ago, and at the soft knock on my door that I've learned to be Dahlia's, I say, "Come in." To my surprise, Daniel walks in with her.

"Hey, girl," Dahlia says, punching me lightly on the arm and sitting on the edge of my bed.

Daniel leans against my desk, and for the life of me, I cannot remember the last time he was even in my room. I can tell he's thinking the same thing as I watch his eyes roam around the space.

"I just wanted to tell you that I'm really proud of you. And I think you're awesome. And I know how hard all that must have been tonight. And after everything you've been through . . ." Tears well, and I watch her roll her eyes as she motions to her stomach. "Hormones," she laughs. "But really, Stella. You've come a long way, and I love you a lot."

I move closer to her on the bed, give her a hug, and whisper, "I love you, too."

But then she straightens and adds, "Oh. And also, I need you to know that I'm still mad at Daniel for not telling you about our engagement. I wish you'd been there."

I pull back slightly, laughing. Dahlia's eyes are narrowed at Daniel, who raises his hands in defense—and then drops them.

"I deserve that," he says solemnly.

My head pulls back in shock, and I look back at Dahlia, who's sitting there with a satisfied smile on her face.

Then she says, "Okay. I need to hit the bathroom one more time before we leave, or I'm not going to make it home."

Daniel's brows furrow. "But we only live fifteen minutes—"

"I will not make it home," she repeats, holding a hand out to him. He laughs, helps her up, and then she scurries out of the room.

Daniel clears his throat, pulling out the desk chair and taking a seat. "So, after tonight . . . I think I just realized that I've been a really shitty brother."

"Oh?" I feign shock, placing my hand on my chest and trying to hide the fact that I actually am surprised.

He gives me a knowing look but continues, "Being four years older isn't an excuse, and I know that. But I just feel like I wasn't around a lot in high school, I guess. And when I was, I feel like I was a real asshole to you. And . . . maybe things would've been different if I wasn't. If I'd tried harder." He shrugs, and I stare at him in disbelief. "So, I just wanted to say that I'm sorry."

"Daniel . . ." I trail off, not entirely sure what to say. "This— this means a lot to me. But honestly, I should be thanking you." His forehead creases, and I laugh. "I mean, you're practically the only person who hasn't treated me any differently after everything that happened. You've played your role of 'annoying older brother' rather well over the years."

He rolls his eyes, laughing, but I swear I can see something like relief flicker across his features.

And again, I realize that maybe this wasn't only my burden to carry. Maybe it hasn't been all this time. Maybe everyone copes in the ways they know how, doing what they can with what they have. And maybe . . . maybe that's enough, for a time.

And this, at least, is a start.

"Goodnight, Stella." He steps closer to me and ruffles my hair, and I shake my head as he leaves.

"Goodnight, Daniel," I call after him.

And as I fall asleep that night, the tears that I cry aren't from sadness at all.

My parents never came up to my room that night. I didn't expect them to. But I'm going to be okay regardless, I know that now. And one day, I hope we *will* be able to talk about it. That we'll get to that place. But even if not, I know . . . I will be okay. Because I can still love them in the ways I know how. And they can do the same.

I think that's the thing about life, about growing up and getting older—learning that the love you're surrounded by won't always look how you thought it would. Maybe it never will.

But the thing that will always be true . . . is that there is always love.

There is always more.

# Epilogue



"Where do you want me to set this?" Maggie says, holding out the small, scratched-up, first-place medal that I've had sitting on my shelf for years.

I smile at the sight of it, saying, "You can just set it on my desk."

I survey the small room, the hallways leading out into the cozy living room and kitchen area. I look into the new apartment I'm renting with Maggie, and I feel brand new.

Maggie told me a few weeks ago that her roommate was graduating. She asked if I wanted to move in, and I immediately jumped on the idea, getting a job at the local library and helping out at the shop to cover rent.

My parents seemed surprised when I told them I was moving out, but they've been supportive, nonetheless. My mom might have joked one too many times about what she could turn my room into, but maybe that's what she needs. What we all need.

We still haven't directly talked about that conversation at the dinner table a month ago, but after a few important talks with

Carol, she recommended we do some family sessions. And, to my complete and utter disbelief—my parents have agreed to go.

Dahlia's eyes went all glassy when I told her, and she said that she and Daniel would be more than happy to come. It won't be easy, I know that. But I think we're finally ready to try.

"Why do you have—"

"Oh, I'll take that—" I say at the same time she does, snatching the captain's armband out of her grasp.

Her mouth drops open as I clutch it to my chest, and she doubles over in laughter.

"Okay, I know that I'm currently unpacking this," she says, motioning to the box in front of her, "but we're going to have to unpack *that*," she points at the band in my hands, "once you get back."

Heat rises up my neck. She laughs again, and I'm thankful when my phone chimes.

"He's here!" I say. I run around the room, frantically opening the boxes splayed throughout.

"Oh, shoot," Maggie says, joining in my search. After a few more boxes, she shouts, "Here! Found them!" and chucks a pair of Converse at my head. I duck just in time and see her cover her mouth, a muffled "sorry" coming from behind her hands.

Stifling a laugh, I trip down the hallway, trying to put them on.

"Have fun! Tell them I say congratulations!" she yells from behind me.

I shout, "I will!" over my shoulder just as a knock sounds.

"Take lots of pictures!" she yells again, and I laugh as I reach the door.

I fling it open to find Bridger beaming at me, already halfway down the hallway before I even shut the door behind me. Laughing again, I race after him. "You're not allowed to run in hospitals, so don't think you're going to get to the room to hold her first."

And as we burst into the cool morning air and run to his car, I can't help the emotion spreading through my chest.

My niece was born today.

Early this morning, we got the text, and the second that visitors were allowed, we decided we would (literally, apparently) scramble across the city to get there.

Bridger still holds the car door open for me, regardless of the speed with which he's trying to get to the hospital. I can see him mouth, "Chivalry's not dead!" through the windshield as he rushes around to his side of the car. I'm laughing when he gets in, and he winks at me, grabbing my hand as he starts the drive.

"How's the book coming along?" he asks once we make it to the highway.

"Still haven't started it yet."

He groans. "Come on, Stel—"

"I know, I know, I just . . . I need to make sure the idea I'm working with is good enough."

"Stella." He gives me a pointed look before flicking his eyes back to the road. "If it comes from your pretty little brain, I already know it is. More than good enough."

I sigh into a smile. The school year starts next week, and as of four days ago, I am officially an English major with a minor in creative writing. It might've set me back a couple semesters, but I know it'll be worth it in the end.

"Oh, also—my prescription is ready. Can we swing by the pharmacy on the way back?"

He reaches over and squeezes my hand. "Absolutely."

I started taking the antidepressants and anxiety medication my psychiatrist prescribed for me after some encouragement from Maggie and Bridger. I told Carol I didn't want the meds initially all those years ago because it felt like giving in, and I didn't want to feel that again—but they reminded me that taking the medication isn't a weakness, but a new kind of strength.

We arrive at the hospital, hurrying through the parking lot.

"You're moving awfully fast for a man with a bum knee!" I shout as he runs ahead, his laughter carrying back to me with the wind.

We finally get up to the room, and the door is already cracked, but we still knock anyway as we hear a soft, "Come in."

We walk into the room, and I suck in a breath at the sight before me. Flowers are on the bedside table, and balloons are tied to the foot of the bed. My parents sit on the couch in the corner as my mom takes a video with her phone, Daniel is beaming down at his wife and daughter, and Dahlia glows with glassy eyes. And then my eyes fall to the small, pink bundle held so lovingly in her arms.

Dahlia looks at us, smiling, tears running down her cheeks. "Stella, Bridger . . . meet Adelyn Stella Reynolds."

I freeze on the spot, unable to see beyond the tears that well in my own eyes, only moving forward by the hand pressing lightly into the small of my back.

"You . . . she—" I'm at a complete loss for words as I look at the beautiful, tiny baby in her arms.

"Do you want to hold her?"

All I can do is nod as she holds her out to me. I gently sit in the chair next to the bed, Bridger leaning in from behind me and reaching his hand over to let Adelyn latch onto one of his fingers with her tiny ones.

"She's beautiful," I breathe, unable to comprehend the sight of her.

"We've always known that if she was a girl, she'd have your name, Stel." She sniffs before continuing, "You've taught us more about life and love and perseverance than we would have ever known if you didn't exist. We're lucky to know you and to be loved by you, and we know that Adelyn is the luckiest girl in the world because she gets to be loved by you, too."

The tears spill down my cheeks, and I wipe them away with my free hand as I look down at the sweet girl in my arms. She's still clutching onto Bridger's finger, and as I glance up at him over my shoulder, I see that his eyes are shining, too.

Adelyn yawns in my arms and my eyes blur all over again because in that moment, I know.

I know then, with a certainty that rattles my bones, that I will make it my life's mission to ensure that this precious life in my arms never once feels the same way I did, in whatever capacity that entails. I know without a sliver of a doubt that her life will be full—full of love, of joy, of every good thing this world has to offer.

But I'll also be there for her when life isn't any of those things, when it's hard and cold and cruel, and she wants to give up.

And I'll give her a hug like I wish I could go back and give my eighteen-year-old self a hug and tell her that this life is worth living. It will be hard and messy and unpredictable, but there is beauty in it all.

There is beauty in the quiet moments after you finish your new favorite book, when you take your first sip of the perfect coffee, when you watch a TV show that makes you laugh so hard tears stream down your face, when the first whisper of a cool autumn breeze rustles your hair, when you hug someone you love more than yourself.

I'll remind her that there are so many places to go, so many things to see, so many experiences to be had, so many people to meet, so much love to give and be given in return . . . so many beautiful reasons to be alive.

To live.

You just have to stick around long enough to see them.

And so that night, when I got home, I sat down at my makeshift desk in the corner of my new room, pulled out my laptop, and opened a blank document.

And I wrote one page.

Then another, and another, and another.

# Author's Note

Suicide and Crisis Lifeline: 988.
Call or Text 24/7.

I wrote this book for the Stellas of the world. So let me just start by saying; if you related to Stella at any point over the course of this book, or if you or anyone you know is struggling with suicidal thoughts—please, *please,* seek out help. You are not alone. Talk with someone you trust. I know that first step is the scariest, but it could make every difference. You are needed here. You have value, you have purpose, and you are so loved. I am proud of you. And just like Stella's—your story isn't over yet. Not even close. I promise you, this life is worth living.

This story is deeply personal to me on many levels, and as someone who has walked through some of the struggles explored throughout this novel, it was of the utmost importance to me to handle these topics with the care, sensitivity, and concern that they deserve, as they are not to be taken lightly. My prayer is that through these pages you were either able to feel seen, less alone, or have gained a better understanding of a loved one who might struggle.

Every single one of our experiences is different, and you never, *ever* know what someone is going through. So—let's be kind to each other. Encourage one another. Empathize with one another. Let someone know they aren't alone. These conversations are *so* incredibly important, and we need to continually come together to support each other and destigmatize mental health.

# Acknowledgments

I think this might be the most surreal part of this entire process. I still can't believe that I wrote a book? And you just got done reading it??? Unreal. What started as a quiet dream tucked away in the corner of my heart, now sitting in the palm of your hands and hopefully tucked away somewhere in your heart, too. As funny as it sounds, I used to dream about writing the acknowledgements, unable to grasp how it would feel to reflect on something that I am so immensely proud of and have the opportunity to thank everyone who has been with me the whole way. Well, here I am, writing it, *still* unable to grasp it. I don't think I'll ever be able to express the gratitude I have for everyone who has helped me get to this point—but I'm going to try. (So buckle up.)

First off, I need to start by thanking my incredible editor, Britt. I am still in awe of how you have loved and cared for this book every step of the way, and all the ways you've helped me make it the absolute best it could be. You've handled my rambling thoughts and chaotic brain like a CHAMP. You are amazing!

Secondly, thank you to Mary Scarlett for quite literally creating the cover of my *dreams.* I still stare at it in absolute awe, everyday. And thank you to Kristen for helping me format this book and making it the beauty that it is. And Joyce, thank you for proofreading!

I especially want to thank my five amazing friends—Brianna, McKenzie, Bethany, Zoë, and Reagan—who read this book in some of its earliest stages (some of you more than once!) and believed in it from the very beginning. Your unwavering excitement and encouragement means more to me than you'll ever know! And a huge thank you to Lucie, Madelyn, Anna, Eryn, and Melissa for reading this story and giving me the most wonderful feedback that helped me to make this book what it is.

To all the incredible authors who have let me babble on and on to them over DM's and have given me encouragement, support and advice when I needed it the most—Hannah Bonam-Young, Kaitlyn Hill, N.S. Perkins, and Taylor Torres to name a few—I am eternally thankful for your kindness and willingness to help.

My Bookstagram friends! From the second I announced this book, I have been blown away by the support and excitement you all have continually had for me. (And by how many of you were telling me you couldn't wait to read it before I even announced the title? Huh???) You guys rock.

To my best friend McKenzie, I DID IT!!!! You have always been the biggest supporter of me and all my (insane??) dreams, and have been the biggest encouragement in my life for the past 15 years. I truly don't know what I would do without your friendship. To the Moon and to Saturn!

Bethany, your belief in me since the second I told you I wanted to write a book gave me the confidence to do exactly that. The encouraging text messages, endless voice memos and the way you've cheered me on through this entire process have gotten me through. I am SO thankful for you.

To Kels, Erin, and Jen—who were like, "duh. Of course you're going to write a book." You guys gave me the courage to take the final leap. Love you all so big!

And a special thank you to Teesha, who believed in something more for me before I dared to believe it for myself. (Look what happened when I stopped looking and started living!!!)

And my girl Shannon—I wouldn't have survived these past four years without you!

To Mr. Spahr—if Stella had had a teacher like you, I know she would've been okay. Thank you for helping me through high school, and making sure *I* was okay.

And finally, my family. I want to thank my sister, Bri—for just being my sister. I could write another book just trying to explain how grateful I am and always have been for you. Thank you for reminding me to leave my fictional worlds every once in a while and be present in my own. You are my best thing. (And Frankie—you are my best brother-in-law!) And my brothers, who are quite literally my favorite people on the entire planet—I don't know what I would do without the two of you. You guys are truly, *truly,* my best friends. Thank you for believing in me and being on my team, no matter what. (And for acting out a scene once so I could make sure it made sense.) I love you both more than you will ever know. Mom and Dad—thank you for loving me. It's your love that is always there to celebrate with me when I succeed, and that acts as my safety net when I make a mistake. Thank you for giving me the space throughout my life to explore, create, and change my mind however many times I need. I am me because of you. And of course, my *amazing* grandparents, who's belief in me has helped me believe in myself. Thank you for your unending support and love all these years!

And Grammy, to whom this book was dedicated. I wish you could have read it. (I'm not entirely sure that this would have been your type of book, though, but when I told my brother as much, he only said, "she would have loved it simply for the fact that *you* wrote it," and he couldn't have been more right.) I miss you everyday.

And, of course, thank YOU. For making it this far, for reading this book, for playing a small part in making this dream come true. To everyone I didn't specifically mention that has touched my life in some way and helped me make it here, you know who you are. Thank you for spurring me on.

Lastly, and most importantly—I want to give thanks to the Lord, for placing this story on my heart and for gracing me with this gift. Glory be to Him, always.

# About the Author

Allie Otoski is an avid reader, writer, daydreamer, and believer. She loves to write stories about flawed yet lovable characters that are, much like all of us, just trying to find their place in this world. A homebody at heart, you can usually find her curled up on the couch with a Cherry Coke and a good book. She lives in Ohio with her family. More Than Just Us is her first novel.